# Dilly's
# Lass

# Rosie
# GOODWIN
# Dilly's
# Lass

corsair

CORSAIR

First published in the United Kingdom in 2015 by Corsair
This paperback edition published in 2024

1 3 5 7 9 10 8 6 4 2

A CIP catalogue record for this book
is available from the British Library.

ISBN: 978-1-4721-5915-1

Printed and bound in Great Britain by Clays Ltd, Elcograf S.p.A.

Papers used by Corsair are from well-managed forests
and other responsible sources.

MIX
Paper | Supporting
responsible forestry
FSC
www.fsc.org    FSC® C104740

Corsair
An imprint of
Little, Brown Book Group
Carmelite House
50 Victoria Embankment
London EC4Y 0DZ

An Hachette UK Company
www.hachette.co.uk

www.littlebrown.co.uk

# *Chapter One*

*Mill House, Nuneaton, February 1919*

Mrs Pegs had just settled down to enjoy a well-earned cup of tea when Gwen the young maid entered the kitchen to tell her, 'There's someone at the front door askin' to see you, Cook.'

Mrs Pegs raised her eyebrows. 'To see *me*?' she asked in amazement.

'Aye, it's a lady wi' a little boy. She's very well dressed an' when I told 'er that Master Farthing weren't to be disturbed an' the mistress were ill, she asked for you. Should I bring 'er through or show 'er into the drawin' room?'

'I'd best come an' see who it is first.' Mrs Pegs sighed as she dragged herself out of the chair. So much fer me tea break, she thought. There's no rest fer the wicked!

She followed Gwen through into the hallway and peered ahead to where a woman stood on the step with her back to her. Just as Gwen had said, the needlecord costume and fancy feathered hat she was wearing looked to be of the finest quality, but she couldn't for the life of her think what the lass might want with her.

'Can I help yer, ma'am?' Her voice cut through the silence – and as the woman turned towards her, still gripping the hand of the child at her side, Mrs Pegs' eyes almost popped out of her head. 'Good God! If it ain't our Bessie . . . But just look at yer! I wouldn't 'ave recognised yer, lass. Why, yer look grand.'

'Hello, Mrs Pegs.'

The woman was amazed to find that Bessie not only looked different but she sounded different too. She was certainly a very far cry from the young maid whom had used to work for her and who had been forced to run away in the dead of night.

But the kindly cook didn't want to think about that for now. She was just delighted to see the girl whom she had once looked upon almost as a daughter. Her glance then fell to the little boy, who was staring up at her from eyes that looked exactly like his father's. Her stomach flipped. The child must be about three years old now, if her calculations were right.

'An' who might this bonny little feller be then?' She tried to keep her voice light.

'This is Roderick,' Bessie informed her solemnly. 'Roderick Ward.'

As Mrs Pegs gazed at her curiously, Bessie went on with a catch in her voice, 'I got married to a wonderful man in Liverpool after I left here, but sadly he passed away last year so I thought I would bring Roderick back to my home town. There was nothing left in Liverpool for us after Malcolm died, and I didn't know where else to go.'

Mrs Pegs could hardly take it all in and her mouth gaped open – but then clamping it shut, she ushered Bessie into the hallway, asking, 'Will you come through to the kitchen, lass? It sounds like we have a lot of catchin' up to do.'

Although she was delighted to see Bessie again she was also feeling very apprehensive. There was no mistaking who the boy belonged to, for he was a younger version of the man who had fathered him, but Bessie had clearly fallen on her feet somewhere along the way if the mountain of expensive luggage that was piled at the side of the door and the way she was togged out was anything to go by.

'I think I'd rather see Mr Farthing first, if you don't mind,' Bessie answered nervously. 'If I'm going to be living around here I think he needs to know why I ran away, so I may as well get it over with.'

'I can understand that.' Turning to Gwen, Mrs Pegs told her, 'The master is in his study. Go an' tell him there's some-one here who needs to speak to 'im, an' that it's very important.'

Gwen rushed off to do as she was told as Bessie stood clutching Roddy's hand. She had dreamed of this moment for so long, yet now it was here she wasn't looking forward to it one little bit.

'The master says I'm to show yer into the drawin' room, miss, an' he'll be along presently,' Gwen said on her return shortly afterwards.

Mrs Pegs squeezed Bessie's hand encouragingly. 'Come through to the kitchen when you're done,' she murmured, and after nodding, Bessie followed Gwen into the drawing room.

When Max Farthing entered the room moments later, his face broke into a smile at the sight of the girl he had fetched from the workhouse to help Mrs Pegs so long ago. Bessie had been just a young lass then and he had grown very fond of her over the years and had been worried when she just ran off with no word of explanation.

And yet he was hardly able to believe his eyes, for the Bessie standing before him was nothing like the girl he remembered. Her hair, which was smoothed into a neat chignon on the back of her head, was shining and she held herself proudly. Her clothes, he noticed, were the height of fashion too and her voice was more refined somehow.

'Why, Bessie. How lovely it is to see you – and looking so well and so grand too. I scarcely recognised you.' His smile expressed his delight at seeing her again, and just for a moment she felt a pang of guilt at the hurt she was about to heap upon him, but it had to be done.

'Actually it's Mrs Ward now. Could you spare me a moment, Mr Farthing?' she enquired.

His smile widened as he glanced down at the child. 'Of course. But who is this handsome little chap?'

'This, Mr Farthing, is your grandson.' Bessie placed a hand on the little boy's thin shoulders.

Max grasped the back of a chair to steady himself and the colour drained out of his face.

'Is – is this some sort of a joke, Bessie? Err – I mean Mrs Ward,' he croaked.

Bessie led Roddy to a chair at the far side of the room, then returning to Max, she lowered her voice and answered, 'It's no joke, I assure you. I ran away because Samuel, your son, had raped me and Roderick here is the result. Can you not see the resemblance to his father?'

Max shook his head in disbelief, but when he looked across at the child he saw the resemblance was undoubtedly there.

'I was afraid that if I had told you I was with child, you would have placed me back in the workhouse,' Bessie explained quietly. 'And that is why I ran away.' She then went on to tell him about the wonderful man she had met and married in Liverpool, and when she had finished, Max sank into the nearest chair and rubbed his hand across his forehead.

He was shocked and disgusted yet again at what his son was capable of, but also unsure what Bessie expected him to do about it.

'Mrs Pegs will verify what I am telling you if you doubt my word,' the young woman went on. 'On the night I ran away I left her a note telling her why I was going. She may well still have it, if you ask her.'

'There will be no need for that.' Max had never had cause to doubt Bessie's word before and he didn't now. 'But I'm not quite sure what you expect me to do about it, my dear. You see, Samuel is married to Niamh now, and she has a daughter to him.'

'You mean Niamh Carey, Dilly's daughter?' Shock registered on Bessie's face but then pulling herself together again, she told him hastily, 'I don't wish to marry your son. But I do think Samuel should acknowledge that Roderick is his. I believe he is his firstborn – unless, of course, there are other women he has taken down.'

Hearing the bitterness in her voice, Max cringed, and yet he could well understand why she should feel as she did. But if only she had told him after the rape had taken place! He could have helped her, and he would never have returned her to the workhouse. Sadly, she had clearly been too frightened to tell him, and it hurt him to think of how terrified she must have been, facing such a terrible situation all on her own.

'I think we need to speak to Samuel as soon as possible,' he said, feeling totally out of control of the situation. 'But meantime, where will you stay?'

'I shall book us both into a small hotel,' she answered and with that she beckoned Roddy to her and bade Max goodbye, before heading back to the kitchen.

Mrs Pegs ushered Bessie to a chair and ordered Gwen, who was clearly enjoying the distraction, to, 'Make a fresh pot o' tea, pet, this one'll be stewed by now.' Then, bending to the child's level she asked kindly, 'An' how would you like a nice glass o' milk an' one o' my special biscuits, eh?'

For the first time she noticed the nervous twitch in the child's eye and the way he glanced at his mother as if for permission before whispering, 'Yes, please.' He was a comely little chap but jumpy as a kitten from what she could make of it.

Within minutes he was sitting docilely at the table with the treats in front of him.

'So how did Mr Farthing take it?' Mrs Pegs asked Bessie.

The young woman shrugged. 'Not well, as you can imagine. It's funny, really. I've dreamed for so long of coming here and getting my revenge, yet I got no satisfaction at all from upsetting the master.' Bessie had removed her hat and after patting her hair she then asked, 'But how are things here, Mrs Pegs?'

The older woman sighed. So much had happened since Bessie had run away and she barely knew where to start. There would be time for all that later though, she decided. For now she wanted to know more about what had happened to Bessie. The poor lass looked thoroughly miserable and Mrs Pegs realised it must have taken some courage for her to face Mr Farthing as she had.

'I wonder now if I've done the right thing coming back here,' Bessie said uncertainly as she glanced across at Roddy. What could she achieve now? Samuel was married and she didn't want to hurt Niamh.

'Mr Farthing tells me that Samuel is married now to Niamh,' she said aloud, and Mrs Pegs gulped and nodded.

'Yes, he is. They've got a house on Abbey Green an' a

little girl called Constance – although we all call 'er Connie.'

'I see,' Bessie said, her voice shaky, 'Did Samuel get Niamh into the family way too?' She could think of no other reason why Dilly Carey's daughter would have married him otherwise. She had been led to believe that Niamh had a sweetheart in Ireland. She and Dilly, who had also worked there as a maid, had been close once and Bessie couldn't imagine her being too happy with the situation.

'I reckon 'e must 'ave,' the older woman said uncomfortably. She didn't want to speak out of turn. 'An' between you an' me I don't reckon theirs is much of a marriage. 'E ain't even there 'alf the time from what I can make of it, but I think that suits Niamh just fine. She never made a secret o' the fact that she didn't want to marry 'im. Dilly is doin' well though. She's come a long way since she worked 'ere as a maid, an' she 'as her own dress shop in town these days, God bless 'er. But now that's enough about what's been 'appening 'ere. That little man o' yours looks fit to drop.'

The child was sitting silently at the table with his head nodding, and Mrs Pegs thought it was no wonder after the long journey he must just have endured. She felt sorry for the poor little chap and suggested tactfully, 'Why don't you come an' snuggle down in the chair by the fire, pet, an' 'ave a little nap while me an' your mam decide what you're to do?'

The child did as he was told after another glance at his mother, and within seconds of Mrs Pegs tucking a warm rug across him, he was sound asleep.

'He's a handsome little boy,' Mrs Pegs commented and Bessie nodded.

'I dare say he is; my Malcolm certainly thought so. The sun rose and set with him.' She sniffed to hold back tears as she thought of the kindly man who had taken her in off the streets, given her a home and a job and eventually married her. Malcolm had been much older than her, a widower, but Bessie had adored him.

Her face crumpled as she remembered and she confided, 'The trouble is, now that Malcolm's gone I'm solely responsible for Roddy and . . .' She forced herself to go on. 'I can't seem to take to him. I know it's wicked – I am his mother, after all, and I should love him! I couldn't wait for him to be born.' She looked sadly towards the sleeping child. 'But then when I had him, I couldn't bear to look at him. Every time I did, I remembered the night Samuel . . .' Unable to go on, she bowed her head and Mrs Pegs patted her hand sympathetically.

'It'll probably come in time. He is your flesh an' blood, after all. You just 'ave to be patient. But what are you plannin' to do now? I'd ask yer to stay 'ere but wi' things as they are . . .'

Bessie sighed as Mrs Pegs' voice trailed away.

'Don't fret about us,' she said. 'I have more than enough money to keep us going for a fair while. The sale of Malcolm's shop has ensured that I can be comfortable for some time, but I quite fancy trying a little business venture of my own although I haven't decided what I want to do as yet.'

Mrs Pegs looked at the large clock on the kitchen wall and commented, 'Shouldn't be too long now afore Samuel calls in. He often does of an evenin' so 'ow about I make you a bite to eat afore 'e comes, eh? I don't need to start dinner for the family fer another 'our or so at least.'

Bessie accepted Mrs Pegs' kind offer. She had no desire to see Samuel but she wanted to get it over with now.

The afternoon was darkening and a thick hoar frost was forming on the grass when the women heard the back door open.

'Hello, Mrs Pegs.' It was Niamh. 'I just popped by as I wanted a word with Max. Is he in?'

Although the mistress had never given the girl the time of day and didn't know her from Adam any more, Niamh still came to see her mother-in-law regularly, especially since Mrs Farthing had been unwell.

Niamh's smile died when she saw how flustered the woman was.

'Is everything all right?' she asked. 'Mrs Farthing isn't worse, is she? I could get the doctor to come back—'

'No, no, it's nothin' like that.' Mrs Pegs flapped her hand impatiently. 'But we 'ave a visitor. It's Bessie – the maid that run away some time back, an' I'm afraid she 'as some news that might shock yer. The thing is . . .'

'It's quite all right, Mrs Pegs. I am more than capable of explaining the situation myself, thank you,' Bessie butted in, more haughtily than she had intended, thanks to her nerves. Taking a deep breath, she then told Niamh as calmly as she could why she had run away.

A wealth of emotions flitted across Niamh's face as she tried to take it all in – and then she erupted. 'If it wasn't for Mr Farthing, I'd get you to come to the police with me and report him,' she said angrily. 'Samuel treats women as if they are dirt, but I don't want to hurt his father.'

Bessie nodded in agreement. Nothing would have pleased her more than to shame Samuel, but by doing that she would shame the whole family too – and she had no wish to do that.

Then suddenly Niamh rushed across to Bessie to take her hands. There was no point in being angry with the girl, after all. She had been wronged too.

'Oh Bessie. I'm so sorry,' Niamh said sincerely. 'But now you and Roderick must come and stay at my house for a few days until you decide what you are going to do and where you are going to live.' Seeing the look of horror that flitted across Bessie's face, she rushed on, 'You mustn't worry about seeing Samuel. Ours is a marriage in name only and he's rarely at home, thank goodness, so you will be quite safe, I promise you.'

Bessie looked uncertain but then she smiled tremulously and replied, 'In that case I would be grateful to accept your invitation, Mrs Farthing. Thank you.'

'It's still Niamh,' the other young woman scolded – and as they looked at each other, they both felt the pain that Samuel had caused them and a bond was forged.

# *Chapter Two*

'But this is just incredible!' Dilly Carey exclaimed that evening as she sat in Niamh's neat little kitchen with her and Bessie. She often called in after the shop was shut to visit her daughter and granddaughter. Bessie had just relayed her story yet again and Dilly was so shocked she could scarcely get her breath. Dilly had never had much time for Samuel and suffered all manner of guilt because she had allowed her daughter to marry him – and yet what would have been the alternative? Niamh would have been branded for life, as would Constance, but even so she was painfully aware that Niamh was still very unhappy. Dilly knew Niamh's heart still belonged to Ben, to whom she had been promised before Samuel had raped her – and Dilly suspected it always would.

'Well, I do sympathise with your predicament, Bessie,' she said briskly now, 'but I hardly think it's appropriate for you to stay here. You must come and stay in the rooms above the shop with me for now. Seamus is convalescing in

11

Ireland with his grandparents, as he suffered shell shock during the war, so you and Roderick can have his room until you decide what you want to do.'

'But, Mammy, little Roderick is fast asleep,' Niamh objected. 'It would be cruel to disturb him tonight. The poor little soul is worn out after all the travelling and there's not much likelihood of Samuel coming home.'

Dilly sighed. It was clear that Niamh had taken to the little boy already, but goodness knew what was going to happen when Samuel found out that Bessie had brought the results of his rape home to confront him.

'Very well, stay tonight then, but tomorrow first thing you must come to me,' she stipulated. 'I've no doubt Samuel's father will have tracked him down and told him all about Roderick by then.'

She shuddered to think how Samuel would take it. He barely acknowledged Constance, not that the little girl lacked in love. Max Farthing, her grandfather, adored her, as did Niamh, and she was a happy, contented little girl. Quite different to Roderick, who seemed to jump at his own shadow.

Bessie nodded. It appeared that her return was causing quite a commotion. But then Niamh clearly loved her child whilst she struggled to feel anything for her Roddy. It all seemed so unfair.

'All right then, Dilly. Thank you, I'll do that just until I decide what we're to do.' As she looked across at her old friend, Bessie found it hard to believe that the woman opposite her was now almost forty-three years old. Dilly was still slim and straight-backed and her face was relatively unlined despite the hardships she had been forced to endure over the years. Her copper-coloured hair had barely a trace of grey in it and Bessie thought she could easily have been taken for someone ten years younger. Niamh was like a younger version of her mother and it appeared that

Constance took after them too. There was no trace of Fergal, Dilly's late husband, to be seen in either the daughter or the granddaughter.

'Mrs Pegs told me that your Kian was killed in the war,' Bessie said then. 'I was sorry to hear that, Dilly. It must be terrible to lose a son. He was a fine young man.'

Dilly's face clouded as she thought of her firstborn. 'Thank you. Yes, he was, and one day I intend to find his resting place and lay some flowers there for him. His regiment are trying to find out exactly where he is buried for me. All I know at present is that it's somewhere in France. But look at the time!' She glanced towards the clock, wanting to change the subject, and rose hastily. 'I must be off but I'll see you in the morning, Bessie. You know where the shop is in Queens Road, don't you?'

'Oh yes, it's the old "Miss Mode's" isn't it?'

'It still is "Miss Mode's",' Dilly grinned making her look younger still. 'I haven't had it for that long and haven't had time to order a new sign to be made for it yet. To be honest, all we sewed throughout the latter part of the war was uniforms, so I'm still in the process of turning it back into a dress shop.'

'And she has some marvellous ideas for it,' Niamh chipped in proudly. 'As well as customers still being able to order a dress and have it made, she intends to stock ready-to-wear items too don't you, Mammy?'

Dilly beamed. 'That's the general idea. In fact, I'm going to Birmingham next week to look over some stock, but I shall still keep two seamstresses on. The ready-made clothes items aren't going to appeal to everyone straight away so I have to be sure that I'll still be able to cater to all my clientele. As it happens I've just acquired the shop next door as well so I shall be able to enlarge the existing shop and knock it all into one to make a more appealing frontage.'

'What she means is a "posher" shopfront,' Niamh tittered. 'Some of Mammy's customers are frightful snobs and she has to pander to them.'

'Snobs or not I need their custom if I'm to make a go of this business,' Dilly said ruefully. She then rose and, shrugging her arms into the sleeves of her warm coat, she kissed both young women on the cheeks and told Bessie, 'Until tomorrow then.'

Once she had gone, Bessie commented, 'She looks really well considering all she's gone through.'

Niamh agreed. 'Between you and me, the shop seems to have given her a new lease of life. After we lost Daddy she took Kian's death very badly, and then when Seamus was injured as well . . . but then Mammy is made of stern stuff, and if her dreams come to fruition she's going to own a whole chain of shops all across the country. I reckon she just might do it as well, with Mr Farthing's help. He's been marvellous to the family, me included. But now how about we treat ourselves to a little glass of sherry? I don't drink very often but I reckon your return warrants it. I just wish I could be a fly on the wall when Samuel learns that you and his son are here.'

The two young women fell silent as Niamh hurried away to fetch the glasses.

Dilly was down on her hands and knees scrubbing the floor in the second shop later that evening when a tap came to the door. The windows had been whitewashed over for privacy during the renovations, but she knew before answering who it would be.

'Hello, Max.' Swiping a lock of hair from her face she ushered him inside away from prying eyes.

'Whatever are you doing?' he asked. 'I thought the builders were coming in tomorrow to knock the connecting door down?'

'They were,' she answered as she wiped her hands down her apron-front, 'but one of them popped in earlier to say that his mate had come down with the influenza so we've put it off until next week.'

She had expected Max this evening although she had already seen him earlier in the day. Max always sought her out when there was a crisis on, and after Bessie turning up so unexpectedly Dilly could only begin to guess how upset he must be.

'Come upstairs,' she said gently. 'I dare say you could do with a nightcap.' She clicked the shop lights off and he followed her up the stairs to where a fire was crackling nicely in the grate in the room that she had transformed into a cosy little sitting room.

After removing her apron and tucking her stray locks behind her ears she crossed to a small whisky decanter and poured two shots into glasses; a large one for him and a smaller one for herself.

'Here you are.' She handed his glass to him, noting that he looked tired. Over the many years they had been acquainted she had come to know his moods, and tonight she could see how weary he was.

'Did you manage to find Samuel?'

He shook his head dejectedly, then took a long swallow of his drink and shuddered. 'No, though I have a good idea where he's hanging around. Robert mentioned when I called into my club that he's been leeching off a widow on the outskirts of town. She's years older than him, by all accounts, but that won't worry Samuel so long as she keeps him in style. I despair of that young man sometimes, I really do. Lawrence is his twin, and has always behaved decently. Where did I go wrong with Sam?'

'You didn't,' she assured him wisely. 'Samuel has always been a law unto himself right since he was a child. He wasn't

15

treated any differently to the rest of your brood and they've all turned out to be fine young people, haven't they? Especially Olivia.'

As their eyes locked, an unspoken message passed between them and Dilly hastily averted her eyes. Even now after all these years it still hurt to think back to the night Olivia had been born, when she had wrapped her in a shawl and taken her to the Farthings to bring up as their own. Looking back, that had been the start of their relationship and it had grown over the years. Sometimes Dilly wondered how she had survived that tragic time. Fergal, her late husband, had been crippled doing his job on the railways, and Dilly hadn't known where to turn to keep them all afloat. Max Farthing and his wife, Camilla, had lost their own baby daughter, Violet, the year before, so when Camilla had offered to buy the child, Dilly had seen no alternative but to go along with the idea. And so year after year, Dilly had been forced to stand back and watch the Farthings bring her daughter up as their own. Dilly had always known that Camilla only allowed her to work in her home on sufferance and because it had been part of their agreement. There was many a time when Camilla would have loved to give her her marching orders, but Max stuck by the agreement and would not allow it.

From then on, Dilly had been forced to watch Fergal deteriorate and Camilla sink into insanity – and during all this, she and Max had grown closer and had drawn comfort from each other. She was painfully aware that he loved her, and truth be told his love was returned, but both of them were too honourable to take their relationship beyond friendship whilst his wife was alive. Now as he lounged back in his chair and stretched his feet out towards the fire with a long sigh, Dilly watched him closely. She could only begin to imagine the turmoil he must be feeling. Although they had never openly acknowledged their feelings for one another, anyone seeing them now might have taken them for an old married couple.

'He's a nice little chap, isn't he? Roderick, I mean,' Max said quietly. 'Fancy having a little grandson I never knew existed turn up out of the blue like that, eh? He seems a timid wee thing though, doesn't he?'

'He does actually.' Dilly frowned. 'But then perhaps he was tired after all the travelling. He might be chirpier tomorrow when he's had a good night's sleep.'

'He might be,' Max conceded. 'But from what I saw of it, he didn't seem to be particularly close to his mother. In fact, he seemed to be quite nervous of her.'

Dilly floundered, unable to come up with an answer before informing him, 'I've told Bessie that she and Roderick can come and stay here with me tomorrow till she decides what she wants to do. It doesn't seem quite right somehow in the circumstances for her to be staying with Niamh.'

'Huh!' Max said wryly. 'I don't exactly know what Bessie is expecting Samuel to do when he learns about Roderick. He doesn't even provide for Connie and Niamh – and they are his legal family.'

When he saw Dilly anxiously chew on her lip he hurried on, 'Not that I mind providing for them, of course. Connie is my grandchild, after all, and there's nothing I wouldn't do for her, as you well know. She's the apple of my eye.'

'But it still doesn't seem fair that you should carry the financial burden of them,' Dilly answered. 'And as Niamh has told you on many occasions, she would be more than happy to return to work.'

'Yes, she has, but I want her at home with Connie, at least until Connie is old enough to go to school.' Max ran a hand tiredly over his eyes and Dilly added another tot of whisky to his glass. He looked like he could do with it. 'The trouble

17

is, I don't quite know what I'm supposed to do about Bessie and her child. I mean, it's been accepted that Connie is my granddaughter – Niamh is married to my son – but how do I explain Roderick? I tell you, Dilly, I could wring Samuel's neck – I really could!'

Hoping to steer the conversation away from Bessie's untimely arrival for a while, Dilly asked, 'How are Camilla and the nurse this evening?'

'When the doctor called this afternoon he said that he thought Camilla seemed a little better, but I'm afraid her nurse is still very poorly with this influenza,' Max said worriedly. 'Camilla isn't quite so bad, although her mental state doesn't help. The doctor mentioned putting her in a home again this afternoon but I can't bring myself to do it.' It had been a rare old day what with one thing and another, and he for one wouldn't be sorry when it was over!

The next morning after breakfast, Bessie began to prepare to move to Dilly's.

'I'll send a cart to pick our luggage up,' she told Niamh and the young woman nodded. She would be quite sorry to see Bessie go and she knew that Connie would too. She had taken quite a shine to little Roderick and was following him about like a puppy.

Having another adult to talk to had made Niamh realise just how secluded she had become. Admittedly, her father-in-law had offered to provide a live-in maid for her but Niamh had always refused up to now. The way she saw it, Max did far too much for them as it was and she was quite capable of cooking and keeping her own house clean. And then of course she had Connie, who more than kept her on her toes as she was now at the age where she was into absolutely everything. For the majority of the time, Niamh was content with her little daughter's company, but sometimes her yearning to see Ben would almost overwhelm her and the loneliness would close in on her.

In her grandmother's last letter, Maeve had told Niamh that Ben was about to take over the blacksmith's business from Sean McLoughlin in Enniskerry and in her mind's eye Niamh could picture the pretty little cottage that came with it. Had things turned out differently, it would have been their home – but that would never happen now. Samuel had put paid to that, and although he had married her she despised him and knew that theirs could never be anything more than a marriage in name only. She'd heard whispers that the rich widow he had recently taken up with owned several jewellery shops across the country, so no doubt he was squeezing every penny he could out of her; that was his way. It didn't trouble Niamh. Whilst he was otherwise engaged he was leaving her well alone and that suited her just fine. The less she saw of him the better, as far as she was concerned. Lately an idea had been forming in her mind and she intended to broach it with her father-in-law at the earliest opportunity. As well as missing Ben she had also greatly missed her teaching job at Chilver's Coton School, and now that Connie was out of her baby stage she was considering going back to it – only part-time for a start, and then she would be able to afford to pay someone to look after Connie without asking any more of Samuel's father.

Niamh turned her thoughts back to Bessie. 'So what exactly are you hoping for from Samuel?' she asked her out-right as she began to clear the pots from the breakfast table.

Bessie chewed her lip. 'To be honest I'm not sure,' she admitted. 'I suppose I just wanted to see him squirm to pay him back for all the pain and humiliation he caused me – but now that I'm actually here I'm not so sure that coming back was such a good idea. I've hurt so many people – you for a start-off – and that was never my intention.'

19

'You haven't hurt me. Nothing Samuel does could ever shock me,' Niamh said stoically. 'But I'm glad you didn't come back expecting him to be sorry for what he's done. Because if you think he'll show you or Roderick any recognition, or that he'll make any monetary recompense, you'll be sadly disappointed.'

'I don't need his money, Niamh. My Malcolm left us more than comfortably provided for, God bless his soul. No, as I said, I just want to see the rat squirm.'

'Well, if you manage to achieve that I hope,' Niamh responded, 'I'm around to witness it.'

The two young women grinned at each other before Bessie bustled away to fetch her son's outdoor clothes.

# Chapter Three

'Ah, so you made it.' Dilly hurried forward to embrace Bessie and Roderick when they appeared in the shop doorway a little later that morning. As usual the child stood mutely at his mother's side as Dilly ushered them towards the stairs.

After throwing open the door to Seamus' room she told Bessie apologetically, 'I'm afraid there's only room for one bed in here but you won't mind having Roderick in with you, will you? He's so tiny he won't take up much room.' She chucked the child beneath the chin as she spoke but he remained solemn-faced as he stared up at her from huge dark eyes that appeared to be too large for his small pinched face. Dilly fought the urge to lift him and give him a cuddle as she went away to fetch an extra blanket. The bedrooms tended to be very cold in winter and she didn't want the poor little mite coming down with a cold, or worse still, to become another victim of the deadly influenza epidemic that was claiming hundreds of thousands of lives. As if the war to end all wars had not claimed enough victims!

Bessie wasn't too happy about the new sleeping arrangements, but not wishing to be impolite she held her tongue. It wouldn't be for long, after all. Once she had shamed Samuel she didn't plan to stay in Nuneaton. She had money and the world was her oyster; she just had to decide where she wanted to go and what she wanted to do now. It was a shame about Roderick though, she thought as she stared down at her son. She felt guilty about the way she felt, or more to the point, *didn't feel* about the little boy. It hadn't mattered so much whilst Malcolm had been alive; he had loved the child enough for both of them and she knew that Roddy, as Malcolm had affectionately nicknamed him, still cried himself to sleep thinking of his daddy. That was one thing she and her son had in common at least, for she still missed her husband dreadfully too.

Her thoughts were interrupted when Dilly bustled back in, saying, 'Now you must treat this as your home for the time you're here. You'll soon get to know where everything is. Unfortunately I have to catch a train shortly to go and view some stock for the shop in Birmingham. Will you be all right until I get back?'

'Perfectly.' Bessie took the hatpin from her hat and removed the feathered concoction with a flourish and once again Dilly was amazed at the change in her. Bessie would never be classed as beautiful in a classical sense, but in her smart clothes and with her new-found confidence she certainly looked very attractive. Dilly wondered what Samuel would make of her when they finally met again, but then had no time to think on it or she would miss her train.

Once Dilly had left, Bessie wandered about the small rooms and frowned discontentedly. Dilly's apartment above the shop was nowhere near as big or as nice as the one she had shared with Malcolm, but Dilly had explained that she was quite happy with it for now as she needed to plough all her money into her new business. Thoughts of Malcolm brought tears stinging to Bessie's eyes as they always did, and once again she felt bereft. She missed the way he had made her feel – as if she was beautiful and important – the warmth of his arms about her and the touch of his lips on hers. She knew that never in her lifetime would she ever again experience a love the like of which she had shared with him, and it frightened her as she pictured herself drifting into a lonely old age. And then of course there was Roderick. Who would want her anyway with a child in tow, even if she was a respectable widow?

Crossing to the small sitting-room window she twitched the curtain aside and gazed miserably down into the street below. Very soon now Mr Farthing would no doubt track Samuel down and confront him about her return; if he hadn't already done so, that was. She sighed. Revenge didn't seem quite so important now, and she had to stifle the urge to grab her bags and run. But she couldn't do that to Roddy, even though she felt no love for him. The poor little mite deserved better than that. She knew only too well what it felt like to be abandoned, for hadn't she spent all of her young life in the workhouse?

Could Bessie have known it, at that very moment Max Farthing was sitting in his gentleman's club gazing impatiently at the clock. It was a rare thing for him to be seen there during the day; he was normally busy attending to one or another of his businesses but he had slept fitfully the night before and during that time he had realised that this would probably be the best time and place to catch Samuel. His son cared little for work or routine and so Max sat on, restlessly tapping his fingers on the arm of the deep buttoned leather chesterfield chair he was seated in.

The minutes ticked away and Max was just about to give

up and leave when the door suddenly opened and Samuel strolled in looking as if he hadn't a care in the world.

'Samuel? Over here, if you please.'

Samuel's head snapped round, and he looked mildly surprised to see his father there. As his son sauntered towards him, Max noted that he was sporting a rather expensive watch chain across his embroidered waistcoat. A present from his mistress, the rich widow, no doubt.

'So, Father, what brings you here at this time of the day?' Samuel took a seat in the chair opposite. Then, clicking his fingers at a passing waiter, he told him, 'Whisky, please.'

'Right away, sir.' As the man hurried off, Samuel turned his attention to his father again.

'I need to speak to you urgently – but not here,' Max informed him grimly.

'Oh yes, what about?'

'Never mind what about. Have your drink and then come with me.'

Samuel shrugged as the waiter reappeared with his whisky balanced on a silver tray. He took it and knocked it back in one go, then rising he said, 'Come on then. I'm intrigued to learn what might be so important.'

After following his father out into the street he looked up and down for a sign of Max's car.

'I'm walking.' Max's voice was heavy with sarcasm. 'The war might be over but in case you've forgotten there are still shortages, including petrol. But never mind, we don't have far to go.'

'My car is just around the corner,' Samuel protested, but when Max ignored him and strode purposefully on, he followed his father just the same, wondering what the hell all this could be about.

'So why have we come here?' Samuel asked a short time later when Max stopped in front of Dilly's shop.

'You'll see soon enough,' his father answered shortly as he went through the shop and headed for the narrow staircase at the back.

With a heavy sigh Samuel stayed close behind, and in seconds Max swung open the door to Dilly's apartment and led him inside.

Then a bedroom door opened and a woman appeared. There was something vaguely familiar about her, although for a few moments Samuel couldn't for the life of him think what it was. And then suddenly, recognition flared in his eyes. '*Bessie!*' he gasped.

But this was not the Bessie he remembered, the timid little thing who would jump to do his bidding. This was a smart, self-assured young woman about town.

'Well I'll be . . .' he said. 'And what brings you back to these parts?'

'I have someone I think you should meet.' She calmly turned and went back into the bedroom, to reappear leading a small boy by the hand. Then crossing to Samuel, she hissed in his ear, 'This is Roderick – your son!'

'My *what*?'

Bessie had the satisfaction of seeing the colour drain from his face like water from a dam.

'I – I don't quite know what stunt you're trying to pull here but that kid is nothing to do with me,' Samuel protested, yanking at his collar. There suddenly didn't seem to be enough air in the room.

The child just stood staring at him, his mouth working and his eyes huge in his pale face. It was clear that he was terrified, and so Bessie gently led him to the bedroom and after coaxing him onto a chair, she closed the door on him.

She then faced Samuel again. Outwardly she appeared to be composed, but inwardly she was quaking as she told him coolly, 'I assure you he *is* your son. Don't you remember the night you raped me in the kitchen? I do – every second of it. Well, he is the result. The reason I ran away was because I was too afraid to tell anyone what you had done, and I was with child!'

'*It's a downright bloody lie!*' Samuel spat as he looked towards his father. 'She's come for a pay-out trying to blame me for some other chap's offspring. Surely you don't believe her word against mine, Father?'

'As a matter of fact, I do.' Max's eyes were boring into Samuel's very soul. 'As it happens, Bessie wrote a letter to Mrs Pegs the night she left, telling her all about what you had done and the unfortunate condition she found herself in, so now the question is – what are you going to do about it?'

'Absolutely bloody *nothing*! It's a lie, I tell you, and I'll not be saddled with a flyblow.'

He felt trapped, and his hands clenched into fists as he glared at Bessie.

Meanwhile, Max narrowed his eyes as he hissed, 'Once again I am ashamed to call you my son. There are plenty of willing women out there for you to paw at, as you well know. You've certainly spent enough time in the town's whorehouse!'

Shock briefly registered in Samuel's eyes. It appeared that his father knew more about his pastimes than he had imagined. But then rage took over and he began to pace up and down the room just as Bessie came out of the bedroom again. She appeared to be very calm and collected. Samuel could almost have believed she was enjoying herself and he had to stifle the urge to smack her face.

'So what *exactly* do you want?' he ground out.

Bessie shrugged nonchalantly. 'To have my son recognised, I suppose. Why should the care of him be left all up to me?'

Samuel snorted with derision. 'Do you *really* think I

would ever admit to being the father of a maid's bastard?'

'You made an honest woman of Niamh, didn't you, and what stock is she from? Hasn't her mother, Dilly, been a maid to your family for years?'

'All right, you two, that is quite enough,' Max intervened then. 'Shouting and arguing is not going to resolve this problem, is it? I suggest you leave now, Samuel, and we will continue this conversation when you've both had time to calm down.'

'Huh!' Samuel turned and stamped away down the stairs without so much as another word as Bessie sank heavily onto the nearest chair. Strangely, the confrontation had been nowhere near as satisfying as she had hoped it would be. She was still the sole carer of Roderick, and every time she so much as looked at him he felt like a great weight on her shoulders, which merely served to increase her misery. If only she could have died with her beloved Malcolm.

'Er . . . are you all right, my dear?' Max asked as he saw the sag of her shoulders.

'Yes. I am quite all right, thank you.'

'Then in that case I too must take my leave, but at least the worst part is over now. Dilly should be back before too long and then you will have another woman to discuss this with. I'm afraid I am not very much good in a crisis.'

'You've been very kind to me,' Bessie whispered to him as she blinked back bitter tears. 'And I'm sorry I have had to involve you in this sorry mess.'

'Everything will come right in the end,' he said gently, feeling very inadequate as he reached for his hat. 'Goodbye for now.'

'Goodbye, si . . . Mr Farthing.'

She watched him leave, closing the door quietly behind him, and once he was gone she lowered her head into her hands and wept.

## Chapter Four

Over in Enniskerry, Maeve Carey was also weeping as Ben loaded the last of his belongings onto the back of the cart.

'Eeh, it don't seem no time at all since you came here as a wean,' she sniffed and Ben put his arm about her and hugged her. Maeve and her husband, Daniel, had taken him in off the streets of Dublin and welcomed him into their family when he was just a child, and he knew that he would never be able to thank them enough for all they had done for him.

'I never thought your leaving would be like this,' Maeve choked. 'I always imagined you and our Niamh would be wed afore you moved into the blacksmith's cottage, so I did.'

Ben hid his pain as he replied. 'I thought the same but it clearly wasn't meant to be, was it? Niamh is happily married to another now.'

'I'm not so sure about that,' Maeve admitted gravely. 'When I popped over to meet Constance, my great-granddaughter, a while back I never saw sight nor sound of Niamh's husband for the whole time I was there.'

'Perhaps he was working away?' Ben suggested as he stared around at the smallholding he had come to love.

'Tish! He works for his father, Mr Farthing, from what I could make of it.' Maeve shook her head. 'And strangely enough, Niamh changed the subject every time I mentioned him, so she did. That hardly sounds like someone in love, does it?'

The conversation went no further when ten-year-old Patrick and eight-year-old Bridie, Maeve's grandchildren, appeared out of the barn and flew towards them, scattering the chickens, who were squawking indignantly, in all directions.

'Ah, you're not goin' so soon, are you, Uncle Ben?' Bridie cried with tears glistening on her lashes and Ben knelt to her level and cuddled her, whilst Patrick looked solemnly on.

'I'm afraid I have to be away now, but I shall be back to see youse all so often you'll barely notice I'm gone. Meantime I want you both to help Gran'ma look after your Uncle Seamus so I do.'

Unconvinced, Bridie sniffed, as Liam, Maeve's youngest son, and his wife Shelagh appeared from inside their cottage. Daniel was striding across the yard too and Ben's throat was full.

Daniel took his hand and shook it firmly, telling him, 'Now you know where we are, lad. We'll always be here should you need us. Don't be a stranger now.'

Shelagh and Liam hugged him then and finally Maeve wrapped her arms about him and whispered, 'Godspeed, me bonny lad. An' think on what we was talkin' about t'other night. You know, about meeting your real Mammy. She's heartsore that she had to give you up when you were just a babe in arms, and just wants to try and make amends, but the final decision is yours, o' course, an' we're here for you no matter what.'

'I'll think on it,' Ben promised, then he was swinging himself up onto the cart. He took the reins and urged the old horse forward to a chorus of, 'Gooodbye, Godspeed!' that followed him all along the track.

Once out on the lane that would lead him to Enniskerry, he took a handkerchief from his pocket and blew his nose noisily. He'd gone no more than a mile or so when it started to drizzle from the dull grey clouds overhead and he pulled his coat collar up to try and keep warm. There was a cold wind blowing that didn't help matters and by the time he pulled the cart up outside Sean McLoughlin's smithy he was shivering and feeling thoroughly miserable.

It seemed like a lifetime ago since he and Niamh had stood outside this place making plans for their future. Jumping down from the cart, he led the horse to the stable and unharnessed him. He then rubbed him down and made him comfortable before making his way behind the blacksmiths to the small cottage that would now be his home.

After inserting the key in the lock he let himself into the small sitting room and struck a match to the fire that Shelagh had laid ready for him the day before. She and Maeve had been there all day making sure that he would have everything he needed, and they had made the place look comfortable and cosy. Shelagh had sewn pretty curtains to hang at the small leaded glass windows and with the leftover material she had made cushions for the small settee that Sean had left for him. Thankfully, Sean had left most of the furniture as it happened, which had saved Ben from having to go out and buy any. The old blacksmith had been widowed some years before, and now that he was retiring and going to live with his daughter in a neighbouring village, he would have no need of it, luckily for Ben. A bright rag rug which Maeve had made lay in front of the hearth and on the wall behind the settee was a pine dresser that the women had stocked with spare pots that they felt he might need. Next to that was a sturdy oak table and four chairs, and beyond them, a curtain at the far end of the room led into a small kitchen. Wide shelves on which stood various pots and pans took up one wall, and beneath the window overlooking the yard was a deep stone sink to which was fastened a sturdy wooden draining board. A range took up most of the other wall and now Ben hastily lit that too as this would be his only form of cooking and heating water.

In truth the cottage was somewhat old-fashioned, and he and Niamh had been full of plans about what they would do to it, but Ben didn't have any heart for it now. He decided he would concentrate on the blacksmith's business. The house would be just somewhere to eat and sleep without Niamh to share it with him. He mounted the staircase that led to two small bedrooms and again found that the women had seen to everything. The front bedroom contained a heavy old brass bed covered in warm blankets and feather pillows, and again there was a fire laid ready to light in the tiny hearth. The only other furniture in the room was an old oak wardrobe and a chest of drawers that had been polished until he could almost see his face in it. It seemed that Maeve and Shelagh had thought of everything. Yet strangely he could feel no excitement nor joy in suddenly becoming the owner of his own home and business. Without Niamh it felt pointless. Admittedly over the last couple of years he had half-heartedly courted a few of the village girls, but as soon as they had begun to talk about bottom drawers and babies he had run a mile. None of them seemed able to match up to Niamh and he doubted now that any of them ever would.

With a sigh he walked back through the empty rooms and headed for the smithy. He had a business to build and the sooner he got on with it the better. Whilst he was busy he didn't have time to dwell on what might have been.

## *Chapter Five*

It was almost teatime when Dilly finally alighted the train in Trent Valley railway station. She was cold and tired but absolutely elated with her day. The supplier she had gone to meet had shown her a range of clothes that she felt would be just perfect for the shop, and Dilly had ordered as many as she felt she could possibly afford. The dresses had been fashionable but very reasonably priced, and she was sure that they would soon become very much sought-after by the women of the town. Of course she would still offer a service to those who wanted their clothes tailormade, but now her mind was buzzing with ideas and she could scarcely wait to talk to Max about them.

On the way home she called in to see Niamh and Constance. Her little granddaughter ran to her and hugged her. Her copper-coloured hair, so like her mother's and Dilly's own, was tied back in a yellow ribbon to match the little dress she was wearing, and she looked adorable.

'Did you have a good day?' Niamh asked as she bustled

about getting cups ready and putting the kettle on to boil.

'I had a wonderful day!' Dilly was almost glowing with excitement. 'In the cities, ready-made wedding dresses are really becoming popular so I'm going to talk to Max about having some in the other shop. I think it could really catch on, don't you?'

'Hmm, I suppose it could,' Niamh agreed thoughtfully. 'It's certainly worth giving it a go.'

Their conversation turned to Bessie then and the recent developments. 'Is Bessie settling in all right?' Niamh asked, 'I would have been quite happy to have her here, you know.'

'Oh yes? And what do you think people would have made of that when word got out that Roderick is Samuel's child? It just doesn't bear thinking about.'

Niamh tossed her head. 'I don't much care what people choose to gossip about any more,' she said firmly. 'This has never been a proper marriage and never will be as far as I'm concerned. To be honest I wouldn't care if I never clapped eyes on Samuel again. Even on the rare occasions when he does come home, he doesn't give Connie the time of day.'

Dilly chewed anxiously on her lip but Niamh went on, 'Actually, I've had an idea too but it would all depend on whether I could get someone suitable to care for Connie for a few hours each week.' She then went on to tell her mother about her hopes of returning to work part-time and was pleased when Dilly didn't scoff at the idea.

'It would get you out of the house. How about Nell?' Dilly suggested. Nell Cotteridge was their old neighbour from their former home in St Mary's Road and both of them would have trusted her with their lives. 'I bet she would be glad of a few extra shillings a week and we both know how much she loves Connie. I can't think of anyone better suited to the job.'

'I think you could be right,' Niamh agreed happily as she measured tea leaves into the heavy brown teapot. 'I might get Connie wrapped up warmly and pop round to put the idea to her today.'

Fifteen minutes later Dilly left and went back to the rooms above the shop to see how Bessie was settling in. It was late afternoon by then and already growing dark when she climbed the stairs to her living quarters.

She found Roderick sitting still as a little statue on the sofa and Bessie putting the finishing touches to a beef stew she had made.

'I hope you don't mind me cooking,' she apologised. 'But I found all the ingredients in the cupboard and thought you might be glad of something warm when you got home.'

'I'm delighted not to have to cook,' Dilly assured her as she slid her coat off and held her hands out to the fire.

Bessie then went on to tell her of her confrontation with Samuel, and Dilly listened intently. Apart from a financial pay-off, she wasn't quite sure what Bessie was hoping for. Samuel could hardly marry her and make an honest woman of her when he was already married to Niamh, and even had he been free she doubted very much whether Bessie would have wanted to be tied to him. The young woman clearly loathed him, which was quite understandable in the circumstances. But Dilly supposed Bessie had returned to the one place she'd thought of as home. The poor girl obviously was lost without her beloved husband.

The three of them sat round Dilly's little table to eat their meal, which was quite delicious, and then Bessie got Roderick ready for bed as Dilly cleared the pots away.

'I must get Niamh to bring a few of Connie's books round for Roderick to look at,' Dilly said. 'The poor child must be bored to death with nothing to do. He's such a good little soul, isn't he?' And then as an idea occurred to her she rushed on, 'You could perhaps take him round to play with Connie for a couple of hours a day? Connie loved having him there and it might bring him out of his shell a bit.'

'He is quiet,' Bessie admitted. 'He's been like that ever since we lost Malcolm. He was very close to him, you see?'

Dilly had noted that Bessie seemed to have no time for the child at all but tactfully refrained from mentioning it. She didn't want to get into a confrontation when Bessie had only just arrived, but she decided that she would address the issue when the time was right.

'I thought I might pop round to see Mrs Pegs if you wouldn't mind keeping your ear open for Roderick for a while,' Bessie suggested tentatively a short time later and Dilly agreed to it readily. If truth be told she would be glad to let Bessie go as she was half-expecting Max to pay a visit and they could talk more freely about the situation if they were on their own.

An hour after Bessie had gone Dilly heard his familiar footsteps on the stairs and, after knocking, he entered the sitting room looking worn out and harassed. Max had his own key to the premises and came and went pretty much as he chose, which suited both of them.

'Bessie's gone to see Mrs Pegs and Roddy is asleep,' Dilly informed him as he sank onto a chair and she crossed to pour him a drink. He looked like he was in need of one.

'What a day,' he sighed as he sipped at the whisky she passed him.

Dilly listened avidly as he told her his version of the terrible confrontation between Samuel and Bessie. She had already heard the story once from Bessie but she listened again, realising that he needed to get it off his chest.

'I hate what he's done and I'm thoroughly ashamed of him, but I don't quite know what Bessie is expecting him to do about it,' he confided.

'I thought exactly the same,' Dilly agreed. 'And I'm very concerned about Roddy. The poor little mite is so quiet. It's as if he knows around his mother he must be seen and not heard.'

'I've noticed.' Max shook his head wearily. 'It looks like there's to be no let-up of problems for you and me, doesn't it, Dilly?'

'Well, at least we both have our health,' she answered, hoping to inject a little light-heartedness into the conversation. She went on to tell him about her day and all the ideas she had brought back with her from Birmingham. Max thought they were excellent and even offered to lend her some more money for stock, but Dilly adamantly refused.

'Thank you, but no. I already owe you for the other shop but I have enough to get me started and I'll go from there. Rome wasn't built in a day, after all.'

Max didn't bother to argue. He knew how fiercely proud and independent Dilly was; that was one of the things he had come to love about her.

At the Farthing household, Bessie found Mrs Pegs all in a lather.

'We've had to call the doctor out again to the missus' nurse – he's up there now with her,' she told Bessie worriedly. 'The missus seems to be slightly improved, but the nurse . . .' She clicked her fingers. 'I wouldn't give *that* fer 'er chances o' survivin'. Poor soul, she seems to be fadin' by the hour.'

'Oh dear – and who will look after Mrs Farthing if anything happens to the nurse?' Bessie asked.

Narrowing her eyes, the cook said, 'I dare say Mr Farthing would 'ave to employ another one.' It seemed cruel to be discussing such things when the poor woman upstairs hadn't even died yet, but then Mrs Pegs had always been practical.

Bessie frowned thoughtfully. She hadn't really decided what she wanted to do with her future yet, but she had no doubt that she could look after Mrs Farthing. From what she'd gleaned, the woman scarcely knew what time of day it was.

'How much nursing does Mrs Farthing need?' she enquired.

'It's more just keepin' an eye on her to make sure she don't 'arm 'erself than real nursin',' Mrs Pegs confided. 'She ain't on no medication as there ain't really nothin' to 'elp her condition apart from a sedative when she starts to get too upset.'

The doctor appeared in the kitchen doorway. He told Mrs Pegs gravely, 'I am going to arrange for an ambulance to come and take Nurse Harris to the cottage hospital. It would be a good idea if you got Mr Farthing to inform her family that she is dangerously ill, and that they should come as soon as possible.'

'I'll tell 'im just as soon as 'e sets foot through the door,' Mrs Pegs promised. 'An' meantime, while we're waitin' fer the ambulance I'll go an' pack a bag wi' everythin' she might need.'

At that moment the front door opened and Olivia appeared. She had been working all day at the Weddington Hall Hospital and she frowned when she saw the doctor there.

'Is Mother worse?' she asked with concern as she unhooked her nurse's cape.

'No, my dear, I'm quietly confident that your mother will make a full recovery. Unfortunately, Nurse Harris is very poorly indeed and I'm just about to send for an ambulance for her now. Perhaps you wouldn't mind going and sitting with her for me until it gets here?' He was aware that the sick room would hold no fears for Olivia because of her being a nurse.

'Of course I will.' Olivia smiled at Bessie. She had heard the day before from Mrs Pegs of Bessie's unexpected return and the reason why she had come, and had been appalled to learn what her brother had done. Bessie had been a part of Olivia's life as she was growing up and she would have liked to go and give her a welcoming hug, but under the circumstances that would have to wait until later.

Olivia disappeared off up the stairs as the doctor left, and Bessie followed Mrs Pegs back into the kitchen. The older woman told her, 'She's turned into a lovely young woman, has Miss Olivia. She's nineteen now, you know. Where does the time go, eh? They turned Weddington Castle into a hospital during the war for injured soldiers and she went there as a VAD just as soon as she was old enough. She's doing her proper nursing training now but for some reason she doesn't seem to be as keen about it as she used to be.'

'Why is that then?'

Mrs Pegs looked thoughtful. 'Can't say for sure but I reckon it's got something to do with Master Oscar. You know they were allus thick as thieves, but then he suddenly announces he's goin' to marry Penelope Merriman an' from then on they ain't been the same.'

'How strange,' Bessie remarked, but then Gwen placed a cup of tea in front of them and for now the subject was dropped.

In a very smart house in Caldecote at that very moment, Penelope Farthing was giving her new husband a hard time. The house, a large Victorian property and a former rectory set in five acres, had been a wedding present from Penelope's father. Max Farthing had paid for all the furnishings, which

Penelope had chosen, and to the outside world they were a very well set-up young couple. But behind closed doors, all was not well.

Oscar had become his father's right-hand man and worked long hours, helping Max to manage his many businesses, much to Penelope's disgust. Their marriage, which had been a very quiet affair, had taken place two months previously. Penelope had wanted a large lavish wedding but because the Farthings were still in mourning for Harvey, Oscar's brother who had been killed in the war, Oscar had insisted that it went ahead with the minimum of fuss.

Penelope had been irked that she couldn't have the extravagant day she had dreamed of, but she wanted Oscar so much that she had finally agreed to his request. Only a handful of people were present at the service in St Nicholas Church. Camilla was too ill to attend, Olivia had declined her invitation, saying that she was needed at the hospital, and Samuel was off somewhere pursuing his latest female conquest.

Even so, Penelope was so aglow with happiness when she walked down the aisle on her father's arm to join her husband-to-be that her otherwise plain face was transformed.

Following the wedding, Max had arranged a meal at a hotel in Manor Court Road, and when this was over the newlyweds moved into their new home. Penelope's father had hired a live-in maid and a cook to ensure that his daughter could continue to live in the manner to which she was accustomed, and that evening the cook presented them with a beautiful meal, served by the maid in the newly decorated and furnished dining room.

Oscar's appetite had fled by then as he stared across the table at the unloved woman he had married and he found, much to the cook's disappointment, that he couldn't eat a thing – although he noted that Penelope ate enough for both of them. It was no wonder she was so plump, he found himself thinking.

Penelope meanwhile kept up a continuous stream of chatter, quite unlike her usual quiet sedate self, and Oscar hoped that he wasn't seeing another side to her. After dinner they had retired to the drawing room but at the earliest opportunity she excused herself and told him shyly, 'I shall just go up and get changed then, dear. Don't be too long before you join me, will you?'

His stomach revolted at the thought of what lay ahead and reaching for the brandy he poured himself a stiff measure followed by another and then another. He had thought that marrying Penelope would rid him of the guilty feelings he had for his sister, Olivia, but in fact he couldn't help but compare his new wife with her and Penelope came out sadly lacking.

Eventually the cook and the maid had retired to their rooms and Penelope, in a stupor of excitement, had crept back downstairs in the expensive lingerie her father had bought her, to seek out Oscar. She'd thought that perhaps he was a little bashful but when she found him almost unconscious with a nearly empty bottle of brandy clutched in his hands she had stormed back to bed in an agony of disappointment. That had been two months ago and still the marriage had not been consummated. Penelope had no idea what to do about it. Her mother was a prude and would never consider talking about what she termed 'unpleasantness'. And so Penelope had gone from day to day, her frustration mounting by the minute until this evening she could hardly bear to even be civil to Oscar.

'You're late,' she snapped the moment he stepped through the door. 'I went ahead and had dinner without you. Cook kept yours warm but I dare say it will be shrivelled up by now.'

'It doesn't matter,' Oscar answered, crossing to the cut-glass brandy decanter. 'I'm not really hungry anyway. We had a bit of a crisis at one of the hat factories in Atherstone and I had to stay behind to deal with it.'

'Well, I suppose that's as good an excuse as any,' Penelope said sarcastically. '*Anything* is better than having to spend time with your wife, isn't it? Do you have any idea how bored I get stuck here on my own day after day with only the servants for company?'

'So go and get a job then,' Oscar said bluntly. 'Lots of women work nowadays, in case you hadn't noticed.'

Penelope's mouth gaped as she stared at him in horror. 'Get a job! But I don't *need* to work!'

'Then stop complaining you're bored.' Oscar was just too tired to argue with her tonight.

'How *dare* you speak to me like that,' she hissed, enraged. 'Why, for two pins I'd tell Daddy how rude you have been to me. And I could tell him about the other thing as well – the fact that we still haven't . . .'

Oscar sighed as he gazed down into his drink. Penelope had appeared to be such a mild-natured girl when they were courting but he had soon discovered that she was a shrew at heart. Not that he placed all the blame at her door. He knew that he was at fault too, but the thought of bedding her made bile rise in his throat. Of course it would have to happen one day – and suddenly he decided that he might as well get it over with. In candlelight he could pretend that she was someone else.

'I shall be up to our room in half an hour,' he informed her coldly and again she gaped.

'B-but the servants haven't gone to bed yet.'

'So? Do you want me to come to you or not?'

'Oh yes,' she said, rising from her chair so quickly that she almost tripped over her skirts. Women were wearing them slightly shorter nowadays but Penelope still insisted on covering every inch of herself from neck to ankle.

She flashed a simpering smile and ran from the room like a child in a sweet shop as Oscar poured himself another stiff drink. He had a feeling he would need it to face the ordeal ahead.

# Chapter Six

'Poor Nurse Harris passed away in the early hours of this morning,' Mrs Pegs informed Dilly late the next afternoon when she popped in to see her.

'How sad.' Dilly hadn't really known the woman as she was usually closeted away with Camilla, but she felt sorry for her all the same. 'So who is looking after Camilla now?'

'Miss Olivia 'as taken a few days off work but I don't reckon she fancies takin' on the job o' carin' fer 'er mam full-time,' Mrs Pegs snorted in a confidential whisper. 'Yer can't really blame the lass though, can yer? I mean, Camilla can be nasty when she turns now, an' she's took to wanderin' about the house. We've 'ad to resort to lockin' her bedroom door 'cos we're feared she might hurt herself. An' when I think o' what a friendly soul she were when I first come 'ere to work an' all! Life can be cruel, can't it?'

'It certainly can,' Dilly agreed sombrely, thinking of all the people she had loved and lost. First of all there had been

Olivia, whom she had been forced to give away so that she could work to feed her other children. Then Fergal who had never really recovered from his horrific accident. Next, Declan her firstborn had decided to stay in Ireland with his grandparents and although he was still alive, Dilly had grieved for him. Kian, her lovely son, had been the next to go, killed in a mindless war and buried somewhere in a nameless grave in France. Soon after that, Samuel Farthing had raped Niamh her beloved daughter, ruining her chances of happiness with Ben in Enniskerry. And finally her youngest, Seamus, had suffered severe shell shock, although Maeve, his grandmother with whom he was convalescing in Enniskerry, reported that he was mending slowly day by day. Yes, Mrs Pegs was right, life could be cruel – and none who knew it better than Dilly Carey. Even so, she tried to stay optimistic. She had the official opening of her shop to look forward to soon and she was determined to make a success of it.

'I might pop up and see Olivia and Camilla, if you don't mind?' she asked then and Mrs Pegs waved her hand at her.

'Go ahead. I dare say the lass will be glad of a bit o' company after bein' shut in wi' her mam all day.'

Dilly climbed the staircase that she had cleaned so many times during the years she had worked there as a maid for the Farthings and paused outside what she knew was now Camilla's bedroom door.

'Olivia,' she called softly through the door. 'It's me, Dilly. Will you let me in, lass?'

She heard footsteps, followed by the sound of a key turning in the lock, and Olivia's lovely face smiled tiredly at her.

'Come in,' she invited, putting a finger to her lips. 'But would you mind keeping your voice down? Mother is sleeping at the moment and I don't want to disturb her.'

As Dilly crept past her, Olivia quickly closed the door again and after locking it pocketed the key.

Dilly glanced towards the bed and her heart swelled with pity. Camilla looked like a shrunken old woman lying there. Her insanity had robbed her not only of her mind but of her beauty, and it was hard to believe, seeing her now, that she had once been quite stunning. Olivia had changed too; she had lost weight and looked drained.

They went and sat opposite each other in chairs placed at either side of the window. The curtains were closely drawn against the cold night and Dilly couldn't stop herself from reaching across and taking Olivia's hands in her own.

'You look tired,' she said quietly.

Olivia shrugged. 'I suppose I am, although it isn't nearly as hard looking after Mother as it is at the hospital.' She chewed on her lip as if she was considering something before bursting out with, 'Between you and me, I'm thinking of moving away and starting a new career.'

Dilly was so shocked and horrified that her mouth gaped open. 'But you've always loved nursing! It's all you've ever wanted to do, right since you were a little girl. And where would you go?'

Olivia sniffed. 'I quite fancy moving to London, though I wouldn't do it until Mother was recovered and Father had found another nurse to take care of her, of course.'

Dilly's heart was beating wildly at the thought of losing this beloved girl but she kept her voice level as she said, 'But the flu epidemic is still raging in London. Think of the danger you would be putting yourself in – and you're very young to be striking out on your own in an unknown place.'

'I can't stay here, Mrs Carey.' There was a break in Olivia's voice and Dilly felt her pain and knew that she was thinking of Oscar. She had never come closer to telling Olivia about her true parentage than she did then – but, she asked herself, what would be the point? Oscar and Penelope were married now, and so even if she was to admit that there was no blood tie between them, they could never come together.

The all too familiar guilt pressed down on her once more and she took a long calming breath before shaking Olivia's hands gently up and down and imploring, 'Please don't get thinking along that track, lass. Your father relies on you and adores you. It will break his heart if you leave and you've worked so hard at your nursing training. It would be terrible if you threw it all away now. At least promise me that you won't get doing anything rash.'

A groan from the bed interrupted their conversation at that moment, and gently freeing her hands, Olivia rose and hurried across to her mother, who was now awake.

'It's all right, I'm here,' she crooned as she lifted a damp cloth from a bowl at the side of the bed and sponged Camilla's sweating brow.

The woman's face relaxed but then as she caught sight of Dilly she stiffened and became agitated again.

'Get – her – out – of – here,' she said quaveringly as she pointed a trembling finger in Dilly's direction.

Dilly was struck dumb with shock. It seemed that even in her present state, and after all the long years they had known each other, Camilla still could not stand to be in the same room as her. Camilla had always been jealous of her and had made no secret of the fact, but surely now she should let the past go?

'It might be best if you left, Mrs Carey,' Olivia suggested quietly as her mother began to thrash about.

Dilly reluctantly rose from her seat and headed for the door. She desperately longed to stay and talk to the girl about her plans for leaving home, but now was not the right time.

'Very well. But please think about what I said. Running away isn't going to solve anything.'

'Get – out – I – say!'

As Olivia attempted to hold her mother down, Dilly beat a hasty retreat. Once out on the landing with the bedroom door closed firmly between them, she sagged against the wall and tears crept down her cheeks. It had been so hard over the years having to watch Camilla be a mother to her own daughter, but she had kept her vow never to tell Olivia the truth. Hard as it had been, at least she had been able to see the girl regularly, but now it seemed that she might well end up losing her for good if she moved away and Dilly didn't know how she was going to bear it. After a while she took a handkerchief from the pocket of her skirt and mopped her eyes, then straightening her back she went downstairs to the kitchen where Mrs Pegs was sitting to the side of the blazing fire snatching a moment.

'Come an' take the weight off yer feet fer a minute,' the kindly woman said, and patted the seat at the side of her. 'Me an' young Gwen 'ere 'ave to take what rest we can when we can at the minute, don't we, pet?'

Gwen, who was stirring a large pan of chicken soup on the range nodded affably as Dilly did as she was told, and Mrs Pegs then asked, 'So 'ow is Bessie an' the young 'un settling in then?'

'It's a bit soon to say,' Dilly said honestly. 'She spends most of her time round at Niamh's. It's perhaps as well because Niamh seems to have taken a real shine to Roderick.'

The cook tutted. 'True, his mam don't seem to 'ave much time for the poor little chap, does she?'

Dilly stifled a grin. She could always rely on Mrs Pegs to say it as it was, offend or please.

'No, she doesn't seem to be very close to her son, but then perhaps she's still grieving for her husband? From what

47

she's told me they were very close and she was very happy with him.'

'Trust you to make excuses for 'er.' Mrs Pegs thumbed towards the ceiling then. 'An' how is the missus?'

'She'd just woken up when I came down and Olivia was tending to her,' Dilly said, deciding not to tell her how agitated Camilla had become. She glanced towards the window then and seeing that darkness had fallen she rose, saying, 'I'd best be off. Bessie promised to cook dinner for me this evening, so having a lodger does have some compensations.'

Mrs Pegs' chest puffed with pride. 'An' a right fine little cook she is an' all, even if I do say so meself. I taught her all she knows.'

Dilly smiled indulgently as she put her hat and coat on, and soon after she was hurrying through the darkened streets on her way back to her little rooms above the shop.

When she arrived home she found not only Bessie and Roderick waiting for her but Niamh and Connie too.

'I hope you don't mind?' Bessie said worriedly. 'But I thought while I was cooking for us I might as well cook for them too.'

'Of course I don't mind, they often come round for their evening meal. Either that or I go round to them, don't I, pet?' She lifted Constance and planted a smacking kiss on her cheek, then frowned. 'I think she's a bit hot, Niamh. Has she been unwell today?'

'Not that I've noticed.' Niamh hurriedly felt the child's forehead. 'Yes, she does seem to have a bit of a temperature. But don't worry, I'll keep a close eye on her.' Then unable to contain her excitement any more she rushed on, 'You'll never believe what's happened, Mammy! Do you remember when I went to that art exhibition in Birmingham last month and took one of my paintings along?'

48

Dilly nodded.

'Well, I received a letter this morning to say that Mr Vaughn – that's the man who owns the gallery – has sold it for *ten guineas*! And there's more. He's coming to the house to look at some of my other paintings. Isn't that just wonderful?'

'It most certainly is,' Dilly agreed proudly. Niamh had loved painting right since she was a little girl and had become quite an accomplished artist. Dilly had a feeling that it was only her painting and her child that had kept her sane since her marriage to Samuel, and she couldn't have been more pleased for her.

'You must show him the portrait you painted of Connie,' Dilly suggested but Niamh shook her head.

'Oh no, I could never part with that one, but I have lots more. There might be some that he thinks are good enough to sell.'

'I'm sure they all will be,' Dilly told her, but then sniffing the air she said, 'Now how about we have our meal. I don't know what you're cooking, Bessie, but the smell of it is making my mouth water.'

In truth, Olivia saying that she might go away had quite robbed Dilly of her appetite, but she had to put a brave face on things. At least until she was in the privacy of her room.

Bessie had actually done them proud. There was a roast chicken and a selection of vegetables as well as creamed potatoes all served with a thick juicy gravy. And then for afters she had made them one of her famous jam roly-polys, with thick creamy custard that stuck to the spoon. Dilly was amused to see that Roderick had seconds but concerned to note that Connie ate hardly a thing.

'I think I might get her home and tucked into bed,' Niamh said as she lifted the little girl onto her lap. Normally Connie would be chasing around after Roddy but tonight she jammed her thumb into her mouth and cuddled into her mother's chest. Her eyes looked feverishly bright and Dilly swallowed the dread that rose in her. What if Connie were coming down with the influenza? She was so small – would she be strong enough to fight it?

'I think that might be for the best,' she said aloud. 'In fact, I'll come with you and stay until she's settled. Leave the dirty pots until I get back, Bessie. The least I can do is clear away and wash up after all your hard work preparing and cooking the meal for us.'

'Oh, don't get worrying about that,' Bessie said. 'You go and make sure the little lass is all right. It's time for Roddy to go to bed anyway and once he has, I'll clear this lot away in two shakes of a lamb's tail. Don't forget it's what I used to do for a living!'

In no time at all Dilly and Niamh were hurrying towards Niamh's home taking it in turns to carry Connie, who clearly didn't feel well enough to walk.

'You don't think she's caught influenza, do you?' Niamh's face was tight with concern.

'Oh, now don't get thinking the worst. It might just be a little cold or something. You know what children are like. She'll be right as rain tomorrow. Children are very resilient and they bounce back in no time. She just needs a warm bed and a good night's sleep, that's all. She's probably just overtired,' Dilly said breezily although she too was very concerned.

Once back at Niamh's, Dilly lit the fire laid ready in Niamh's bedroom. They had both decided that it might be best if Connie slept with her mother that night so that Niamh could keep an eye on her, and soon after Connie was tucked into bed with a stone hot water bottle tucked in by her feet. She didn't even ask for her bedtime story which worried Niamh even more.

'It usually takes me ages to get her off to sleep,' she fretted as she stared down at the child who had dropped off in seconds and was deeply asleep.

'Well, they do say sleep is the best cure for all ills,' Dilly pointed out as she took her daughter's elbow and led her from the room. 'Now we'll make us a nice cup of tea and if she's still sleeping peacefully when we've had that, I'll get off. But don't get worrying. I'll be back first thing in the morning to check on you both.'

She was wondering if Max might have called round while she was away. He did most evenings and tonight she had been looking forward to seeing him after what Olivia had told her. Not that she intended to tell him of the young woman's plans to leave before Olivia had spoken to him herself. Half an hour later she was speeding back towards the shop and she arrived just in time to see Max letting himself out of the door.

'Ah, Bessie said you'd gone round to Niamh's. Connie isn't very well, is she?' he said when he spotted her.

Dilly shook her head. 'No, she seems quite feverish but she was fast asleep when I came away.'

Dilly suddenly realised that whilst Bessie was staying with her, she and Max would no longer be able to spend so much time together – at least, not alone – and it saddened her.

'Let's go and sit in the shop for a while,' she suggested. 'You can tell me what sort of day you have had then.'

They trooped inside and sat down. 'I'm sorry it's so cold, we'll have to keep our coats on,' Dilly apologised. 'But we can't really talk upstairs with Bessie there. Have you managed to speak to Samuel again about what he intends to do?'

'Briefly, but I'm afraid I'm no further forward with anything.' Max took a packet of cigarettes from his pocket and lit one. It was a sure sign that he was worried as he only

51

usually smoked cigars. 'He's still strenuously denying that the child is anything to do with him although you only have to look at the mite to see that Roderick is the spit of him. What am I going to do, Dilly?'

Dilly dragged her coat more closely about her. It really was terribly cold and her breath was hanging on the air in front of her like steam.

'I honestly don't know,' she said. 'I think you'll just have to give them both some time. So much has changed since Bessie went away. I don't for one minute think Bessie came back for money,' she went on. 'I believe her late husband left her quite comfortably off. Not rich, of course, and she's already said that she'll have to consider getting another position at some point, but I think she came back more to show Samuel what he had done. As a kind of revenge, if you know what I mean? I don't suppose you can blame her for feeling bitter, can you?'

'Not really,' Max said with a shudder. 'It must have been awful for her to run away as she did, but the sad thing is I would have helped her if she had only told me of the predicament she was in. I'm not so heartless that I would have turned her out on the streets.'

'Well, I'm sure things will sort themselves out given time,' Dilly reassured him although deep down she was concerned for Bessie and Roddy too. The couple then went on to talk of the alterations that would shortly be taking place in the shop, and so the evening passed until it was time to say good night.

# Chapter Seven

By the middle of the following week Dilly's premises were really beginning to take shape. The two shops had now been knocked into one and the sound of the builders hammering and sawing echoed off the walls from morning till night. Normally Dilly would have been ecstatic to see all her plans coming to fruition but Connie was now seriously ill and she was spending as much time as she could round at Niamh's house helping to care for her. Dr Beasley was reluctant to send the child into hospital because the flu she was suffering from was so contagious. And so Dilly and Niamh were nursing the child round the clock and Niamh was almost beside herself with worry. Bessie had offered to help but Dilly had declined it because she didn't want little Roddy to be exposed to it too.

'She's not getting any better,' Niamh wept one frosty February morning when Dilly took a cup of tea up to Connie's room for her.

Dilly desperately wanted to reassure her daughter but as

she looked at the little girl lying on the bed the words stuck in her throat. She was beginning to fear the worst. Connie's eyes were feverishly bright and every breath she took seemed to be an enormous effort.

'You're doing all you can,' Dilly said instead as she gently stroked her daughter's back.

'But it's not enough. I think I'm going to lose her, Mammy.' Niamh stifled a sob as she continued to sponge her daughter's brow.

'Well, Dr Beasley should be here soon,' Dilly replied helplessly. He had called every day to check on the patient but there was nothing more he could do now, as both women were painfully aware.

'I asked Mr Farthing to let Samuel know how ill she was yesterday. He is her father, after all, and I thought he just might bother to come and see her but he hasn't put in an appearance as yet,' Niamh said bitterly.

'Well, that's no surprise, is it? He's too busy gallivanting about with that Lilian King, his rich widow,' Dilly answered grimly.

At that moment they heard the sound of someone rapping, down on the front door. 'That will be the doctor now, but Mary will let him in,' Dilly said.

Max had employed a local girl to move in and take over the housework whilst Connie was ill, and she was proving to be worth her weight in gold. Mary was a good-natured girl, plump and cheerful, and Niamh had come to rely on her already. Mary wasn't pretty in the conventional sense. Her hair, which was thick and a lovely brunette colour, was inclined to curl wildly and her mouth was wide but it was her eyes which were her saving grace, for they were a deep chestnut colour heavily fringed with long dark lashes.

Sure enough, seconds later they heard the sound of

footsteps on the landing and the doctor entered accompanied by Max who had arrived at the same time.

'How is she today?' Max asked, directing his question at Dilly.

Behind Niamh's back, Dilly shook her head. 'Not good this morning but let's let the doctor take a look at her, eh?'

The physician did just that as they all looked on gravely, then with a sigh he straightened from his small patient and faced them all. 'I'm afraid she's deteriorated further since yesterday. If this fever doesn't break soon and her temperature doesn't start to come down . . .'

There was a stunned silence. No one questioned him, for they all knew exactly what he meant.

As the day wore on Connie became more and more restless and Niamh frantically sponged her down, refusing to leave her side for a second, even to eat. And then suddenly at teatime the little girl calmed down. Her eyes opened and as they fastened on her mother she bestowed on her an angelic smile.

'Mammy, she knows me again. I think she's over the worst,' Niamh said ecstatically.

Delighted that the fever had finally broken, Dilly gazed down on her precious granddaughter – but still a cold hand closed about her heart and she shuddered for no reason that she could explain.

Niamh continued to sit by her daughter's bed, holding Connie's little hand tight in hers as Dilly flitted silently about the room gathering up the dirty bedlinen and taking it away for Mary to wash.

And then to everyone's surprise, Samuel arrived at about seven thirty.

'I thought I should come and see how she is,' he mumbled, looking uncomfortable.

Dilly was peeved to see him but Max looked so pleased

that his son had made the effort to come that she didn't have the heart to say so. Max himself had been there with his granddaughter since early that morning.

'Would you like to go up to her?' Dilly asked, hoping to keep the peace.

'Er . . . yes, I would if that's all right.'

Dilly noted that he didn't look particularly over-enthusiastic and suspected he'd only come because his father had ordered him to, but she ushered him up the stairs all the same.

In Connie's room he stood awkwardly in the doorway staring across at the pathetic little figure on the bed.

Niamh glanced over her shoulder and when she saw him standing there she frowned.

'I think she's a little bit better,' she said eventually for want of something to say.

He inched into the room, keeping a good distance from the bed, and Niamh felt an overpowering bitterness towards him. He was probably afraid of catching the infection himself if she knew him, but then she felt guilty. For whatever reason, he'd bothered to come at least.

They remained silent for some time watching the child's chest rise and fall painfully with each breath until he suggested, 'Why don't you go downstairs and have a cup of tea, Niamh. You look tired and I can watch her for a while.'

Niamh's first instinct was to refuse but she was tired and she supposed leaving Connie alone for just a few minutes couldn't do any harm. And Samuel would be there to watch over her, after all.

'Just for a little while then,' she said. She felt as if she could fall asleep on her feet and wondered how much longer the nightmare was going to go on.

Once downstairs, however, she began to have misgivings. What if Connie were to wake and find herself alone with

Samuel? He was almost a stranger to her. Dilly didn't seem any too happy with the arrangement either but she didn't comment for fear of hurting Max's feelings.

It was Max who made them all a drink and carried it into the sitting room, but they had barely sipped it when they heard a shout from upstairs and they all leaped from their seats and made for the doorway.

'I er . . . think she's stopped breathing,' Samuel told them as they raced into the room. He was the colour of putty and Dilly saw that he was shaking.

*'Nooooo!'* The sound that came from Niamh was so heartrending that both Dilly and Max knew that they would never forget it for as long as they lived.

'What happened?' Max demanded as a nerve in his eye began to twitch.

'I don't know! She began to thrash about all of a sudden and then she just went limp.'

One glance at Connie told them that Samuel was right. Her eyes were wide and staring as if something had shocked her, and her tiny hands were clenched into fists.

Her mother gathered her little body into her arms and sobbed broken-heartedly. Staring towards the bed, Max noted the rumpled pillow and the overturned water glass. Connie had been fine, she'd been sleeping peacefully. How could this have happened? Grief rose in his chest for his beautiful little granddaughter.

'I should never have left her,' Niamh wailed and all Dilly and Max could do was look helplessly on.

'Drink this. I insist,' Max ordered as he pressed a glass of whisky into Dilly's hand.

It was now the early hours of the morning and Niamh was finally asleep, helped by the powerful sedative the doctor had given her. Dr Beasley had been shocked. He'd never heard of such a relapse. Normally once the fever broke, a patient made a full recovery. The undertaker had been and taken Connie's slight body away to the chapel of rest and now there was nothing more they could do for the time being, apart from wonder how they were ever going to face the days ahead.

'We don't seem to have much luck, you and I, do we, Dilly?' Max said musingly as he stared into her exhausted face. 'Every time things start to go smoothly, something happens to knock us back.'

Dilly shrugged. 'It's nothing to do with luck. It's life – and life can be cruel,' she muttered. 'I learned that a very long time ago.' She was thinking back to the day Fergal had had his accident and all the hardship that had followed. And yet strangely she had begun to think lately that her luck had changed, that she could finally now have some time to chase her dreams. How wrong could I have been? she thought ruefully, for nothing could compare to the heartache of losing her beloved little granddaughter. She just couldn't contemplate never seeing her again; never feeling her chubby little arms about her neck or her wet sticky kisses on her cheek. The child had been violently conceived against her mother's will, and throughout the pregnancy Niamh had not wanted her – and yet from the moment she was born they had all adored her.

'Would you like me to stay here tonight? I could sleep on the sofa in case Niamh wakes and needs anything,' Max offered, pulling her thoughts sharply back to the present.

'Dilly shook her head. 'Thank you, but no. I shall stay. You get yourself home. Olivia will be worrying where you are.'

Max frowned. 'Of course – Olivia. Oh, Dilly, however am I going to tell her what's happened? You know how much she loved Connie.'

'We all did – but she'll accept it in time,' Dilly said brokenly.

Max bowed his head. Again he was astounded at how strong Dilly could be in a crisis. She had suffered so much in her life; most women would have folded under the pressure but not Dilly. She somehow always managed to fight back from whatever was thrown at her. He knew he must do the same for both their sakes.

'Very well, I'll be on my way then. As you say, if Olivia is still awake she will be concerned about me. I shall be back first thing to take care of all the arrangements. But please try to get some sleep, Dilly. You look utterly worn out.' That was an understatement. Dilly's red-rimmed eyes had huge dark circles beneath them and her face was strained and white as death.

'I will be fine,' she told him as she helped him on with his coat. 'It's Niamh we have to worry about. And perhaps you should check that Samuel is all right?' He had left, grey-faced, some time earlier.

'Oh yes – yes, of course,' Max said. His son hadn't even crossed his mind but he supposed Dilly was right. 'I'll get Mr Jackson to try and track him down first thing in the morning. There's no point in getting Jackson out of bed tonight, is there?'

When his voice cracked, Dilly placed her arms about him and gave him a quick hug before pulling away abruptly. There was nothing she would have liked to do more in that moment than fall into his arms, bury her head in his chest and sob her heart out, but whilst he was a married man she would never do that.

'Off you go then and be careful. It's thick fog out there – look.' They both stood on the step for a moment staring into the swirling mist. Their moods were as bleak as the weather but then Max strode away and in seconds he was lost to sight as Dilly silently closed the door behind him and finally let the tears that she had bottled up all evening flow down her cheeks in rivers.

Mr Jackson finally managed to track Samuel down the following morning. It wasn't hard. Rumour was rife about Lilian King, the rich widow he was having an affair with, and seeing as everyone knew where she lived it was the first and most obvious place to look.

Mr Jackson was a gentle-natured, elderly man who had served the Farthing family loyally for many years, and when he was shown into the morning room of Samuel's mistress he removed his cap and said bluntly, 'Your father 'as asked me to tell yer to come straight 'ome, Master Samuel. There's funeral arrangements to be made fer your little girl.'

Samuel was enjoying a cigarette and a second cup of strong coffee to try and assuage the effects of a hangover and he frowned. 'Are you sure it's about Constance? If it's about that little baggage that's turned up like a bad penny trying to hoist her bastard onto me you can tell my father that I've said all I'm going to say on the matter,' he snapped rudely.

''Tain't nowt to do wi' Bessie,' Jackson retorted. He longed to tell the good-for-nothing exactly what he thought of him, but it wasn't his place. How could anyone be so callous when they had lost their little daughter only hours before?

Samuel sighed with irritation. 'Oh, very well. Tell Father I shall be there as soon as I've bathed and changed, although I really can't see why they need me to help with the arrangements.'

Jackson turned without a word and left the room wishing with all his heart that he was a few years younger. There was nothing at that moment that would have given him greater pleasure than to be able to give that young man the pasting he deserved.

'Did you manage to find him, Jackson?' Max asked hopefully the second the old man stepped foot through the door.

'I did that, Mr Farthin', an' he'll be along shortly.' Jackson forbore from telling him exactly where he had found him. That would have been too much like rubbing salt into the wound, and the way the kindly man saw it, the poor bloke had enough on his plate to cope with at the moment.

'Thank you, Jackson. I greatly appreciate it. I shall see that there's a bonus in your wage packet come Friday.'

'Ain't no need for you to be doin' that,' Jackson protested. 'I were glad to do anythin' I could to 'elp, precious little though it were. An' Mr Farthin', the missus said to tell yer she's hearty sorry to 'ear about little Connie. She ain't stopped blartin' since I told 'er this mornin'. But now I'll be gettin' on if yer don't mind. I'm sure you've things to do.' And with that he let himself out of the room, leaving Max to stare forlornly into the heart of the blazing fire.

Thankfully, Olivia had been fast asleep on the small bed they had placed in her mother's room when he had got in the morning before, and as yet he hadn't seen her. Even so he knew that he couldn't put off telling her for ever, so he slowly peeled himself out of the chair and wearily made his way upstairs. His clothes were crumpled and he was badly in need of a shave as he hadn't bothered to go to bed, but he was sure that Olivia would forgive him for his appearance when he explained the reason why.

Samuel arrived at the house just before lunchtime and went straight to the drawing room where he found his father waiting for him with a grim expression on his face.

'So what do you want me to do now?' the young man

61

asked disinterestedly as he leaned against the wall and examined his nails. 'I've already told Jackson that if you want to speak to me about Bessie I have nothing more to say.'

'It isn't about Bessie although I haven't finished on that subject either, not by a long shot. This morning I need to speak to you about your daughter and what you intend to do about the funeral!'

'Why?'

'Because she was your daughter, that's *why*! Haven't you got a heart? Niamh shouldn't have to face this on her own.'

Samuel looked momentarily stunned before stammering, 'I – if this is your idea of a joke, Father, I have to say I find it in rather poor taste! You know as well as I do that Niamh and I are married in name only. I married her because you forced me to! The thing is, now that Constance is dead there's no need for us to be married any more, is there? We could get a divorce.'

'You sicken me. How could you even talk of such things at a time like this?' Max wiped a hand across his weary eyes. 'And I assure you, it's no joke.' His shoulders sagged as he said, 'You could at least go and offer a word of comfort to your wife and help her to plan the funeral.'

Samuel looked suitably ashamed for a moment but then said gruffly, 'I'm sorry about what happened to the kid, but I wouldn't have a clue of how to go about organising something like that. Couldn't you do it for me, Father? You're so much better at that sort of thing than me.'

'I've had to be, haven't I?' his father ground out from between clenched teeth. 'I had to organise your wedding, find somewhere for you all to live – not that you're ever there. I pay the household bills for you as well as your wages – and for what? When was the last time you even set foot in any of the factories, eh?'

'I er . . . I've just been a bit busy,' Samuel told him cagily.

'Well, I warn you that things are going to change from now on,' Max said with a frightening calm. 'As soon as this funeral is over you will start acting like a man or I shall cut you off without a penny – and I mean it this time. And where will you be when your rich lady friend tires of you then, eh? I've already sent Lawrence a telegram, so no doubt he will head straight back from Whitby to be here for the funeral – and you are bloody well going to be there too or you'll have me to answer to! Now get round to see Niamh and get out of my sight! I can hardly bear to look at you and I'm ashamed to call you my son.'

'Now look here, Father,' Samuel objected hotly. 'That's a bit harsh, isn't it? It's hardly my fault that the kid has died, is it? At least I went to see her!'

When Max took a threatening step towards him, Samuel shot from the room like a bullet from a gun, leaving the door swinging open behind him. He had rarely seen his father in such a towering rage and was only too glad to make his escape. At the end of the drive he looked back at the house and paused to turn his coat collar up, and for the first time the full force of what he had done hit him. He could still almost feel the feeble struggle the child had put up as he'd pressed the pillow down across her face. It had been for a pitifully short time in her weakened state and then she had lain still. He felt no remorse. Constance had been the reason he'd been forced into the marriage, and to his mind now that she was gone there was no reason for them to go on with this farce any longer. Even so, he supposed that he should keep up appearances for the time being at least, so with a sigh he turned reluctantly in the direction of the house his father had bought as a wedding present for him and Niamh.

*

Back in the house, Max leaned heavily on his desk with his head bowed as a picture of the overturned glass and the rumpled pillow on Connie's bed flashed in front of his eyes. But then he pushed the suspicions aside: they were just too terrible to contemplate.

# Chapter Eight

The following morning in the smallholding in Enniskerry, Maeve Carey, Dilly's mother-in-law, was rolling pastry on the kitchen table when she glanced towards the window to see the telegram boy cycling down the lane with his legs pumping the pedals like pistons.

'Eeh, Daniel,' she croaked at her husband, for ever since the war that sight could strike terror into her heart. 'There's a telegram boy heading for the house, so there is. Would you go an' see what he wants? Me legs have gone all of a wobble.'

Daniel nodded. Luckily he had just come in for his mid-morning cup of tea but like his wife he felt apprehensive as he went towards the door.

The lad had just swung down from the saddle when the front door opened. He handed Daniel the envelope then clambered back on his bike and whizzed away without a word.

'What's to do then?'

Maeve turned just in time to see Liam, her youngest son, enter the kitchen. He had been working in the barn when he too had seen the lad approaching. His mother had no time to answer him, however, for Daniel came back into the kitchen and held the envelope out towards Maeve as if it might bite him.

Flapping her hands in panic, she backed away, and with a sigh, Liam told his father, 'Ah, give it here. It might be somethin' or nothin'.' He quickly slit the envelope with his thumb and after withdrawing the single sheet of paper, he hastily read the message it contained.

'I – I'm afraid it is bad news, Mammy,' he breathed as tears started to his eyes.

Maeve's hand flew to her mouth. 'Is it our Dilly or Niamh?' she asked fearfully.

Liam shook his head, avoiding her eyes. 'No, it's not them. It's wee Connie. She got the influenza an' she . . . she's died. Dilly is askin' us if Seamus or any of us want to go over for the funeral.'

Maeve made the sign of the cross on her chest as tears erupted from her eyes. 'But she were just a little wean,' she choked.

Seamus, who was sitting huddled beneath a blanket in the chair by the fire, began to cry. He was having one of his lucid moments and understood only too well what had happened. The bodily injuries he had received during the war had healed now, but mentally he was still very unstable and still suffered from horrendous nightmares that would have his gran'ma scuttling along the landing on many a night.

'M-Mammy an' our Niamh will be distraught,' he said throatily and laying a comforting hand on his shoulder, Maeve nodded agreement as tears continued to spurt from her eyes.

'They will that, me fine boy, but we'll have to help them as much as we can, so we will.'

'Perhaps Niamh could come and stay here with us for a while when the funeral's over?' Daniel suggested.

His wife glared at him. 'Oh aye – and just how do you think that would affect our Ben?'

'Perhaps you're right, woman,' Daniel said then. 'First thing in the morning I'll send a reply to the telegram and I'll go and book some tickets on the ferry. But how many of us should go? Someone should stay here to take care o' the beasts.'

'I'll stay, Daddy,' Liam offered. 'Shelagh is close to her time with the wean now so she'd not be up to the journey anyway, an' it would mean keeping the other two off school. Why don't just you an' Mammy go? Seamus could stay here with us too, so he could. You know how distressed he gets if he goes out of his routine.'

'I reckon you're right, although we should let Declan know – he might want to come too.' Maeve broke into a fresh torrent of weeping. It was so hard to think that she'd never see her great-granddaughter's impish little face again, and if it was affecting her so badly she dreaded to think how poor Dilly and Niamh must be faring. It was every parent's worst nightmare come true.

'And what about Ben?' she said then, as an afterthought. 'I know he and Niamh aren't together any more but he might want to come and pay his respects.'

Daniel nipped at his lip with his teeth as he considered what she had said. 'I'll mention to him what's happened and leave him to decide what he wishes to do. That way, he won't feel under any pressure. I'll call into the blacksmith's first thing when I go to Enniskerry to send the telegram.'

'That might be for the best,' Maeve said quietly and so it was agreed.

Ben's face crumpled the next morning when Daniel passed on the grave news about Connie. Niamh had broken his heart when she had married Samuel, but he still cared deeply for her and now he grappled with his conscience. Should he make the journey with Maeve and Daniel, or should he stay well away? He couldn't see Niamh's husband being very happy if he turned up – but then if he didn't, would Niamh think that he didn't care?

'I feel in a bit of a quandary,' he confided to the man who had been the nearest thing to a father he had ever known. 'What do *you* think I should do?'

'Whatever your heart tells you to do,' Daniel answered wisely. 'You and Niamh were very close once and it might comfort her to have as many friendly faces about her as she can get. But saying that, if it would make you feel out of place or unhappy then you should stay away. I could pass on your condolences if you'd like me to.'

Ben ran his hand across his face as he stared off into space, then making a hasty decision he told Daniel, 'No. Get me a ticket too, please. But I'll not stay. As soon as the funeral is over I'll make my way back here. No doubt you and Maeve will want to stay on for a few days.'

'Just as you like.' Daniel turned to go but paused at the door to look back over his shoulder and say, 'You've got a heart o' pure gold, so you have, son. That's why me and Maeve love you so.'

The following morning found Maeve, Daniel and Ben on the ferry in very choppy seas. The sky was grey, as were the waves, and on the horizon they seemed to merge into one. The ferry had gone barely any distance at all before Maeve was hanging over the rail depositing her breakfast into the sea.

'Eeh, lass, you've gone a funny green colour,' Daniel said with concern as Ben scooted off to try and find her a glass of water. It was bitterly cold and he looked enviously towards the passengers who were seated inside but it never even occurred to him, or Ben for that matter, to leave her side.

Maeve flapped her hand at him. 'I'll be fine, so I will. I just have to find me sea legs. Get yourself inside why don't you, out of the cold.' She straightened then and after wiping the back of her hand across her mouth she said worriedly, 'I've just thought of something. We can stay with Niamh, but where will Ben stay? It wouldn't be right for him to stay there. I dare say her husband wouldn't allow it anyway and he can't stay with Dilly if Bessie is there – unless he's a mind to sleep on the sofa.'

'I'm sure he wouldn't mind that, but let's just get there first afore we start to worry about trivial things like that, eh?' Daniel answered but then he said no more as they saw Ben swaying towards them across the deck balancing a glass of water that was sloshing everywhere.

It was a huge relief to all of them when their journey from Ireland was nearly over and their train was pulling into the station in Nuneaton.

'I'll flag us a cab, shall I?' Ben offered, for Maeve looked worn out.

'There won't be any need for that, lad,' she said. 'Niamh's house is only a stone's throw away on Abbey Green and we can walk there in minutes.'

It was late afternoon now and the streets were already dark as they hurried along, keen to get out of the biting cold.

'I shall be glad to get a nice hot cup o' tea inside me, so I shall,' Maeve muttered.

Hands thrust deep into the pockets of his overcoat, Ben remained silent, his thoughts confused. Now that it was too late, he wondered if he had made a big mistake in coming here. He had spent the last few years desperately trying to push thoughts of Niamh to the back of his mind and now here he was about to open up all the old wounds again. It was going to be hard seeing her with the man she had chosen over him, but there could be no turning back now.

He was so deep in thought that it was almost a shock when Maeve suddenly opened a gate leading to a neat detached house. The curtains at the downstairs windows were shut but a glimmer of light shone through them and he had the sudden urge to turn and run.

As if she had picked up on his apprehension, Maeve gently squeezed his arm. 'You and our Niamh were good friends once, lad. She'll appreciate the fact that you've come to pay your respects, just wait and see.'

He swallowed and managed a weak smile as they approached the door and Daniel rapped on it. Seconds later, Dilly opened it and fell into Maeve's arms, hugging her tightly. Maeve was concerned to see how pale her daughter-in-law looked, but then what else could she have expected under the circumstances?

'It's all right, we're here now, lass,' Maeve crooned as she rocked Dilly to and fro. 'But now let us in, won't you, pet. It's enough to cut a body in two out here, so it is an' we're right tired an' thirsty.'

Remembering her manners, Dilly quickly ushered them all into the hallway and through to a cosy lounge where a large fire was crackling in the grate.

'Sit yourselves down,' she urged, trying her best to hide her surprise at seeing Ben. 'I'll get Mary to make you all some tea and get you some sandwiches to tide you over until we can get a proper meal on the go.' She smiled at them apologetically. 'To be honest, Niamh and I haven't really had much of an appetite but I'm sure Mary will rustle something up.'

Mary entered the room then and smiled at the visitors saying, 'Shall I make some tea, Mrs Carey? And will the visitors be staying?'

'Yes on both counts, pet. At least my mother and father-in-law will be staying . . .'

'It's all right,' Ben piped up, greatly embarrassed. 'I can find a lodging house, I'm sure.'

'You'll do no such thing, my fine lad.' Dilly wagged an indignant finger at him. 'You'll come back with me later on to my rooms above the shop. Unfortunately you'll have to sleep on the sofa as I already have Bessie and Roddy staying with me temporarily but I'm sure you'll manage for a few nights.'

When she saw him glance about the room she explained, 'Niamh is upstairs resting. The doctor gave her some tablets to take but she should be down soon and I'm sure she'll be pleased to see you all.'

Ben smiled weakly, hoping that things might not be as bad as he'd feared. At least Dilly was giving him a warm welcome.

'Mary seems a nice girl,' Maeve commented as Dilly collected their coats and hats. They had left their bags in the hallway.

'She is. To be honest I don't know what we'd have done without her over the last few weeks,' Dilly said. 'Max – that is, Mr Farthing – hired her to come in and help when Connie took ill, and between you and me I think she likes living here. She comes from a very large family and every Friday she takes her wages off proud as punch to her mammy. I have an idea Niamh might keep her on now. She's sort of become part of the family and she'll be company for Niamh once the funeral . . .'

'Ah pet.' As Dilly's voice broke, Maeve reached over and hugged her again but then Mary trundled a loaded tea trolley into the room and Dilly pulled herself together with a great effort. The family tucked into the cheese sandwiches and the sponge cake Mary had baked that afternoon hoping to tempt Niamh to eat. At least it wouldn't go to waste now.

'I just 'eard Mrs Farthing moving about upstairs,' Mary informed them as she poured tea into dainty china cups. 'So I popped up and told her that you 'ad all arrived and she said to tell you she'll be down just as soon as she's tidied 'erself up.'

'Thank you, lass,' Dilly answered and Mary smiled and disappeared back to the kitchen where she just happened to have a nice piece of pork all ready to pop into the range. She had some fresh vegetables to hand as well, so she decided she'd cook them all a dinner fit for royalty. They deserved it in these tragic circumstances.

In the lounge everyone heard Niamh's footsteps on the stairs but when she appeared in the doorway Maeve was shocked at the sight of her. Her clothes hung off her to the point that she looked gaunt, and her eyes were dull and lifeless. As they settled on her grandmother, they filled with tears again and in seconds Maeve had hurried over and caught the girl to her chest.

'There, there now, me wean,' Maeve said gently as tears washed down her own cheeks. 'This is just the worst thing in the world that could have happened to be sure, but we have to stay strong now and give the little lass the sort of send-off she deserves, don't we?'

'The funeral is the day after tomorrow at St Mary's Church in Manor Court Road,' Niamh gasped out.

Maeve bit her tongue. She would have preferred her granddaughter to have had a Catholic funeral but under the circumstances she didn't feel able to say so. Things were bad enough as it was, and no doubt the Good Lord would welcome the wean into heaven whichever way she got there.

'We'll all face the day together,' Maeve informed her granddaughter, and then Daniel stepped forward and he too gave Niamh a cuddle although he found that he was too choked to offer any words of comfort. It was when he finally released her that Niamh looked up and caught her first glimpse of Ben – and for a moment she blinked thinking that she must be seeing things.

'B-Ben . . . is it really you?'

He crossed the room in two strides and self-consciously took her hands in his.

'I er . . . hope you don't mind me coming, Niamh,' he said softly. 'But when I heard about what had happened I thought you might need all the support you could get. We are still friends after all, aren't we?'

'Always.' She stared up at him, hardly daring to believe that he was really there. She was afraid to blink in case he disappeared and she had imagined him.

'Why don't we all go an' give Mary a hand with the dinner,' Maeve suggested, guessing that the two young people might be glad of a little privacy. It was the first time they had seen each other since Niamh had written to Ben telling him that she was going to marry Samuel, and the older woman realised how awkward they must both feel.

'Good idea.' Daniel shepherded Dilly and Maeve towards the door. 'We might be able to cadge another cup o' tea out of her if she isn't too busy.'

Seconds later the door closed behind them but Ben continued to hold on to Niamh's hands as he stared into her face. Even in grief she was still as beautiful as he remembered her and his heart broke all over again as he thought of how she had chosen another man over himself.

'Why don't we sit by the fire?' Niamh said eventually when she managed to drag her eyes away from him and he instantly dropped her hands as if they had burned him. Had she seen what he still felt for her in his eyes? He hoped not; he certainly didn't want to add to her problems.

'So . . . how have you been?' Niamh asked as she clasped her hands to try and stop them shaking.

'Oh, very well. I've taken over the blacksmith's now and it's doing quite well considering there are only the old farm horses left to shoe,' he said ruefully. 'I reckon it will take years to build the horse population up again. The war had a lot to answer for, and not just in human lives.'

Niamh nodded in agreement. She could still clearly remember the day the Army had turned up at the beginning of the war to take the Farthing family's horses away and the pain it had caused them. The animals had never been seen again but then as Ben had pointed out, few horses had survived the battles. It was very sad.

'And how have you been?' Ben asked, then realising how ridiculous that must sound under the circumstances, he added swiftly, 'Before this happened, I mean. I expected your husband to be here?'

Niamh regarded him solemnly and making a sudden decision she told him quietly, 'My husband and I rarely see each other, Ben. It is a marriage in name only. It always has been. He did come to see me yesterday to discuss the funeral arrangements but I think it was only because his father insisted, and I doubt we shall see each other again now until the day of the service.' There seemed little point in keeping up the farce any longer, now her beloved child had died.

As Ben's head snapped up she saw the shock registered on his face. 'B-but I thought you were happily married? Especially when little Constance came along.'

Niamh shook her head. 'I'll tell you all about it one day,'

she promised and they then lapsed into silence, each locked in their own thoughts.

In the kitchen as they sat around the large scrubbed oak table, Maeve's thoughts were also on Samuel. 'So where is Niamh's husband then?' she asked bluntly. 'I thought he'd be here comforting her.'

'It's a long story,' Dilly replied wearily. 'But I doubt we'll see him now until we get to the church for the funeral.'

Maeve's eyebrows rose into her hairline but after a warning glance from Daniel she pressed her lips together. There was something not quite right here and she was determined to get to the bottom of it before she went home, if it was the last thing she did.

# Chapter Nine

'Come on now, lass. You sit there an' I'll get Mary to bring you a nice cup of tea, shall I?'

Maeve stared at her granddaughter fearfully as she pressed her into a chair. They had just returned from the funeral and she feared for the young woman's sanity. The day was dark and dismal to match the mood of the mourners who had attended, and now Maeve was just glad that it was over. Niamh had not shed so much as a single tear but had held herself rigidly throughout the service and the interment in the churchyard. Even so her eyes were bleak, and every time Maeve looked at her she could feel the girl's pain.

Under strict instructions from his father, Samuel had attended but Maeve had noticed that for all the comfort he gave to Niamh, he might as well not have been there. Ben had stayed discreetly in the background and now he too stared anxiously at Niamh. Samuel had disappeared as soon as the burial was over but the rest of the mourners would be arriving shortly, or at least those that chose to come to the house to sample the wonderful spread Mary had somehow managed to lay on. Despite the fact that the war was over there was still a shortage of food but the lass had miraculously conjured up a feast. There were pies and pickles, home-baked bread and a selection of cakes and pastries; Mary had stayed up almost the whole of the night before, getting it all ready.

Dilly was throwing coal onto the fire and Daniel was hanging everyone's coats up. Seconds later, the first guest appeared and before they knew it the house was teeming with people all keen to express their condolences and get into the warm. It had been a lovely service but Maeve had a feeling that Niamh hadn't heard a word of it. She had been too busy staring numbly at the tiny white coffin placed in front of the altar, lost in her memories.

*Poor lamb, how will she ever get over this loss?* Maeve asked herself as she ushered the guests towards the tables. Max had supplied wine and whisky for those that wanted it, but most people seemed to be happy with a hot drink after being out in the biting wind. They drifted towards Niamh but then quietly drifted away again when they found her staring blankly into space.

Finally Ben could stand it no more, and threading his way through the assembled guests until he reached her, he took her elbow and led her away firmly to the kitchen, saying, 'Come on. I think you need a bit of peace and quiet.'

Niamh stumbled mechanically after him, scarcely seeming to know where she was but once away from the crowded room she took a deep breath as she sank down onto one of the kitchen chairs. Mary was rushing in and out ensuring that the plates of food were kept piled high, and so Ben personally crossed to the heavy brown teapot and poured them out a cup of tea each. He added three heaped teaspoonfuls of sugar to Niamh's then handed it to her ordering, 'Now get that down you. I won't leave your side until you do.'

Obediently she raised the cup to her lips and after taking a few sips he was relieved to see a little colour seep back into her cheeks. It was the first time they had been alone together since the night he had arrived and there was so very much he wanted to say and ask, and yet the words stuck in his throat.

'Better?'

Niamh nodded and flashed a wobbly smile and his heart broke afresh for her. He could only imagine what she must be feeling, but he was helpless to relieve her pain. He had a horrible feeling that she was bottling everything up, but he supposed that everyone grieved in their own way. The day before, Dilly and Maeve had discreetly slipped up to Connie's room and placed all her things in the loft, saying that it would be less painful for Niamh if she didn't have to see the child's things lying all over the place. Ben wasn't sure that he was in agreement with them. Perhaps Niamh should have been allowed to do it in her own time when she felt ready? But then he had never had to deal with a situation like this before and so he had kept his own counsel. He had also been concerned to see the distance between Samuel and Niamh at the church. Oh, they had stood together in the front pew, and yet they might have been a million miles apart, for they never so much as looked at each other once throughout the service. In one way he was pleased because he knew it would have been very hard to see Niamh close to anyone else. And now their time together was limited because he was due to leave for the ferry on the first train out of Nuneaton the following morning – and who knew when he might see her again?

'Niamh, I know this probably isn't the right time to ask,

but I have to know: why did you throw me aside to marry Samuel? I thought we had something special.'

She stared at him dully for a moment then said, 'I didn't throw you aside. I had no choice but to marry Samuel. You see, he . . . he raped me and Connie was the result. When I found out I was with child I was beside myself with fear and shame but Mr Farthing made him do the honourable thing and marry me.'

Ben looked horrified and his hands balled into fists. 'So why didn't you *tell* me? I'd have come over here and murdered the bastard and I would have taken care of you – and the baby. *Surely* you know that?'

Niamh shrugged. There seemed little point in hiding the truth from him now. It was over and done with. 'And what would that have achieved? You would have got yourself into trouble and then you would have been saddled with another man's child to bring up. It would hardly have been fair on you, would it? And I cared too much for you to do that.'

'You did? You mean you never stopped loving me?' he asked incredulously.

'Never, but what good will it do now? I've lost Connie so I married him all for nothing.'

'But it needn't be like that.' Ben grabbed her hands as hope flared in him. 'You have no reason to be tied to him now. You could get a divorce and we could be together again.'

Niamh's head wagged from side to side. 'Samuel came to see me when Mammy wasn't here yesterday and asked me the same thing. But what you're both forgetting is that my gran'ma an' most of my family are staunch Catholics. They would disown me if I even spoke of divorce. It's not allowed in the Catholic faith. They'd be ashamed of me. Samuel wasn't best pleased with my answer, needless to say.'

'Sure I've been brought up as a Catholic too,' Ben pointed out desperately. 'But if it means a choice between you and the Church, there'll be no contest. You'll win every time, Niamh. I still love you, I always will. Oh, I'll admit I've taken a few lasses out since we split up, but none of them ever measured up to you. So what do you say? Pack your bags and come away with me now. You'll never be happy with him, you know you won't.'

Niamh groaned as the bitter tears she had valiantly held back all day finally burst from her like water from a dam. 'I still love you too,' she wept. 'But it's hopeless. I'm married to Samuel now for better or for worse and there's no going back.'

She watched the hope die in his eyes and longed to take him in her arms, but her own grief for Connie was so great at that moment that she couldn't deal with Ben's too.

'Is there nothing at all I can say that will make you change your mind?' He was standing now looking down at her as if he had the weight of the world on his shoulders.

Too choked to speak, Niamh merely shook her head.

'In that case I may as well be on my way now. I'll get back to Dilly's and do my packing. Early start in the morning, you know.'

'Th-thank you for coming. It meant a lot.'

He inclined his head and left without another word, and once he had gone Niamh gave way to her grief and sobbed as if her heart would break. She had lost the child and the man she adored, and now she would be tied in a loveless marriage for the rest of her life. It was a terrifying prospect. Life barely seemed worth living.

Dilly returned to her rooms above the shop late that evening after staying behind at Niamh's to help Mary and Maeve put the house to rights when the last of the mourners had finally departed. Bessie, who had attended the funeral, had been back for a while to put Roddy to bed. Nell Cotteridge had kindly looked after him for the day and now Dilly sank into the fireside chair opposite Ben's and said quietly, 'I've been dreading today. To be honest I'm glad it's over now.'

'Yes, quite.' Ben's voice was clipped and as Dilly narrowed her eyes and stared at him it suddenly dawned on her that Niamh had finally told him the truth.

'Niamh told you why she married Samuel, didn't she?'

He gritted his teeth and nodded before exploding, 'Why didn't you tell me what had happened, Dilly? I would have married her and loved the child as my own.'

'I know you would,' Dilly answered tiredly as she wiggled her shoes off her swollen feet. 'I told Niamh that, but she wouldn't let me tell you. She said it wasn't fair to saddle you with another man's child.'

Ben slammed a fist into his open palm as his temper erupted but then it subsided as quickly as it had come. 'Well, it's done now, isn't it?' he said resignedly. 'And at least I know that she didn't end with me because she didn't love me any more. It just seems such a waste though. I've always felt that me and Niamh were made for each other.'

Dilly decided not to answer. She didn't want to rub salt into the wound. Heart-weary the familiar feeling of guilt settled about her like a cloak.

# Chapter Ten

*April 1920*

'You get off, dear, I can finish off here and lock up,' Dilly told her trusty assistant Jayne late one afternoon in early April.

'Oh, right you are, Mrs Carey, thanks. Me and Dave are going to the cinema house tonight so it'll give me a bit more time to get ready if you're quite sure.'

'Of course I am. Now off you go and don't be late in the morning.'

'I won't,' Jayne Richards promised cheerfully as she snatched her coat from the sewing room that had been created at the back of the shop. The area also served as a staffroom for the two other women whom Dilly now employed to make the garments she sold in the shop. Both of them had been gone for a good half hour now, eager to get home to their families and get their husbands' meals on the go. Jayne Richards was twenty years old, tall and slim as a reed with short fair hair that she painstakingly fixed with the newly invented bobby pins each night before going to bed. The effect created the tiny spit curls that were so popular amongst the younger generation with their fashionably bobbed hair. Dilly had found her assistant to be a godsend as Jayne was always aware of the very latest styles.

Today was actually a very special day and Dilly was hoping that Max would call in on his way home. After the traumatic year that had just passed it was nice to have something good about to happen and Dilly found herself humming as she turned the Closed sign on the door and locked it. Max had his own key but she knew that she would be in the shop putting it to rights for some time yet as she and Jayne had had quite a busy day.

As she turned to admire her little empire, a smile formed at the corner of her lips. The shops had been very tastefully refurbished. The part she was standing in housed the ready-made garments that were selling as fast as she could order them, and they hung on a number of rails that covered one entire wall. A large gilt cheval mirror was placed next to two fitting rooms where women could go to try their garments on, and this side of the shop was decorated in elegant shades of duck-egg blue and cream. Dilly found the colours had a calming effect on herself and everyone who entered, and was pleased with her choice. The other side of the shop was divided by a thick cream curtain, and beyond that was Dilly's bridal section where two or three wedding gowns were displayed at any one time on mannequins in the full-length window. She had chosen a soft ivory colour for the walls in there that suited the gowns she stocked and was thrilled with the response this particular department had received.

Since the end of the war, people seemed to have abandoned caution and embraced their freedom, and now that food and materials were becoming more easily obtainable, women in particular were prepared to welcome the new fashions that were flooding the market. Coco Chanel and Jean Patou were two designers that Dilly was exceptionally influenced by, and although the majority of her customers could never have afforded to buy the designers' original work, she was always happy to copy the fashions for those that wanted them, which kept her two seamstresses busy in the back room from morning till night.

Crossing to the large brass till on the end of the counter, under which she also kept a stock of very attractive scarves and gloves, Dilly was just about to open it to remove the day's taking when the sound of a key in the lock made her glance up.

Her face broke into a smile as she saw Max enter and he smiled in return, saying, 'You're looking very chipper today. What's put you in such a good mood?'

'Oh, you'll see – but come upstairs first before I tell you. I've got a hotpot slow cooking if you fancy joining me for a bit of dinner.'

'How can I refuse an offer like that?' Max grinned. 'You know how I love your hotpots.'

Dilly removed the money from the till and Max followed her up the stairs trying not to ogle her legs in her new shorter-length skirt. She certainly had a very good pair of ankles for a woman her age, he found himself thinking.

Once in her cosy lounge, Dilly ushered him into a chair before pouring him a generous measure of scotch and telling him, 'I'll just go and check if the meal is ready and if it is we'll talk when we've eaten.'

'Yes, ma'am!' Max thought briefly of Mrs Pegs, who would also have a meal ready for him. He knew he would have to eat it even if he had to force it down, otherwise he would never hear the end of it. No doubt he would suffer from heartburn all night for over-indulging but it was worth it if he got to spend a little time alone with Dilly.

She returned minutes later with two steaming plates which she placed on the small table against one wall and once they were seated she asked, 'So how is Camilla?'

'About the same,' he sighed. 'But I have to admit, Bessie is doing a fine job of caring for her. She seems to have a calming effect on her somehow. And it must be nice for you to have your living accommodation to yourself again.'

'It is nice,' Dilly said. 'Although I have missed having Roddy about the place. He's very happy with Niamh looking after him though, and I think it's done her good to have another child to focus on. I know how much she still misses Connie.'

'Well, at least he's brought her out of her depression and that must be something to be thankful for,' Max pointed out as he loaded his fork with hotpot.

He had employed Bessie some months before, after she had implored him to give her a trial with Camilla, and Niamh had instantly stepped in to offer to care for Roddy in her absence. In fact she had insisted that both Bessie and Roddy should move back in with her, seeing as she had so much room to spare.

'Me and Mary rattle around this house like two peas in a pod,' she grumbled. 'So you'd be doing me a favour, and having Roddy here would keep me occupied through the day.' And so it had been agreed that Bessie would have two nights a week off when Olivia and Max would keep their eye on Camilla, so that Bessie could return to Niamh's to see her son. The arrangement had worked very well, and just as Max had said, Niamh did seem to be more her old self.

Once they had finished eating, Max rubbed his full stomach contentedly and then remembered: 'So what were you going to tell me that's put you in such a good mood?'

Dilly's eyes sparkled as she dabbed at her mouth with a napkin before rising from the table and hurrying off into the bedroom. She returned seconds later with a large envelope, and after plonking it down in front of Max she told him bossily, 'Open that.'

His eyes popped when he withdrew a large amount of banknotes. 'So . . . what's this then?'

'It's the rest of the money I owe you for the shops,' she said delightedly. 'Do check it. I think you'll find it's all there.'

He glanced at her, amazed.

'I told you we were doing well,' she laughed. 'And I'll do even better now that I can concentrate on buying extra stock.'

'But I told you that there was no rush to pay this back,' he objected.

'A deal is a deal,' Dilly said firmly. 'You were kind enough to get the shops for me and I wouldn't feel as if they were really mine whilst I still owed you money. Please take it, Max. I'm fine really.'

Max knew better than to argue with her. Dilly was a very determined woman when she set her mind to something.

'Actually, I have my eye on another shop now – in Birmingham,' she went on. 'My supplier told me about it and I went to look at it yesterday. The premises are very run down, but with a bit of work it could be wonderful.'

'Look, Dilly, I don't want to interfere and tell you what to do, but please be careful. You don't want to try and run before you can walk.'

Her laugh tinkled around the room. If anyone else had said that to her she would have taken offence and put them immediately in their place, but she knew that Max had only her best interests at heart.

'Don't worry,' she said, 'this shop is only for lease – well at the moment anyway – so I wouldn't be taking on anything I couldn't get out of if it wasn't profitable. I've already spoken to the landlord and he's told me that I could rent it for just a year to start with. That should be long enough for me to know if I could make it pay. It's right by the Bullring as it happens so it's in a prime location, and seeing as the train goes right through to New Street station it's also very easy for me to go backwards and forwards to it.'

Max held his hands up, defeated. He knew when to back off. 'It sounds to me as if you've already made your mind up about it but if you need any help financially . . .'

'I don't, but thank you for offering,' she told him primly, then changing the subject she said, 'Olivia seems a little brighter since she joined the local amateur dramatic society, doesn't she? I think it's done her the power of good – getting out of the house I mean.'

Max nodded – but then after glancing at the clock he suddenly remembered that Oscar was calling by to see his mother that evening. 'I ought to be off,' he said regretfully. 'Oscar is coming round tonight and Samuel is bringing the books for me to look at. I've got him collecting the rents from the properties I own now. Perhaps he'll enjoy that more than he did working in the offices.'

Dilly doubted that young man would take kindly to any type of work but she tactfully refrained from saying so.

After she had helped Max on with his coat, she went downstairs ahead of him to see him out, saying, 'Tell Mrs Pegs I'll pop in tomorrow, will you? The seamstresses have almost finished the skirt she ordered so I need her to have a final fitting.'

Max promised that he would and after closing the door behind him, Dilly hurried upstairs to read the letter that had arrived from Enniskerry that morning.

As she had thought, it was from Maeve and she snuggled down in the chair to read it.

*Dear Dilly,*

*I hope you are well as we all are. Everyone sends you their love as always. Seamus has been out helping Daddy with the cows today so we are thrilled that he is venturing outside now and taking a little more interest in things. He still has bad days, of course, but as we were told, this is normal for someone who has suffered shell shock.*

*Patrick and Bridie are growing like weeds and little Kian is into everything now.* (Dilly had been very touched when Liam and Shelagh had decided to call their latest addition to the family after the dear son she had lost in the war.) *Declan and Roisin are still very wrapped up in each other and I'm now going to share a secret with you. I shouldn't really, as Declan wanted to tell you himself but you are to be a grandma again, Dilly. Roisin is with child, God love her. Isn't that wonderful news? The baby is due in October so you must put some time aside even though you are so busy to come over round about then.*

*Ben is well but still no sign of a ladylove yet. I wonder if he will ever get over our Niamh. Do give the dear heart our love. I hope she is coping with the loss of our lovely little Connie.*

*Daddy went into market and bought two fine new bulls today so hopefully in the not too distant future we'll have some fine healthy calves on the way . . .*

Dilly read on but it was hard to concentrate after discovering she was to become a grandma again. Tears filled her eyes as she thought of how thrilled Fergal would have been, but she quickly blinked them away. She had learned long ago that it did no good to look back with regrets, only forward with hope for the future.

I must set the sewing ladies on making some little nightgowns, she thought excitedly and raced straight back down into the shop to scout around and see if there was any flannelette material there that would be suitable.


Max got home just as Oscar arrived and they went into the study together where Max poured them both a glass of port.

They bent over the ledgers that Oscar had brought with him for a time until Max commented, 'You seem a little preoccupied this evening, son. Is everything all right?'

'I suppose you may as well know, Father,' Oscar said glumly. 'Penelope informed me this evening that I'm to be a father – sometime in November, I believe.'

'Why, that's wonderful news! Congratulations, son.' Max slapped him heartily on the back.

Oscar grinned ruefully. His father could have no way of knowing how abhorrent Oscar found his wife, nor the fact that they had only lain together three times since their wedding day – and then it was only because of his wife's insistence. It had come as a shock to say the very least when Penelope had triumphantly revealed that she was having his child – but Oscar supposed he would love it when it arrived. The child would be a part of him, after all.

The door opened then and Lawrence limped in. He had been badly injured during the war and doubted he would ever walk again without the use of his stick, but then he counted himself lucky that at least he had come home. Thousands of other young men from the town hadn't been so fortunate, including Harvey, his brother, and Kian, one of Mrs Carey's sons. It was just a month to his wedding to Patty

Newcombe, the young nurse whom he had met in the field hospital after being wounded, and he could hardly wait.

'Your brother has just announced that he's going to become a father and I'm to become a grandfather again,' Max told him, and Lawrence instantly pumped his brother's hand up and down.

'Well done, matey!' he exclaimed just as Olivia entered the room.

'Well done for what?' She had washed her fashionably shorter hair earlier in the evening and in her calf-length waist-skimming dress she looked very attractive.

'Bro here is going to be a daddy,' Lawrence crowed and Olivia went white; she gripped the back of a chair, as she stared at Oscar.

He lowered his eyes, unable to meet hers, and eventually she choked out, 'You . . . you must be very pleased.' Then, not waiting for an answer, she turned and bolted from the room, almost colliding with Samuel who had come with his father's rent books.

Once the door was firmly closed between them, Olivia chewed on her knuckle as she pictured Oscar and Penelope in bed together. She often tortured herself with such thoughts, but then snatching up her coat she slammed out of the house. How he could make love to that horse-faced bitch she had no idea. She knew that she was being unkind but she couldn't seem to stop herself. Blinking rapidly, she rushed on. It wouldn't do to be late for rehearsals. She and the rest of the actors and actresses in the Dramatic Society were due to put on a show the following month, so she would think about that instead. She loved being part of the drama group and looked forward to the evening rehearsals; they distracted her from thoughts of Oscar.

Michael Freeman, a young man who lived on Manor Court Road, met her on the way to the theatre and fell into step with her. He'd had his eye on Olivia ever since the first time he had seen her but being a little shy he hadn't yet plucked up the courage to ask her out.

'It's a lovely evening, isn't it?' he said conversationally.

'Yes, I suppose it is,' Olivia replied. She'd never taken much notice of Michael before, but now as she glanced at him she saw that he was actually quite attractive. He was very tall and slim with blond hair and an easy smile. He was also a very a good actor and had been in the Amateur Dramatic Society for years, one of their stars. She'd heard that his father owned a number of houses in the town and was quite well off, but she'd never been interested enough in him to find out any more.

'I er . . . was wondering if you might let me take you out one evening?' he asked suddenly. 'We could perhaps go dancing? Or if you'd prefer, I could take you for a meal or to a show.'

As usual when young men showed an interest in her, Olivia opened her mouth to refuse but then for some reason changed her mind. Wasn't it about time that she started to get out and about and enjoy herself? Ever since Oscar had married Penelope she had moped about the house, only leaving it to go to work or more recently to the Amateur Dramatic Society meetings. Perhaps it was time to get on with her life.

'I'd like that,' she answered quietly and was rewarded with a dazzling smile. Michael could hardly believe his luck. Olivia was easily the prettiest girl he had ever set eyes on.

'Wonderful. How about this Friday evening then? Just name what you'd like to do.'

'Oh, we could perhaps just go for a quiet meal somewhere.'

Suddenly Olivia wished that she hadn't been so hasty in her reply. Michael was a lovely fellow but she had no romantic interest in him whatsoever, so she was just being cruel, leading him on to believe that she did. But then she could always explain to him whilst they were out on Friday that she was only looking for friendship. She would make sure that Oscar knew that she had a date though, one way or another. She'd done with moping about for him, she told herself fiercely – and yet somehow the words didn't quite ring true.

# Chapter Eleven

The following week when the customer Jayne Richards had been serving had left the shop, Dilly seized her chance for a private word.

'Jayne, pet, I have a proposition to put to you.'

Jayne looked at her curiously.

'The thing is, when I went into Birmingham yesterday I signed the lease for that shop I told you about. Now obviously it's going to take at least a month to get it up and running and stocked, but then I was wondering . . . how would you feel about managing it for me? I clearly can't be in two places at once so I need someone I can trust and you fit the bill admirably. I would, of course, pay all your travelling expenses and it would mean a rise in your wages, too – so what do you think?'

Jayne was flabbergasted but delighted. 'But who would help you here?' she asked. 'We're getting quite busy now and I doubt you'd manage it single-handed without running yourself into the ground.'

'I've already thought of that,' Dilly answered with a grin as she deftly tidied the drawer containing the gloves and scarves. It seemed a never-ending task. 'I'm going to ask Niamh if she would come in and help out. She's clearly abandoned her idea of going back to work at the school part-time and she seems to have lost interest in her painting for the time being.'

'But doesn't she look after Bessie's little boy during the day?'

'Yes, she does, but he'll be starting school eventually and she'll need something to fill her days. Until then I thought we might get Nell Cotteridge to care for him while Niamh is here with me – if she'll agree to come, that is. I'm sure it would do her good to get out of the house more. She's become rather reclusive since she lost Connie.'

'Hmm.' Jayne stared off into space for a moment or two but then her face broke into a wide smile. 'In that case I'd love to manage the shop in Birmingham. Imagine that, eh? *Me* a manageress! Me mam will be tickled pink when I tell her. Thank you, Mrs Carey. I won't let you down, I promise.'

'I know you won't,' Dilly assured her. 'But now we'd better get on. We have another delivery of clothes coming this afternoon so we're going to be busy.'

Beaming fit to bust, Jayne was only too happy to oblige.

In the Farthing residence at that moment, Bessie had just appeared in the kitchen to share a cup of tea with Mrs Pegs. Camilla was asleep for now, so Bessie was making the most of it.

'How is she?' Mrs Pegs asked as she beckoned to Gwen to fetch her the tea pot.

'Fast asleep but I don't know how long it will last.' Bessie yawned. 'Her sleep pattern is all over the place at the moment; she had me up half the night and now she's snoring her head off.' She yawned again, and Mrs Pegs thought how tired she looked.

'Between you and me I think she's getting worse,' Bessie confided. 'She talks to the boys as if they are in the room with her and as if they are still little. I can't help but feel sorry for her now. I reckon the master will have to put her in a home eventually because she's not safe to be left alone any more. I caught her this morning standing on the windowsill as if she was going to jump out so I'll have to have a word with Mr Farthing later on. We need the windows to be screwed shut or some bars put across them at least, else she's likely to do herself a mischief. The trouble is, you only have to turn your back on her for a second now and there's no saying what she might be up to.'

'It is a shame,' Mrs Pegs agreed. 'I'll tell yer what, if I ever get like that I want yer to shoot me out o' the way an' be done wi' it! I can't think of anythin' worse than losin' all your marbles.'

'Neither can I.'

'But anyway it's yer day off tomorrer so yer can get some rest an' see that lovely little lad o' yours. How is he?'

'Oh, fine I believe,' Bessie said. 'Niamh takes very good care of him.'

'Even so, he's still your child an' he needs to see yer.'

'I know that and I *do* see him.' Bessie was instantly on the defensive as guilty tears sprang to her eyes. 'The trouble is, I reckon he prefers Niamh to me now, not that I can blame him. She's so good with him whereas I—'

'But he's likely to, ain't he?' Mrs Pegs interrupted. 'He spends more time with her. I sometimes wonder if this is the right job fer you, wi' you havin' a little 'un. Surely somethin' wi' fewer hours where yer could spend more time wi' little Roddy would suit yer better? You've openly said yer don't need to work full-time since that nice husband o' yours left yer comfortably off.'

'But I *like* working here,' Bessie said. 'While I'm busy I don't have time to think and when I don't think I don't miss Malcolm so much.'

'We all 'ave us crosses to bear,' Mrs Pegs said stoically. 'But we 'ave to get on wi' things an' from where I'm standin' you should be puttin' that little lad first. I don't mean to be harsh, Bessie, but Malcolm is gone an' there's no bringin' 'im back, but little Roddy is still 'ere an' he needs his mam!'

'Don't you think I'm aware of that?' Bessie stormed, standing up so abruptly that her chair almost overturned. 'I didn't come down here for a lecture. I *do* try with Roddy . . . *I do*! I lie awake every night hating myself for not being closer to him, but I don't know how to change things. I think I must be unnatural. Mothers are supposed to love their children, aren't they? But all I see when I look at Roddy is his father!' With that she banged out of the room.

When Bessie had gone, Mrs Pegs scrubbed at her eyes with her knuckles wondering if she had been too hard on the young woman. There was a time when this house had rung with the sound of laughter, but that seemed like a million years ago now.

It was the following week when Dilly told Niamh, 'I was thinking of going over to visit the family in Ireland. I shan't have time once the Birmingham shop has opened and I don't want to wait until Declan and Roisin's baby is born. Why don't you come with me? I know they would all love to see you and a little break would do you good.'

Niamh, who was playing with Roddy and his bricks in front of the fire, looked up and frowned. 'But I can't come, Mammy. Who would look after Roddy while I was gone with Bessie at work?'

Dilly sighed. More than ever she was convinced that Niamh needed to get out and about again, and a trip to Ireland would bring the roses back to her cheeks.

'I've no doubt Mary will manage fine,' she said confidently. 'Won't you please at least think about it?' She'd expected a firm refusal so was shocked when Niamh nodded.

'All right then. It would be nice to see Gran'ma and Granda, and I do get a little tired of staring at the same four walls.'

Dilly was delighted. Niamh had scarcely left the house since losing Connie and hopefully this would be the start of her having more of a social life again. She was far too young to lock herself away. The time since Connie had died had not been easy for any of them, least of all Niamh, and the girl had struggled with all sorts of emotions – grief, anger and utter heartbreak – but now it was time for her to get on with her life, as far as her mother was concerned.

That same day, Dilly took a lease on another small shop that had become vacant in Abbey Street. It was conveniently close to her dress shop and this one would be used as a sewing room where the seamstresses could make copies of the ready-made clothes she had purchased and also put together some of her own designs. Already the small area at the back of the shop where they had sewed was proving to be inadequate for the amount of work they were taking on. Dilly hoped this would keep the cost of stocking her shops down, and the seamstresses she employed were more than happy to be so busy. Dilly knew that this latest venture would stretch her finances to the limit but considered it would be worth it in the long run and was prepared to take the risk. Already she had bought bales of suitable material that the women would make into dresses of various styles and sizes. It would also ensure that she could still cater to the clients who preferred bespoke garments. And so, all in all, she was feeling happy that evening as she stood in her little domain and admired it. She was still standing there when Max arrived, looking harassed.

'Is something wrong?' she asked.

'What? Oh no, everything's fine.' He forced a smile before looking around and commenting, 'I must say, this place is really looking lovely now. No wonder it's becoming so popular with the local women. You clearly have an eye for business.'

Dilly flushed at the praise. She was thrilled with the way the shop was doing and prayed that the one in Birmingham would do as well.

'Would you like to come upstairs for a drink?' she asked then and looked vaguely surprised when Max shook his head.

'Thank you, but I won't this evening if you don't mind. Samuel sent a message to say that he needed to see me at home and so I've no doubt that will mean trouble. I only ever see him nowadays if he wants something. He's been so taken up with his lady friend Mrs King that he doesn't even come to see his mother any more. Never mind, I'll call in again tomorrow evening, shall I? I should have more time then. Good night, Dilly.'

'Good night, Max.' Dilly watched him leave then set about tidying the clothes rails before making her way to her rooms upstairs. She had been about to tell him of her proposed trip to Ireland but she supposed it could wait.

'So . . . to what do I owe this honour?' Max asked his son sarcastically an hour later as Samuel entered his study.

Samuel flipped his hat carelessly onto a small table before dropping into the nearest chair.

'Well, the thing is, I find myself in a bit of a pickle, Father.'

Max sighed. It was just as he had thought and he wondered how much this latest 'pickle' was going to cost him.

'My friend Lilian . . . well, we've had a little tiff and—'

'I take it *Lilian* is the widow you've been seeing?' Max snapped before Samuel could go on. 'I don't know how you have the brass neck to even mention her to me. You're a married man, although you certainly don't act like one. Isn't it about time you grew up a little and paid your wife some attention?'

'Now that's a bit harsh,' Samuel objected. 'You know as well as I do that Niamh prefers me to stay away from her. So what's a chap to do? I don't intend to live like a monk.'

Max couldn't argue with that. More than ever now he wondered if he had done the right thing when he had forced Samuel to marry the girl. They clearly had no time for each other and now that Connie was gone it all seemed so pointless – as if they had both thrown their lives away for nothing.

'So what's wrong then?' he asked resignedly.

'I need to borrow a bit of money. Just for a while. I'll pay you back, of course.'

'How much is a bit?'

'Fifty pounds.'

'*Fifty pounds!* You call that a bit?' Max barked.

'It's only till Grandmother's allowance comes through at the end of the month,' Samuel told him sheepishly.

Max's late mother-in-law had left all the children a sizeable sum of money that was paid to them monthly, but Samuel had always spent his before he'd even got it, as well as his wages.

'What the hell have you wasted fifty pounds on this time? Cards – horses?'

'Something like that,' Samuel muttered, lowering his head. He hated having to come cap in hand to his father but the chap he owed the money to wasn't the sort that would wait.

'Very well,' Max sighed eventually. 'But I want it straight back at the end of the month. Is that clear?'

'Quite clear,' Samuel said sullenly.

Max strode to the safe and after unlocking it he counted fifty pounds out and handed the notes to his son.

Samuel then rose from his seat, saying, 'Good night, Father.' With that he was gone, leaving Max to shake his head in despair. One of these days that young man was going to get his comeuppance, that was for sure.

Outside, Samuel stood uncertainly looking up and down the road. There would be no point in going back to Lilian's that evening. She'd chucked him out on his arse good and proper and all because she'd found out that he'd had a little fling with one of her maids. He supposed he had no choice but to return to the house his father had bought for him and Niamh. It was better than having to sleep on one of his friends' sofas, or go back into the house cap in hand again begging for a bed for the night. He'd done quite enough grovelling for one night! But he didn't relish the thought of having to see Niamh again one little bit and he had an idea she would be none too pleased to see him either.

Niamh was playing with a wooden train on the hearthrug with Roddy when Mary admitted Samuel, and her mouth gaped with shock. 'Wh-what are *you* doing here?' she stuttered

'It's my house, in case you'd forgotten,' Samuel growled back churlishly. 'And I shall be staying here for a while.'

'Not in my bedroom you won't!'

Picking up on the tense atmosphere, Roddy cringed into

Niamh's side as Samuel stared at him in disgust.

'So where *am* I supposed to sleep then?'

'In the spare room. I'll have Mary make the bed up for you,' Niamh responded coldly.

'Suit yourself. And tell her to get me a meal as well. I haven't eaten since lunchtime.'

Feeling as if she didn't have much choice, Niamh went to find Mary with Roddy clinging on to her. She could only pray that her husband's stay would be a short one, and suddenly she was glad she had agreed to go to Enniskerry with her mother the following week. Anything would be better than being forced to spend any time with him!

# Chapter Twelve

'You're doing what?' Dilly asked in amazement the following morning when Niamh called into the shop.

'I'm bringing Roddy with us to Gran'ma's and Granda's.'

The firm set of her daughter's chin told Dilly that there would be no use arguing. 'But why? He would be perfectly safe with Mary.'

'I know that, but Samuel turned up and stayed last night. I think he and his mistress have fallen out so he could be there for a time – and I don't trust him with Roddy. He clearly doesn't like the child. I just popped round to the Farthings to see Bessie and she has no objection to him coming with us.'

Dilly doubted Bessie would care if she never saw the boy again, but she didn't say it. Instead, she nodded. 'Very well then, if you think that will be best.' Secretly she had been hoping to get Niamh away from the child for a while. Her daughter needed some time to herself. Still, at least she was still agreeing to go, and that was a major step forward in itself. A customer entered the shop then and Niamh departed, promising that she would see her mother later.

In the Farthing household, Mrs Pegs was fussing over Olivia who was sitting at the kitchen table with a face the colour of putty.

'Perhaps yer should let me get yer father to fetch the doctor in to have a look at yer?' the kindly woman suggested but Olivia quickly shook her head.

'No, no, I'll be fine, Mrs Pegs – honestly. I've probably just got a tummy upset or something. I'll be right as rain in a few days. In fact, I'm feeling better already, so I'd best get changed and get myself off to work.'

Mrs Pegs thoughtfully watched the girl leave the room. Poor soul, she seemed to pick up every cough and cold that was going around lately – but then it was hardly surprising. She didn't eat enough to keep a sparrow alive.

Upstairs in her bedroom, Olivia leaned heavily on her dressing table. Oh, what a fool I've been, she thought. But there was nothing to be done about it now. Her mind drifted back to the first night she had met Roger Bannerman at the Amateur Dramatics Society. It was mere days after she had found out that Penelope was carrying Oscar's child and her head had been in a whirl. Her little fling with Michael Freeman had been very shortlived. Truthfully, Olivia had found him quite dull and had finished their relationship almost before it had started, but Roger had paid her a lot of attention. He was courteous and flattering as well as being extremely good-looking and she'd thought, Why not! Oscar was living *his* life, so why shouldn't she live hers? And so had begun a whirlwind romance. He had wined and dined her, bought her flowers, and she'd found that it was quite nice to feel wanted again. Until she had turned up to a rehearsal one evening and Jean Miller, one of the older members of the society, had pulled her to one side.

'I don't wish to interfere, my dear,' she had said worriedly, 'but I couldn't help but notice that you and Roger are becoming close. You're such a nice girl I felt I should tell you that he's a married man. Were you aware of the fact?'

'No, I wasn't!' Olivia had gasped, thinking what bastards men were. Then, pulling herself together, she said, 'Thank you for telling me, Mrs Miller. Rest assured I shan't be seeing him again.' And she hadn't, but she whipped herself for being such a fool as to fall for his lies. She could only begin to imagine how her father would feel if he discovered she had been seeing a married man. She had briefly considered telling him about Roger before someone else did, but had discounted that idea almost immediately. In the cold light of day she knew that she had only used Roger as he had used her to take her mind off what she considered to be Oscar's betrayal – and look where it had gotten her.

Her feet dragged as she made her way to Weddington Hall Hospital and she racked her brains about the best road to take. And then it came to her – she would go away. Not run away but go in an organised manner with her pride still intact. But where to go, that was the question. London? Yes, she thought. Drury Lane! She had a considerable amount of money put by, for she always saved her wages and allowances, unlike Samuel. There would be more than enough for her to rent a room somewhere while she tried to find a job in one of the theatres there. She'd been feeling restless for some time and this was just the spur she had needed to make her do something about it. All she had to do now was speak to her father and put her plan into action, maybe even that very evening, for there was no time like the present. She would have a word with Dilly Carey too. She'd always been able to speak easily to Dilly for some reason. With her mind made up, her heart felt lighter

That evening over dinner, Olivia eyed her father before saying cautiously, 'I was thinking of going away for a time, Father.'

'What?' Max almost dropped his knife and fork. 'What do you mean, going away? Going away where?'

'I thought it might be nice to work in London for a time,' she answered cagily. 'I quite fancy a change from nursing so I might try my hand at working in a theatre. I've loved being in the Amateur Dramatic Society and theatre work is so much more exciting than nursing.'

Max frowned. 'Don't you think you're a little young to be taking such a big step? London is a big place for a young woman alone, and you don't know anyone there. Lord knows what might happen to you.'

'Rubbish!' Olivia scoffed. 'I'm quite old enough to leave home, Father, and I'm quite able to take care of myself. Women have had to grow up fast since the war started and I need a break. I'm not saying I'll never return to nursing but I want to try something different while I'm young enough to enjoy it.'

'So take a holiday then,' he grunted, horrified at the thought of his daughter all alone in a big city. 'London isn't all it's cracked up to be, believe me. There's many a young woman come unstuck after going there.'

'Even so, I've made my mind up and I intend to give it a try,' she answered with steely determination.

'And when were you planning on going?'

'Within the next couple of weeks. In fact, I'm going to give my notice in at the hospital today.' She reached across the table and gently squeezed his hand. 'It won't be for ever,' she promised.

Max's shoulders sagged but he knew better than to argue with Olivia when she'd made her mind up about something. She could be as stubborn as a mule and she had seemed to enjoy her nights at the local Dramatic Society. More than he'd realised, if what she was proposing now was anything to go by.

'Then I shan't forbid it but I can't pretend to be happy with the idea. Can't you just think about it for a while longer?'

'I have thought about it for months and it's what I want to do.'

'But where will you stay? And why do you need to change careers? You worked so hard to become a nurse.'

'Oh, I shall probably rent a room somewhere for a short time,' she said airily. 'I have plenty of money saved up so I certainly shan't starve or end up on the streets, if that's what you're worried about.' Seeing his dejected expression she ended, 'And it will only be for a time. *Please* let me go with your blessing, Father. I . . . I need to do this.'

Max knew how unhappy Olivia had been since Oscar had married Penelope and as he stared into her strained face he sighed.

'Very well then. But there is one proviso. I have a business colleague in London who I'm sure would put you up until you found somewhere suitable to live. Will you agree to that at least? I need to know that you're safe, and Neville Green and his wife are a lovely couple. What do you say?'

'I'll think about it,' Olivia answered reluctantly. She doubted she would need to stay with them for long anyway. Surely there would be dozens of rooms vacant in such a big city? 'Thank you, Father,' and for now the subject was dropped.

'She's doing what!' Dilly gasped when Max gloomily told her of Olivia's plans later that evening.

'She seems set on going and apart from locking her in her room I can't see how I can stop her,' Max said, sounding depressed. 'But at least she's agreed to consider staying with some friends of mine until she finds somewhere suitable to live.' It just seemed to be one thing on top of another at present. He had thought when his children grew older, the worry about them would lessen but that certainly hadn't proved to be the case with his family.

Dilly began to pace up and down the room, her joined hands pressed tightly into her waist. 'I shall try speaking to her. Perhaps I can get her to change her mind?'

'You're more than welcome to try, but I very much doubt you'll manage it. She's obviously been thinking about this for a time and I don't think anyone could persuade her against it now.'

'I shall try anyway,' Dilly said obstinately, as fearful as Max was. Olivia had led such a sheltered, protected life that the thought of her heading off alone to the streets of London was terrifying.

The following week, Dilly, Niamh and Roddy set off for Enniskerry. Dilly had tried on two occasions to speak to Olivia about her proposed plans but the girl was adamant that she was still going and Dilly was afraid that she might decide to leave while she was away in Ireland. Not that there was anything she could do about it. Olivia had made her mind up and nothing was going to change it.

'Is anything wrong, Mammy? You seem preoccupied,' Niamh said as the train taking them to the ferry rattled along the track.

'No, it's nothing, pet,' Dilly assured her, forcing a smile. 'I was just hoping that Jayne can keep the shop running smoothly whilst we're away.'

'Oh, will you please stop worrying about work,' Niamh

scolded. 'We're only going to be gone for a few days, so relax. Jayne is more than capable, as you well know.'

'Yes, of course she is,' Dilly answered, then turning her attention to Roddy she pointed out some cows grazing in a field to change the subject.

Daniel was waiting for them with the cart when the ferry arrived in Dublin that evening. He greeted them warmly as he threw their bags into the back. Roddy was almost asleep and when Daniel peered at him curiously, Dilly whispered, 'I'll explain all about him later on.'

Niamh climbed into the back with Roddy as Dilly sat up front with her father-in-law and he steered the horse towards the farm.

'I'm so looking forward to seeing everyone,' Dilly told him. 'Especially Declan and Roisin. Isn't it wonderful news about the baby?'

Daniel's face clouded. 'Ah, well, there's been a few setbacks in that direction so there has,' he confided. 'Only this morning Declan fetched the doctor out to Roisin. She's been quite poorly since she discovered she was carrying the wean and the doctor has made her put her feet up. Maeve and Shelagh have been keeping their eye on her so we're hoping things will improve.'

'I see.' Dilly was concerned but tried to stay positive. Lots of women were unwell during the first months of their pregnancy so maybe things would settle down for the girl.

Looking over his shoulder, Daniel saw that Niamh and Roddy had both dropped off to sleep. Lowering his voice, he asked, 'How has she been?'

'Up and down, you know. Good days and bad days, but that's to be expected.' Dilly then went on to tell him all about Roddy as the horse trotted along.

'Sure, life can be a cruel thing,' her father-in-law said

sadly. 'There's our Niamh losing little Connie who she idolised, an' you're telling me this little mite's mother can't take to him. It doesn't seem fair, does it?'

Dilly agreed. She then went on to ask him about Seamus and the rest of the family, and the journey passed quickly as they caught up on all the news.

As they pulled into the cobbled yard Daniel frowned when he saw the doctor's trap there again. He helped Dilly down and she rushed into the kitchen to find Maeve softly crying.

'Aw lass,' she said, opening her arms to her. 'What a terrible greeting 'tis for you. Sure, poor Roisin has lost their baby. The doctor is in with her now. She and Declan will be heartbroken, but there was nothing could be done to prevent it.'

As Dilly thought about all the tiny baby clothes she had brought for them, packed carefully away in her bag, her heart sank but then her eyes settled on Seamus who was sitting at the side of the fire and she hurried over to cuddle him, saying, 'Why look at you. Don't you look grand? You're putting weight back on and there's some colour in your cheeks again.'

'I-I'm feelin' better, Mammy,' he answered, clearly pleased to see her.

Shelagh entered the room then and after giving Dilly and Niamh a hug she whispered, 'The doctor has just left. He's told them to wait a few months and then try again, but they're terrible upset, so they are. It's so sad.'

The men had built yet another small cottage for Declan and Roisin to live in next to Shelagh and Liam's, and Dilly headed for the door, saying, 'I'd best go and see them.'

Shelagh gently caught her arm. 'I wouldn't just yet,' she advised. 'I reckon they need a little time alone. I've done all the cleaning up and made sure they have everything they need, so I'd wait till morning to give them time to come to terms with things if I was you.'

'Very well.' It was sensible advice. Dilly unbuttoned her coat as Maeve bustled away to serve the meal she had ready, but for the rest of the evening they were all subdued as they thought of the baby that had died before it had had a chance to live.

Niamh and Roddy had retired to bed when Declan came round to his grandparents, to see his mother. Roisin had cried herself to sleep and Shelagh was sitting with her until he got back. His face was strained, his eyes red-rimmed, and Dilly hugged her son to her, wondering at how he now towered above her. He was so like his father when she had first met him that just to look at him brought a lump to her throat.

'Aw, Mammy,' he sobbed as he clung to her. 'I can't believe that we've lost our wee wean.'

'These things happen from time to time, sadly,' Dilly murmured as she stroked his thick black hair. 'But they usually happen for a reason. It could be that something about the child Roisin was carrying was not quite right.'

'We wouldn't have cared if it hadn't been perfect!' Declan said passionately.

'No, you probably wouldn't,' his mother agreed patiently. 'But you are both fit and young and there will be other babies in time, although of course you'll never forget this little one. You have to grieve then put it behind you as best you can and try again.'

'Easier said than done,' Declan sniffed as his gran'ma pressed a glass of poteen into his hand.

'Get that down you, lad,' she ordered. 'A drop o' the hard stuff will do you a power o' good.'

Declan drained the glass in one swallow before handing it back to her and swiping the back of his hand across his mouth. 'So where is Niamh?' he asked then.

Dilly gestured towards the door that led to the stairs. 'She's turned in with Roddy, Bessie's little boy, but I'll tell you all about him tomorrow.'

'Do you mean the Bessie that used to work for the Farthings? The maid who ran away?'

Dilly nodded and they then went to sit on the sofa. Declan rested his head on her shoulder as she held him tight and offered what comfort she could. It was a terrible start to the visit but Dilly was still glad that she had arrived when she had. At least she was there to offer a helping hand over the first, most difficult days of their loss.

## *Chapter Thirteen*

The following morning Niamh left Roddy with Maeve and told them all that she was going for a long walk. Maeve was only too happy to oblige as she felt the fresh air would do the girl good. Niamh had always been pleasantly rounded but she was now painfully thin and her clothes hung off her.

'I'll put some meat back on her bones afore she leaves if it's the last thing I ever do – even if I have to force-feed her, so I will,' Maeve declared and they all smiled, knowing the determined little woman was quite capable of doing just that.

Niamh meanwhile was meandering along the road leading to Enniskerry wondering if it would be appropriate to pay Ben a visit. Deep down she acknowledged that he was the only reason she had agreed to come on the trip. She hadn't seen him since he had attended Connie's funeral but a weight had lifted when she'd confessed about Samuel and they had become friends again and were once more easy in each other's company. Just knowing that he was so close was enough to set her pulse racing and she knew that she still loved him; would always love him – not that there could ever be more than friendship between them now. She was a married woman, but if she could just see him from time to time, she felt she would have something left to live for. Constance had left a huge hole in her heart. She supposed that in time Ben would meet a lass and marry, and she dreaded it – even though she knew it was unreasonable of her to feel that way.

Shortly after, she turned a bend in the lane and the roof-tops of Enniskerry came into view. Her heart began to thud painfully with anticipation as she quickened her footsteps.

Samuel stared down at the money in his hand as he ran his tongue across his dry lips. Ten pounds – all he had left after paying off his latest gambling debt. Now he was considering whether or not to risk it on another card game. If he lost that too he would be broke until the end of the month, for he sensed that he'd get no more out of his father for a while and Lilian was still refusing to see him. The silly cow, he thought. Didn't she realise that he was a young man with needs which she was far too old to satisfy?

He glanced around the drawing room of the house that his father had bought for him and Niamh to live in just before their wedding. It felt more like home to him whilst Niamh was away in Ireland and he reckoned it would be worth a pretty penny. He enjoyed being the master of his own home, and he'd liked having Mary running about after him. But he'd like the money the house would fetch more. Trouble was, his father had never actually handed him the deeds to it and he wondered if Niamh had them. The way he saw it, she didn't need to live there now that the kid was gone. She could clear off and go and live in a hovel for all he cared. It was bad enough that he had been forced to marry one of their ex-servant's daughters, but they'd nothing to tie them now that he'd made sure the brat was out of the way.

His thoughts moved on to the business he had looked at that day. He was sick and tired of working for his father. Sick of being at Max's beck and call the whole time and spoken to as if he was still a child – but if he were able to buy his own business . . . With his mind made up he rang the bell at the side of the fireplace.

'Yes?' Mary made no secret of the fact that she didn't like him, and the feeling was mutual.

'Get me something to eat straight away. I shall be going out early this evening.'

Mary turned without a word. There had been no please or thank you, but then she didn't expect it from Samuel. As far as she was concerned, he was uncouth and she could understand why Niamh wanted nothing to do with him. She was also aware of the reason why Niamh had been forced to marry him and of the fact that he was Roddy's father too. When Niamh had first left for Ireland, Mary had felt quite nervous at the thought of being alone in the house with him, but then she'd started to take a knife to bed with her and she vowed that she would use it if he so much as put a foot wrong with her – not that he'd tried anything up to now and it wouldn't pay him to!

In the drawing room Samuel was pacing up and down with his hands clasped behind his back as he contemplated the evening ahead. There would be some good poker players there and the stakes would be high. But then he wasn't averse to a little cheating if he could get away with it. He briefly thought about raiding Niamh's bedroom to see if there was anything there worth taking, but decided against it. Mary watched him like a hawk and anyway, as far as he knew, the only pieces of jewellery that Niamh possessed were her plain gold wedding band and a small sapphire and diamond ring that she wore all the time on her other hand. He had no idea who had given it to her and didn't much care, so he would just have to go with what he had in his pocket and hope that Lady Luck would smile on him.

Tomorrow, Samuel decided, he would search for the deeds of the house. He reasoned that they must be here somewhere. If he won this evening and sold the house, he need never be accountable to his father again. He imagined Niamh's face if he was able to snatch the house right from under her nose. She would be furious, no doubt, but he didn't care. He had never had any feelings for her, or the child she'd carried for that matter, but hopefully soon he need never set eyes on her – or his father – again.

In a happier frame of mind he clipped the end from a cigar and lit it.

Olivia stared around her bedroom thinking how much she would miss it when she left.

She had just been to say goodbye to her mother but she needn't have bothered; Camilla had just stared off into space, not even aware that she was there. Bessie had given her a hug though and wished her all the best. Now her father was downstairs waiting to run her to the station. She wished that she had had the chance to say goodbye to Dilly Carey but she was in Ireland and once Olivia had decided what she wanted to do, she had also decided that she might as well get on with it and put her plan into action. She would have liked to have seen Oscar and said goodbye to him too, but she knew that it would have been too painful. It was time to put the feelings she had for him aside now, once and for all.

Max was clearly upset about her decision and Mrs Pegs and Gwen had openly wept when she'd told them that she was going. However, Olivia was determined not to let anything sway her; she couldn't afford to. Packing the last of her things into the big leather suitcase, she swung it off the bed then after a last glance around she staggered along the landing with it and carried it down into the hall. Her father's face was strained but he merely lifted it without a word and carried it out to the waiting car. Olivia followed him meekly and clambered into the passenger seat, keeping her eyes straight ahead. She knew if she so much as blinked she would break down in tears – and that would never do.

They were driving through Abbey Green when her father broke the silence to implore, 'Is there *nothing* I can do to make you change your mind, dear? I'm so worried about you going off like this. Once you've left the Greens you don't have anywhere to live'

'I shall be fine,' she said with forced gaiety.

'Then just promise me at least that you'll telephone me and let me know that you've arived safely.'

'Of course I will.'

They were approaching the station now and drew the car to a halt and helped her out before fetching her suitcase from the boot.

'Don't come in with me, please,' she said suddenly. 'I have my ticket and I'd rather say goodbye here.'

'But I . . .' Max's voice trailed away as he saw the determined set of her chin. 'Very well then,' he said resignedly. 'But you will—'

'Yes, I'll telephone you,' she promised, forecasting what he had been about to say.

It was then he pressed a large envelope into her hand, saying, 'Put that away safely in your bag. You may need it.'

'But what is it?'

'Some extra money . . . just in case.'

'But I *have* money,' she objected.

'Well, take it anyway – please. Just for emergencies, eh? It will make me feel a little better. I've phoned Neville Green and their maid will be waiting for you at Euston. But just in case you miss her you have their address safe, don't you?'

'Yes, Father,' Olivia told him as she patted her bag. 'Now will you *please* stop fussing? I'm a big girl now, you know.'

As she reluctantly rammed the envelope into her bag he stared at her, thinking how grown up she looked in her smart suit and hat. They were a light bronze colour and set her copper hair and eyes off to perfection. Fear gripped him again then. Olivia was so attractive and so naïve in many ways and it was common knowledge that there were unscrupulous men in London who preyed on young girls. Would she be able to keep herself safe? Should he put his foot down and haul her back home kicking and screaming? Yet he knew that wasn't an option, Olivia had clearly made her mind up and he had to let her go. She was a young woman now.

'Stay safe and keep in touch,' he said, dragging her into his arms and squeezing her. 'And remember, if anything should go wrong – anything at all – you only have to telephone or write and I shall come and fetch you.'

'I know,' she said chokily as she kissed his cheek. 'Goodbye for now, Daddy.' And then she lifted her suitcase and walked away, and he could only stand helplessly and watch her go.

When Olivia alighted from the train at Euston station, she stared about her dumbfounded. The whole place was teeming with people and she didn't even know which way the exit was. She would meet Mr and Mrs Green's maid at the pre-arranged place, but she had no intention of going back with her. As she had told her father, she was a big girl now, and kind as the couple's offer of letting her stay with them was, she wanted to stand on her own two feet. She felt rather guilty and devious about letting her father and the Greens down, but after apologising to the maid and telling her to let her employers know that she had made alternative arrangements, Olivia emerged onto the streets of London.

It was a marvellous day with the sun riding high in a cloudless blue sky, and Olivia suddenly realised that she was hot and thirsty. She wondered if she should have taken her father's advice and planned her trip a little more thoroughly. She felt conspicuous standing there with her heavy suitcase at her feet, and yet a glance around her assured her that no one was even looking at her. It was as if she was invisible, just one of many of the surging crowd. Spotting a small cart that appeared to be serving faggots and peas she approached it.

'What can I sell yer then, me little sparrer?' a big rosy-cheeked woman in a large floppy hat enquired pleasantly.

'I was wondering if you could tell me where I might get a cup of tea and if you knew of any rooms to rent,' Olivia croaked. Already she was wondering if she should have taken the Greens up on their offer after all?

'Well, there's any number of tea rooms along that road there, but what part o' London did yer want to stay in?' The woman was concerned. Olivia was clearly a well-bred young lady if her voice and her clothes were anything to go by; she'd be a target for any unscrupulous types if she wasn't careful.

'I . . . I'd like to stay close to Drury Lane,' Olivia stammered.

'Ah, yer want the Covent Garden area then. You'd no doubt find somewhere along Wellington Street or Russell Street. A lot of the actors an' actresses stay there. Is that what you've come to be, luvvie?'

'Something like that,' Olivia answered with a tremulous smile.

'Then in that case I'd suggest yer find yer lodgin's first before you go out an' about. It ain't safe to be luggin' a suitcase around, hereabouts. There's some right nasty people who would cut yer throat fer sixpence. An' don't get goin' out on yer own at night neither, luv. It ain't safe fer a young woman on her own 'ere. Why don't you go an' get a cab, eh? There are some parked over there – look. It ain't far to Covent Garden from 'ere – just an 'op, skip an' a jump.'

Olivia's eyes followed the direction the woman was pointing in and when she saw a number of horse-draw cabs she smiled at her gratefully.

'Thank you very much – I'll do that. Goodbye.'

'Bye, luvvie . . . and take care, mind!' The woman was approached by a customer then and she turned to serve them as Olivia set off.

Minutes later, the girl was sitting in the back of a cab.

'Where to, miss?' The driver plonked Olivia's case onto the floor of the carriage.

'The Covent Garden area, please.'

'Any particular place?'

'Er . . . I'm looking for lodgings close to the Theatre Royal. A lady at the station said I might find some in Wellington Street or thereabouts.'

'Right, y'are, young lady.' The driver tipped his cap before scrambling up into his seat and before she knew it he was guiding his horse past an enormous church – St Pancras, it was called – and along a wide busy main road past Holborn underground station, where he made a right turn.

Olivia clung to the seat feeling very small and insignificant, and at that moment she would have given everything she owned to see a familiar face as the doubts crept in. What if she wasn't able to find anywhere to stay? What if she had all her money stolen? She would never be able to go home with her tail between her legs, not for months at least – her pride would not allow it. Word was bound to get out sooner or later about how Roger had duped her, and she knew that she wouldn't be able to bear the shame.

Eventually the driver drew the horse to a halt and jumping down from his seat he came to open the door for her, saying, 'This 'ere is Wellington Street, miss.' He lifted her case onto the pavement and once she had paid him and he had driven away, Olivia looked about uncertainly, wondering where she should begin her search. The houses on either side of the street were enormous – great towering places three storeys high. She was beginning to wish that she hadn't packed so many clothes now. She wouldn't be able to carry the case about for long but she supposed she would have to start somewhere. She had gone no more than a few yards when a sign in one of the windows caught her eye. *Room To Let*.

After dragging the heavy case up the steps she knocked at the door and seconds later an elderly lady opened it and peered at her.

'Yes, what're you wantin'?'

She certainly wasn't the friendliest of creatures but plastering a smile to her face, Olivia said politely, 'I noticed the sign in your window and I'm looking for a room.'

'Have you got the money to pay for it?' the woman asked suspiciously. Her grey hair looked as if it hadn't been washed for months and the clothes she was wearing were no cleaner.

'Yes, I have,' Olivia said boldly, flushing with annoyance. 'But I'd like to look at the room first if I may.'

The woman sniffed but held the door open and as Olivia stepped past her the overpowering smell of stale urine and something else quite unfathomable hit her. The wail of a baby crying came from a door further along the hallway and the sound of an argument wafted down to her from the first floor.

'There's a room just come vacant along 'ere,' the woman informed her. 'But be warned, they don't last long. It'll be snapped up in no time.'

After fiddling with a bunch of keys she threw a door open and Olivia gasped as she stepped into the room. The smell was atrocious and what appeared to be an elderly person's clothes were scattered about the dingy room.

'You could sell them,' the old woman told her as if she was doing her an enormous favour. 'The old chap who lived 'ere passed away this mornin'. The funeral directors 'ave just been to take 'im away, though who'll pay for the funeral I've no idea. Anyway, the room is ten bob a week – take it or leave it.'

'I'll leave it, thank you,' Olivia managed as she backed out into the hallway.

'Well, you'll get nowhere cheaper round 'ere,' the woman said grumpily. 'But suit yerself.' With that she went and flung the front door open as Olivia snatched up her case and beat a hasty retreat, the door slamming shut behind her.

Out on the pavement again, Olivia felt dejected. If she didn't find somewhere soon she would have to book into a small hotel for the night. There was no way she could lug her heavy case about with her for much longer. She tried two more houses along the same street advertising rooms to rent but with no success. One was so small she felt claustrophobic and the other was just as dirty as the first she had looked at, as well as being much more expensive. It was beginning to look as if the money her father had forced on her might be needed, after all. Feeling thoroughly disheartened, she lifted her case and struggled on.

# Chapter Fourteen

When Olivia reached the end of the road, keeping a keen eye open for rooms to rent, she literally collided with a young woman coming the opposite way and her suitcase went flying across the pavement, although due to its thick leather straps, thankfully it didn't burst open.

'Oh, I'm so sorry,' the young woman gasped as she bent to retrieve the case.

'No, it should be me that's sorry, I wasn't looking where I was going.' Suddenly overcome, Olivia blinked rapidly to hold back tears.

'Are you heading anywhere in particular?' the girl asked kindly.

'Actually . . . I just arrived here in London and I'm looking for somewhere to stay but I haven't had much luck yet,' Olivia gulped.

'Mm, I see. Do you have a job here then?'

Olivia shook her head. 'Not yet, but I'm hoping to go into theatre work. I don't really mind what sort of work it is as

I'll try anything, but I need to get somewhere to stay first.'

'In that case I just may be able to help you. I'm Fiona Rivers, by the way.' The girl held her hand out and hope sprang into Olivia's eyes as they clasped hands in greeting. 'I'm a violinist in the orchestra at the Palace Theatre and I live in a theatrical lodging house in Russell Street. I'm just on my way home from rehearsals. I happen to know that one of the actresses is leaving today to get married, so her room might still be going if Queenie, that's the landlady, hasn't already let it. Would you like to come with me so we can ask her? It isn't that far.'

'Oh, that would be perfect,' Olivia said ecstatically. 'If the room is going to be vacant I could move straight in.'

The girl stared at her thoughtfully before saying, 'You could, providing Queenie hasn't already let it out so don't go building your hopes up. Decent rooms to rent around here are like gold dust.'

'This is really very kind of you,' Olivia said sincerely.

They fell into step and as they moved along Olivia stared at her new friend from the corner of her eye. She was very fashionably dressed and Olivia suddenly felt quite dowdy. Fiona's curled blonde hair was level with her chin, with a side parting. Her dress was fairly straight and calf-length and her shoes were high-heeled.

'Everyone who stays at Queenie's has something to do with the theatre,' Fiona told her with a smile. 'And Queenie is lovely, sort of a mother figure to us all although you might get a shock when you first meet her. She's rather . . . how can I put it? Colourful would be an apt description, I suppose.'

'I'm just grateful that you're going to so much trouble for me,' Olivia answered as Fiona paused in front of an enormous three-storey house with railings round it.

'This is it,' she told Olivia. 'That's the kitchen down those steps there. We get our meals in with the price of our rooms and Mrs Gordon the cook is very obliging. She has to be, as most of us work unsociable hours. Come on, let's go and see if that room is still available.'

As they climbed the steps leading to the front door, and Fiona fumbled about in her bag for her keys, Olivia offered up a silent prayer that it would be. She'd taken to Fiona and felt safer somehow after meeting her.

They stepped into a large hallway and Olivia blinked in surprise. Someone was playing a piano in one of the rooms that led off it and there appeared to be lots of people bustling about. It wasn't at all what she had expected. Everyone seemed to be very friendly and she began to feel a little less tense.

'Queenie's room is over here. Let's go and see her,' Fiona said. 'Leave your case there, it will be quite safe.'

She crossed to a door and rapped on it and almost instantly a woman's voice shouted, 'Come in.'

Fiona opened it and stepped inside as Olivia closely followed, and then as she was confronted with Queenie it was almost all she could do to stop her mouth from falling open. A middle-aged woman was sitting in a large chair; it needed to be large because she was absolutely enormous. Her hair, which had clearly been dyed, was a bright carroty red, piled on top of her head and curled, and her dress was so low-cut that her breasts looked in danger of spilling out of it. Her face was heavily made up with rouge and powder, and as she raised her arm it jangled from the many bangles she wore. Her plump fingers were heavily ringed too, but for all that her smile was kindly as she greeted Fiona.

''Ello, dearie, and what can I do for you?'

'I was wondering if you had anyone lined up for Carol's room yet?' Fiona asked. 'I just bumped into this young lady here around the corner and she's looking for a job in the theatre and somewhere to stay.'

'Is she now?' Queenie lifted a long cigarette-holder to her lips and drew on her cigarette as she eyed Olivia up and down.

'I have money to pay for a room until I get a job,' Olivia assured her swiftly.

'Do yer now, dearie.' Queenie blew a cloud of smoke into the air before asking, 'An' just what sort o' theatre work were you after?'

'I really don't mind. I'll work on sets or in wardrobe. I'll even just clean if I have to, but eventually I'd like to go on stage. I have done a little acting – and I can sing too.'

Queenie, who was a very good judge of character, saw at once that this young lady was quality from the tip of her nose to the toes of her shoes, although her clothes were a little outdated for London. She was certainly pretty enough to make it onto the stage.

'My rates are fifteen shillin's a week, but that includes havin' yer clothes laundered an' all yer meals. How does that sound?'

'It sounds wonderful,' Olivia assured her with a beaming smile.

'In that case you'll have to look at Fiona's room – they're all much the same but I can't show yer Carol's 'cos she ain't even gone yet.'

'Oh, I don't mind waiting until she has. I have nowhere else I have to be,' Olivia said honestly.

'I could take her through to the kitchen and scrounge a cup of tea off Cook while we're waiting,' Fiona suggested then and Queenie nodded.

'You do that.' Queenie addressed Olivia again then, saying, 'But I expect two weeks rent up front an' no gentleman callers.' She sniffed. 'As Fiona will tell yer, I run a respectable establishment 'ere an' I don't stand for no jiggery-pokery. If I wanted that, I'd run a knockin' shop.'

125

Olivia nodded eagerly.

'You'd best go an' show her your room then,' Queenie advised Fiona with a wink at Olivia. 'An' tell Mrs G when yer go to the kitchen that there'll be another for dinner tonight.'

Flashing Queenie a grateful smile, Olivia followed Fiona from the room feeling as if she had fallen on her feet. Things were looking up.

It was late that evening when Olivia telephoned home and Max himself answered. He had been pacing up and down the hallway, almost beside himself with worry following a call from the Greens, who had informed him that Olivia was not with them. She had sent word via their maid that she would not be staying with them, and had later despatched a taxi to deliver a note she had written telling them that she had found a suitable room and would not need to impose on them.

'Where the hell are you?' Max demanded when he heard her voice. 'I've been out of my mind with worry ever since Neville telephoned to say you wouldn't be staying with them!'

'Now calm down, Daddy,' Olivia soothed. 'I'm perfectly all right and I've found a wonderful place to stay.'

'Where exactly?' he snapped.

'Somewhere very safe. That's all you need to know for now,' Olivia answered, standing her ground. 'But if you keep on shouting at me I shall put the telephone down and I won't bother getting in touch again. You're talking to me as if I were a young child instead of a young woman.'

'I'm sorry, darling, it's just that I've been so afraid. 'Max was instantly contrite as well as being very relieved to know that she was safe. 'But why shouldn't I have the address of where you are staying?'

'Because I know you. If you took it into your head, you'd turn up on the doorstep to check on me,' Olivia told him with the hint of a smile in her voice. 'What I will tell you though is that the place where I am lodging is very respectable and the lady who owns it is very strict with her tenants. They are all theatrical people and I've made a friend already. Her name is Fiona and she's in the orchestra at one of the local theatres. Do try to understand, Daddy. I've been spoiled by you and Mummy all my life and I just want to prove to myself that I can stand on my own two feet. Will you allow me to try?'

'I don't really have much choice, do I?' Max answered grudgingly. 'But just promise me that you'll write and telephone me regularly, and that if you do need help you'll get in touch immediately.'

'I promise.' Olivia's voice was soft. 'But I must go now. I'll write to you very soon. Good night, Daddy.'

'Goodn—' Max sighed as he realised that the phone had gone dead in his hand.

# Chapter Fifteen

Max was in a good mood. He had just been to the tailors with Lawrence for the final fitting for his wedding suit and Dilly was due back the next day. He'd missed her. Trouble was, he himself would be leaving for Whitby the following week for the wedding so they'd only have a few days before he was off again. Still, he didn't begrudge Lawrence, or Patty, his time. Lawrence had become his right-hand man and Max was proud of him. There was one son he didn't need to worry about, at least.

Lawrence clearly adored the very ground that Patty walked on and it was obvious that his feelings were returned. It was a real love match, and Max hoped that the pair of them would happily grow old together. Patty was a lovely girl and after the wedding she would be moving to Nuneaton with Lawrence to continue her nursing at Weddington Hospital. Max had bought them a fine little cottage in the village of Caldecote as his wedding present to them. He had been prepared to buy them a much grander house but Patty had fallen in love with the cottage at first sight and could hardly wait to move in. It was situated on the edge of the grounds to Caldecote Hall and had a lovely sunny sitting room and a large garden. It was ideally situated for both Patty and Lawrence to get to work and Max was sure the lovebirds would be happy there.

A lump formed in his throat as he remembered how Lawrence had looked in his wedding suit in the tailors. It didn't seem two minutes since he was reading him and Samuel their bedtime stories and tucking the twins into bed – a reminder that time passed all too quickly.

He sat down at his desk, deciding to get some of his paperwork out of the way, but before he had even started the door opened and Samuel walked in with a broad smile on his face.

Max frowned. 'Why aren't you at work?' he wanted to know.

'I'm just going there now, but as I was passing I thought I'd pop in and see how Mother is.'

Max didn't believe him for a second. Samuel rarely called by unless he wanted something and he wondered what it was this time. More money probably!

He didn't have to wait long to find out.

Samuel sat down and ran his finger down the crease in his trousers before saying casually, 'You wouldn't happen to know where Niamh keeps the deeds to the house, would you? It occurred to me the other day that I've never actually seen them. I checked the safe but they weren't in there.'

'They wouldn't be, because I have them,' Max answered.

'Oh really? Then perhaps I ought to take them home and keep them safe.'

Instantly guessing what his son was up to, Max grinned sardonically. 'There would be no point in you keeping them because the house is in my name.'

'*What!*' Samuel was outraged. 'But why would it be in your name? It's my house!'

'Your house to live in, yes, but I own it,' Max replied calmly. 'And do you know why? It's because I couldn't have trusted you not to sell it and leave Niamh with nowhere to go.'

'Why . . . that's preposterous,' Samuel stuttered. 'What sort of a man do you take me for, Father?'

'The sort of man who would risk losing the shirt off his back if the mood took him. Just as you did in that poker game the other evening, although I hear you came out of that one very lucky, upsetting a few rather unsavoury characters along the way, I believe. Don't ever think I don't come to hear what you get up to, Samuel.'

Colour flooded into Samuel's cheeks. Yes, he had been lucky thanks to a little bit of cheating. In fact, what he had won added to what the house was worth would have set him up – but now here was his father telling him that he didn't actually own the property, after all.

'So you don't even trust me enough to let me have my own home in my own name now?' he said, hoping to play on his father's finer feelings.

Max snorted with derision. 'I wouldn't trust you as far as I could throw you,' he told him bluntly. 'I love you because you are my son, but until you prove yourself you're not going to get another penny out of me!'

'In that case you can keep your bloody lousy job!' Samuel roared.

'Brave words – but exactly what will you live on? Your ill-earned winnings and your grandmother's allowance will hardly keep you in the style you're accustomed to.'

'As it happens I plan to buy my own business – a tattoo parlour!'

'*A what?*' Max burst out laughing. 'But you don't know the first thing about tattooing.'

'As it happens tattoos are becoming very popular, especially with the mill workers and the miners,' Max retorted. 'There's already a chap there that actually does the tattoos so all I'll have to do is sit back and take the money each week.'

'Surely you could come up with a more lucrative idea than that?' Max scoffed.

Lost for words, Samuel's hands clenched into fists and turning about, he stormed from the room, slamming the door resoundingly behind him.

All the way down the drive he fumed. No wonder he hadn't been able to find the deeds to the house even though he had almost tipped it upside down, much to Mary's distress. And the way his father had laughed at his proposed business venture! He clearly couldn't see what a lucrative business it was to go into. But I'll show him and make him eat his words, Samuel promised himself.

Back at his house he let himself in and headed straight for the drawing room where he poured himself a stiff whisky. Mary was polishing in there and eyed him cautiously before scuttling from the room. Someone had upset him good and proper by the looks of it.

Minutes later she was back to say, 'There's someone here to see you.'

'Who is it?' he grunted.

'A Mr White.'

Samuel froze. 'Tell him I'm not in,' he hissed.

'Can't do that,' Mary said in an off-hand manner. 'He knows you are here 'cos he said he'd seen you come in, a few minutes ago.'

'Very well, show him through,' Samuel muttered, but before Mary had a chance to do so, the person in question suddenly pushed past her and shoved her roughly back through the door.

'What's this then, Snowy?' Samuel forced a smile although his heart was thudding. Snowy White was an unpleasant individual and one of the sharpest card players around. 'Care for a drink?'

'I ain't come 'ere fer a drink, Farthin'.' Snowy's eyes scanned the room and he grinned craftily. 'Nice little gaff you've got 'ere,' he remarked.

Samuel squirmed. Snowy was enormous, with hands like hams. His nose was spread across his face and Samuel could smell the rank scent of him even from across the room.

'So what can I do for you?' he asked, trying to keep his calm. Sweat had broken out on his brow and his knees were knocking.

'Well, now . . . the thing is, yer took a lot o' money off me an' quite a few more blokes the other night an' I ain't too fuckin' 'appy about it, as it 'appens!'

Samuel gulped. 'That's the way it goes,' he bluffed. 'Winner takes all – you know that Snowy.'

'So they do, but they shouldn't, not when they've cheated – an' I 'appen to know you did.'

'If you believe that, why didn't you say something at the time?'

''Cos I got to thinkin' yer could perhaps be worth a lot more than the fifty quid yer stole off me. Everyone knows yer old man is one o' the richest blokes in town, so 'appen it'd be worth yer while payin' me to keep me bleedin' gob shut. I don't reckon the other blokes that played would be none too 'appy if they knew about the cards you 'ad 'idden up yer sleeve, do you?'

'S-so how much are we talking about?'

'Ooh . . . I reckon five 'undred quid would be enough to keep me quiet . . . fer now!' Snowy answered menacingly.

'Five hundred pounds! You must be mad!' Samuel choked. 'Where do you think I could get that sort of money from? I didn't even win that much!'

'From yer old man, like I said,' Snowy said calmly as he picked his nose with a tobacco-stained finger. 'The thing is, I don't reckon he'd like to see 'is son 'ave a little accident, do you?'

Samuel yanked at the collar of his shirt as sweat trickled down his face. He had no doubt at all that Snowy meant business. 'I'd need some time to get it together.'

'You've got till tonight. I'll meet yer in the alley that runs alongside the Union Wool an' Leather Mill by the holdin' pond at midnight. There'll be no one about by then. No one will go down there after dark anyway. An' make sure yer come on yer own wi' the money. No fuckin' tricks else I'll make sure yer wish yer'd never been born.' With that he sauntered from the room and let himself out as Samuel sank onto the nearest chair before his legs let him down.

That evening in Enniskerry, Dilly stroked Seamus' hand as they sat together by the fire in Maeve's cosy kitchen, enjoying his company. She'd hoped to persuade him to go home with her but he seemed reluctant.

'It ain't that I don't want to come home, Mammy,' Seamus assured her. 'But the thing is I'm able to do a few jobs about the place now when I have a good day. Gran'ma and Granda ain't as young as they used to be any more; they're both in their sixties an' although Granda still does more than his fair whack, it's Declan an' Liam that do the lion's share o' the work now. Every morning I collect the eggs, and at night I shut the hens away so as the foxes won't get 'em. I feed the pigs an' clean out the sties an' all, an' sometimes I even get to help with milking the cows. You do understand, don't you? I know I'm not fit enough to take on a full-time job yet if I were to come home, but here I can go at me own pace an' I feel as if I have a purpose.'

'Of course I understand,' Dilly said gently and she smiled; she could see such an improvement in her son that it did her heart good. He was so much better than he had been in the dark days in Weddington Hall Hospital but he still had a long way to go.

'Where's our Niamh got to again?' Maeve complained then as she carried a large pan of stew to the table. 'This is ready to serve, so it is.'

The words had no sooner left her mouth than the door burst open and Niamh appeared. Her hair was loose and she was breathless.

'Sorry I'm late, I forgot the time,' she told her grandmother.

Maeve grinned. 'Well, you're here now so make yourself useful and get the cutlery out, would you?'

Dilly looked at her daughter. She'd been out tramping the hills again no doubt but there was some colour in her cheeks and she seemed brighter than she had since Connie's death. This little break away had clearly done her good.

'I've walked for miles,' Niamh told them as she laid the knives and forks on the table and kissed Roddy's cheek. Ben had called round twice since they had been there and Dilly had been relieved to see that the pair of them were now easy again in each other's company. Maeve confided that Ben had been walking out with a girl from the village for a time, so Dilly hoped that both of them could be able to move on now.

'And what have you been up to, young man?' Niamh asked Roddy.

He flashed a broad smile. 'I've been round at Roisin's an' we've been doin' a jigsaw together. She's ever so good at it.'

'You think Roisin is good at everything,' Niamh answered with a grin. 'I always know where to find you don't I?'

134

The little boy grinned before rushing on, 'An' Declan let me help feed the pigs an' all.' Then suddenly his face dropped and tears formed on his lashes as he whispered, 'I wish we didn't have to go home.'

'I'm afraid we have to,' Niamh told him. 'But we can always come back again another time.'

Slightly heartened, Roddy nodded, already planning the next visit in his mind.

After the meal Dilly went along to Declan and Roisin's cottage to say her goodbyes, leaving Niamh to help her grandmother with the dishes and Daniel reading a story to Roddy. They would be leaving early the next morning to catch the ferry and she wanted to spend a little more time with them before she left.

'How are you feeling, pet?' she asked as she took a seat at the side of her daughter-in-law. Roisin was still pale but she was dressed today, and although she and Declan were still devastated at the loss of their child, at least they seemed to be slowly coming to terms with it now.

'A little better, so I am,' Roisin replied quietly, her brilliant blue eyes sad. 'And Declan and I have decided that we're going to try again for another wean just as soon as the doctor says it's wise to.'

'I'm sure everything will be fine next time.' Dilly thought of the tiny baby clothes she had brought with her. She had given them to Maeve and asked her to put them safely away until they were needed. 'Niamh and Roddy will be round shortly,' she told the young couple then. Niamh had spent a lot of time with Roisin during their brief stay and the two had become firm friends. Being of a similar age they had a lot in common, and after what Niamh herself had been through she had been a tower of strength to her sister-in-law. Roddy had gone a long way towards raising the couple's spirits too as they seemed to have taken a great shine to the boy. The whole family had, if it came to that and Roddy had seemed like a different child, delighting in the animals and the lush green fields.

'Shall I make you a drink, Mammy?' Declan offered.

Dilly shook her head. 'Oh no, thank you, pet. I've just ploughed my way through one of your gran'ma's dinners an' I couldn't manage another thing.'

Declan laughed. 'She sent some of her stew round for us an' all, so she did. Me gran'ma is the only person I know who could make even a salad fattenin', to be sure. But now come on, Mammy, tell us about how the shop is doin' and about the new one in Birmingham.'

So Dilly told them all about what had been happening back at home and the time just seemed to fly by. Niamh and Roddy joined them an hour later and Dilly then kissed them both soundly, promising to visit again just as soon ever she could. She then popped into Shelagh and Liam's cottage to say goodbye to the weans, picking her way through the chickens that were pecking in the yard as she went. It had been a good visit apart from the sad news of Roisin and Declan's baby, and she was thrilled to see how well the farm was doing. The cowsheds were now full of big healthy cows and in the fields were a fine flock of sheep. Huge fat pigs grunted in the sties and it was all down to her in-laws' hard work. She thought briefly of how proud Fergal would have been to see it. They had achieved their dream and she just hoped now that one day she would be able to achieve hers.

'I hope Niamh doesn't keep Roddy up too late,' Maeve fretted when she returned to the kitchen. 'The little chap has an early start ahead of him in the morning, so he does, an' he'll need a good night's sleep.'

'I'm sure they won't be long now,' Dilly told her and went to place a pan of milk on the fire for some cocoa for them all. The visit seemed to have passed in the blink of an eye.

## Chapter Sixteen

At eleven-thirty that evening, Samuel stole down the stairs and paused at the bottom of them to listen. There was nothing but the sound of the grandfather clock to be heard. Everywhere was as still as a grave and he was relieved that Mary was clearly in bed, fast asleep. Making his way to the kitchen, he fumbled about in a drawer then tucking something deep into his coat pocket he let himself out of the back door as quietly as he could.

Just as Snowy had said, the streets were deserted and he hurried on until he came to the alleyway that led up past the Union Wool and Leather Mill. It was eerily quiet and Samuel shuddered. Word had it that this place was haunted and people shunned it at night. The mill loomed up out of the darkness. It was a forbidding place even during daylight hours, but at night-time it looked even more sinister and Samuel's heart began to thud in his ribcage. He blundered his way along, however, and within minutes he was swallowed up in an inky darkness. Something suddenly broke from the thick overgrown laurel hedge to one side of him and rushed across his foot, and Samuel had to bite his lip to stop himself from crying out. It had probably been a rat. They grew as big as cats round here and the place was overrun with them. He waited for his heart to steady to a more normal pace and then cautiously moved on again, and as he did so the sound of the clock in the market square chimed midnight in the distance.

At last the hedge ended and Samuel found himself beside the large holding pool that supplied the mill with its water when the river was low. The moon sailed from behind a cloud, turning its surface to silver as he stared into the gloom.

'Have yer got it then?' Snowy's voice almost made him jump out of his skin as the large man suddenly appeared from the shadows.

'Yes, I've got it.' Samuel prayed that his nerve wouldn't fail him as Snowy stepped closer. It was too dark to see his face, just his outline. Samuel felt in his coat pocket for the knife he had taken from the kitchen drawer and licked his dry lips as his fingers closed around it. He would have only one chance at this and if he failed it would be God help him!

Snowy drew closer and, choosing his moment, Samuel drew the knife back and with every ounce of strength he possessed he lunged forward. He felt a slight resistance as the blade came into contact with the leather waistcoat Snowy was wearing but then it was through and it slid into his chest like a knife into butter.

'What the . . .' Snowy gasped as he clutched at his chest where the knife was still lodged as Samuel quickly backed away.

Samuel felt bile rise in his throat as Snowy stared at him in amazement. There was something dark trickling from the side of his mouth and his chest. He was clutching the knife which was still embedded in him as he slowly sank to his knees and Samuel stepped back so quickly that he almost fell as he realised that it was blood. It appeared to be black in the dim light. Snowy made a horrible gurgling sound then and dropped heavily onto his side, then after jerking convulsively a few times he lay quite still.

Samuel's heart was pounding but pulling himself together with an enormous effort he glanced anxiously about before bending and tugging the knife from Snowy's chest. He had to get rid of it somehow – and Snowy too if it came to that. He must try and make it look as if he had been robbed.

Grimacing with disgust, he bent and emptied the man's pockets of any money he could find, then grabbing him beneath the arms he began to drag him towards the holding pool. At the edge of it he paused to catch his breath before pushing with all his might. Snowy plopped into the water and began to float across the top of the pool and now Samuel really did have to place his hand across his mouth to stop himself from being sick. It was then he noticed that the gloves he was wearing were covered in blood and he drew them off with a shudder. But what was he to do with them? He couldn't take them back to the house – Mary would be sure to find them. Ramming the knife into one of them, he began to feel around the bank of the holding pool for some decent-sized stones. When he had filled both gloves with rocks he then threw them into the pool as well, sighing with relief as they instantly sank.

The sound of an owl hooting made him start, and keen to be away, now he hastened back down the alley keeping his eyes peeled for a sight of anyone. A mist had come down and with his head bent he hurried through the town until he reached the house on Abbey Green where he silently let himself in again. Hopefully Mary would have no idea that he had even been out, so should anything be traced back to him she could confirm that he had been indoors all evening.

Once in the privacy of his room, Samuel quickly stripped his clothes off and slid into bed, shivering uncontrollably. But he didn't regret what he'd done for a single minute. Snowy had asked for all he had got, as far as Samuel was concerned. On the way back he'd briefly thought of just clearing off where nobody could find him, but then common-sense had taken over and he'd realised that that would be the worst thing he could do. It would look too suspicious if he should go missing the very night someone he knew was killed. Now he just had to bluff his way through the next couple of weeks until everything calmed down and then he could get out of this Godforsaken place for good.

His thoughts unexpectedly turned to Constance then and his shivering increased as he recalled the way his daughter had looked at him just before he had placed the pillow over her small face. And there was something in his father's expression when he had entered the room after-wards; could it be that Max suspected he had murdered the child? All for nothing, as things had turned out because he was still tied to Niamh as surely as if they were bound together with rope. He'd been convinced that Constance's death would free him – but he'd been wrong. And now he had committed a second murder. As before, Samuel Farthing felt that he'd had no choice. Snowy had been threatening him. All he could do now was pray that he would get away with it once again.

The sound of Mary singing woke Samuel the next morning and he blinked as he rubbed the sleep from his eyes. She was clearly in a good mood, no doubt because Niamh was due home that day. As the events of the night before flashed in front of his eyes he flinched before clambering out of bed. He realised that he must act as normally as possible.

Mary had a full English breakfast ready for him in the dining room and under normal circumstances Samuel would have devoured it, but today he was so nervous that he had to force every mouthful down.

'I'm off out,' he informed Mary casually soon after he had finished.

'Right y'are. Will you be wantin' a meal this evenin'? I shall be cookin' for Niamh an' Roddy.'

'Yes, I shall be back.'

As he left, closing the door quietly behind him, she frowned, perplexed. He'd been almost civil to her this morning, which made a change. With a shrug she went about her business as she pondered what she should prepare for dinner.

Niamh and Roddy arrived home at the same time as Samuel. Dilly had declined Niamh's invitation to join them for a meal as she was keen to get back to the shop and see that everything was in order. She was also secretly hoping that Max might call in. She'd missed him, although she would never tell him so.

The shop was spotlessly clean when she let herself in but then she had expected it to be. Jayne was a good worker and Dilly was sure she would make a perfect manageress in the Birmingham shop. She passed through and went upstairs to her rooms, suddenly feeling a little lonely. She had been surrounded by family for a few short days but now it came to her that she was completely alone again. Giving herself a mental shake, she hurried to fill the kettle at the small sink. She should be used to being alone by now, and feeling sorry for herself wouldn't do her any good at all. Dilly had found over the years that keeping herself busy was better than any medicine the doctor could prescribe, so the way she saw it the sooner she got back into her routine again the better.

It was almost eight o'clock that evening when she had almost given up on him that Max suddenly appeared carrying a bunch of colourful chrysanthemums.

'Jackson was cutting some for the house and I thought you might like a few as well,' he said self-consciously as he handed them over to her. 'But now tell me all about your trip. Did it go well?'

'It did eventually but it didn't start very well.' Dilly's face clouded. 'Roisin lost the baby the first day we got there and she and Declan were very upset as you can imagine.'

'That's awful – the poor girl,' Max said sympathetically.

'I think they'd begun to come to terms with it by the time we left and strangely enough Roddy seemed to have a lot to do with it. He spent almost all his time round in their cottage with them once Roisin began to feel a little better, and she and Declan took a real shine to him. But other than that, everyone was fine. Seamus is looking better and even helping out on the farm a little now. Niamh looks better for a break too. She went out for lots of long walks in the hills and I think she in turn is coming to terms with losing Connie now. But that's enough about us. Tell me what's been happening here.'

Max swallowed, wondering how Dilly was going to take the news about Olivia's sudden departure. She hadn't even had the chance to say goodbye to her and he knew that she would be worried sick about the young woman who was her daughter.

'Well first of all, Samuel and I had a blazing row and he told me where to put my job.'

Dilly raised her eyebrows. 'But you and Samuel are always having words,' she pointed out. 'I'm sure he'll be back with his tail between his legs in no time.'

'I doubt it. He's informed me that he's going to invest in his own business. A tattoo parlour, no less.'

'A *what*!' Dilly's eyes stretched wide with shock. 'But what does Samuel know about tattooing?'

'That's exactly what I asked him but he seemed intent on going ahead with this madcap scheme so let him get on with it.' Max ran a hand through his hair, a habit he adopted when he was worried about something.

'*And?*' prompted Dilly.

'What? Oh, and er . . . something else happened while you were away too,' Max muttered. Dilly had been through so much during the years that he'd known her that he hated having to give her yet more bad news, but he was wise enough to know that it would be better if she heard it from him. He had been trying to postpone breaking it to her, but now he was keen to get it over and done with.

'Olivia left for London just after you went to Ireland.' There, it was said and all he could do now was watch the different emotions flit across her face. Shock – horror – fear and finally despair.

'Left for London?' she repeated faintly. 'But . . . she said she would give herself a little more time to think about it! Whereabouts in London is she? Have you heard from her? Is she all right?'

'Yes, I heard from her the day she left,' he reassured her hastily, for Dilly had gone terribly pale. 'I'd arranged for her to stay with some friends of mine but instead she's found herself a room in a nice lodging house in the Covent Garden area and now she's looking for a job in a theatre.'

'But she's so young to be so far away from home, and . . . I didn't get to say goodbye to her,' Dilly said brokenly.

'She won't be gone for long, I'm sure,' Max said kindly. 'And between you and me, Dilly, this might be the best thing she could have done. You know how badly she took it when Oscar married Penelope. Then when she heard that Penelope was carrying his child it was the final straw. In London she might meet a nice young man who will make her forget all about the feelings she has for her brother and—'

'But Oscar *isn't* her brother, is he?' Dilly said bluntly. 'The trouble is, she must never know that or everything we've done will all have been for nothing. She would never forgive me for giving her away at birth and she would never forgive either of us for lying to her all these years. I often wonder what we set in motion all that time ago, Max, and yet I swear I only did what I did because I thought it would be for the best, for both her and my other children.'

'You really shouldn't whip yourself so,' Max said quietly, resisting the urge to draw her into his arms. 'We all did what we thought was for the best. How were we to know that she and Oscar would develop feelings for each other?'

Dilly brushed away a tear then and her chin set in the determined way he had come to love.

'Well, there's nothing else for it, is there?' she said matter-of-factly. 'I shall just have to go to London, find her and bring her back.'

'Oh, Dilly.' Max's voice was loaded with sadness. 'We both know that you can no more do that than I could stop her going. Olivia is a young adult. We have to give her some breathing space, but let her know that we will always be here for her. Think of it, my dear – how would it look if you were to go haring off after her? Don't you think she would find it rather strange, for as far as Olivia knows, you are merely an ex-servant.'

Dilly's shoulders sagged as she saw the sense of what he said, but all the same the thought of the girl being all alone in a big city filled her with fear.

'I know you are right,' she admitted reluctantly. 'But

even so you must promise me that you will keep in constant touch with her.'

'That goes without saying. Now how about we have a drink and try to calm down. It's a different world today, Dilly, to what it was when you and I were Olivia's age. The war changed everything, especially for women, and I doubt things will ever go back to being as they were. Look at you, you're a prime example, buying shops and making a success of them. Who would ever have thought it?'

'I suppose you're right,' she said gloomily, but it didn't make her feel any better.

In Niamh's house, Mary was feeling bewildered. Samuel had joined Niamh and Roddy for the meal she'd had ready for them when they got home and he'd been civil to Niamh for the first time that Mary could remember.

As Niamh helped her to clear the dirty pots into the kitchen, Mary commented on it.

'So what's up wi' His Lordship then?' she said cryptically. 'He's been very pleasant tonight, ain't he?'

'I suppose he has.' Niamh deposited the pots onto the wooden draining board. She'd actually felt quite uneasy finding Samuel still in the house when she returned. She'd hoped that he'd have cleared off again by then and like Mary she couldn't understand his sudden civility.

'P'rhaps he wants to try an' make a go o' your marriage?' Mary suggested.

Niamh snorted. 'There's no chance of that. There's nothing between Samuel and me; never has been and never will be as far as I'm concerned. I dare say he's just staying here to lick his wounds after the widow dumped him. But don't be fooled, I've no doubt he'll have someone else on the go in no time – and the sooner the better as far as I'm concerned. But anyway, I'm going to go and get Roddy tucked in now, Mary, he's tired out after his journey. Can you manage?'

'O' course I can,' Mary scoffed. 'That's what I'm paid for, ain't it?'

Once Niamh had gone she set about putting the kitchen to rights. The plates had all come back empty so they'd clearly enjoyed the meal she'd cooked for them. She wished she knew where her favourite knife had got to though. It had taken her twice as long to peel the vegetables when she hadn't been able to find it. Still, I dare say it will turn up, she thought and hummed merrily as she plunged the pots into the hot water she had ready.

## Chapter Seventeen

The next evening, the local paper was full of the body that had been found floating in the holding pool next to the Union Wool and Leather Mill. It had been identified as the body of Richard White, known locally as Snowy White, and when Mary found the paper and glanced at it as she was tidying up, her hand flew to her throat. The police were appealing for anyone who knew of Mr White's last movements to come forward to help with their enquiries. Mary's mind raced back to the visitor who had come to see Samuel. Hadn't he introduced himself as Snowy White? He'd looked a shifty character, to be sure. She'd heard raised voices during his visit and had assumed that Samuel must owe him money. Samuel was getting quite a reputation about the town as a gambler, and she knew from what Niamh had told her that his father frequently had to pay off his debts. She chewed on her lip as her mind raced on. He had been stabbed, the report said, and on the very evening her favourite knife had gone missing. Could it be that this was the murder weapon?

She was so lost in her thoughts that she didn't hear Samuel come up behind her, and when he snatched the newspaper from her hand, she started.

'Shouldn't you be going about your business?' he barked.

'I were just readin' about the bloke that's been stabbed,' Mary said boldly. 'Didn't he come to see you that mornin'?'

'I did see Snowy that day, as it happens,' Samuel blustered as he broke out in a sweat. Mary was clearly no fool. 'It's quite appalling isn't it?'

'Aye it is,' she said thoughtfully, then: 'Yer wouldn't happen to know where me favourite kitchen knife is, would yer? It went missin' the same day as this man were stabbed.'

'Just what are you inferring?' Samuel growled in a panic. 'Do you think that *I* had something to do with his murder? If so, you must be mad. Snowy and I were friends.'

'Well yer didn't sound very friendly to me from what I could hear of it,' Mary dared.

Samuel grasped her arm then and Mary flinched as he lowered his face to hers. His good mood clearly hadn't lasted long.

'I'm afraid you have a rather overactive imagination,' he ground out. 'And I'll tell you now, if you should repeat to anyone else what you've just said to me, I'll make you regret you were ever born. Do you understand me?' He shook her then until her teeth rattled. Terrified now, Mary nodded.

'Good!' Samuel released her abruptly and she rubbed her arm, sure that it would be bruised.

Half of her wanted to run to Niamh and tell her what he had just said to her, but the other half was too fearful. She loved working there and was sure that her job would be the first to go, should she cross him. Perhaps it would be best to try and forget all about it.

Niamh entered the room then and Mary scooted away like a cat whose tail was on fire.

'What's wrong with Mary? She looked upset,' she commented.

Samuel waved a hand airily. 'Oh, I just told her off for reading the paper when she should have been doing her jobs.'

'Mary works hard and more than earns her keep,' Niamh retorted. 'And I'll thank you to leave her alone in future. That's if you're planning on staying here for any length of time. Do you mind me asking what your plans are?'

'Don't worry, I shan't be here for much longer. As it happens I'm going to buy my own business. A tattoo parlour.'

It was all Niamh could do to stop herself from laughing aloud. What did Samuel know about tattooing? But then as long as he left the house she really didn't care what he did so she wisely held back from antagonising him.

The following morning, two police officers called at the house asking to speak to Samuel. Mary showed them to the drawing room without a word.

'What did they want?' Niamh asked her when she entered the kitchen.

'They said they was questionin' everyone as knew that chap that were murdered,' Mary mumbled, keeping her head down.

'I see.' Niamh shrugged and went about her business.

The following week, Max, Oscar and Lawrence set off for Whitby for the wedding. It was a beautiful morning in early August and they were all in good spirits.

They'd decided to make the journey by train and as they settled into their seats, Lawrence grinned.

'Just think! When I come back, I shall be a married man and have my wife, Mrs Farthing with me,' he said happily.

Max smiled back at him. Lawrence and Patty were so compatible, he doubted he would ever have to worry about those two; they were made for each other. Unlike Oscar and Penelope. Oscar would be standing as Lawrence's best man and Max had an idea he would be quite relieved to get away from Penelope for a while. Since the start of her pregnancy she had become a semi-invalid, insisting that she be waited upon hand and foot and generally making Oscar's life a living hell. Max had booked them into a hotel for the night before the wedding, then he and Oscar would return the morning following the marriage whilst Patty and Lawrence stayed behind in the same hotel for a week's honeymoon.

'All ready for the ball and chain to be fitted, are you?' Oscar joked as the train rumbled along.

'Can't wait!' Lawrence responded and it was clear from the look on his face that he meant it.

Patty was waiting at the station for them when they arrived and she threw herself into Lawrence's arms.

'Mum has a meal ready for all of you at the cottage,' she told them when she finally managed to escape Lawrence's embrace.

'Oh, but we can eat at the hotel; we don't want to put her to any trouble,' Max said. 'She must have more than enough to do as it is, with the wedding tomorrow.'

Patty shook her head, setting her bright red curls dancing. The sunshine had brought out the freckles across her snub nose and Lawrence thought she looked adorable.

'She wouldn't hear of it. But come along, we can drop your cases off at the hotel on the way. I have a cab waiting outside. And you did remember to bring my dress, didn't you?' she ended anxiously.

Max laughed as he pointed to the largest of the cases. 'Do you really think Dilly would have let me come without it?' He knew how much trouble Dilly had gone to in the making of the dress. Patty had had her final fitting on her last visit to them and since then, Dilly had worked on it personally, determined that it should be just perfect. He felt sad as he thought of her back at home. It would have been nice for her to be there to see Lawrence and Patty wed, although he could understand her reluctance. Best not give folks anything to talk about, she'd said when he invited her, and he supposed she was right. He also felt sad that Lawrence's mother couldn't be there but Camilla was locked in a world of her own now and scarcely knew him half of the time. It would have been just too difficult to try and bring her. She was far happier at home with Bessie looking after her. Olivia had also declined his invitation the last time he had spoken to her on the telephone. She had secured a job at the Palace Theatre as a dresser to the actresses and was worried about taking time off so soon after starting. That only left Samuel, and knowing that he and his twin brother did not get on, nobody had even bothered to invite him. And then of course there was Harvey, and as Max thought of him a lump formed in his throat. His brave lad had died in the war, tending the horses he loved, but he would never be forgotten, and Max hoped that Harvey would be smiling down on them from heaven the next day.

Pushing his gloomy thoughts aside, he hailed a porter and once their cases were carefully loaded onto a trolley, he and Oscar followed the young couple along the platform. The smell of the sea air greeted them as they stepped into the cobblestoned streets, and Max inhaled deeply. This was Patty and Lawrence's special time and he wanted to make it as perfect as he could for them.

The marriage took place the next day in a tiny church perched high on the hillside overlooking Whitby Bay, and Max was sure that the young couple could not have chosen a more picturesque venue. Patty looked stunning in the dress that Dilly had worked on so diligently, and Lawrence was handsome in his new suit. It was a quiet affair with only Patty's family, themselves and a few close family friends present as the young couple had requested. Max had, however, insisted that they allow him to provide a meal at the hotel that he and Oscar were staying in, and as a surprise he'd had an elaborate three-tier wedding cake made for them too. When the service was over the wedding party snaked down the hill, their laughter ringing in the air as folk left their cottages to shower them with rice and good wishes.

The hotel staff had gone to great pains with the room where the meal would be served and when they entered Patty crowed with delight on seeing the beautiful cake.

'You really shouldn't have gone to any more expense. You've done so much for us already,' she scolded but Max waved aside her thanks. She and Lawrence could barely keep their eyes off each other, which was just as it should be.

Patty's dress was truly beautiful. It was a smooth white satin, that fell to just below her ankles. The dropped waist was intricately beaded with crystals and pearls which had taken Dilly hours and hours to do, every single one of them stitched on by hand. The sleeves were sheer, again edged with pearls and crystals, and Patty had had the same ones woven into her thick red hair, which she wore piled into gentle curls on the top of her head. Wine flowed and the atmosphere was light. Oscar slightly bodged his wedding speech because of nerves, but no one minded and Max was almost sad when the meal finally came to an end.

Patty's mother and father, Mr and Mrs Newcombe, couldn't thank Max enough for all he had done. They were a lovely couple with no airs and graces whatsoever, and Max couldn't help but wonder what Camilla would have thought of their tiny cottage and their down-to-earth ways.

But then he supposed that had she been of sound mind, no one would ever have been good enough for her children.

'Your daughter has been the making of my son and I owe her a great deal for the way she looked after him when she was nursing him during the war,' Max told Patty's parents, and he meant every word of it.

'I shall miss her though when she goes to live in the Midlands,' Patty's mother sniffed, blowing her nose noisily on a scrap of lace hankie. Hilary Newcombe was an older version of her daughter with the same red hair and friendly nature, whilst Brian, her father, was a great gentle bear of a man with muscles built up through years of hard work.

'Ah, but at least we'll know she's being well looked after,' he comforted his wife now with a smile at Max.

The bottom tier of the cake was duly cut by the newlyweds and the other two were carefully packed away into stout boxes. 'For the christenings of your first two infants,' Hilary teased them, causing Patty to blush as red as her hair.

'Give them a chance!' Oscar said and everyone laughed uproariously. It had been a truly beautiful wedding.

'Well . . . this is it then, my lovely girl,' Hilary said eventually as the guests started to drift away.

'Not really. Lawrence and I will be staying here for another week before we leave, and of course we shall be calling in to see you,' Patty told her as her mother clung to her hands. Most of her things had already been forwarded on to the little cottage in Caldecote that would soon become their home, and the rest of the things were now in their room at the hotel.

'Of course you will,' Hilary said emotionally, stepping away from her.

It was her father's turn then and he too had tears in his eyes as he bent to kiss her, wondering when his little girl had grown into such a beautiful young woman.

'You just make sure you take good care of her now, me lad, else you'll have me to answer to,' he told Lawrence sternly then as he shook his hand, but his eyes were smiling. A blind man on a galloping horse could have seen how much the young man adored her.

'I will, I promise,' Lawrence answered solemnly.

And then there was only Lawrence and Patty, Oscar and Max left in the room. The staff were clearing away the dishes by then and feeling in the way, Max suggested to Oscar, 'Why don't we go and get changed and do a bit of exploring then, son, and let these two lovebirds have some time to themselves. I quite fancy a walk up to the Abbey ruins.'

'Sounds good to me,' Oscar agreed and they all walked upstairs together before parting to go to their separate rooms.

Once in the privacy of their suite Patty started to feel nervous. She was a virgin and was apprehensive about what lay ahead of her. What if she didn't enjoy the sexual act? But she needn't have worried. Lawrence closed the curtains and then slowly undressed her, and no one saw them again for the rest of the day, apart from one maid who took a snack up to them in their room later that evening.

'Well, I'd say that went rather well, wouldn't you?' Max said as he and Oscar were on their way home on the train the next day. They had encountered Patty and Lawrence in the hotel dining room during breakfast but the newlyweds had eyes for no one but each other.

'Couldn't have gone better,' Oscar agreed wistfully, thinking of his own wedding. It had been a dismal affair and the marriage he was now trapped in for life was no better, as far as he was concerned. As he stared from the carriage windows at the fields and hills rolling past, Olivia's face appeared in front of his eyes but he pushed the image away. He hoped that wherever she was she was happier than him, but he also worried about her. It would do no good breaking his heart for something that could never be. He just had to get on with his life now.

# Chapter Eighteen

'That's it then, you can put the Open sign on the door now,'
Dilly said the following week as she patted her hair into
place. The streets outside were teeming with people and
Dilly hoped that some of them would come in to look at
the clothes she and Jayne had displayed about the shop on
mannequins. The whole place was very tastefully decorated,
and because it was situated on the outskirts of the Bullring,
they should catch a lot of passing trade.

Soon the bell above the door tinkled and a young woman
entered, pointing to the dress on the mannequin in the
window. Jayne rushed forward to serve her as Dilly stood
back with a satisfied smile on her face. Many of the clothes
in the shop had been made by the seamstresses back in
Nuneaton and Dilly had priced them to sell. She was a firm
believer that ordinary working-class women should be able
to afford pretty clothes, and with her flair for colour and
fashion she hoped to carve a niche for herself in the clothing
market.

'Crikey, my feet feel as if they're on fire,' Jayne sighed when they finally put the Closed sign on the door that evening. 'We must have sold almost a quarter of the stock already.'

Dilly was delighted with their first day but dismayed all at the same time. 'I think we have,' she fretted, 'which makes me think I may need to set on another seamstress over here to keep up with demand. It's no good having a shop with no stock in it, is it? Do you think there would be room for a sewing machine in the back room if we tidied it up a little? I don't want to have to be carting stock here on the train every day. It would be much easier if we could have someone sewing on the premises.'

'I'm sure there would be enough space,' Jayne said, peering into the room Dilly had mentioned. 'And there'd still be room for bales of material if we were to put deep shelves along that wall. Shall I place an ad in the window?'

'Yes,' Dilly replied. It would be an added expense that she hadn't allowed for, but then if trade continued as it had today it would more than pay for a seamstress to work on the premises and still return a profit.

'So how did your first day go?' Max asked that evening. He only had time to call in for a fleeting visit as he had arranged to meet a business client, but he was eager to know how Dilly's new venture had taken off.

'Extremely well.' She smiled broadly. 'So well in fact that we sold about a quarter of the stock. I've instructed Jayne to put an ad in the window for a seamstress to work over there.'

Max shook his head in amazement. It was becoming increasingly clear that Dilly had a very good business head on her shoulders, and he had no doubt at all that in time she would indeed build up her own little empire. She certainly worked hard enough and he felt she deserved to do well.

'I've found it hard to settle down since I got back from Patty and Lawrence's wedding,' he told her then. 'And I must admit I'm not in the least bit in the right mood for entertaining prospective clients this evening. I'd much rather have stayed here and told you all about it. Patty looked absolutely stunning in the dress you designed for her, and the couple were so happy.'

'You already have told me all about it,' Dilly teased. 'And in so much detail, in fact, that I can almost imagine I was there.'

'I just wish you had been,' he said quietly, then inclining his head he hurried away and she stood silently and watched him go.

Over in Niamh's house, Niamh was watching Mary clear the dinner table. The girl hadn't seemed to be herself at all for the last few days and Niamh was concerned about her. She was usually such a cheerful soul but just lately she seemed edgy and solemn.

'Is everything all right, dear?' Niamh asked gently.

Mary nodded keeping her eyes on the job she was doing. 'Yes, fine, thank you. Why wouldn't it be?'

'I don't know,' Niamh shrugged. 'You just seem to be a little jumpy, that's all.' As a sudden thought occurred to her she scowled before asking, 'Samuel hasn't . . . well . . . touched you or done anything to upset you, has he?' After what he had done to her and Bessie she didn't trust him an inch.

'Oh no, no,' Mary hastened to tell her. 'He ain't laid so much as a finger on me. It'd be the worse fer him if he tried to.'

'That's all right then.' But Niamh still looked thoughtful as the girl scuttled from the room with the big wooden tray full of dirty pots. What with Mary not being herself and Samuel still hanging around, Niamh sometimes wished that she hadn't bothered to come home. Roddy was being difficult too, constantly asking her when they could go back to see Roisin again. He had clearly taken as much of a shine to her as she had to him, which Niamh found surprising seeing as he was such a quiet little soul normally.

Samuel had just gone out and secretly Niamh hoped that he'd stay out. It unnerved her having him in the house but all she could do was hope that his stay wouldn't last for much longer. Sighing, she lifted the newspaper and instantly her eyes were drawn to the latest report on Snowy White's murder. It seemed that the police had now questioned everyone who had seen Snowy on the day he had been attacked, but were no nearer to discovering who was responsible. She doubted they would waste too much time on their inquiries. It was a well-known fact that Snowy White had a list of convictions as long as his arm. Dropping the paper back onto the small table, Niamh gave a lengthy yawn. She would be going into the shop tomorrow to help her mother so she decided to get an early night.

At the Farthing residence, Samuel let himself in the front door with his key. From something that Niamh had said he knew that his father would be out this evening, so it was a good time to raid his mother's old bedroom to see if there was anything of worth there.

As he made for the stairs, Mrs Pegs appeared from the kitchen and he bestowed a winning smile on her. 'Ah, good evening, Mrs Pegs. I just need to get a few things from my old room but I won't disturb you, so do go about your business.'

Mrs Pegs eyed him warily. She always wondered what Samuel was up to when he was civil. But then he was the son of the house, so she could hardly stop him from going upstairs, could she? And with a nod she disappeared back to where she had come from to enjoy a cup of cocoa with Gwen.

On the landing, Samuel paused to listen but all was silent. He approached his mother's old room first and quietly let himself in. Her jewellery box still stood on the dressing table so he rifled through it, pocketing any trinkets that he thought might be of any value. Next he searched the wardrobe. There was a wonderful mink coat hanging there that he was sure would fetch a pretty penny, but it was too bulky to sneak out of the house so he decided that he would leave it where it was for now. His mother would certainly never wear it again. She was as mad as a hatter now. After a thorough search of that room he then crept along the landing and sneaked into his father's room. He doubted he would find any money there. Max locked all his takings away in the safe, but perhaps he might just have left the key lying about . . . Samuel sighed with disappointment. He should have known that his father would not be so lax although he had pocketed a rather nice pair of gold cufflinks. Samuel was fairly sure that the police had no inkling it was he who had killed Snowy but now he was keen to get as far away as he could, so the more money he could raise for his new future the better.

He was searching through the final drawer in his father's tallboy when his hands closed around a small tin box. Curious, he took it out and laid it on the bed. It was locked but the key was in it so he quickly turned it and opened the lid, disappointed to see that all it contained were papers. The first he glanced at was his mother and father's marriage certificate and he let it flutter down onto the bedspread. Then came birth certificates, Oscar's, his and Lawrence's, and Harvey's. Violet's was there too, along with her death certificate. He guessed that the last one must be Olivia's but when he withdrew it and glanced at it, his mouth fell open. For a moment he stared at the document in stunned disbelief but then he broke into a broad grin and pocketed it hastily before returning everything else to the tin box exactly as he had found it. What a turn-up for the books! He would have his father over a barrel now and suddenly he could scarcely wait to see him.

When Max returned home late that evening he was unpleasantly surprised to find Samuel lounging in his favourite chair in his study with a glass of his finest port in one hand and a cigar in the other, looking like the cat that had got the cream.

'Well, that didn't last long, did it?' Max said cryptically. 'Seeing as how you told me to "Keep my job" not so very long ago and said that you never wanted anything to do with me again. To be honest, Samuel, I don't think I wish to speak to you at the moment. I've had a rather long day and I'm tired.'

Samuel grinned at him slyly. 'Oh, I think you'll want to talk to me when you hear what I have to say,' he answered glibly.

'And just what is that supposed to mean?'

'I've been putting two and two together and suddenly things that I've always found rather strange have started to make sense. It's almost like the pieces of a jigsaw finally falling into place.'

Max sighed as he helped himself to a drink. 'Can you just get to the point and stop talking double Dutch!'

'All right then. I've always found it rather odd that you've taken such a keen interest in Dilly Carey and now I think I know why.'

Samuel had the satisfaction of seeing the colour drain from his father's face and went on, 'She is – or was, after all

– merely a servant here and yet you've always shown her rather preferential treatment and treated her as your equal.'

'All human beings are equal, it's just that some are more fortunate than others,' Max blustered.

'Hmm, that's a matter of opinion.' Knowing that he had the upper hand, Samuel was enjoying himself immensely. His father was positively squirming in his shoes but he wasn't done with him yet, not by a long shot.

'I found it strange to say the least when Dilly Carey suddenly started buying shops, and I got to thinking . . . someone must be buying them for her, or at least loaning her the money to buy them. That someone wouldn't happen to be you, would it, Father?' When Max's lips set in a grim line Samuel went on, 'And if it *was* you, why would you lend all that money to a servant? Perhaps you are more than friends? Or could it be that there's something else between you that binds you together?'

'This is quite preposterous. *How dare you!*' his father roared.

'Oh, I *dare*,' Samuel retorted. It was nice to see his father so discomfited. 'I always wondered why you and Mother suddenly took to sleeping in different rooms and why Mother was always so protective of Olivia when the Carey woman was about. I had the feeling that mother would have gotten rid of her years ago but perhaps you wouldn't let her? And perhaps *that's* the reason why Mother is as she is now, because she knew that Carey was your bit on the side?'

'That's not true!' Max denied hotly. 'Dilly Carey and I have never been anything other than friends. I admit I helped her to buy the first shop with a loan, but she has repaid that in full – and I only did it because I thought she deserved a break. It's been hard for her, bringing her family up all alone since her husband died.'

'But it goes much deeper than that, doesn't it?' Samuel smirked, playing his final hand. 'I happen to know something about Olivia's birth that would really put the cat amongst the pigeons should it ever become common knowledge. Olivia isn't *really* my sister, is she? Olivia is Dilly Carey's child! Were you the father?'

Max thumped heavily onto the nearest chair as blood thundered in his ears. Samuel knew – but how? They had all always been so careful.

'Of course I wasn't.' He was shocked that Samuel could even think such a thing. Deciding that his son should know the truth too, he began, 'Dilly and her husband Fergal were on their beam ends. Fergal had been seriously injured on the railways and would never work again. Things got so bad that Dilly was afraid she would have to put her children into the orphanage and she had another on the way. One night when Dilly came to wait at table at one of your mother's dinner parties your mother noticed that she was carrying a child. Camilla, as you are aware, was beside herself with grief after losing Violet, and unknown to me she offered to buy Dilly's unborn baby. I was horrified when she first told me what she had done, but I was so worried about your mother's sanity that in the end I agreed to it. And so Camilla and I unofficially adopted Olivia and brought her up as our own – but Dilly has never stopped loving her. How could she?'

Samuel was staring at him thoughtfully as he absorbed what he had heard. 'If Olivia ever found out, she would hate you and the Carey woman for the rest of your lives, which leads me to what I want to ask you. You see, the thing is, I want to move away – right away from here – so I'm going to need some money, more than I have. If you really want me to keep your secret I'm sure you'll give me my inheritance now, Father. After all, you owe it to me. You've always cared more about the others than you have about me. Good-goodie Oscar and my saintly twin Lawrence and Hero Harvey!'

'Th-that's not true!' Max spluttered. 'I've always loved *all* of my children.'

A silence settled between them then that seemed to stretch for an eternity. This was what Max had always dreaded happening. Should the truth come out now it could no longer affect Camilla, which was one blessing at least as she was beyond understanding these days. But as Samuel had said, it would destroy Olivia and Oscar – and Dilly too, if it came to that. But then if he allowed Samuel to blackmail him, where would it end? Knowing his son as he did, Max was aware that he wouldn't stop coming for money until he had bled him dry. Perhaps he should call his bluff?

Suddenly coming to a decision, he looked his son in the eye.

'I'm sorry you had to find out about this,' he said as calmly as he could. 'But I'm afraid you're going to have to wait for your inheritance, the same as the rest of your siblings are. I refuse to let you blackmail me, Samuel, so do your worst. But before you do, I beg you to think of the heartache you will cause. Also, I should tell you that should you carry out your threat, you will never get another penny piece from me. I shall cut you out of my will and disown you, so I ask you to seriously consider this before you do anything rash.'

Samuel leaped out of his chair, his face a grimace. 'You're going to regret this,' he hissed, and before Max could respond he stormed from the house, leaving all the doors flapping open behind him.

# Chapter Nineteen

'It's from the War Office,' Dilly told Niamh with a catch in her voice as she stared at the envelope in her hand the following morning.

Nell, her trusted neighbour from her days back in the courts, had popped in to see her, and she said in her usual forthright way, 'Well, open it then, woman. It can't bite yer.'

With trembling fingers Dilly slit open the envelope, and within a sheet of official-looking notepaper she found Kian's identity disc. Tears filled her eyes as she scanned the page, and at last she told them, 'They are informing me where Kian is buried in France. At last I shall be able to go and say a proper goodbye to him.'

'Ah, God rest 'is soul,' Nell muttered as she hastily made the sign of the cross on her chest. Little did Dilly know that the son she thought of as a war hero had once killed the prostitute called Madge Bunting who had been blackmailing his mother. But it was a secret that Nell would take to her grave. As far as she was concerned, Kian had done the town a service the day he had killed Madge, for she had been the scum of the earth. Far better for Dilly to remember him as the kindly son she had nurtured.

'That's grand,' Nell agreed, laying a gentle hand on Dilly's arm. 'But first you have to get your little empire truly up an' runnin', lass. It's time to look forward, not back. That's what Kian would have wanted you to do.'

'You're right.' Dilly sniffed, swiping at a tear as she looked around the shop. 'But one day I *will* go, Nell. And I'll lay flowers on his grave and tell him how proud I am of him.'

The shop bell tinkled then and instantly Dilly was professional again as she glided forward with a smile on her face to ask, 'May I help you?'

Nell winked at Niamh then slipped away, pleased that Dilly's prayers had finally been answered. It had destroyed her, not knowing where Kian's resting place was but one day now, hopefully in the not too distant future, she would be able to make the journey to say her final goodbye.

Samuel staggered from the gentleman's club late that afternoon much the worse for drink. He felt sick but above everything else he felt angry. How *dare* his father refuse him? Max clearly didn't believe that he would carry out his threat – but he'd show him. He turned in the direction of Abbey Green but then changed his mind. He couldn't face seeing his wife's face and feeling like an intruder in his own home for a moment longer. His self-pity increased. That was another thing his father had forced him into – his farce of a marriage to a servant's daughter – and he hadn't even allowed him to have the house he had bought for them in his own name.

Hailing a cab, he decided to go and see if his little widow had calmed down enough to forgive him yet. If she hadn't, he'd spend the night in the local whorehouse. At least the women there made him feel wanted. And then tomorrow he would plan his revenge. His mind raced. Dilly Carey could clearly do no wrong in his father's eyes. Perhaps that was the way to hurt him – by hurting *her*? All he had to do now was plan how he was going to do it.

Max seemed preoccupied and not at all his usual cheery self the following evening when he called in at the shop.

'Are you feeling unwell?' Dilly asked with concern.

Max had wrestled with his conscience all day wondering if he should tell her about the argument with Samuel but finally had decided against it. It would only worry her, and knowing his son as he did, Max hoped that he wouldn't have the guts to follow his threats through. He would be too afraid of being cut out of his will altogether.

'Oh, I just have a slight headache, that's all,' he said vaguely. 'But how has your day been?'

Dilly showed him the letter she had received from the War Office and he was glad, knowing how much this would mean to her.

'And on top of that, Jayne reported when she came back from Birmingham this evening that she'd had another very good day of sales. I shall have to go over there again tomorrow with more stock until we can get a new seamstress set on.'

'But how will you manage it?'

Dilly chuckled. 'I have two rather heavy suitcases of clothes already packed to go. It's not ideal but I shall get a cab to and from the station so I shan't have to carry them far. I shall buy in some more ready-made clothes too to keep us going. But now – have you eaten? I have some rather nice lamb chops upstairs if you'd care to share them with me.'

'I'd love to but Mrs Pegs will have my dinner ready and I don't want to upset her.'

'Of course not . . .' Dilly paused then before asking, 'And have you heard anything from Olivia?'

She asked the same question every single time she saw him and he sensed how much she was missing her.

'Not today, but then she may telephone this evening.'

'Has she given you her address yet?'

'I only know she's in the Covent Garden area. I don't have a specific address but she sounds fine, honestly, and she knows where I am if she needs me.'

'Of course she does,' Dilly answered, flushing slightly. She supposed she shouldn't question him; after all, she had given up the rights to Olivia many years before, but she hoped that she and Max now shared the sort of relationship where they could speak to each other about anything.

A little later, Max departed and Dilly settled down to go over her books. The success of the Birmingham shop had taken her by surprise, not that she was complaining. She was delighted and prayed that things were finally working out for her.

The next few days passed in a blur. Dilly was back and forwards to Birmingham most days making sure that Jayne had enough stock, and Niamh was happy to keep the Nuneaton store going in her absence. She'd told her mother that Samuel hadn't shown his face back at the house for a few days and was clearly relieved about it.

'To be honest I wouldn't care if I never clapped eyes on him again,' she confided and Dilly could quite believe it.

When Saturday evening arrived and Dilly turned the sign on the shop door to Closed, it was almost a relief. It had been a very hectic week and she was looking forward to having Sunday off. She tidied the shop and made herself a light meal then settled down to listen to the wireless.

Eventually she retired to bed and although she had intended to read for a while she fell asleep almost as soon as her head hit the pillow.

In the early hours of the morning something woke her and she stretched and yawned. A glance at the curtains told her that it was still dark outside, so she burrowed down beneath the blankets again, intent on going back to sleep. But for some reason she felt restless and after a few moments she turned on her back and looked towards the window again. It was then that she noticed a smell and leaning towards the bedside table she fumbled for the matches and lit the oil lamp. Smoke was seeping beneath her bedroom door. Dilly gasped as she realised that there was a fire, and leaping out of bed she hastily pulled her dressing robe on. It was then that she heard a shout from the road outside. 'FIRE!' and it was in her shop.

Sobbing with fright, she hurried to the bedroom door and threw it open. The landing was full of thick black smoke but after covering her nose and mouth she fumbled her way through it to the door that led to the stairs. She inched it open but then instantly slammed it shut again as bright orange flames licked towards her. The whole of the shop downstairs must be on fire – there would be no way out there. Hurrying back to her bedroom she forced herself to stay calm as she tried to think what she should do. Put something across the bottom of the door – yes, that was it – to stop the smoke from entering the room. Hastily snatching a towel, she rolled it up and jammed it along the gag at the base of the door.

Crossing to the window then, she threw it open just as someone burst into the back yard.

'My shop is on fire!' she called down to them in a

wobbly voice. She could vaguely make out more than one person now.

'Aye, we know it is, lass,' someone answered. 'Don't be scared. We've sent for the fire engine and we're going to get you down from there. Someone has gone for a ladder but in the meantime, d'you reckon you could clamber out onto the roof?'

Dilly stared in horror at the roof some feet below her. Thankfully it was flat but it looked an awful long way down. People were shouting and appearing from all directions as she told herself not to panic. Despite the towel she had laid down, the room was fast filling with smoke now and she started to cough, feeling light-headed.

'Come along now,' the calming voice urged again. 'Climb onto the sill and then lower yourself down.'

Hearing the urgency in the man's voice Dilly took a deep breath and climbed into a sitting position on the sill. She could hear the sound of the fire now and knew that if she delayed for much longer, it might be too late.

'That's it . . . well done. Now turn around and hang onto the sill as you lower yourself down. We can get to you then. Look – here's the ladder now.'

Dilly heard the clunk of the ladder as it was propped up against the lower roof and with every ounce of courage she could muster she turned and clung to the sill before letting her legs dangle down below her as wave after wave of dizziness washed over her. She heard someone clattering up the ladder and striding across the flat roof, then they were gripping her around the knees as they coaxed, 'That's it, now let go, pet, I've got you. You'll be safe in a minute.'

The din of the fire engine's bell pierced the air as Dilly fearfully did as she was told then suddenly darkness rushed towards her and she knew no more.

Dilly slowly opened her eyes then blinked and hastily shut them again as she began to cough. The light was so bright – but where was she?

'It's all right, Mammy, you're safe now.' Dilly recognised Niamh's voice. She was holding her hand and she sounded frightened, so with an enormous effort Dilly opened her eyes again and tried to focus on her daughter's face.

'Wh-where am I?' She started to cough again as Niamh lovingly stroked her hand.

'You're in hospital, but don't worry – you're going to be fine. You inhaled a lot of smoke, but once you get that out of your system you'll be good as new,' Niamh said tearfully. There was someone standing behind her and as her vision cleared, Dilly saw that it was Max. His face was drawn and he looked as if he hadn't slept for a month.

'You gave us a right old scare there, Dilly,' he said with a catch in his voice.

Dilly was confused. Smoke? Niamh had said she'd inhaled a lot of smoke – what did she mean? Then suddenly it all came rushing back and she gasped.

'*My shop* . . . something woke me up! There was smoke coming from under the door and when I tried to get out there were flames licking up the stairs . . . it was on fire!'

'Don't get worrying about the shop. You got out safe and sound and that's the main thing, thanks to the man who spotted the flames on his way home from the night-shift at the pit,' Max said soothingly.

Dilly felt as if she was caught in the grip of a night-mare. She had worked so hard to get the shop up and running.

'How bad is it?' she managed to ask between bouts of coughing. Max and Niamh exchanged a glance and her stomach sank. Their expressions gave her the answer.

'The shop is the least of our worries at the moment,' Niamh said, squeezing her mother's hand but Dilly shook her head in despair.

'Is – is it all gone?'

'Well, the downstairs is gutted but the fire engine managed to contain the blaze before it took a hold upstairs, although I doubt we'll be able to salvage much. Everything will be smoke damaged. But Mammy, you got out alive and that's all that matters.' Niamh's eyes were raw from crying and Dilly felt guilty that she was the cause of bringing her yet more heartache. She had gone through so much already since losing Connie.

'How did the fire start?' she asked then.

'The firemen are looking into that,' Max said somewhat reluctantly. 'But it appears that it was started in the back yard.'

'Deliberately?' A cold hand closed around Dilly's heart but Max was saved from having to answer when a nurse in a crisp white apron swept into the room, closely followed by a doctor.

'Ah, so you're back with us then!' the nurse said with satisfaction, then turning towards Niamh and Max she told them firmly, 'Could you leave the room please while the doctor examines her?'

Max and Niamh almost collided at the door in their haste to do as they were told and for the next few minutes the doctor subjected Dilly to a thorough examination.

'You're a very lucky woman,' he told Dilly eventually as the nurse stepped forward to tuck the blankets back around her. 'No burns thankfully, so once your lungs have cleared you should make a full recovery.'

'When can I go home?'

The doctor chuckled. 'Oh, I dare say in a couple of days' time if there are no complications, which there shouldn't be, all being well. But I'd just like to keep my eye on you until then.'

*A couple of days!* It sounded like a life sentence to Dilly. However, she knew she had no option but to do as she was told for once.

'Now no arguing, you're going to come and stay with me for a while,' Niamh told her bossily two days later as she unpacked the clothes she had brought for her mother to go home in.

'They're not mine,' Dilly said breathlessly as she dragged herself to the edge of the bed. Her chest was still tight from all the smoke she had inhaled and the doctor had warned her that it could be a few weeks before she felt fully well again. Dilly supposed that she should be grateful to be alive, but she couldn't help fretting about her shop. She wouldn't rest properly until she had seen it for herself and assessed the full extent of the damage. Perhaps it wouldn't be as bad as she feared.

'They *are* yours,' Niamh told her. 'Peggy and Hilda have been up almost all night since the fire occurred stitching you new clothes. I hope you'll like them.'

Hilda and Peggy were the two seamstresses Dilly employed in the shop in Abbey Street, and a lump formed in her throat to think of how much trouble they had gone to on her behalf, bless them!

'Does that mean that all my clothes were destroyed?'

Niamh kept her voice cheerful as she laid the clothes out on the bed.

'Well, I think some of them are salvageable, but everything smells of smoke so we'll have to go through them and see what we can save when you're feeling up to it. For now you have more than enough to be going on with, believe me.'

Dilly felt as weak as a kitten and actually allowed her

173

daughter to help her dress. Everything fitted beautifully, and she knew it was down to the keen eyes of Peggy and Hilda. They seemed to have a flair for knowing what size someone was just by looking at them. The dress that Niamh had brought in for her today was one of the styles that were selling well in the shops, and even in her weakened state Dilly couldn't help but admire the fine workmanship that had gone into the making of it. Niamh had brought in one of her own coats for Dilly to wear over her new dress, and a pair of her own shoes. Luckily she and Dilly were the same size so with luck they would fit her comfortably until they could get around to buying her some new ones.

'Right, I think we're all ready to go now,' Niamh said brightly when she'd brushed Dilly's hair. 'Max has the car outside waiting to drive you to my house so we'd better not keep him waiting.'

'I want to go and look at the shop first,' Dilly said.

Niamh looked worried. 'But the doctor said you weren't to overdo things. You should rest for a few days first, Mammy.'

'I want to look at the shop!' Dilly repeated. 'And if you won't ask Max to take me, then I shall walk there myself.'

Niamh lifted the small bag containing Dilly's nightclothes. 'The shop it is then,' she sighed. She knew better than to try and argue with her mother when she had made her mind up about something. Dilly Carey could be as stubborn as a mule.

# Chapter Twenty

'So what do you think, Doctor?' Daniel asked as he screwed his cap in his hands.

''Tis broken, to be sure,' the doctor replied gravely. 'She'll need to be taken to the hospital to have it set in plaster, I'm afraid, Daniel.'

'Oh, how could I have been so clumsy,' Maeve groaned as she thumped the arm of the chair in frustration. 'And right in the middle of harvesting too! Sure I couldn't have picked a worse time to go me length, now could I?'

'You couldn't help tripping over,' Shelagh said soothingly. 'And them cobblestones in the yard are always slippery after we've had a shower.'

'I'll go and bring the trap round,' Daniel said. 'The sooner we can get that leg set the better I'll be feelin' about it.'

The doctor snapped his bag shut and made for the door, saying, 'Try not to jolt her about too much on your way in, there's a good man, else she'll be in agony, the poor creature.'

'But how long will I have to keep the plaster on for?' Maeve asked him as he was about to step out of the door.

'I should think six or seven weeks at least depending how the break heals.'

'Six or seven weeks!' Maeve was horrified. 'But this is our busiest time of the year!'

The doctor gave her a wry grin. 'I'm afraid accidents have a habit of happenin' at the worst possible times, so they do, but I'm sure there's enough of you to get by. Good day, Maeve. I'll call in to see how you're getting on the next time I'm passing, but if you need me in the meantime you only have to shout.' With that he was gone.

Angry tears ran down Maeve's cheeks. 'Sure, amn't I a clumsy old bugger to be fallin' over!' she cursed and Shelagh couldn't help but grin. It was rarely that she heard her mother-in-law swear.

'Now don't you go feeling bad about it,' Daniel said sternly. 'As the doctor pointed out, we'll get by. If need be I'll write and ask young Niamh to come over and give us a hand again but we'll see how we go on first, eh? Meantime let's be thinkin' of getting you to the hospital, woman.' And with that he was off to saddle the pony and get the trap ready – although how he was supposed to get Maeve there without jolting her with all the potholes in the lanes he really didn't know.

As Max drew the car to a halt in front of the shop, Dilly gasped. The front windows had imploded with the heat of the fire and beyond the gaping holes all she could see was a blackened shell. She had feared it would be bad, but nothing could have prepared her for this. Tears stung at the back of her eyes. The beautiful gowns that had graced the mannequins in the bridal shop were now nothing but piles of ashes blowing about the charred floors in the gentle breeze. Even the counter was beyond saving.

'I told you it was too soon for you to come,' Max said, angry at himself for bowing to her wishes. He should have put his foot down and driven her straight to Niamh's but then Dilly was a force to be reckoned with when she'd made her mind up and he had no doubt she would have carried out her threat and walked there by herself.

'I want to go in. Is it safe?' she asked dully.

'But surely you can see all you need to from here?' Max didn't want to prolong her agony for a second more than was necessary. At least she could go away and come to terms with the worst now. He half-expected her to argue but she didn't.

'All right. We'll come back another day.' Dilly's face was the colour of bleached linen and he was suddenly fearful. She had gone through so much in her life but could this be the straw that broke the camel's back? Dilly had worked tirelessly to turn the little shops into the classy establishments she had created and now they were gone in a puff of smoke. Worse still was the suspicion that was niggling away like a worm in the back of his mind. The fire officer had confirmed that the fire had indeed been deliberately started in the back yard, and had asked if Dilly had any enemies. Max had truthfully been able to answer that she did not. But *he* did! Samuel would have known that if he hurt Dilly he would hurt him, but Max didn't want to believe that his own son could be capable of such a wicked act. Had Dilly not woken up on the night of the fire she could quite easily have been burned to death – and then the police would be looking for a murderer rather than an arsonist. No, it couldn't have been him, Max tried to convince himself . . . but the doubts remained.

Now he steered the car away from the kerb and drove to Niamh's as quickly as he could. Dilly looked in need of a good hot cup of sweet tea or something stronger if he could persuade her to have it.

'Here we are then,' Niamh said as Max parked outside her house. 'Let's get you inside, eh, Mammy? Roddy and Mary are longing to see you.'

She helped her mother from the car then while Max got her bag she led her towards the front door. Dilly walked beside her woodenly, too numb to feel anything.

Mary and Roddy gave her a rapturous welcome but Dilly was feeling so defeated that she barely acknowledged them as she went to sit in the chair by the window.

'She just needs time to come to terms with everything that's happened,' Max told Niamh, seeing how concerned she was. Niamh had never seen her mother looking so defeated and she prayed that Dilly would find her fighting spirit again.

Dilly remained in the seat by the window for two days, only leaving it to pick at her food when Mary served it, or to go to bed.

'It's as if she's given up,' Niamh told Max tearfully when he visited that evening.

'Right, then – we need to do something about it,' he said determinedly. Crossing to Dilly he told her, 'Dilly, I think it's time I got the builders in to start putting the shop to rights now, or would you prefer to put it up for sale? Of course it wouldn't be worth what you paid for it in the state it's in, but—'

'*What?*' Her head snapped round. 'But why ever would I do that?'

'Well . . .' Suddenly a spark of the Dilly he had come to know and love shone in her eyes.

'Thank you for your offer,' she said primly, 'but I'm not quite a charity case just yet, and furthermore I have *no* intention of selling either of my shops. In fact, I might go round there tomorrow and look at exactly what needs doing.'

'I could take you,' he volunteered but she shook her head.

'I appreciate the offer but I think I'd rather go alone, if you don't mind. I can look and see if there's anything salvageable upstairs while I'm at it.'

Niamh and Max exchanged a satisfied smile and for now the subject was dropped.

Sure enough, when Mary came down the stairs to start the breakfast early the next morning she found Dilly in the kitchen already dressed for the outdoors.

'But you haven't had anything to eat yet,' Mary protested.

'I shall be fine,' Dilly told her. 'I'll probably be back in no time, so you just see to Niamh and Roddy.' With that she left by the back door as Mary tutted disapprovingly.

As Dilly neared the charred remains of her shop she fingered the key in her pocket but she needn't have bothered. The front door was all but gone, eaten away by the flames, and she could step over it into the black cavern beyond. Picking her way through the ashes, she made for the stairs. One side of them was partly gone so she gingerly stayed close to the wall as she climbed up, testing one step at a time.

Just as Max had said, the firemen had managed to stop the fire before it entered her living quarters, but everything was smoke damaged. It was as if some giant hand had swept in and painted everything the colour of midnight. It was a very depressing sight and yet she instantly realised that there were lots of things that she might be able to save. The pots and pans for a start off. They would be as good as new after a good wash.

Moving across the room, she entered her bedroom. Again it was smoke damaged but nowhere near as badly as the living room, so perhaps some of her clothes might have escaped? She was right. When she opened the wardrobe door she found them all still hanging there, reeking of smoke but after a good soak and a wash, the majority of them should be as good as new. Dragging a bag from the bottom of the wardrobe, she began to fill it with her favourite things. She had sat about feeling sorry for herself for long enough. It was time to pick up the pieces and start again – and up here would be as good a place as any. Dilly tore down the curtains in the bedroom and the sitting room then, and tossed them onto the floor. She would begin now to decide what was worth keeping and what had gone beyond saving.

By mid-morning she was black from head to foot but she didn't care. Dilly had never been afraid of getting her hands dirty, nor of hard work. She'd decided that the small sofa and chairs in the living room could be saved if they were reupholstered, and she was quite happy to tackle that job herself. After all, how hard could it be? she reasoned. The walls and paintwork would all need doing again, but then Dilly was confident she could do that herself too and it would take no time at all to run up new curtains. The more she did, the more confident she felt that with time and a lot of hard work she could get everything back to where it had been. The fire officer had told her that he thought the fire had been deliberately started but Dilly didn't want to dwell on that. She'd prefer to think it had just been a group of kids larking about. If she allowed herself to believe otherwise, she knew she might never have the confidence to return there.

By lunchtime she was tiring so she set off back to Niamh's toting her bag of smoky-smelling clothes. After filling a tin bath in the yard she deposited all the clothes into it to have a good soak then hurried off to have a thorough wash and change. She really did look a sight but she felt better about things already so she knew that the morning's work had not been wasted.

She went to bed early that evening determined to get a good night's rest, and first thing the next morning she arrived back at the shop again in the work dress that she had borrowed from Mary.

Hands on hips she stood in the shop wondering where to start. Should it be upstairs or down here? Eventually she decided that the shop was the most important. The sooner she could open it again, the sooner it would be earning. She could always stay with Niamh for a while longer so the living quarters weren't quite so important. She nipped along the road to the hardware shop where she purchased buckets, sweeping brushes and everything she thought she might need to begin the clean-up, then she set to with a vengeance. First off, she had to clear all the charred debris out into the yard but it wasn't as difficult as she'd feared. The shelves were so brittle that they fell apart when she touched them so she soon had them ripped from the walls and stacked outside. The counter was another matter. That was heavier and she knew that she would need help to move it, so for now she just had to clean around it. Tonight she would speak to the carpenter about replacing the windows and the door so that she could secure the place again. By mid-morning the air was thick with dust and soot and Dilly had to peer through it to see who it was who had just come to stand in the empty doorway.

'Good Lord, is that you, Dilly? Whatever are you doing?'

She smiled and relaxed when she recognised Max's voice.

'What does it look like I'm doing? I'm getting the place ready to open again, of course,' she replied.

'But you can't tackle this lot alone – and do you have any

idea how much it's going to cost to get it all shipshape again?' Max said, appalled.

'The shop is paid for now,' Dilly pointed out practically, 'so it's mainly a question of getting it cleaned out, redecorated and restocked. Jayne is still doing a roaring trade at the shop in Birmingham so I can afford to use some of the profits from over there to get this place up and running again.'

Max blew out a breath. Dilly never failed to astonish him. A couple of days ago he'd been fearful that this latest disaster had broken her spirit – but here she was as strong as ever again.

'In that case, I shall give you a hand,' he said, shrugging his jacket off.

'But you can't do anything in those clothes,' Dilly objected. 'They'll be ruined!'

'So be it. Now what do you want me to do first?'

He had rolled his sleeves up and seeing that he meant it, she chuckled. 'Well, you can start by fetching some more clean water and helping me to wash the walls down if you're quite sure? Oh, and I need to get this counter out into the yard too. It's too heavy for me to move on my own but I'm sure we'd be able to shift it between us. I'm afraid it's beyond saving, so that will be another job for the carpenter. I intend to go and see him tonight.'

For the next couple of hours the pair worked side by side and Dilly was more grateful to Max than she could say.

'I'll get Jackson to come round with the cart tomorrow to shift all that debris from the back yard,' he told her, and thankfully she didn't object as he'd half-expected her to. She was such an independent devil sometimes but then that was one of the many things he admired about her.

By mid-afternoon the thick dust was affecting Dilly quite badly and she was coughing. Her lungs were still not fully clear of the smoke she'd inhaled so Max put his foot down saying, 'That's enough for today then. No sense in overdoing it and making yourself ill, now is there?'

Straightening from the bucket of water in which she'd been in the process of wringing a cloth out, she burst out laughing. He was black from head to toe but then she supposed that she couldn't be much better.

'Good grief! What will people think when we go out onto the road looking like this?' she giggled.

'Since when have you worried about things like that?' Max asked with a twinkle in his eye. 'Now come along and I'll run you home in the car.'

For once Dilly did as she was told but she didn't intend to let that be the end of it. After a rest she would go and see the carpenter and instruct him to start work just as soon as possible.

# Chapter Twenty-One

After a good night's sleep Dilly was raring to go again but as she hurried along Queens Road and the shop came into view, she frowned.

Tim Graves the carpenter was there replacing the doorframe as she'd asked him to, but it looked as if someone else was inside the shop too – in fact, quite a few people from what she could see of it. As she drew level her mouth dropped open in amazement. Nell was inside, attacking the walls with a bucket of soapy water with a vengeance, and so were a few other people.

'What's going on?' she asked as she stepped past Tim.

Nora Myers, a woman who had once lived by her in the courts flashed her a toothless grin. 'Well, we all heard about what 'ad 'appened an' we thought you'd be glad of a bit o' help, lass. There's too much work 'ere fer you to tackle on yer own an' yer know what they say "many 'ands make light work" so me an' the neighbours 'ere decided to come an' give yer a hand. Whoever started this fire should be

strung up by the balls when they catch 'im! He could 'ave killed yer!'

Dilly felt a lump form in her throat. These were all women who barely had a penny to their name and yet they had all turned out to help her from the goodness of their hearts. She wouldn't forget it.

She rolled up her sleeves and joined in. By lunchtime the new windowframes were installed and Tim had gone off to order the glass which he informed her should be ready to install the next day. 'At least you'll be able to lock the place up and make everywhere secure again then,' he told her and she smiled at him gratefully. 'Then soon as ever you've painted the walls I'll come back in and get cracking on putting new shelves up and building new fitting rooms.'

Niamh arrived shortly afterwards with a basket full of sandwiches which the women shared between them, then she too set about helping.

By teatime the whole place had been thoroughly scrubbed and Dilly sighed with satisfaction.

'We can start the painting tomorrow,' she told Niamh, 'and with a bit of luck we should be ready to open again in two or three weeks. Hilda and Peggy are working flat out making new stock for the shop, bless them. Of course I shall have to buy in some bridal clothes for the time being because they take longer to make, but everyone has been so kind.'

'Mm, everyone except the lousy sod that started the fire,' Niamh retorted angrily. 'I just wish I could get my hands on them whoever they are. I'd show them!'

Dilly laughed. It was so rare to hear her placid-natured daughter get on her high horse but in this case she felt much the same. However, as yet the police had no clue who the culprit or culprits were, and it was looking now as if they would never find out who'd done it. Dilly just prayed that whoever it was wouldn't come back again.

*

When Niamh and Dilly got home that evening, tired but satisfied with what they'd achieved, Mary pointed to the mantelpiece. 'A letter came for you today,' she told Dilly as she started to dish up the evening meal. 'And it's got an Irish postmark so it's probably from your in-laws or Seamus perhaps?'

'Oh, I'll save it to read after dinner,' Dilly answered. 'But first, I think Niamh and I need to go and get washed and changed. We look as if we've both done a double shift down the pit!'

The meal Mary had cooked for them was delicious and both women did it justice, hungry as hunters. There was a lovely crispy leg of pork served with roast potatoes and vegetables followed by one of Mary's rice puddings topped with nutmeg.

'Oh dear, I'm so full I feel as if I might burst,' Dilly groaned when she had finished. 'The sooner I can get back into my own rooms the better or I'm sure I shall end up being as fat as a pig with all your lovely cooking, Mary.'

The girl flushed with pleasure at the praise and started to carry the dirty pots into the kitchen, a spring in her step.

Dilly settled down to read her letter then, but as she scanned the page, her cheery smile faded. Maeve had written to inform her that she had broken her leg after falling in the farmyard.

'But it's their busiest time of year,' Niamh said worriedly as her mother read it out to her. 'How will they manage with Gran'ma out of action?'

'Shelagh and Roisin are probably having to do a lot more,' Dilly said, but she was as concerned as Niamh. Shelagh had the children to see to as well and Maeve would never ask for help, she was too independent. Dilly could imagine that her mother-in-law would be pulling her hair out with frustration, having to sit there and be waited on.

'Perhaps you should go and stay for a while to give a hand – that's if you wouldn't mind?' Dilly suggested.

Niamh bit her lip. 'But how will you manage then, with all that work in the shop to do?'

'From what I saw today, Nell has rustled me up more than enough willing helpers,' Dilly chuckled. 'So I think perhaps you'd be needed even more in Enniskerry than you are here at the moment.'

'But what about Roddy?'

'I'm sure Bessie wouldn't mind you taking him with you again,' Dilly answered. 'To be honest, I think she almost likes him to be away – and I know that Roisin would love to see him again.'

'In that case I'll write to Gran'ma tonight and tell her that I'll be there within the next few days. If I do it now, and go and put it in the postbox, it will go first thing in the morning. But are you quite sure that you can manage?'

'Quite sure,' Dilly promised with a smile and so it was decided.

Roddy danced from foot to foot with excitement the next morning when Niamh told him that they would be going back to Ireland.

'See Roisin an' the chickens,' he said happily, and both Niamh and Dilly noted that he didn't seem in the least bit concerned about leaving his mother. But then it wasn't as if he saw much of her. On her one day off a week she rarely spent much time with him and he seemed far happier now in the company of Mary or Niamh, which both women thought was rather sad.

As Niamh and Roddy set off for the railway station two days later, Samuel was skulking in a small room in the back streets of Manchester. He stared morosely from the grimy window as he sucked noisily on his cigarette. He almost regretted setting the fire in Dilly's yard. It had seemed like a good idea at the time – after all, how better to get back at his father than through his fancy piece? – but then once the flames had taken hold and he'd seen Dilly trapped through her bedroom window, he had panicked. He knew that someone had seen the flames, and had run for the railway station, intent on getting as far away as possible, as soon as possible. The mail train bound for Manchester had been waiting at the platform at the time so he had just jumped aboard and eventually ended up in this dump. Every day he had bought newspapers and pored over them looking for a report of the fire, but up to now he had seen nothing, so he had no idea if Dilly had survived. He'd thought to use the fire as a blackmail threat to his father but had soon realised that he might have alienated himself altogether if Max suspected that it was him that had started it.

Slamming his fist onto the windowsill he cursed. Everything was going wrong. His plan to free himself from Niamh had backfired when she'd informed him that a divorce was out of the question, which meant he'd killed Constance for nothing – not that he mourned her. He'd never wanted the child in the first place. Then he'd had to do away with Snowy. A messy business – but what choice had he had? His father had called his bluff when he'd tried to blackmail him about Olivia's true parentage – and then the fire! He wasn't even sure if it would be safe to go ahead with buying the tattoo parlour now. The police could be searching for him even as he stood there – and it was a daunting thought. Worse still was the realisation that the money he had wouldn't last for ever and he might need to find a job – a real job, which would entail him getting his hands dirty.

Everything was a mess and at that moment he couldn't see a way out of it!

'The lovebirds are back and settling happily into their little cottage,' Max told Dilly that evening as they sat together in Niamh's sitting room. 'And Patty loved the curtains you made for them. She asked me to thank you.'

'I'm so relieved that I went and hung them before the fire, otherwise they would have gone up in flames along with everything else in the shop,' Dilly answered as she strained tea into two china cups. She'd spent another day at the shop, which was now secure again with a new door and windows. Half of it was also painted and the carpenter was busily erecting shelves on the walls that were finished.

'It looks as if Tim is going to have to build me another staircase too before I can move back in,' she told Max, handing him his cup. 'Apparently the fire weakened one side of it and he doesn't think it's safe.'

'So why don't you just stay here then? There's more than enough room and I know Niamh enjoys your company.' Max wasn't at all happy with the idea of her being alone again. What if whoever had set the fire decided to come back? She would be very vulnerable. He was still trying to convince himself that it couldn't have been Samuel, yet the thought plagued him day and night, especially as his son seemed to have disappeared off the face of the earth. It was just too much of a coincidence.

'I love staying with Niamh but I'm used to my own space now,' Dilly told him. 'And practically it makes far more sense for me to live on the shop premises.' She lifted one of her fashion magazines then – they were her only indulgence – and showed him a photo, asking, 'What do you think of that design? It's called *Harper's Bazaar* and is by Erté, but do you think the women of Nuneaton are ready for it?'

Max peered at a picture of an ankle-length dress with a flowing cape. 'It's no use asking me. I'm afraid I wouldn't have a clue about women's fashions,' he chuckled.

'Hmm.' Dilly stared at it thoughtfully. 'I might show it to Peggy and Hilda and ask them what they think. It would be quite economical to make and if we did a contrasting colour for the cape, it could look quite striking . . .'

It was nice to hear her making plans again and Max smiled indulgently. Dilly was back on form and he couldn't have been more relieved.

In the kitchen in Enniskerry, Niamh was making cocoa and soda bread for everyone's supper. Roddy was perched on Roisin's lap and from the chair at the side of the fire, where she sat with her leg propped up on a stool, Maeve couldn't help but notice that Roisin couldn't stop smiling.

'So what's put you in such a good mood then, lass?' she enquired.

Roisin glanced at Declan before shrugging. 'Oh, I don't know. I'm just feeling happy again, so I am,' she answered as she nuzzled Roddy's neck, sending him into fits of giggles. He had been like her little shadow ever since he and Niamh had arrived.

'It's right glad I am to hear it,' Maeve told her, looking around at her family with a smile of contentment. It was lovely to have Niamh there again; she just wished it could have been under different circumstances. She felt as if she was neither use nor ornament sat there with her plastered leg propped up, but then she knew she shouldn't grumble. There were lots of folk far worse off than she was, so she'd count her blessings.

By the beginning of October Dilly had the shop open again and was doing a brisk trade. She had replaced as much of the stock as she could afford to, but the seamstresses were having to work long hours to meet demand. Niamh had said in her last letter that Maeve should be having her plaster cast off any time now and Dilly was looking forward to having her home. She was missing both Niamh and Olivia, although Max made sure that he told her every time Olivia rang. He said that she sounded happy and Dilly could only pray that it was true.

Olivia had told her father that she had changed her job and was now working at the London Hippodrome as a make-up artist, and Max reported that Olivia sounded as if she was really enjoying it. Dilly was hoping that Olivia would eventually give her father her full address so that she could pay her a surprise visit, pretending that she'd come to London for the day on a shopping trip and had decided to look her up.

Dilly found it strange that Olivia hadn't disclosed exactly where she was living, but didn't say as much to Max. She knew that he was worried about Olivia too, and she didn't want to add to his fears. Instead she offered Max another cup of tea and their conversation continued comfortably as they sat in front of the fire.

Up to a point, Olivia was enjoying living in London. It was so different from the life she had known back in the quiet market town in the Midlands. There was so much to do there for a start-off, and she and Fiona went out together regularly on their days and evenings off, which were rare as they both tended to work rather unsociable hours. There were theatres to visit, the Palace Theatre, the Shaftesbury Theatre and the Theatre Royal to name but a few. Then there were the sightseeing trips that Fiona insisted she should take her on. Olivia's eyes widened at her first glimpse of Buckingham Palace and Trafalgar

Square. She had only ever seen them in books before and was enthralled.

'How about we do a trip on the river?' Fiona suggested one day and Olivia was only too keen to agree.

In no time at all they were settled on a boat and as it chugged along, Fiona pointed out places of interest to her. 'That's the Tower of London over there,' she said. 'It's where people were imprisoned before having their heads cut off. Look – can you see Traitor's Gate?'

'Charming,' Olivia responded dryly and the two girls grinned at each other. When the river trip was over they then visited the Houses of Parliament followed by St Paul's Cathedral, which had Olivia gasping with admiration.

'It's like another world,' she breathed, and Fiona couldn't help but notice the sadness in her voice. For some reason that she hadn't divulged, Olivia never seemed to be truly happy although she was a nice girl. Fiona just hoped that one day her newfound friend might trust her enough to tell her what was tormenting her so. In the meantime, Fiona continued to introduce her to as many new sights as she could.

There were ballets and operas, even casinos. The lifting of wartime restrictions had created all sorts of nightlife in the West End and entrepreneurs were opening clubs, restaurants and dance halls to cater for the new crazes of jazz and dancing. Yet despite her exciting new life, Olivia could never quite get away from the ache in her heart. She missed Oscar every single day.

Often she had to stifle the urge to hop on a train and go back home – but of course she knew that she couldn't, and so she did her best to settle into her new life and tried, unsuccessfully, to put thoughts of her brother from her mind.

# *Chapter Twenty-Two*

It was mid-October when someone rapping on the front door of Niamh's house brought Dilly springing awake in the early hours of the morning. Since the fire she had been a very light sleeper and she was suddenly glad that Mary was there to answer the door. Putting her robe and slippers on, she hurried downstairs just in time to see Mary admit Max.

'Oh goodness, what is it now?' She immediately feared the worst. But she needn't have worried. Max was beaming from ear to ear.

'Oscar just left,' he gabbled excitedly. 'Penelope has given birth to a baby boy. They're going to call him George.' Then suddenly his face fell. 'Oh dear, I should have waited until the morning to tell you instead of dragging you both out of your beds, shouldn't I?' he said repentantly.

Dilly laughed as she grabbed his hand and shook it heartily. 'No, of course you shouldn't! Congratulations, Grandpa Max, what wonderful news. It's time something nice happened, isn't it? How are mother and baby, by the way?'

'Very well, by all accounts, although Oscar says Penelope won't let the baby out of her sight. I hope she's not going to spoil him.'

'It's a little soon to be worrying about that, seeing as he's only just been born isn't it?' Dilly teased. 'I was just the same when mine were born. I wanted to hold them and . . .' Her voice trailed away as her thoughts flew back to the night when Olivia had been born, but then turning to Mary she forced herself to be cheerful as she said, 'I think this calls for a drink, don't you, Mary? I believe it's customary to wet the baby's head.'

'You two can if you've a mind to, but I'm off back to me bed,' Mary grumbled and with that she turned and walked away, leaving them to it.

'Don't worry about a drink,' Max said hastily, suddenly conscious that Dilly was in her nightclothes. She looked very pretty and natural, and more than anything in the world he would have loved to put his arms about her.

Dilly suddenly became embarrassed too and so she didn't press him to stay as he made for the door.

'Do give them both my best wishes, won't you?' she said as he strode down the path and he nodded before climbing into his car and driving away.

Once she had closed the door, Dilly leaned against it and stared off into space. She had sensed the need in Max tonight but worse still, she had wanted him too. But it was useless. Whilst Camilla was alive nothing could ever come of their feelings for each other, so she pushed him firmly from her mind and went back up to bed.

In Maeve's little cottage in Co. Wicklow, Niamh was restless too. More than ever now she knew that she could never stop loving Ben and she knew that he felt the same – yet what could they do about it? Although she and Samuel were married in name only, she was tied to him for life, for her faith would never allow them to divorce. That day when she had gone into town shopping, she had called to see Ben as she often did – unbeknownst to Maeve, who would have frowned on such a thing. She had agreed to meet him the following afternoon as well. He was going to close the blacksmith's for a few hours and they were going to walk in the hills.

Niamh knew that what she was doing was wrong yet she couldn't seem to help herself. A dozen times that night she had told herself firmly that she wouldn't go, that nothing could come of it, and yet she knew that she would be there in the place they had agreed to meet, away from prying eyes. As yet they had done no more than hold hands and stare at each other longingly – but how long will I be able to keep that up? she asked herself gloomily. She wanted him more than life itself and longed to be his, but if she gave herself to him she would be committing a mortal sin and her soul might never find its way to heaven. 'I won't go!' she muttered as she burrowed beneath the blankets and sleep finally claimed her.

The following morning, Niamh set about her chores and by lunchtime the meal was ready to be served and the place was gleaming. There was a nip in the air now that autumn had come and the leaves were falling from the trees like confetti at a wedding but the place was still beautiful.

'I thought I might go for a good long walk this afternoon,' Niamh said innocently as she was mashing the potatoes. Why did I say that? she scolded herself silently and yet deep down she had always known that she would go.

'I'm pleased to hear it, lass,' Maeve answered. 'You've gone through the whole place like a whirling dervish this morning, so you have. I've no doubt Roisin will be happy to look after Roddy while you're gone. A bit of fresh air will do you good and blow the cobwebs away.'

Niamh avoided looking at her. She was ashamed and hated lying to her gran'ma but she couldn't seem to help herself where Ben was concerned. Maeve's plaster had now been removed and she was pottering about again and Niamh knew that soon it would be time to go home.

Lowering her head, she got on with the job in hand and soon after the men came in hungry for their dinner and she had no time to think of anything but filling them up.

By two o'clock the pots were washed, dried and returned to their rightful place and Maeve told her, 'Why don't you slip off now, lass? There's nothing for you to do until teatime apart from a bit of ironing – and that can wait, so it can, although I might sit at the table and have a go at it myself. I realise you must be missing your mammy and be keen to get home now.'

'I'll gladly stay as long as you need me, Gran'ma,' Niamh assured her but she still skipped off to her room without protest to get ready. It only took her a matter of minutes to wash her hands and face and brush her hair, and then she looked at herself critically in the mirror before pinching her cheeks to bring a little colour to them. That'll have to do, she thought, snatching up her shawl, then she bowled downstairs, planted a kiss on her gran'ma's cheek and was on her way. After climbing to the top of the rise she saw Declan and Liam working in the fields below her then turned and made her way down the other side towards a small copse.

She had gone no more than a little way into it when Ben stepped out from behind an enormous oak tree.

'Hello, alanna.'

Her face lit up at the sight of him and without a word they fell into step as they moved further into the copse. In the centre of it was a large pool and there was nothing to be heard but the sound of the birds and the breeze sighing through the trees. Autumn had kissed the leaves with gold and they were drifting down to form a carpet beneath their feet.

As one they sat down and Niamh hugged her knees and sighed with contentment. 'It's so peaceful here. You could almost think we were the only two people in the whole world.'

'If only we were,' Ben said softly. 'Then all would be right with the world.'

They watched a fat water rat run down the bank and plop into the pool and Ben laughed. 'Creatures have it easy, don't they? They love where they like. There are no complications for them as there are for us.'

Niamh nodded sadly and then she felt Ben untie the ribbon that held back her hair so that it fell in shimmering copper waves about her shoulders.

'I know I shouldn't say this but I still love you,' he sighed. 'I always have and I always will. Oh, I've tried walking out with other lasses but they can never hold a candle to you.'

'I still love you too,' Niamh admitted with a catch in her voice. 'And I hope you know that I would never have married Samuel if I'd had another choice.'

His hand moved to her cheek then and when he drew her towards him she went willingly. His lips gently brushed hers and before they knew it they were lying side by side and she was wrapped in his arms as it had been meant to be. At one stage he would have pulled away but Niamh clasped him to her.

'No, don't stop,' she pleaded. 'I've waited too long for you, Ben. I want to belong to you.'

'Are you quite sure, me darling girl?' His face was concerned as he pulled himself up onto his elbow to stare down at her. Niamh's initiation to sex had been brutal and humiliating on the terrible night that Connie had been conceived, and she had often wondered if she would ever be able to give herself willingly to a man, but all her fears fled now like mist in the morning as Ben gently stroked her breast. Her nipple hardened and she groaned with longing.

'Quite sure.' Her voice was husky with her need of him and he said no more but loved her as she had never been loved before.

Every touch led her to new heights of passion and when he finally entered her she felt as if she would die with joy. He had awakened feelings that she had never known she had, and she moved with him until they reached their climax. At last she felt that she was completely his for all time.

'I didn't hurt you, did I?' he asked when it was over and she lay curled against his broad chest.

'It was wonderful – I never knew that I could feel like that.'

'But what do we do now?' he asked and she heard the pain in his voice. 'I don't think I can bear to let you go back to that beast.'

'I have no choice.' Niamh was coming back down to earth with a bang. 'I'm Samuel's wife by law – but my heart will always belong to you.'

'Then you must divorce him.'

Despair coursed through her. 'You know that I can never do that. The Catholic Church would never countenance it and besides, it would break the family's hearts. They'd disown me. But don't worry, I shall come to see you as often as I can, and when I do, we'll make time to be together. That's the best that I can offer you.'

'Then that will have to be enough because I'd rather have

a few snatched moments with you than a whole lifetime with someone else.'

In a sombre mood now they dressed and began to walk back through the copse hand in hand.

'I should tell you that I decided this week that I'm going to meet my mother,' Ben told her then. 'Maeve received another letter from her so I think it's time.'

'Then I hope it goes well for you.' Niamh squeezed his hand, remembering how as a child he had longed to find out who his parents were. She was pleased that after his mother had tracked him down his wish would finally be fulfilled.

'It will be strange because I felt bitter towards her when she first contacted Maeve, wondering why she hadn't done it years ago. But now that I've grown up I realise that sometimes things happen to people that they can't change. You and I are a prime example, I suppose, for if Samuel hadn't raped you we would be married by now.'

Niamh nodded; he was right. She hoped with all her heart that meeting his mother would bring him a measure of peace. Dear Ben deserved that at the very least.

'Why, you're looking bright-eyed and bushy-tailed, me darlin',' Maeve commented when Niamh entered the kitchen.

'Oh, I enjoyed my walk.' Niamh hurried away to her room to hang her shawl up as she hugged the time she had spent with Ben to herself. She knew that from now on she would never be the same again and thoughts of him would help her through her darkest hours.

# *Chapter Twenty-Three*

*Late October 1920*

'Look, Dilly – a squirrel!' Roddy said excitedly, pointing at a tree as they strolled through Riversley Park late one afternoon. The days were shortening and Dilly knew that they should head for home soon. Mary had gone to visit her mother and Niamh was minding the shop so Dilly had taken the opportunity to get the child out for a little fresh air. She was in a happy mood as Seamus had surprised her by returning with Niamh from Ireland. He was now staying at Niamh's house with them as Dilly still hadn't gone back to her rooms above the shop yet. He had settled very well and it was lovely to have him home although he was still a long way from being able to take up any sort of full-time employment as yet.

'Yes, pet, I see him.' Dilly smiled at Roddy indulgently. He raced off ahead of her, so intent on watching the squirrel that he wasn't looking where he was going and cannoned straight into a gentleman who was walking towards them.

'Whoa there, laddie,' the man said, catching him by the shoulders so that he wouldn't fall.

'I'm so sorry,' Dilly apologised as she hurried towards them. 'I'm afraid he wasn't paying attention. Say sorry to the gentleman immediately, Roddy.'

'S-sorry, sir,' Roddy muttered contritely.

The man chuckled and Dilly thought that he looked vaguely familiar. He was tall and well dressed in a smart suit, beneath which he wore a crisp white shirt and one of the ties that men seemed to be favouring rather than cravats nowadays.

'Oh, don't tell him off, please. He was only being a boy,' the man said with a wink at Roddy. Then, 'It's Mrs Carey, isn't it?'

'Yes, it is. Do I know you?'

'Not really, but your dress shop was a favourite of my wife's. She died six months ago, unfortunately.'

'Oh, you must be Mr Price,' Dilly answered as she recalled his wife. 'I was so sorry to hear of her death. She was a lovely lady.'

'Yes, she was.' He became silent for a moment but then fixing his smile back in place he raised his hat and said, 'Well, I mustn't keep you any longer. Good day, Mrs Carey, sir.'

Roddy giggled; he'd never been called sir before but he liked it. The man bowed and moved on and taking Dilly's hand, the little boy chattered, 'He was a nice man, wasn't he, Dilly?'

'Yes, he was, pet,' she answered, and intent on getting home and into the warm she pushed the incident from her mind.

The next time she encountered Mr Price was two weeks later. It was a blustery day and Dilly was arranging a dress on the mannequin in the shop window when the bell above the door tinkled. She turned to see an attractive young woman and Mr Price enter the shop.

'Good morning.' Dilly beamed, genuinely pleased to see them. The young woman had often visited the shop with her mother and Dilly liked her.

Mr Price removed his hat and returned her smile. 'I'm hoping you'll be able to help us, Mrs Carey,' he said. 'My daughter is getting married in June next year, but so far she hasn't been able to find a gown that she likes. I'm afraid she has quite a distinct idea of what she is after, and seeing as she and my wife set great store by your flair for fashion I wondered if you might be able to come up with a design that would please her.'

'Well, I shall certainly do my best,' Dilly answered. She had made many bespoke gowns for his wife and knew that the cost was no object. Mr Price owned a very lucrative solicitors practice in town and was highly regarded. 'Perhaps we could begin by looking through the pattern books so that you can show me what sort of design and material appeal to you,' Dilly suggested. 'And then if need be, we could combine a few ideas to come up with your perfect dress.'

'That sounds wonderful,' the young woman smiled so Dilly hurried away to get the book and opened it on the smart new counter that the carpenter had made for her.

The girl turned the pages slowly, studying each dress intently. 'I like the top of that one but I don't like the skirt, it's too full,' she told Dilly, pointing at a certain design. 'I was wanting a straighter skirt, perhaps heavily beaded?'

Dilly eyed her up and down. She certainly had the figure for the design she had in mind, for she was quite tall for a girl and slender as a reed.

'That could certainly be done.' Dilly turned a few more

pages and pointed to the skirt of another dress. 'Was that anything like you had in mind?'

'Yes, that's exactly what I want,' the girl said excitedly.

'Then we shall be looking at a satin lining with a chiffon overlay to get that effect,' Dilly told her. The style that she wanted was going to mean hours of work, but Dilly knew she was quite capable of doing it. Indeed, she had handmade Patty's dress very successfully. 'We could perhaps do a scalloped hemline?' she suggested then. 'But do you want short or long sleeves and would you like ivory or white for the colour?'

'Short sleeves, I think, seeing as the wedding is in early June, and I think I'd like white. What do you think, Daddy?'

'That's far too many "thinks" for me to cope with.' He chuckled. 'You must have exactly what you want, my dear. I'm afraid I am but a man so have no idea at all about ladies' fashions, but thankfully Mrs Carey seems to know exactly the sort of look you're hoping for, so I'm happy to step back and just pay for it. That's the easy bit, from what I can see of it.'

'Would you like me to give you a rough idea of what it might cost?' Dilly asked. This was probably going to be one of the most expensive dresses she had ever taken on, and she intended to make this one personally. Thankfully her sewing machine upstairs had survived the fire and would be as good as new after a thorough clean.

'Not at all,' he assured her. 'I'm just grateful that you seem to understand what she wants. It's all gobbledegook to me!'

'Then what I need to do next is visit my supplier in Birmingham to get some samples of really good quality fabric for you to choose from. Once we've done that I shall show you some sketches and we can go from there. How does that sound, Miss Price?'

'Oh please, Mrs Carey, call me Eleanor,' the young woman said. 'And it sounds just wonderful. You're the first person I've spoken to who seems to understand what I'm looking for.'

'I promise you shall have the dress of your dreams if I have anything to do with it,' Dilly vowed. 'But now let's see . . .' She consulted her diary. 'I could have the samples here for you by next Tuesday if I go to Birmingham on Monday, so what day would you like to come in and look at the designs? I shall start work on them straight away.'

'Wednesday then,' Eleanor chirped brightly. 'The sooner we get started on it the better as far as I'm concerned.'

'Wednesday it is then. Shall we say about eleven o'clock?'

Dilly showed them to the door where Mr Price shook her hand warmly. 'Thank you, Mrs Carey. This is the happiest I've seen my girl since her mother died. It's hard for her not to have her mamma here to help her choose her dress and plan the wedding, so could you but know it you've just taken a great weight off my mind.'

'It's my pleasure,' Dilly assured him and with a little bow he was gone.

'I've been commissioned to design and make Eleanor Price's wedding dress,' Dilly told Max proudly that evening.

'Is that Henry Price the solicitor's daughter?'

Dilly nodded as Max lit a cigar. 'Nice chap, Henry is,' he commented. 'He lost his wife not so long ago, I believe, and he's a brilliant solicitor. He has a lovely house in Hartshill down by the castle ruins. I see him at my gentleman's club sometimes. He only has the one child and I heard she's marrying one of his partner's sons. Seeing as he's very wealthy, you should feel honoured that he's chosen you to make her dress. I'm sure that he could afford a London designer if he wanted to.'

'I know,' Dilly answered, 'but I'm determined to make this the best dress ever, even if I have to stay up working on it every single night from now until next June.'

'I've no doubt it will be quite amazing.' Max knew what Dilly was like when she had set her mind to something, and his daughter-in-law Patty had looked so radiant in Dilly's creation.

'So I've decided it's time I put my rooms above the shop to rights now. I've been so busy downstairs that I haven't paid much heed to up there, but after work each evening now I'm going to start on the paintwork.'

'There's no need for you to do that,' Seamus piped up from his chair at the side of the fire. 'I'm quite well enough to slosh a bit of paint about now. I can always rest if I get tired so I'll go and buy some paint tomorrow and get started on it straight away. It shouldn't take long now that you've washed all the walls.'

'Oh, that would be wonderful, pet.' Dilly smiled at him affectionately. 'And I can get Hilda and Peggy to run up some new curtains for me.'

'What's this then? You're not plannin' on leavin' us, are you?' Mary asked as she carried a tea tray into the room.

'Probably not for at least another couple of weeks,' Dilly answered, taking the tray from her.

Mary's face fell. 'I'll miss yer,' she muttered forlornly and Dilly couldn't help but notice how her eyes strayed to Seamus. It was then that it hit her and she could have laughed aloud. Mary was smitten, bless her, but Dilly had been so busy that she hadn't noticed. Admittedly she'd been pleased to see how well they got on together. Seamus always seemed brighter when Mary was about because she made him laugh. But now . . . how could I have missed it? she asked herself. She wondered if Seamus felt the same and was tempted to give him a little prod in the girl's direction.

She couldn't think of anyone she would sooner have as a daughter-in-law than Mary, for the girl had a heart of pure gold – but then she thought better of it. If it was meant to be, it would be without any intervention from her – and even if she and Seamus did move back to the rooms above the shop, it wasn't as if they were going to be a million miles away, was it?

She caught Max's eye then and without a word being said she knew that he had read her mind. Things were looking up again at last and Dilly was determined to put the last few awful months from her mind.

The very next morning as promised, Seamus arrived at the shop loaded down with as many tins of paint and paint-brushes as he could carry. He was eager to start, saying, 'I'll go up and get changed, then I'll begin on the sitting room.'

Dilly smiled at him gratefully before returning her attention to the customer she was serving, an elderly lady who was after a warm pair of gloves. Dilly had already laid every pair she had in the shop on the counter before her but the woman was finding it difficult to choose.

'If I may make a suggestion, the navy-blue wool pair would match your coat and hat beautifully.'

'Hmm, do you know, I think you may be right, my dear. I'll take them.'

Dilly stifled a sigh of relief and hastily wrapped them up before the woman could change her mind again.

By lunchtime Seamus had painted two walls and the place was beginning to look better already, but he looked tired.

'That's enough for today,' Dilly said bossily, taking the paintbrush from his hand. 'Get yourself round to Niamh's and have a rest. I've no doubt Mary will have some lunch ready for you.'

'But what about your lunch?'

'Mary always packs me some sandwiches to bring with me, bless her. In fact, I shall have them now with a nice cup of tea while the shop is quiet, so be off with you and leave me in peace!'

With a grin Seamus went into the bedroom to get changed and once he'd gone Dilly sighed with satisfaction as she looked around. Soon she would be back in her own little home and life would return to normal.

Eleanor Price returned the following week as arranged to look at the sketches Dilly had drawn and the material samples.

The young woman beamed with pleasure at Dilly's sketches as her father backed towards the door, keen to make his escape.

'It looks as if you two ladies are going to have your heads bent over those for some time so I'll call back for you in an hour, shall I?'

'Yes, please, Daddy.' Eleanor was busy inspecting the various crystals and pearls that Dilly had laid out and he smiled indulgently as he slipped away.

'I think this satin and chiffon would work well together,' Dilly advised. 'I'm afraid it is the most expensive but it hangs beautifully when it's made up, although of course the choice is yours.'

'Oh I entirely agree, Mrs Carey,' Eleanor said immediately, then leaning towards her she added quietly, 'Thank you so much for all the trouble you're going to for me. It's been quite daunting trying to choose things for my wedding without Mummy here to help me. She would have loved coming to advise on the dress. But at least I have you now.'

When tears welled in her eyes, Dilly's kind heart went out to her and she squeezed her hand gently. The poor lass!

A girl needed her mother at a time like this but she would do all she could for her now.

'It's all sorted,' Eleanor told her father when he returned. 'I've chosen the design I want and Mrs Carey has taken all my measurements so she'll be starting on the dress very soon now.'

He blew out an exaggerated breath of relief. 'Thank goodness for that. I might get a bit of peace now.' But his eyes were twinkling and Dilly could see how much he adored his daughter.

They left the shop in a happy frame of mind and when the shop doorbell tinkled later that day she glanced up and was shocked to see a local florist holding the largest bunch of roses she had ever seen.

'For me?' she gasped, wondering who on earth they could be from. They were clearly hot-house grown, and must have cost a fortune. She slid the little card from amongst the blooms and blushed as she read, *With thanks for making my daughter smile again, kind regards, Henry Price.*

For the first time she allowed herself to admit what a handsome man Henry was. He was probably a few years older than her and his once dark hair was now peppered with grey, but his eyes were kindly and a lovely violet blue, the same as his daughter's. He was tall and stately-looking too, but then Dilly scolded herself: he was merely being kind, there was no sense in reading any more into the gift.

Smiling to herself, she went about her work and when she closed the shop she carried the roses home and got Mary to stand them in a vase for her.

'Got an admirer, have you, Mammy?' Seamus teased when Mary stood the blooms in pride of place in the middle of the sideboard.

'What's this about an admirer then?'

Max had just entered the room and Dilly felt herself blushing. 'It's just Seamus being silly. Henry Price sent them to me as a thank you for agreeing to make his daughter's wedding dress.'

'Did he now?' Max crossed to the flowers and plucked the small card from amongst them. Dilly couldn't help but notice that he didn't look at all pleased as he read it and wondered suddenly if he might be jealous. Angry with herself for having such thoughts, she changed the subject, asking, 'How is Camilla? I haven't had time to pop round and see her for a while.'

Max took a seat opposite Seamus, 'I'm afraid she's beginning to get rather aggressive from time to time now,' he said worriedly. 'But I have to say Bessie is marvellous with her. In fact, she seems to be the only one that Camilla will respond to now. Bessie has endless patience with her and I don't know what I'd do without her. She's proved to be an absolute godsend!'

If only she could be that way with Roddy, Dilly thought, but she didn't voice this aloud.

'It's strange,' Max went on. 'Bessie says that Camilla has times when she can talk quite lucidly about things that happened in the past and yet she can't remember what she did the day before. Dr Beasley still seems to think that she would be better off in an asylum but I'm not so sure.'

'Only you can make that decision,' Dilly said wisely. 'After all, you know her better than anyone else.'

'I did,' he said slowly. 'But to be honest she's like a different person now. I don't recognise her at all. Still, on a happier note, little George is coming along a treat. I had a rare visit from Penelope today when she brought him to see me, and he's a grand little chap. He's the spitting image of his father at that age actually. Oscar seems to be quite taken with him although he and Penelope don't appear to be getting along any better. I was hoping that the baby would bring them closer.'

'I think I'll go through to the kitchen and see how Mary is getting along with the dinner,' Seamus interrupted, and Max watched him go with a thoughtful expression on his face.

'Those two, by contrast, seem to be getting along rather well, don't they?' he asked and Dilly chuckled as she picked up a piece of sewing she had brought home from the shop to work on.

'They do – but then Mary is a lovely girl. How are the newlyweds doing?'

'Oh, still very lovey-dovey,' he grinned. 'And long may it last. Patty has started at the hospital and loves it and Lawrence is back at work now too.'

'And still no word from Samuel?'

Max shook his head, his face drawn now. 'Not so much as a dickey-bird. But he'll turn up like a bad penny no doubt when his money runs out.' He felt tempted to tell Dilly that Samuel knew that Dilly was Olivia's mother, but decided against it. Dilly would only worry about it as he himself was doing.

Dilly had no doubt that Samuel would reappear when he wanted something, and didn't look forward to seeing him again at all. Lawrence's twin brother had turned into a thoroughly disagreeable young man, there was no denying it.

# Chapter Twenty-Four

It was a week later when Eleanor Price and her father visited the shop again. Dilly was surprised to see them as they'd agreed that there was no rush to get busy on the dress until after Christmas, even though the beadwork would mean hours of laborious stitching.

'Good morning,' she greeted them.

Eleanor beamed. 'Oh, Mrs Carey, I'm afraid I've come to ask you to take on even more work if you're able to.'

When Dilly raised an inquisitive eyebrow she rushed on, 'The thing is, I'm planning on having four little flower girls and two page boys, and I was wondering . . . seeing as you're making my dress, do you think you might be able to make their outfits too?'

'Well, I . . .' Dilly was a bit taken aback. 'What sort of outfits did you have in mind?' she asked then.

'I've done a rough sketch of what I'd like the girls to wear here.' Eleanor produced it with a flourish. 'I'm afraid it's nowhere near as good as the sketches you did, but I'm sure it will give you the general idea.'

Dilly studied the drawing and thought that contrary to what Eleanor had said it was actually quite good. The dresses had round necks and fitted waists that flared into very full skirts. There were short puffed sleeves and a wide sash at the waist, and they made an attractive picture.

'They look straightforward enough,' she said cautiously. 'And what age are the flower girls?'

'They're my little cousins and they range in age from five to nine years old.'

'And what about the page boys?'

'They'll be six and seven.' Eleanor produced another drawing and again Dilly was impressed.

'Ah, so you want silk shirts and matching waistcoats and trousers?'

Eleanor nodded. 'Yes, but again I'm going to need your help there. I'd thought of having lilac for the girls but then that would clash with whatever colour the boys were wearing and I really don't think they'd take kindly to wearing lilac, do you?'

'Not at all,' Dilly agreed with a smile. 'So why don't you stick to white satin for the girls' dresses and the boys' shirts, then we could use perhaps blue sashes for the girls' waistbands and blue velvet for the boys' waistcoats and trousers. We could also do a chiffon overlay for the girls so that they tie in with your dress. Royal blue might look very attractive against the white. What do you think?'

Eleanor mulled the idea over then nodded enthusiastically.

'Freesias will be in season in June,' Dilly went on, 'so the girls could perhaps carry some lilac and blue ones to tone with the sashes on their dresses and in their posies and they would smell wonderful. You could use the same flowers for decorating the church and the tables at your reception then too if you wanted to.'

'Oh you are so clever!' Eleanor impulsively stepped forward and gave her a hug as Henry Price looked on indulgently.

'Does this mean you are willing to take on the extra work then, Mrs Carey? I know it would make my daughter very happy if you would agree.'

Dilly's mind raced ahead. This would be the biggest commission she had ever taken on, and it would mean a tremendous amount of work, although she could let Hilda and Peggy help with the girls' dresses and the boys' outfits. The rooms upstairs were almost ready for her to move back into again now, thanks to Seamus, so she could work on them in the evenings as well as in the day when the shop was quiet.

'Very well, I accept,' Dilly told them. 'I shall fetch you some samples of material back from the suppliers the next time I go to Birmingham and then I shall need them all to come in for fittings, but what you have to understand is that children of their ages grow all the time so I won't be able to finish their outfits until just before the wedding. I know when my children were that age they seemed to shoot up at least half an inch a month!'

'I hadn't thought of that,' Eleanor said, and she then wandered off to look at the clothes on the rails as Dilly smiled at Henry Price.

'Thank you so much for the lovely roses but there was really no need,' she said, and felt herself blush like a schoolgirl.

He waved aside her thanks with a broad smile. 'You are very welcome,' he told her, then his face became serious as he lowered his voice to confide, 'Eleanor was going to postpone the wedding to be honest because it will only be a

213

year since her mother died. But rightly or wrongly I told her that I thought she should go ahead with her plans. It's what Emma would have wanted and this mourning period is rather outdated since the war, don't you think? So many people lost loved ones but they just had to get on with things.'

'You're right,' Dilly said quietly. 'I lost my son as it happens but I still had to earn a living, hence this shop.'

He looked around before saying, 'It's a credit to you, Mrs Carey, and yet another sign of how times are changing. Who would have believed a few years ago that women could be successful in business? I must admit I'm rather traditional and like to think of the man as the wage earner, but I also agree it's high time women were given equal opportunities. My wife felt the same. In fact, she was an active member of the Suffrage Movement. It isn't easy for anyone at the moment, is it? The country isn't recovering as quickly as we had all hoped it would after the war, and many women are finding it hard now that those men that came back are returning to their jobs. The women did a brilliant job of keeping everything running while the men were away and have become used to a measure of independence now. But oh dear, I'd better get my wallet out. It looks as if Eleanor has found a dress she likes.'

Dilly would have enjoyed carrying on with their conversation, but she went to help Eleanor, who was having difficulty deciding between two dresses.

'Hmm . . . I love this pink one, but the blue is lovely too,' she mused, holding them both at arm's length. 'What do you think, Mrs Carey? Which one should I try on?'

'Try them both, darling,' Mr Price prompted affectionately. 'I won't have you to myself to spoil for much longer so I'm going to do it whilst I may.'

Eleanor tripped happily away to the changing rooms and

while she was gone Dilly said suddenly, 'Would you like a cup of tea while you're waiting, Mr Price?'

She was instantly embarrassed. She had never offered a customer refreshments before, but then she had never been commissioned to make so many outfits for one person before so she hoped that it would be all right and that Mr Price wouldn't think she was being forward.

He smiled, revealing very straight white teeth. 'A cup of tea would be very welcome,' he answered. 'I'm afraid Eleanor can be some time when she starts to try clothes on. And do please call me Henry. We're going to be seeing quite a lot of each other in the build-up to the wedding with all the fittings, et cetera, and Mr Price is so formal.'

'I – I'll try to remember – Henry.' Dilly came over all flustered. 'Will you excuse me while I go and make the tea?' And with that she fled into the little room at the back to put the kettle on to boil.

When she returned with a laden tea tray shortly afterwards, Eleanor was admiring herself in the long cheval mirror that stood to one side of the fitting room. She was wearing the blue dress and it certainly suited her and fitted like a glove.

'Oh dear, I've already tried the pink one on and that was lovely too. I don't know which one to choose now.'

'Then have them both,' her father urged her, as Dilly poured the tea with a shaking hand. For some reason she was suddenly all of a dither round him. 'Now go and get changed, darling. I'm in court with a client this afternoon and after I've had this lovely cup of tea I shall have to drop you off back at home, I'm afraid.'

As Eleanor skipped away to do as she was told, Dilly couldn't help but remark, 'She's a charming girl, an absolute credit to you and your wife if I may be so bold as to say so, Mr . . . Henry.'

'Why thank you, Mrs Carey. My wife and I were very fortunate because, even though Eleanor was our only child and we rather spoiled her, it never affected her lovely nature. I'm going to miss her terribly when she's married. Still at least I'm happy with her choice of husband. Paul is the son of one of my partners in the law firm and he adores the very ground she walks on, I'm pleased to say.'

Dilly couldn't help but sigh with regret as she recalled Niamh's wedding day. The poor girl had looked like a lamb being led to slaughter . . . but she supposed it was too late for regrets now.

'I suppose you ought to call me Dilly if I am to use your Christian name,' she said then, feeling ridiculously shy.

'Dilly! How charming, it really suits you,' he told her, and to her annoyance she found herself blushing again. Thankfully the mood was broken when Eleanor emerged from the fitting room and Dilly hurried forward to take the dresses from her and wrap them up.

'Would you mind me being very forward and making a suggestion?' Mr Price said then, and Dilly looked at him questioningly. 'The thing is, whilst the bags you are using for the clothes are quite adequate, I can't help thinking that something a little more elaborate might draw in more customers. If I can use an example, my wife always used to insist on shopping at a certain London store when we visited the capital because they had rather nice bags with the name of the shop emblazoned on the sides. It's pure snobbery, of course, and smarter bags would cost a little more to have made, but ladies like to be seen to be shopping at smart establishments, and little touches like that can set them apart from the rest. I do hope that I haven't offended you? That wasn't my intention.'

'No, you haven't,' Dilly said, staring thoughtfully at the plain brown carrier bag in which she had just placed

Eleanor's new dresses. She'd never really taken much notice of them before but now that Henry had mentioned it she saw that they did look very cheap indeed. The sort of thing that people would probably use for shopping in the market.

'And may I also suggest – perhaps a nice hand-painted sign above the shop, something classy? Apart from the clothes displayed in the window, no one would know this is a ladies' dress shop at present.'

'Do you know, Henry, I think those are excellent ideas.' Dilly used his Christian name more easily now. 'I hadn't really given a lot of thought to the finer points, as I've been too busy getting the shop up and running, especially after the fire.'

'As it happens, a very good friend of mine happens to be a brilliant sign-writer. Would you like me to ask him to call and see you?'

Dilly hesitated. All of the things he had suggested were going to cost money and she was still trying to fully restock the shop after the fire, but then her chin came up and she told him, 'Yes, please. I'd appreciate that. I just have to decide what I'm going to call the place now.'

'Nothing too elaborate,' he suggested. 'You don't want people to think that it's too expensive for them to walk through the door.'

She nodded, her mind already racing ahead as she took the money for the dresses and bade them good day. She then wandered around the shop trying to look at it through a customer's eye. Yes, she decided, Henry was quite right. It was time to move on to the next stage.

Dilly was telling Niamh and Seamus about Henry's ideas that evening when Max appeared. As Seamus rose to get him a drink, Max raised an eyebrow and asked, 'So what's all this then?'

'I was just telling them that Henry Price made a couple of very good suggestions today when he came to the shop with his daughter. They've now asked me to make the flower girls' dresses and the page-boy outfits as well as the wedding dress.'

'Oh, it's *Henry* now, is it?'

Ignoring the hint of sarcasm – or was it jealousy in his voice? – Dilly hurried on to explain and when she was done, Max had the good grace to acknowledge the man's shrewd business sense. 'He's quite right and I've had an idea too.'

'Really? What is it?'

'As you know, I have a couple of hat factories in Atherstone. Most of the finished hats go to London but I wondered, seeing as you seem intent on doing bridalwear, if it wouldn't be a good idea for you to have a few hats in the shops? I could let you have them at a very reasonable rate on a sale-or-return basis for a time if that would help.'

Max would willingly have supplied Dilly with a selection of hats for no charge at all, but knowing how fiercely independent she was he knew better than to offer.

Dilly's mind was doing overtime as she mulled this over. 'Perhaps I could start to stock mother-of-the-bride outfits too?' she said slowly. 'What do you think, Max?'

'Well, there's certainly nowhere around here that offers that service so I think it's a very good idea. You could always give it a try, and if it doesn't work out you haven't really lost a great deal, have you? But then you would be offering a complete wedding package to a bride: her outfit, the mother's and the attendants' too. I have a feeling it could be very lucrative indeed. But remember, you will be catering more for the upper classes, so the outfits would have to be very good quality.'

'Actually, I don't agree,' Dilly said. 'I would like to cater for all classes. Why shouldn't working-class families be able to have a nice wedding on a budget too?'

Max smiled. He had a feeling that even if Dilly went on to become a millionaire she would never forget her roots and he couldn't fault her for that.

'Would you let me get just a few outfits together before I decide on the colour of the hats?' she asked then and he nodded.

'Of course. The milliners at my factory will even make up your own designs in your choice of materials if you'd like them to.'

Dilly was getting really excited now and that night she couldn't sleep as ideas raced around in her head. At last everything seemed to be coming together – if only Olivia would leave London and return home, where she belonged!

# Chapter Twenty-Five

*Mid-November 1920*

'Are you quite sure that you won't change your mind and come back with me?' Dilly asked Seamus one last time. She was ready to return to her rooms above the shop now but Seamus had decided to stay with Niamh. Dilly wasn't really surprised, the way Mary waited on him hand and foot. She had an idea the girl would have walked to the moon and back for him if he had asked her to, and now she suspected Mary's feelings were not one-sided. She'd noticed the way her son's eyes would follow the girl about the room and she thought it was no bad thing.

'He'll be fine here, Mammy,' Niamh assured her. 'And you know you are more than welcome to stay too – but saying that, I can understand you wanting to be in your own place again. If Seamus stays here though you'll be able to set your sewing machine up in his room and give yourself a little more space in the sitting room.'

'There is that in it, I suppose.' Dilly kissed both of her

children soundly. She had already said goodbye to Mary, who was now upstairs putting Roddy to bed. 'Ah, here's Max now,' she said as she saw his car pull up outside. 'Good night, both.'

Lifting her bag, she carried it outside and once Max had placed it on the back seat she climbed into the passenger seat at the front beside him.

'Looking forward to going home?' he asked as he started the car and pulled away from the kerb. It was a bitterly cold night and the frost on the pavements sparkled in the headlights.

'I am, but after the fire I'm a little nervous too in case whoever started it decides to come back again,' she admitted.

'I don't think that will happen.' Max frowned grimly as he thought of Samuel. There had still been no sign of him and the longer he stayed away, the more convinced Max was that it had been his son who had started the fire. The cowardly side of him half hoped that his son would never return, for if he did and Max had proof that he had been the arsonist, he didn't know how he would live with himself.

In Enniskerry, Ben was pacing nervously up and down the small living room in his little cottage behind the blacksmith's, for very soon now he would be meeting his birth mother for the first time.

He paused to glance about and inwardly groaned, wishing now that he had made more of an effort to tidy the place up. He could turn his hand to most things and prided himself on being a good blacksmith, but when it came to housework he knew that he failed dismally. Every now and again, Shelagh or Roisin would descend and scrub the place from top to bottom but it soon looked as bad again. In truth he had little interest in the place. It was just somewhere to lay his head – although he knew his attitude would have been very different if things had worked out between himself and Niamh. She would have kept the place as neat as a new pin and taken pride in it. He shook his head – it was no use dwelling on that now. Then the tap on the door that he'd been waiting for echoed around the small room and he gulped and yanked at his collar, suddenly regretting that he'd ever agreed to this meeting in the first place. He coughed to clear his throat then straightened his spine. It was too late to go back now – and how hard could it be? If he and the woman who called herself his mother didn't like each other then they need never meet again.

Grasping the door handle he swung it open then stared in shock at the lady standing there. It was like looking at an older female version of himself and he had to stop himself from slamming the door in her face.

'C-come in,' he said hoarsely.

She stepped into the light and he instantly saw that she looked just as nervous as he felt. Her eyes were full of tears and she was blinking rapidly to stop them from falling.

'Hello, Benjamin . . .' she faltered. 'It's so wonderful to meet you at last. There have been times when I feared this day would never come.'

He bit back the hasty retort that sprang to his lips. Surely she wasn't trying to make him feel guilty when it was she who had abandoned *him* when he was just a tiny wean? Maeve had explained why she had done it and at the time he had felt a measure of sympathy for her, but suddenly the resentment and the hurt were back and he wanted to verbally lash her.

'Sit down.' He motioned to a chair and she perched on the edge of it like a frightened bird that might take flight at any second as she clutched her bag.

'I'm so grateful that you agreed to see me – I know I don't

222

deserve it,' she said in a small voice and a solitary tear slid down her cheek. She wanted to grab him and hold him and tell him how very much she had yearned for him over the years, but Elizabeth McFarren was a wise woman and sensed that he wasn't ready for that.

'I was just about to make some tea. Will you join me in a cup?' Ben couldn't think of anything else to say to her and was relieved when she nodded. Making the tea would give him something to focus on rather than just standing there looking like a tongue-tied fool. Crossing to the kettle, he pushed it into the heart of the fire, glancing at her from the corner of his eye. She was dressed like a real lady. Who would have thought that he, the ragged little soul that had run away from the orphanage all those years ago, could have been born to someone like this?

'Are they making you comfortable at the hotel?' he asked then as he arranged two cups and saucers on a small tray and spooned tea leaves into the heavy brown tea pot.

'Very, thank you. They are so kind. Benjamin I—'

Her words were halted when the kettle started to sing and Ben hastened to snatch it from the fire.

Sometime later when he had handed her a drink an uncomfortable silence settled between them until Elizabeth eventually took a deep breath and broke it. 'I do realise how difficult this must be for you and I'm very grateful that you agreed to see me. You must feel quite bitter towards me and I don't blame you for that. My only excuse is that when I had you I was very young and foolish, and I couldn't see any other option but to let you go. If it's any consolation to you, I can truthfully say that there has never been a day when I didn't think of you, and in my own way I have probably suffered as much as you have – which serves me right. But the reason I have come here today is to tell you that I will be leaving Ireland soon. I should have gone

223

months ago but I couldn't bring myself to leave until I knew if you would see me or not.'

Benjamin raised an eyebrow. This was their first meeting and here she was telling him that she was going away again. It would have been laughable if it hadn't been so painful, but she shocked him then when she went on, 'I never came here expecting you to fall into my arms and call me Mother. I gave up that right long ago. But what I would like is for you to think of me without bitterness. That is the best I can expect.'

She took a nervous sip of her tea and returned her cup to the saucer, which was wobbling dangerously. 'I wanted you to know that when anything happens to me, I have named you in my will as my sole heir.'

Ben opened his mouth to object as pride surged through him but she held her hand up to silence him. '*Please* don't deny me that. At least I can leave with the satisfaction of knowing that you will be well set up then. The other alternative is . . . you could come with me and we could try to build a relationship.'

'Come where?'

'I am going to live with my sister and her husband in New York. She's been asking me ever since Lionel, your half-brother, was killed in the war. But I couldn't go until you had made a decision about whether you would see me or not.'

There were genuine tears in her eyes again now, and despite the fact that he had been determined not to like her, Ben felt himself softening, although it hurt him to know he had a half-brother he had never been allowed to meet. Life didn't always run true to plan as he and Niamh had found to their cost, and it must have been the same for her. If what she said was true – and she seemed an honest person – then she had been made to pay all her life for one mistake.

'If you should decide to come with me, you would be made very welcome,' she told him. 'My sister knows all about you and would love to meet you. And I believe there are endless possibilities there for a young man like yourself. Will you at least consider it?'

Ben sighed before shaking his head. 'I thank you for the opportunity but I have me business here an' me fami . . .' His voice trailed away but she nodded in understanding.

'You were about to say "your family" and that is just what they are. Maeve has been far more of a mother to you than I ever have, and I shall never be able to thank her enough for the way she's cared for you. When I went to see her, she told me that you had grown into a young man that any mother could be proud of – and she was right. I know that I could never take her place in your affections, but I was hoping that you could at least come to regard me as a friend. Do you think you could ever do that, Benjamin?'

He stared at her soberly for a moment before nodding. 'Yes . . . I think I could, but it will be difficult if you're going to be living on the other side of the ocean.'

'Not at all,' she disagreed. 'We can write to each other and I shall visit you at least once a year if you'll allow me to. And who knows? Perhaps in time you'll feel able to come and join me.'

Ben doubted that would ever happen. It would mean he would never get to see Niamh again and he knew that he couldn't bear that. At least here he got to see her occasionally and that was what kept him going.

'Won't you tell me a little about your childhood now?' she asked hopefully and before Ben knew it he was doing just that, and he realised with the telling that it hadn't been all bad, after all.

'Father Donahue was always kind to me when I was in the orphanage,' he confided, 'and it was him who had a hand in me coming to Enniskerry with the Careys. From then on I never felt truly alone again and it was the best thing I ever did.'

She hung on his every word and was so easy to talk to that soon he found himself telling her all about Niamh and what had happened to her.

'So now she lives alone and barely sees her husband?'

He nodded.

'Then why doesn't she get a divorce and come to you? She clearly still loves you, from what you've told me.'

'Huh! She's a Catholic. Can you imagine what Father Donahue would have to say about that, or the Careys for that matter? The Catholic faith doesn't believe in divorce.'

'So what?' She tossed her head and he saw a little of his own spirit in her. 'I gave you away because of what everyone would say and I've regretted it every day since. My husband was a good man – you would have liked him, I'm sure – and looking back now, although he would have been shocked and hurt at my one indiscretion, I believe he would have forgiven me eventually and accepted you as his own. What I'm saying, Ben, is don't make the mistake that I did by worrying too much about what other people would say. Be true to your heart even if it means living in sin together!' Seeing the shock on his face she realised that she had gone too far and ended hastily, 'I'm sorry. I shouldn't have said that, but I hate to see you so unhappy.'

Strangely enough, the tension between them eased then and soon they were chattering away about anything and everything and the time just seemed to fly by. Eventually Elizabeth glimpsed the small clock on the mantelpiece and gasped.

'My goodness, it's a quarter to twelve. I'm so sorry if I have outstayed my welcome – and with you having to get up early in the morning too.'

'It doesn't matter,' Ben assured her and he meant it. As the night had gone on he had found himself relaxing in her company and he liked her.

She was rising now and he said hastily, 'I'll walk you to the hotel.'

'Oh no,' she protested. 'I've taken up quite enough of your time as it is and you must be ready for your bed. I shall be all right on my own really.'

But Ben wouldn't hear of it. He was already reaching for his coat and she was secretly pleased. Every second she spent with him was precious, something to remember when she sailed for New York.

A thick freezing fog had fallen when they stepped out of the cottage and the paths were so slippery with frost that she would have fallen if Ben hadn't caught her.

'Tuck your arm in,' he offered and she did so gladly, revelling in the warmth of him. She was finally walking out with the son whom she had missed every single day of his life.

Their footsteps echoed on the deserted streets and soon they came to the hotel entrance.

'When are you leaving?' he asked.

'I'd booked in for a week,' she told him truthfully. 'But if having me here makes you feel uncomfortable, I shall leave early.'

He found that he didn't want her to go. 'No, there's no need to do that,' he said. 'You could perhaps come to the cottage again tomorrow evening. I could make us a meal although I have to admit I'm not much of a cook. Maeve always teased me that I could burn water.'

'In that case, if you don't mind me taking over your kitchen for an hour or two perhaps I could come and cook for you? I could have a meal ready for when you close the smithy?'

227

'That'd be grand,' Ben answered and was shocked to realise that he meant it.

'Right, I shall go shopping tomorrow and see you late tomorrow afternoon. Good night, Ben – and thank you. This evening has been one of the best of my life.'

Without warning she stood on tiptoes and kissed his cheek before tripping into the hotel, and once she was gone from sight he fingered his cheek with a wide smile on his face. His mother had just kissed him good night for the very first time in his life – and he'd liked it.

# Chapter Twenty-Six

True to her word, Elizabeth arrived at the blacksmith's mid-afternoon the following day.

'Do you mind if I go into the cottage and make a start on preparing the meal?' she asked.

He was amused to see that she was carrying a large shopping basket that looked to contain all manner of goodies. 'Not at all, the door is unlocked. I'm sorry if the place isn't as tidy as it should be. I'm not very good when it comes to housework. Maeve is always scolding me about it.'

'Oh, don't worry about that. I shall be too busy cooking to take much notice.'

Now that their initial meeting was behind them they were less formal with each other and he thought she looked younger.

'I'll go and make a start then and perhaps bring you a cup of tea through, shall I?'

Ben grinned. 'You're spoiling me, so you are – but thank you, that would be much appreciated.'

She turned, picking her way carefully across the icy ground. Ben glanced at the sky through the window. It looked full of snow and he wondered whether, if it came down, would it delay her departure? He half-hoped that it would. But then he turned his attention back to the job in hand. The sooner it was finished, the sooner he could close; he was looking forward to his meal that evening.

Hands on hips, Elizabeth stood in Ben's kitchen and eyed the chaos. Clothes were flung across the backs of chairs and the sink was full of dirty pots. She smiled. Her other son, Lionel, had been untidy too but then he'd had a maid to clean up after him whilst her husband was alive. She could still have afforded one but chose to look after herself now. First things first though, she must get the meal prepared before she tackled anything else. She lifted two large steaks from her basket and a selection of winter vegetables. By four o'clock it was very dark outside but inside the cottage the fire was blazing merrily and the tantalising smell of meat slowly cooking filled the room. The vegetables were bubbling on the hob and Elizabeth had closed the curtains. She had scrubbed the kitchen from top to bottom and the dirty clothes were now sorted into a pile. With Ben's permission she would return to wash them tomorrow, although she didn't want him to think that she was interfering. The quarry tiles on the floor were gleaming in the light from the oil lamp, and earlier on, she had taken the rugs outside and after hanging them across the line, had beaten them to within an inch of their life.

At five-thirty the door opened and Ben stepped into the room only to stop and stare about in amazement. For a moment he wondered if he had come to the wrong house.

'I hope you don't mind, but once I'd got the meal on the go I thought I'd tidy up rather than sit about,' his mother told him nervously.

The smell of the meal was making his stomach grumble with anticipation and he smiled. 'I don't mind at all. In fact, I'm very grateful – but you shouldn't have gone to so much trouble. Maeve always tells me off for being such an untidy devil.'

'Well, wash your hands and the meal is ready to serve,' she told him then and it was as if they had known each other for years. 'There's steak and onions, mashed potatoes and winter cabbage, then I've done a semolina pudding for after.'

Ben did as he was told, and once the food was on the plates, Elizabeth removed her apron and joined him at the table.

'You must let me pay you for all this,' Ben said, longing to tuck in.

'You'll do no such thing,' she retorted, placing a glass of ale in front of him. 'It was my pleasure, though it might not be yours when you try it. I'm afraid I had a cook for many years so I'm not really very good at it although I can manage simple things.'

'It's delicious,' he told her minutes later with his mouth full of tender steak. 'As good as Maeve makes. I've missed her cooking, it's true, but this is lovely.'

Elizabeth had noticed the many times he had mentioned Maeve but she wasn't jealous – just grateful to the woman for all the kindnesses she had clearly shown to Ben in her absence.

The meal was a relaxed affair. They spoke of everything from farming to politics, and with every minute that passed Elizabeth was more proud of him. She had had no hand in his upbringing but he had grown into a fine young man.

After the meal he rose to help her clear the table but she shook her head and ushered him towards the fireside chair. Throwing another log onto the fire she told him then, 'You're to sit there now and smoke your pipe. I'll fetch you another glass of ale as well. I shall do the dishes tonight.'

Sensing that she wanted to do it, Ben did as he was told thinking how nice it was to have company. His thoughts turned to Niamh then and how things might have been, but he impatiently dismissed them. His mother would be gone again soon enough and who knew if he would ever see her again – and so he determined to make the most of the time they had left together.

Maeve came into town with Daniel the following day on the horse and cart. She was longing to know how Ben's meeting had gone with his mother, so the instant Daniel dropped her off she made a beeline for the blacksmiths.

'Well?' she said as she stepped into the workshop. 'How did it go?' The snow had held off up until now although it was bitterly cold, but it was as warm as toast in there with the furnace going.

Ben grinned. He'd wondered how long she'd be able to keep away. 'Why don't you go and ask her yourself. The last I saw of her, she was feeding my bedsheets through the mangle in the wash-house. She's going through the whole place like a tornado, you should see her!'

Maeve's face showed her relief. 'Well, that's grand then, to be sure. I reckon I'll go and have a cup of tea with her.' With that she turned about and headed for the cottage. Elizabeth had Ben's bedding pegged on a line stretched across the yard by then and Maeve saw that it had already frozen solid. By, they were in for a bad winter if she was any judge. Thank goodness they'd managed to get all the animals down into the fields surrounding the barns.

Elizabeth had her back to her when Maeve quietly let herself into the cottage, and glancing about she was impressed to see how clean and orderly everywhere looked.

'Somebody's been busy if I'm not very much mistaken,' she said.

When Elizabeth spun about it was all Maeve could do not to laugh aloud. She looked nothing like the smart lady who had visited the farm: she was wearing a huge apron that almost buried her, and some of her hair had come loose from its pins and was curling attractively around her face. Something smelled nice too – beef stew if Maeve wasn't very much mistaken.

'Oh Mrs Carey, how lovely to see you,' Elizabeth said. 'Do forgive the state I'm in. I've been doing a bit of tidying up for Ben.'

'More than a bit, from what I can see of it,' Maeve answered approvingly. 'He's not the tidiest of men, is he? And do call me Maeve.'

'Thank you – I will. I was just making a pot of tea to take a cup over to Ben. Will you stay for one?'

'I'd love to.' Maeve took off her coat and neatly folded it across the back of the chair as Elizabeth bustled about preparing the cups and the teapot.

When Elizabeth had taken Ben his tea the two women sat at the table to drink theirs and Maeve commented, 'It seems that you two are getting on well together. I'm pleased.'

'So am I,' Elizabeth said frankly. 'And I can't thank you enough for getting him to agree to meet me. I'm sure you had a hand in it.'

Maeve shrugged. 'Ben needed to know where he had come from and to meet his own mother,' she said practically. 'But how long are you planning on staying?'

Elizabeth then told her of her plans to go to New York, concluding, 'I suppose I was half-hoping that Ben would decide to come with me, but I realise now that it was too much to ask. To be honest, now that we're finally getting to know each other a little there's nothing I'd like better than to stay here close to him, but my sister is very ill and . . . Well, if I don't go soon it may be too late and then I would never be able to live with myself. You do understand, don't you?'

'Of course I do,' Maeve said sympathetically. 'Does Ben know that your sister is ill?'

'No.' Elizabeth wrung her hands together. 'I thought if I told him, he might think that I was playing on his sympathy. If he had decided to come, I wanted it to be because he wished to be with me – if that makes any kind of sense?'

Maeve nodded. Things were going well between them from what she could see of it, but there was still a very long way to go. Until a few days ago they had been strangers and Maeve knew Ben well enough to know that he wouldn't go haring off anywhere with someone so soon, even if that someone was his birth mother.

'Take it one day at a time, lass,' she advised comfortably.

'I will,' Elizabeth promised. Every minute she spent with her son was precious and she didn't intend to waste a single second of it.


'So what do you think?' Dilly asked as she stared up at the smart new sign hanging above her shop.

'I think it looks just right,' Henry Price said approvingly.

'It took some time for us all to come up with a name that everyone approved of,' Dilly explained truthfully. 'But yes, I think it does look right now.'

The sign was painted in red with large gold lettering, and it read:

*Dilly's Designs*
*Ladies' bespoke, ready-made, and quality bridalwear specialist*

Dilly clasped her hands in excitement before catching Henry's hand and almost dragging him into the shop, eager to show him the new bags she had commissioned. They too were red with gold lettering and string handles, and they looked very chic and elegant.

'I should think the ladies will be coming in just to get a bag,' he teased, but Dilly wasn't done.

'I've had two more chairs put into the bridalwear section so that the mothers can sit in comfort while the daughters try on the dresses. And I've also started offering tea whilst they wait.'

'It seems you've thought of everything.'

'I just hope it pays off,' Dilly said, sober again now. The changes had been expensive and she could only keep her fingers crossed that they would be worth it.

'Max – that is, Mr Farthing – suggested that I should set up a service to the mother of the bride too,' she went on then. 'He's kindly said he'll supply me with hats from his factory in Atherstone, so I already have the seamstresses working on some outfits. The first two should be ready tomorrow and I'm going to put one in the window.'

'Excellent idea.' Henry took the silver watch and chain from his waistcoat pocket. 'I'm so sorry but I really do have to dash,' he told Dilly. 'I have a client coming to see me at the office in less than half an hour and if I don't go now I shall be late.'

'Of course. Thank you for coming to see the sign. I'd never have thought of it so I'm very grateful to you.'

He crossed to the door then paused before saying awkwardly, 'I have two tickets for a show at the theatre in Coventry on Friday evening. Eleanor is always off out with her young man and I've got rather bored with sitting in alone staring at the same four walls. I don't suppose I could persuade you to accompany me, could I?'

Dilly was so taken aback that for a moment she was speechless but then she blustered, 'The theatre? I er . . . I've never been to the theatre before. I wouldn't know what to wear – and how would we get there?'

'I'm sure you would look charming whatever you chose to wear and we would go in my car. Coventry isn't so far, you know?'

Dilly's first instinct was to refuse the invitation, but then as she saw the hopeful look on Henry's face the words died on her lips. He was obviously missing his wife and she felt sorry for him.

'I suppose I could go,' she croaked, not at all certain that she was doing the right thing. What would Niamh and Seamus say when they knew she was gadding off out with a gentleman?

'That's wonderful. I shall pick you up from here at about seven-thirty then if that's suitable?' He was beaming and once again it struck Dilly how handsome he was.

'Thank you. I'll see you on Friday evening then.'

Henry left the shop with a spring in his step but Dilly had no time to dwell on what she'd agreed to because a young woman and her mother entered at that moment and she was soon busy serving them.

'Hmm, going to the theatre, eh?' Seamus said with a twinkle in his eye that evening. 'And about time too. You never go out socially, you're always working so the change will do you good.'

'I couldn't agree more,' Niamh chipped in as they all sat at the table waiting for Mary to serve them.

Although Dilly had moved back into her rooms above the shop she still went round to Niamh's to have her evening meal with her family most evenings. She let out a sigh of relief. She'd been worried about telling them but they seemed to have taken it very well, seeing as it would be the first time she had gone out with a gentleman since their father's death. That seemed so very long ago now and she felt sad as she thought of Fergal.

'In actual fact, Seamus and I were only saying the other day that you should get out more,' Niamh told her. 'You're still quite young, Mammy, and still very attractive too.'

Dilly squirmed with embarrassment. 'I don't want you reading more into this than there is,' she said more sharply than she had meant to. 'Mr Price and I are going out together merely as friends, so don't be getting any romantic notions. I only agreed to go because he's clearly missing his wife and I felt sorry for him.'

'Well, for whatever reason you're going I hope you enjoy it. But have you thought what you're going to wear?' Niamh asked.

Dilly suddenly felt alarmed. No, she hadn't given a thought as to how she should dress, but now that Niamh had asked she started to panic. What did women wear nowadays to go to the theatre?

'How about that lovely light-blue dress that Hilda and Peggy made for you after the fire?' Niamh suggested.

'Isn't it a little plain?'

Niamh shrugged as Mary started to load their meals onto the table. 'We could soon smarten it up with a few pearls stitched around the dropped waistline. You could wear your navy coat as well and they'd go together a treat. I could sew the pearls on if you're too busy in the shop while I'm here in the day with Roddy.'

'It seems an awful lot of trouble for you to go to, just for one night out,' Dilly said. 'Not that I'm not grateful for the offer, of course,' she ended hastily.

'What's this then? Off somewhere nice, are you?' Mary asked affably.

'Ma's going to the theatre on Friday evening with Mr Price,' Seamus informed her with a grin.

'Well, how lovely!' Mary exclaimed, then with a shy glance at Seamus, 'It just so happens that me and Seamus are going to the pictures that night too.' She had hardly stopped smiling since he had asked her and now it was Dilly's turn to grin. She'd wondered how long it would be before the two of them realised that they were drawn to each other. It was as clear as the noses on their faces.

'In that case we'd better find an outfit for you too,' she said. 'Why don't you come round to the shop tomorrow? I think I might have just the dress for you.'

Mary looked worried. 'It's right kind o' you to say so, Mrs Carey, but the thing is . . . I hand most o' me wages to me mam each week. Me dad don't earn much, see, so's I helps out wi' what I can.'

'We won't worry about that for now,' Dilly said kindly. 'Just come round in the morning. The one I have in mind is very cheap and I have an idea it would slot on you perfectly.'

'But I have Roddy to look after,' Mary fretted. She only usually got one new dress a year – that was if she was lucky – and even that was usually from the rag stall in the market.

'Then bring him with you.' Dilly was not going to be put off.

'All right then,' Mary sighed resignedly. 'But even if it fits I'm not sayin' as I'll have it.'

'We'll see,' Dilly responded. First thing in the morning she intended to alter the price on the dress she had in mind to such a ridiculously low cost that Mary wouldn't be able to resist it.

# Chapter Twenty-Seven

After dinner, as they all sat enjoying a cup of tea, Mary suddenly remembered, 'Oh, there's a letter for you on the mantelpiece, Mrs Carey. Niamh has already had hers.'

'Oh really?' Dilly looked at Niamh questioningly, wondering who it might be from.

'Oh, mine was from Ireland as well,' she mumbled, then set about helping Mary to clear the dirty pots into the kitchen before getting Roddy ready for bed.

At the mention of Ireland the child's ears pricked up and he beamed. 'Go see Roisin?' he asked hopefully.

Dilly smiled as she ruffled his hair. He had put weight on and although he was still slight he looked much healthier than he had when he had first arrived with Bessie.

'Not yet, sweetheart,' she told him.

Niamh glanced up from loading the tray then and said quietly, 'Actually, Mammy, I was going to speak to you about that. I was wondering if you'd mind if I spent Christmas in Ireland this year with Gran'ma and Granda

239

now that Seamus is here to keep you company? I could take Roddy with me if Bessie didn't mind.'

'Oh.' Dilly was taken aback. Niamh had never wanted to spend Christmas away from home before but then she was a grown woman now, so how could she refuse?

'Of course I have no objections if that's what you'd like to do,' she told her. 'And Roddy can always stay here with Mary if Bessie doesn't want him to go.'

'Me go!' Roddy said with fierce determination and they all smiled. It appeared that he would rather spend his time with Roisin than his mother but then that was hardly surprising. Bessie barely bothered with him, and Dilly had an idea that she'd be glad to get rid of him for a while. Christmas or not!

'We'll see, but now off you go and get ready for bed while I read my letter, there's a good boy.'

Roddy immediately did as he was told. He was such a lovely child it was no wonder they were all so fond of him.

Dilly settled herself into the chair then with the latest missive from Maeve, and she had read no more than a few lines when her face broke into a delighted smile.

'Why, Roisin is expecting another child,' she told Seamus joyously. 'Isn't that wonderful? Maeve says she's very early on and Declan is making her keep her feet up and rest. Let's hope that all goes well this time. Ooh – and Ben met his mother and they got on well,' she carried on as Seamus listened.

'I must let Maeve know that I'm back in the rooms above the shop when I reply,' she said when she'd finished reading out the news. 'She can start sending her letters back there then.'

She was in a happy frame of mind as she made her way home a short time later. Mary and Seamus were getting along, Declan and Roisin had something to celebrate and

Christmas was just around the corner. She supposed she ought to think about doing some Christmas shopping but as yet she'd been so busy putting her rooms to rights and getting the shop back to normal again that she hadn't had time to think about it. Every night now she was busily working on the clothes for Eleanor Price's wedding, and as well as that she also spent one day a week in the shop in Birmingham with Jayne whilst Niamh kept the Nuneaton one open. The Birmingham shop was doing far better than she had ever dared hope, although she concentrated on selling more everyday clothes there rather than bridalwear. Another day a week was spent visiting her suppliers and restocking on material for the seamstresses who were now working six days a week to meet demands.

Seamus had proved to be a great help. He always went with her to the suppliers and carried the heavy bales of material back to the shops, and she felt it was giving him a purpose. He had also started to look around for a job, and she took this as yet another sign that he was feeling stronger, although she was slightly concerned that he wasn't quite ready for that yet. He certainly looked vastly improved physically but Dilly knew that he still had a long way to go mentally. Only days before, Niamh and Mary had had to rush along the landing to him in the middle of the night because he was in the grip of a terrible nightmare. Poor lad, she could only hope it would ease with time but the doctor had told her that it would take a long while so she had all the patience in the world with him. During the war he had seen sights that no one should ever see and she rightly guessed there could be no quick cure for that.

As soon as she arrived home that evening she sorted out the dress she had in mind for Mary. It was a warm burgundy colour in a very fine wool with long sleeves, perfect for the cold winter and she was sure it would be just right for Mary.

How to get her to accept it was the problem. The girl was no fool and would know after looking at the other dresses that Dilly had reduced it especially. Dilly considered letting a little bit of the hem down but abandoned that idea immediately. Mary would see through this ruse, and she was far too proud to accept charity. Then an idea occurred to Dilly and she hurried away to fetch her scissors. Turning the dress inside out she made a tiny hole on the inside of the hem. The damage would be invisible when it was being worn and very easily repaired, but she could tell Mary that because it was imperfect she had been forced to reduce it.

She then turned it back the right way and placed it on its hanger before taking off the price tag and replacing it with one that was half of the original cost. She removed that one too then and reduced it to a quarter. Finally satisfied, she was just about to hang it up again when the door opened and Max appeared.

'Hello, what are you up to?' he smiled. 'You nearly jumped out of your skin then. Are you doing something you shouldn't?'

Dilly grinned, looking slightly guilty. 'I suppose I am actually.' She went on to tell him what she'd done and why, and when she'd finished he shook his head.

'You really are a most remarkable lady,' he said, amused. 'I think you must have a heart as big as a bucket although how you manage to squeeze it into that slim frame I'll never know.'

'Rubbish,' she scoffed. 'I'm just playing matchmaker, that's all. If she's going to woo my son she has to look her best, doesn't she? But now would you like a drink? I think I'm done down here for this evening.'

He followed her up the narrow staircase and once in the tiny sitting room he held his hands out to the fire as she poured them both a small glass of sherry.

They were seated either side of the fireplace when she mentioned, 'As it happens, Mary isn't the only one who'll be going out on Friday night. Henry Price has asked me to go to the theatre in Coventry with him and I've agreed.'

'You've *what*?' Max was so shocked that a little of his drink slopped out of his glass and onto his trousers, causing a red stain to spread across his leg.

'I'll get a wet cloth quickly else that will stain.' Dilly hastily scuttled away to get the cloth. When she handed it to him he dabbed at his trousers angrily, his face set in grim lines.

'Why on earth have you agreed to go out with Henry Price? If you'd wanted to go to the theatre I would happily have taken you. I've offered before but you've always turned me down, so why should he be different? You barely know the man!'

Dilly's anger had risen to match his now and her back straightened as she told him: 'I would have thought it's perfectly *obvious* why I couldn't go with you, Max. Just in case you've forgotten, you're a married man! People gossip about us as it is, but imagine what they would say if I was seen brazenly going out with you! And as for Henry Price – it was you yourself who told me what a nice gentleman he was. He's also a widower, so why shouldn't we go out together?'

'Because . . .' Max spluttered, lost for words, and then to her horror he stood up and after snatching up his coat he slammed out of the room. She heard his heavy footsteps pounding down the stairs and the sound of the shop door banging resoundingly behind him.

Dilly leaned heavily on the back of the chair with her hand to her throat. She had never in all the time she had known him seen Max so angry. What on earth had she done to so upset him? Then suddenly it hit her like a blow: *Max was jealous!* Tears pricked at the back of her eyes as she tried to imagine the situation reversed. She would have been jealous too, for all the good it would have done. Their feelings for each other had simmered silently between them for years, but they both knew that whilst Camilla was still alive there was nothing they could do about it.

Her anger dispersed, to be replaced by despair. Perhaps it was time to start getting out and about again as Niamh and Seamus had suggested. The longer she remained foot-loose and fancy free, the longer Max would harbour hopes that they might come together. A picture of Henry Price's face flashed in front of her eyes. He was a kind, handsome man and yet she couldn't rid herself of the guilt she felt each time she remembered Max's reaction. She angrily swiped a tear away with the back of her hand. What was wrong with her, for goodness sake? Henry Price was just a friend, nothing more, and he had only asked her to accompany him because he was lonely. Well, she would go and Max could go to hell, she told herself defiantly and with that she swept into the bedroom to search out the dress Niamh had suggested she should wear.

Samuel had been living in a small room in Birmingham for two months. He'd been forced to flee Manchester after being caught cheating in a card game. But his money was fast running out now and he was getting desperate. He barely had enough left to pay the rent for the next week and knew that he was going to have to do something.

It was a bitterly cold day as he set off for a walk. Even braving the cold was better than sitting in the depressing rented room. He headed for the Bullring. There were plenty of cheap places to eat there and his stomach was rumbling ominously. It was as he was nearing the outskirts of the large market that a newly hung sign above a shop window caught his attention. It was quite eye-catching in red with bold gold letters that read

*Dilly's Designs*

He stopped abruptly, his hands thrust deep into his coat pockets as an idea occurred to him. He'd known that Dilly Carey was planning to open a shop here somewhere – could this be it? If it was, it must mean that she hadn't perished in the fire he had started. And if she was still alive, perhaps it would be safe for him to go home. The fuss about Snowy White's death must have died down by now, surely? He'd been such a well-known rogue that it was doubtful the police would have searched for his killer for long. Truth be told, they'd probably been glad to see the back of him.

The sky was overcast – an eerie grey colour that threatened snow as he cautiously approached the shop window. The lights were on within and he recognised the young woman inside, who was busily serving a customer, as Dilly Carey's assistant from the Nuneaton shop. What was her name now? Jayne something or other if he remembered correctly, but there was no sign of the Carey woman.

He crossed to the other side of the road again while he decided what to do. A group of raggy-arsed children were singing carols and the youngest held his cap out hopefully to him but when Samuel growled he quickly backed away.

People were teeming everywhere, women laden down with shopping bags or with children clinging to their skirts, and men who walked purposefully, probably on their way to their jobs. Samuel stroked his chin; he badly needed a shave and he didn't smell very nice either. He couldn't remember the last time he'd had a nice hot bath. There was an indoor bathroom at the place he was lodging at, but the last time he'd ventured into it he'd found a large rat sitting in the bathtub and he hadn't ventured in there again.

Making a decision, he took a comb from his pocket and dragged it through his greasy hair, wincing as the teeth caught on the knots. There was only one way to find out what was going on and that was to go into the shop and ask, but first he'd get something to eat. He entered a small café and ordered tea and toast. It was all he could afford but it would fill a hole. When the down-at-heel, harassed little waitress served him he gobbled it down and drained his mug in seconds, then feeling slightly better he headed for the shop again. His mouth felt like the bottom of a birdcage, probably from the ale he'd downed the night before, but there was nothing he could do about it for now.

Jayne was showing a customer a selection of scarves when he entered and he began to wander about the shop looking at the various clothes on display. When the woman had made her purchase and left the shop, Jayne then turned her attention to Samuel.

'Good morning, sir. May I help you? It's very cold out tod . . .' Her voice trailed away as recognition dawned. 'Why, it's Mr Farthing, isn't it? Dilly's son-in-law.'

He flashed a charming smile as he chose his words carefully. 'Yes, it is. I've been working away but on the way home I thought I'd pop in and see how the new shop is doing.'

'Oh . . .' Jayne had been led to believe that he'd cleared off after a row with his father but she supposed it was none of her business. 'It's doing really well,' she said, trying not to stare at his grubby, dishevelled clothes.

'And the one in Nuneaton?'

'That's doing really well too. Dilly runs that one with help from Niamh. It's re-opened again now. Did you know that there was a fire there?' She seemed to recall he'd cleared off round about that time but couldn't remember if it had been before or after the fire.

'Really? No one was hurt, I trust?' he said, feigning surprise.

She shook her head. 'No. Thankfully a man passing by spotted the fire and called for the fire engine. Dilly was very lucky, thank goodness, but it could have been very different.'

'Well, that's something to be grateful for at least,' he answered. 'But now if you will excuse me I should get on. Good day.'

'Good day, sir.' As he left the shop, Jayne shuddered. There was something about that young man that she really didn't like, but then yet another customer entered the shop and she thought no more about him.

Outside, Samuel paused. So Dilly was alive then. Perhaps he could risk going home? The thought was so tempting. He visualised the delicious meals Mary cooked, the clean clothes all laid out ready for him to step into and the soft bed. A bath full of hot water. He'd almost forgotten what it felt like to feel clean. He knew that Niamh wouldn't be particularly pleased to see him, or his father for that matter, but he didn't much care. The Carey woman was alive and no one could prove that it was he who'd started the fire, could they? He wondered what time it was. He'd long since pawned anything of value, including his Hunter watch; their father had bought him and Lawrence one each for their twenty-first birthday. He gauged it to be still quite early in the morning. If he were to catch a train now, he could be home for lunchtime. There didn't seem much point in returning to his lodgings to collect his things. There was nothing of any value there and the landlord could whistle for the rent he owed.

Feeling more optimistic, he set out for New Street station.

# Chapter Twenty-Eight

Mary was clearing away the lunch pots and Niamh was again busily working on the dress her mother would be wearing that evening when she went to the theatre with Mr Price. She'd almost finished it now and was quite proud of her efforts. The beadwork had completely transformed it from a very plain day dress into something quite stylish.

'What do you think?' she asked, holding it up to show it to Mary.

'I think it looks lovely,' Mary answered with a smile. 'I dare say you'll be popping it round to her now, will you?'

Niamh was just about to answer when they heard the back door open and close.

'I wonder who that could be?' Niamh mused and her question was answered when Samuel strode into the room.

He smiled disarmingly as if he'd only been gone for ten minutes before saying, 'Don't look so surprised. I do live here, you know.'

'Not for some time you haven't,' Niamh responded shortly.

'But surely you're just a little bit pleased to see me?' he smirked, then before she could answer he told Mary, 'Get me some lunch. I've been travelling and I'm hungry. You can run me a bath afterwards and sort me out some clean clothes.'

Mary glanced uncertainly towards Niamh and when she nodded, the maid sighed and hurried away to do as she was told. She'd thought the peace and quiet was too good to last.

'Aren't you going to ask me where I've been?' Samuel asked then.

Roddy had shot across to Niamh and was clinging to her skirts in fear of the man.

'Where you go and what you do are really no concern of mine,' she answered gruffly. 'And to be quite honest, I'm not in the least interested.' With that she took Roddy's hand and marched from the room as Samuel took a seat at the table. Not the best of homecomings, he shrugged, but at least he would be comfortable and warm again. Now all he had to do was think about how he was going to get around his father.

It was a pity his bastard was still in the house, he thought as he glanced around the room noting the easel that stood at the side of the window. It looked as if Niamh had resumed her painting again. There was a partly finished landscape on the canvas and he grudgingly had to admit that it was quite good – not that he would ever tell her that. But where was Mary with his food? The lazy bitch had better pull her socks up now that he was home else there'd be hell to pay!

Niamh arrived at the shop less than an hour later with Roddy in tow and Dilly saw at once that something was troubling her daughter.

'I've brought your dress,' Niamh informed her. 'Though why you couldn't have treated yourself to a new one from the stock I'll never know. You are allowed to treat yourself now and again, you know.'

'Someone got out of bed the wrong side this morning,' Dilly teased as Roddy ran across to Niamh and threw his arms about her waist.

'The nasty man has come home, Dilly,' he told her and the smile slid from her face as she glanced at Niamh questioningly.

'The nasty man? He's not talking about Samuel, is he?' Now she suddenly understood why Niamh was in such an ill humour.

'I'm afraid so. He strode in as bold as brass about an hour ago, throwing his weight about. We all hoped that he'd gone for good.'

'Oh I see.' Dilly took the dress that Niamh had so painstakingly worked on and admired it. 'Why would I want a new one anyway when you've made such a lovely job of this?' She had very mixed feelings about the evening ahead, particularly as Max hadn't called in since the night she had told him about it. She wanted to be angry with him but instead she'd found that she'd missed him.

'Here you are, you can play with these while Niamh and I go through to the back for a cup of tea.' Dilly took a bag of marbles from a drawer behind the counter and Roddy happily settled on the carpet to play with them as the two women disappeared off into the back room.

'So where did he say he'd been?' Dilly asked when Roddy was out of earshot as she hung her dress on the back of the door and filled the kettle.

'He didn't,' Niamh answered flatly. 'And truthfully I really don't care. I was hoping he'd never come back. But I'll tell you something: he looked filthy and he stank. I reckon he's only returned because he's run out of money. He'll no

250

doubt be trying to get back into his father's good books now.'

'Hmm, you're probably right,' Dilly answered as she warmed the tea pot. 'But at least you'll be out of his way for Christmas, and so will Roddy. I'm pleased you're going to Enniskerry now. Mary and Seamus can come to me for their Christmas dinner if they like and Samuel can fend for himself. He doesn't deserve any better. But isn't it sad for Roddy? He only knows his father as "that nasty man"!'

'He doesn't need to know him as anything else,' Niamh retorted. 'I don't think Bessie has ever told him that Samuel is his father and truthfully I don't blame her. I think Malcolm, Bessie's husband, was the nearest thing to a father that child has ever had, so let him hold on to his happy memories of him.'

They'd almost finished their tea when a customer came into the shop and Niamh left with Roddy, saying that she was going to call in and see Mrs Pegs. The prospect of being at home with Samuel for the afternoon was more than she could face.

Dilly closed an hour early that afternoon and lugged the tin bath that she kept in the yard through to the small back room. It was just too much to try and lug it up the stairs. She then boiled kettle after kettle of hot water until there was enough to bathe in and quickly undressed. It was bitterly cold in there so she didn't intend to take any longer than necessary to perform her ablutions. She thoroughly washed her hair and scrubbed herself from top to toe, then clambered out and dried herself on the towel she had ready. She was shivering by then and decided that the water in the bath could wait to be emptied until the next morning. Hurrying upstairs in her dressing gown, she sat by the fire and dried and brushed her hair until it shone – and then a glance at the clock told her that it was time to start getting ready. She pinned her hair up and applied the minimum of make-up before slipping her dress and shoes on. She then surveyed herself critically in the mirror.

'Not too bad for an old bird,' she decided with a wry grin. Her nerves were kicking in badly by then, but of course it was far too late to let Henry down now. There was still over an hour to go before he was due to pick her up and she wondered if she should eat something, but then decided that she was too tense to swallow. She began to pace up and down – and jumped when the door suddenly opened and Max appeared. He had his own key and must have let himself in.

'You made me jump,' she told him as he eyed her appreciatively.

'I thought it was time I came round and apologised for my rather childish behaviour the other night,' he said. 'I didn't want you to go off tonight without my telling you so. I've er . . . brought you this as way of apology. I hoped it would look nice on your coat.'

When he held out a corsage of hothouse cream rosebuds her heart melted and she instantly forgave him.

'Why, it's lovely. Thank you. But I'm not going for a while yet. Have you time for a quick drink? There was something I needed to tell you.'

He watched somewhat anxiously as she poured them both a small glass of port. He hoped that she wasn't going to tell him not to come here again, although it would be his own fault if she did. He had behaved abominably, like a sulky schoolboy.

'I'm only telling you this because it may then be less of a shock to you than if he just walked in,' Dilly began.

'Who are you talking about?' he asked, looking bewildered.

'Samuel . . . he's back. He arrived at Niamh's just after

lunchtime. She said he wandered in as if he'd just been down to the corner shop.'

'I see.' Max's lips set in a thin line. 'Well, thank you for telling me. I wonder how long it will be before he comes to try me for another hand-out. That's all he would have come back for, going on his past record. He's probably broke again.' He threw back his drink in one go then rose, saying, 'I mustn't keep you. Henry will be here soon. And Dilly, my dear, I hope you have a nice evening. You've had so much unhappiness in your life it's time you had a few pleasures.'

Then he was gone, and as he clattered off down the stairs she stared at the lovely corsage he had bought for her.

Dilly and Henry had a wonderful evening and on the way home Dilly couldn't remember when she'd last enjoyed herself so much. Henry had been the perfect gentleman, taking her to the cocktail lounge in the interval of the show, and now she felt a little tipsy. But as they neared the shop she began to feel nervous. Should she invite him in for a last drink or would that appear too familiar? It was so long since Fergal had wooed her that she couldn't remember what she was supposed to do now. She needn't have worried though, for as Henry smoothly drew the car to a halt he took her gloved hand and kissed it gently.

'Thank you so much for coming with me tonight,' he said softly. 'I'd forgotten what it was like to go out and enjoy myself. I'm afraid I've become a bit of a recluse since . . . Well, thank you again. Now I ought to be getting home. If Eleanor gets back before I do she'll be worrying.'

'It should be me thanking you,' Dilly told him, her eyes sparkling. 'I've had such a lovely time.'

'I wonder . . .' Henry paused as if he was choosing his words cautiously. 'Could we go out again some time? Only if you're not too busy, of course,' he added hastily.

Dilly smiled at him shyly. 'I'd like that. Good night, Henry.'

He watched her let herself into the shop before driving away and Dilly stood for a moment as the silence surrounded her. She was still a little jumpy at night-time since the fire. The least noise could make her start awake and break out in goosebumps, but she had forced herself to stay there, and each night now was becoming a little easier. Eventually she took a deep breath, steeled herself and made her way upstairs to get ready for bed. Once she was tucked in she snuggled down beneath the blankets and her last thought before she fell asleep was of Max. He'd clearly been upset when she'd informed him that Samuel had turned up again and she hoped that there wasn't yet more trouble ahead for him.

'What do you mean – you're going away for Christmas?' Samuel thundered the next morning when Niamh informed him of her plans over breakfast.

Niamh cut up a sausage for Roddy before answering coolly, 'Just what I said. Roddy and I are going to spend Christmas with Gran'ma and Granda on the farm.'

'But I've only just come home!'

Niamh grinned. 'I'd hardly call this your home. It's somewhere you come to lay your head when you've nowhere else to go.'

Samuel scowled. 'So what am I supposed to do then?'

'Well, I rather imagine you'll want to spend Christmas with your mother and father,' she answered. 'If not, Mary will be here to cook for you and Seamus. I'm sure you'll manage.'

She scraped her chair back from the table then and once Roddy had finished his meal she took his hand and left the room without giving Samuel so much as another glance and went to join Seamus and Mary in the kitchen.

'So how did your evening go?' Niamh asked her mother when she, Seamus and Roddy called in at the shop later that morning. Niamh had been shopping for presents to take to Ireland with her and was in fine spirits.

'It was lovely,' Dilly answered truthfully. 'I really enjoyed it, but how is Samuel behaving?' She'd expected Niamh to remain upset at his untimely return but today she seemed to be remarkably calm about it.

Niamh shrugged as Seamus took Roddy into the back room to put the kettle on. 'All right as far as I can see,' she said. 'But to be honest I'm not really that concerned. No doubt he'll be off again as soon as the fancy takes him. The sooner the better, that's what I say – but he's got to face his father first and I don't imagine he'll be looking forward to that. Did you warn Mr Farthing that he was back?'

'Yes, I did. And between you and me, I don't think he will be any more pleased to see him than you are. Max has enough on his plate at the moment with Camilla, without having to wonder what Samuel will be getting up to again.'

'Is she no better?'

Dilly shook her head. 'Not according to Bessie – but then she'll probably tell you herself. She's due home this evening, isn't she?'

'Yes, she is. Mrs Pegs is going to keep her eye on Camilla so Bessie can get her Christmas shopping done.' Niamh frowned. 'Won't it be awkward for Samuel having both the women he raped sitting down to dinner with him this evening?'

'He's so thick-skinned I doubt it will bother him,' Dilly answered sadly. Niamh then went on to show her the presents she had bought for the family in Ireland and the subject was closed.

# Chapter Twenty-Nine

Samuel was on his way to his former home and he was not in a good mood. He had to face his father at some point so he supposed he might as well get it over and done with. He didn't fancy the thought of having to eat humble pie one little bit, but then it was highly unlikely that Max would be home at this time of day. He could always look in on his mother if he wasn't, and that might go some way towards softening his old man up when he heard about it.

'Oh, it's you,' Mrs Pegs said coldly when he entered the kitchen a short time later. He'd lost his front-door key months ago and reminded himself to ask his father if he could have another. He'd see what mood he was in first though.

'Not exactly the warmest greeting I've ever had,' Samuel answered, helping himself to one of the mince pies the cook had just taken from the oven.

She scowled, hoping it would burn his mouth then returned to what she was doing as Samuel made his way into the hall.

As he'd thought, there was no sign of his father so he went upstairs and tapped on his mother's bedroom door. He heard the sound of a key in the lock then it swung open and Bessie's mouth pressed into a straight line when she saw who it was.

'What do *you* want?' she asked bluntly.

Samuel chuckled as he straightened his tie and flattened his hair. 'Why, I've come to see my dear Mamma, of course. Now remember your place, woman, and move out of my way.'

He swept past her as Bessie silently fumed. I'll have my day with that one, just see if I don't, she promised herself. Meanwhile, Samuel had crossed to the chair by the window where Camilla was sitting staring vacantly out over the gardens. A little shock coursed through him at first sight of her. She seemed to have shrunk and suddenly looked very old and fragile.

'How are you, Mother?' He deliberately kept his voice cheerful as he addressed her but when she turned to look at him there was no recognition in her eyes.

'I came to see Father but he's obviously at work.'

There was nothing to show that she had even heard him and after a moment he turned to Bessie and asked, 'Is she always like this?'

'Most of the time.' Bessie was busily folding the clean linen that Gwen had brought up to her and was putting it away in the tallboy. Camilla was becoming incontinent and Bessie felt as if she spent half of the time changing the bed and her patient now. 'When she does talk she tends to get quite violent now,' she ended.

Samuel was horrified. This wreck in front of him barely resembled the attractive, vibrant woman he remembered. He suddenly thought back to what she had been like when he was a child and had a vision of her leaning across him as she tucked him and Lawrence into bed after reading them a story. He could remember the smell of the perfume she had worn and the way she would pick him up and cuddle him if he fell over. Looking back now, he supposed the gradual change had taken place after he and his brothers were sent away to boarding school. She had become very nervy and highly strung then; perhaps that had been the start of her decline into madness? He knew that she had never forgiven his father for depriving her of her boys.

He stood there staring at her for a few moments as the happier memories flooded back, then turned abruptly and left the room without another word. He instantly heard the door being locked behind him and shuddered, praying that he would never end up in that state. From the welcome he'd received, he doubted that his family would nurse *him* with such loving care.

In a thoroughly bad humour he went down to the library and poured himself a stiff whisky and then another. Then he left the house heading in the direction of Lilian's street. His mistress would have had time to calm down during the preceding weeks and would surely have started to miss him now – and if that was the case, then the whole lot of them could go to hell as far as he was concerned. Admittedly he had a roof over his head and food provided by his father, but he didn't have a penny in his pocket and that went sorely against the grain with Samuel.

The walk took some time; he had no money for a cab and he didn't recognise the young maid who answered the door to him.

'Can I 'elp you, sir?' she asked.

Brushing her aside, he stepped into the hallway as if he owned the place.

'Ere, you can't just march in like that. The mistress won't like it,' the girl choked in a panic. She was supposed to announce any visitors – and because she was new, she was keen to make a good impression.

'Where is she?' Samuel barked, making the girl shake with terror.

'She's in the drawing room but she's—'

Ignoring her, Samuel strode along the hallway, head held high, then plastering a smarmy smile on his face, he threw open the drawing-room door and stepped inside.

'Hello, darling,' he began. 'I'm afraid I couldn't keep away any longer. I've missed you so much. Have you missed . . .' The rest of the words stuck in his throat as he saw Lilian sprawled on the chaise longue with a handsome young man at her side feeding her grapes.

'This is my nephew,' Lillian said quickly as she heaved herself up onto her elbow. Then, her face hardening, she snapped, 'What are *you* doing in my house? I thought I told you never to come here again.'

Nephew my arse, Samuel thought darkly as he glared at Lilian's latest lover. Since when did nephews feed their aunt grapes? Her clothes were dishevelled too – and so were his, if it came to that. Yet when Samuel spoke his voice was calm and he managed to look upset.

'Could we not speak alone?' he forced himself to ask.

She gave a quick shake of her head. 'What would be the point? I have nothing I wish to say to you.' The young maid who had admitted him had come to stand behind him and was wringing her hands in distress.

'Show this . . . *gentleman* out this instant,' the woman commanded her. 'And make sure that he is never allowed into this house again.'

'But I couldn't stop 'im, ma'am. 'E just barged past me an'—'

'*Now!*' the woman roared, and sensing that she wasn't going to change her mind, Samuel spun on his heel and strode away, his face crimson with rage.

As he stamped off down the drive, tears of humiliation stung his eyes. Who did the silly old cow think she was anyway? She should be grateful for the attention he'd shown her. The sop she had dancing attendance on her now was still wet behind the ears, but what did Sam care? He'd show her. He'd show them all, if it came to that!

By the time he was halfway back into town his anger had dissipated and he was feeling miserable. He'd have no choice but to go to his father for help again, although begging for hand-outs made him cringe. No doubt he'd get a load of 'I told you so's' from the old man but he could stand that as long as Max coughed some money up.

For the second time that day, he made his way back to the family home and as he marched through the kitchen, he told Mrs Pegs, 'I shall be dining with my father tonight.'

She said not a word but once he'd gone she grinned to herself. She wouldn't mind being a fly on the wall when Mr Farthing did set eyes on him.

And she wasn't far wrong, she thought with amusement when the master came in some time later, not if the commotion issuing from the study was anything to go by. And it serves the bloody little upstart right, she thought as she winked gleefully at Gwen who was busily mashing the potatoes with butter just the way Mr Farthing liked them.

'So . . . you've decided to show your face again then, have you?' Max asked his son. 'Money ran out, did it? How much are you after this time?'

Samuel bowed his head and tried to look repentant but it didn't cut any ice with Max – he knew his son too well.

'My business venture didn't pay off,' Samuel told him meekly, hoping to play on his sympathy.

'Hmm, so I ask again – how much are you after and what do you intend to do to earn it?'

Whilst Samuel had been waiting for his father to come home he had drunk steadily throughout the afternoon and now he was feeling light-headed and queasy.

'I'll work for you again, of course I will,' he responded. 'I'd never have cleared off as I did in the first place if things hadn't been so impossible here. Can you begin to imagine how awful it is to be tied to a woman who despises you? Niamh can't even speak to me civilly half of the time.'

'Don't you *dare* to bring Niamh into this!' his father ground out, his voice rising dangerously. 'Why, you are my son but I'm ashamed to say you aren't fit to lick her boots. It's her I feel sorry for, if anyone.'

Samuel quickly changed the subject. 'But will you just give me one last chance to redeem myself?' he pleaded. 'I'll work all the hours God sends to prove to you that I'm going to be different from now on. I *swear* I will.'

Max wavered. He still loved his son – the boy was his own flesh and blood, after all – and yet he doubted he meant a word he was saying. But Samuel had picked up on his hesitation and now he hurried on, '*Please*, Father, just tell me what you want me to do and I'll do it. I want you to be proud of me.'

'We'll talk again after dinner,' Samuel informed him, and side by side they went into the dining room.

When Samuel left the house that evening, he was seething with suppressed rage. He still hadn't got so much as a penny in his pocket because his father had said that the only time he would pay him was when he'd earned it. He was to start the very next morning sweeping floors at the mill in Attleborough. Just the thought of it brought Samuel out in a cold sweat. He'd be a laughing stock, the gaffer's son sweeping floors. But his father had him over a barrel, and had he refused, Samuel knew that he'd have been kicked out for good. His mind was racing as he tried to think of a way out of his predicament. For now he would have to go along with his father's wishes, but there must be *some* way he could get his hands on some cash?

It was as he was lying in bed that night dreading the day ahead that an idea of how he could obtain a good deal of money occurred to him – and suddenly he was glad that Niamh would be going to Ireland for Christmas. What he had in mind would take some careful planning, but if all went well he hoped that he might be able to disappear – never to return again.

Dilly was serving a customer when the postman arrived the following morning. She thanked him as he handed her the mail then shoved it behind the counter until she had time to read it. Both of her shops had been very busy in the lead-up to Christmas and already she was hoping that if trade continued as it was, she might be able to buy the shop in Birmingham rather than rent it in the not too distant future. She was in a happy mood when Niamh burst in mid-morning, and she wondered what could have happened to make her daughter look so elated.

'Have you had a letter from Ireland this morning?' she asked breathlessly when Dilly had finished serving yet another customer. The woman had left the shop with a spring in her step, carrying one of Dilly's creations tucked safely into one of the smart new bags.

'I don't know, I've been too busy to go through my mail as yet,' Dilly said, lifting the pile of letters that had arrived. Then, 'No, it doesn't look like it.'

'It's Roisin, she's having another baby,' Niamh trilled excitedly. 'Isn't that grand news, Mammy?' Dilly of course

262

already knew but had refrained from telling Niamh as yet in case she tempted fate.

'It certainly is,' Dilly beamed. She knew that Declan was over the moon with the news and prayed that this time there would be a happy outcome. She could see no reason why there shouldn't be, as Roisin was young and healthy.

'How are things at home?' she asked then. She knew how hard it must be for Niamh to have Samuel under the same roof again.

The girl shrugged nonchalantly. 'I don't see that much of Samuel if that's what you're asking,' she replied. 'And being as Roddy and I are leaving for Ireland in a couple of days I shan't have to see him over Christmas either, which is a relief. But what will *you* do, Mammy?'

'Bessie has already asked me round to your house with her and Seamus for Christmas dinner, and Mrs Pegs invited me there too so I'm not short of offers,' Dilly assured her. She didn't want the girl to feel guilty for going away. She could have told her that Henry had also invited her to dinner at his house but she didn't want Niamh to start reading more into their friendship than there was. Henry had taken her out for a lovely meal the evening before and once again she'd thoroughly enjoyed his company, but she had no intention of becoming romantically involved with anyone. She was far too busy building up her little empire. But the real reason she hadn't accepted anyone's offer as yet was because she was hoping that Olivia would come home for Christmas and she might get to spend a little time with her.

'Roddy must be getting excited now,' Dilly said then and Niamh nodded.

'That's rather an understatement. I think he'll burst before we get to Ireland. He's so looking forward to seeing everyone again, especially Roisin. He adores her and I think she's got a huge soft spot for him too. I have an idea he'll be a little jealous of this baby when it finally comes. But I still can't believe that Bessie didn't want him here with her for Christmas. I would never have agreed to spend Christmas apart from . . .' Her voice faltered as she suddenly remembered other Christmases with Connie and her eyes welled with tears. At least in Ireland there would not be constant reminders of her little girl, which was just one of the reasons why she wanted to go.

'So how are the dresses for the wedding coming along?' she gulped, keen to move on to another subject.

'Very well. I've shoved Seamus' bed against the wall in his bedroom and moved my machine in there so that I have more room to work. I do a little each evening, mainly on the chiffon overlays. If I can get them done it won't be so hard to fit them over the dresses then. The beadwork takes hours but I'm quite enjoying it. And now that Seamus is going to the suppliers and keeping both shops stocked for me, that's a great help too.'

'I think it's doing him good having something to keep him occupied,' Niamh confided. 'It's not too hard work so it doesn't tax him but it gives him a purpose to get up each morning. In actual fact I've decided that I'm going to go back to work at the school too after Christmas. Now that Connie . . . Well, I can't just sit at home painting and earning nothing for ever, can I? My father-in-law has been more than generous but I want to start contributing towards the upkeep of the house now.'

'That's more than admirable, but I'm sure Max wouldn't expect it of you,' Dilly said gently.

'I know that, but as I said, I feel as if it's time to start getting my life together again.'

Dilly was secretly proud of her and thought going back to work would do her the world of good. Mary was more than capable of looking after Roddy – in fact, Dilly thought she'd enjoy having him to herself for a few hours each day. They were all very fond of him and Max adored him. It was just sad that neither his mother nor father had time for the dear little fellow.

They chatted on for a while and then Niamh left to get some shopping that Bessie had asked for as Dilly set about tidying the shop.

While Niamh was shopping, Samuel was enduring his first day in the mill – sweeping the floors under the amused glances of the trained men. Even so, the idea that had come to him the evening before was growing and he had every intention of setting his plan in action that very night. Thankfully he knew just the man who might be able to help him and he frequently glanced at the clock, praying for his shift to end.

'All right, Farthing. It's time to clock off,' the supervisor told him eventually and Samuel drew himself up to his full height to glare at him.

'It's *Mr* Farthing to you,' he snapped.

'Not according to your father, lad. He told me I'm to show you no preferential treatment whatsoever, so if surnames are all right for the rest of the men, then it's all right for you.'

Samuel fought to bring his temper under control. The supervisor was clearly enjoying himself but he vowed he'd wipe that smirk off his face if it was the last thing he ever did. Slinging his broom down he turned to leave but the supervisor told him sternly, 'Oy, you put that away before you go. Don't leave it there for someone to trip over. You know where the broom cupboard is.'

Samuel forced himself to bend down and snatch the broom up, painfully aware that a number of the men were watching what was going on with grins on their faces. He stalked away and slung it into the cupboard before joining the queue waiting to clock out after their shifts, his humiliation complete.

# Chapter Thirty

Once outside, Samuel took a great gulp of fresh air and tried to calm himself before setting off for the working men's club in town in search of the man who might be able to help him. Once there, he walked across the sawdust-scattered floor through a haze of cigarette smoke and ordered a glass of ale at the bar. Sure enough the chap he wanted was sitting playing dominoes at a table to one side of the fire, so after his drink was served Samuel sauntered over to him. He didn't know the man personally but his reputation went before him.

'I've got a little matter I'd like to discuss with you,' Samuel said and the man looked up at him suspiciously.

'Oh yes? An' what would that be then?' He was slightly bemused. Samuel was dressed as a worker yet his voice was that of a gentleman.

'I'd like to discuss that with you in private.'

'Would yer now?' The man took a drag of the cigarette that had been dangling from his mouth. 'Then sit yersen over there an' I'll join yer when I've finished this game.'

With what dignity he could muster Samuel did as he was told – something he wasn't used to doing at all. But then he didn't have much choice at the moment.

He was aware of men staring at him curiously, but he gazed into the fire and waited. It seemed an age but at last the man he'd come to see rose from the table and came towards him plonking himself down at the table next to him.

'Me glass is empty,' he said rudely. 'An' I find it 'ard to discuss business wi'out a drink in me 'and.'

Samuel felt colour creep up his neck as he fumbled in his pocket praying that he had enough to refill the chap's glass. He just managed to scrape the price of a pint of ale together and when he'd placed it in front of him he then went on to explain what he wanted of him.

'An' yer sayin' that yer can't give me the money for doin' this here an' now? So how do I know I'm goin' to get it?' the chap questioned warily.

'You'll get it – and a bonus, I swear it,' Samuel told him.

The chap narrowed his eyes then decided. 'Fair enough. Write down the exact details on that there bit o' paper an' it'll be ready in a couple o' days. But I warn yer, it won't change 'ands till I'm paid fer it.'

Samuel wrote down the details that were needed, then after pushing the piece of paper across the table he said, 'I'll be here the same time the day after next then. Good evening.' With that he walked back out into the bitterly cold air.

'Now are you quite sure you've got everything?' Dilly fussed as she stood on the station platform with Niamh.

The young woman grinned. 'Yes, Mammy, I have everything but the kitchen sink, judging by all this luggage.' Glancing down at the two bulging bags containing all the presents and hers and Roddy's clothes, she joked, 'I reckon my arms will reach down to my ankles by the time I've got this lot over to Ireland. But look, here's the train. Come here, Roddy, don't get going too near the edge of the platform.'

The child obediently did as he was told as the train drew in and Dilly rushed forward to open a carriage door for them. 'Now, Bessie did prepare you some food to eat on the way?'

'She certainly did, enough to keep us going for a week, I should think. It's in one of the bags somewhere, but now will you stop fussing, Mammy?'

'Sorry, lass.' Dilly leaned in to plant a kiss on her cheek then bent to do the same to Roddy, who was impatient to board the train. She helped Niamh to lift the bags, then once they were settled in an empty carriage she stood on the platform and waved them off, suddenly wishing that she'd gone too. It would have been nice to see the family but then she was very busy and didn't want to have to shut the shop. Just for a second she stared wistfully along the track before hurrying back to open up. It seemed that almost every woman in Nuneaton wanted a new dress to wear for Christmas and she was only too happy to supply them.

That evening, after yet another horrendous shift at the mill, Samuel made his way to his parents' house. His father had flatly refused to advance him so much as a penny piece until he'd completed his first week, but somehow he had to raise the money to pay John Tompkinson, the chap who was arranging the documents he needed. It was only the day before that it had occurred to him that Bessie had money. If he remembered correctly, her late husband had left her some – so perhaps it was time to start being nice to her? The way Samuel saw it, needs must – and he could be a charmer when it suited him.

Mrs Pegs raised her eyebrows when he opened the back door and walked through the kitchen. 'I ain't cooked for yer, if that's what you've come for,' she said boldly. 'I need a bit o' notice.'

'Oh no, it's quite all right,' he said pleasantly. 'I shall be eating with Seamus and Mary but I just thought I'd pop in and see Mother on my way home from work.'

'Since when 'as *he* been so concerned about his family?' the woman remarked to Gwen when he'd left the room. She sniffed. 'I reckon he must be after sommat again.'

Samuel took the stairs two at a time. On the landing, he paused to smooth his hair down before tapping gently on Camilla's bedroom door.

'Oh . . . it's you again,' Bessie said ungraciously when she opened it. 'I'm afraid this ain't a good time to come visitin'. Your mother is havin' a bad day.' A sudden crash confirmed what she'd just said, and as she turned hastily to see what had happened, Samuel stepped into the room, closing the door behind him.

'*Why* won't you bring Violet to me?' Camilla wailed as Bessie rushed over to her. She had swept a row of perfume bottles from the dressing table and the cloying scent was filling the room. Her hair was standing on end and with the look of madness shining in her eyes she put Samuel in mind of a witch.

'Now then, I think it's time you had your tablet, don't you?' Bessie soothed as she took one from her apron pocket. She then led the woman gently towards the bed and lifting a glass of water, she held the pill out to her.

'Who is that?' Camilla asked, pointing a wavering finger at Samuel. 'Tell him to go away. I want Violet.'

'It's me, Mother.' Samuel took a faltering step towards her but she shrank away from him.

'I don't know you,' she screeched. 'Go away this minute.'

Bessie caught her firmly round the waist as the poor soul began to lash out and somehow managed to shove the tablet into her mouth.

'There now, that's better, isn't it?' She seemed to have all the patience in the world as Camilla coughed and spluttered. 'Now swallow that, there's a good girl and 'ave a little drink to wash it down. You'll start to feel better in no time, I promise.' Holding the glass to Camilla's lips she managed to pour a little into her open mouth and within seconds the woman had become calmer.

'Now how about a little rest?' Bessie suggested then, sitting her on the edge of the bed and swinging her legs up. Camilla's eyelids began to flutter before they closed and Bessie sighed with relief as she straightened.

'She'll sleep for a while now,' she informed Samuel shortly as she bent to start cleaning up the mess. 'So you may as well leave.'

'You're very good with her.' Samuel stayed exactly where he was as she stared at him suspiciously.

'Cut the flannel. What do you want?' You could always trust Bessie to say what she thought. He'd also noticed that she'd slipped back into the local dialect.

'I don't want anything. I was merely passing a comment.'

'Hmm – an' I'm a monkey's uncle. Is it money yer after?'

'Well, as it happens a small loan wouldn't come amiss,' he muttered, deeply embarrassed.

'So why have you come to me? Go an' ask yer father.' It was taking her all her time to even speak to him after what he'd done to her.

Samuel's face set in grim lines. 'Don't speak to me like that,' he growled. 'Remember – your name would be mud in this town if I was to let it be known that Roddy is my bastard! As it is, everyone thinks you're a respectable widow, that Roddy was your husband's—'

'How *dare* you!' Bessie snatched up the poker from the fireplace, hands on hips, her eyes flashing, and Samuel was so surprised he took a step back from her.

'You almost ruined my life the night you raped me,' she hissed, hatred in every word. 'But worse still, that resulted in a child being born who I can't love! Did you hear me? *I – can't – love – him!* How do you think that makes me feel, eh? It's unnatural, but every time I look at him I see *you*. Poor little mite, it's not even his fault! And now you have the audacity to come here with your threats demanding money. Well, you can bugger off 'cos I tell you now, if I was to see you lying in the gutter on fire I'd not piss on you to put the fire out. Now get out afore I hit you wi' this!' Suddenly all the humiliation and hurt she had bottled up over the years was spewing out of her and she raised the poker threateningly as bright colour stained her cheeks.

Like the coward he was, Samuel was so shocked at Bessie's outburst that he almost stumbled in his haste to leave the room. Once out on the landing he slammed the door behind him and let his breath out in a hiss. Bessie had made it abundantly clear that she wouldn't help him.

Then it came to him. The figurines in the china cabinet – they must be worth a small fortune. Hurrying down the stairs, he crept into the sitting room and after making sure that he was alone he opened the door of the cabinet and pocketed two of what he hoped were the most valuable items. His father probably wouldn't even miss them, and if Samuel got a move on, he'd be in time to reach the pawnbrokers before they shut.

In town, he was offered a fraction of what the pieces were worth. There wasn't much call for expensive figurines, as the pawnbroker went to great pains to tell him, but at least it would be enough to pay Tompkinson. Samuel then set off for the club and found the chap he was looking for sitting in exactly the same seat as he'd been in before. Samuel sat down with his ale and after a while Tompkinson sauntered over to him.

'Have yer got the readies then?' he asked.

When Samuel nodded, the other man took a document from the inside pocket of his overcoat and shoved it across the table.

Samuel quickly examined it then smiled. 'It's perfect,' he told him, sliding the banknotes under the table towards him.

'Pleased to be o' service,' Tompkinson said, surreptitiously counting the money. 'But if yer up to mischief an' it should misfire, don't try blamin' it on me,' he warned, licking his blackened teeth.

Transaction concluded, Samuel wasted no time in getting the hell out of there. The whole place stank of stale ale, body odour and dirt, and he couldn't get away quickly enough. Even so he couldn't stop smiling as he headed for the house on Abbey Green. If all went to plan, he should be able to leave the area in no time – and this time he'd make sure that he never set had to set foot in the place again.

'Aw, me darlin' girl. Sure it's wonderful to see you so it is,' Maeve said as a very weary Niamh entered the kitchen later that evening. 'But look at you, you're worn out, poor lass. Sit yourself down, an' I'll fetch you a nice hot cup o' tea.'

Daniel came in then carrying Roddy who had fallen asleep in the trap on the way back from the port and now he laid him gently down on the sofa.

'I reckon this one is out for the count.' He chuckled. 'I don't mind bettin' we won't hear a peep out of him now till morning. But come on, woman, where's me tea? It's blowin' a blizzard out there an' it's enough to slice you in two, so it is.'

Niamh felt as if she had never been away as she listened to the gentle banter. Her grandparents had the sort of marriage that she would have had with Ben, she was sure, but it was no use pining about that now. What was done was done, and at least she was here safe and sound. There had been times on the ferry when she'd wondered if they'd make it, for the sea had been rough and the boat had bobbed about like a cork. Poor Roddy had been sick almost the whole way, but she hoped that when he woke up he would feel better. It never failed to amaze her how resilient children could be.

'So how is everyone?' she asked as her gran'ma placed a steaming mug of tea into her cold hands.

'Right as rain,' Maeve informed her brightly. 'Roisin is positively glowing, though I'd sooner they'd have waited a bit longer before trying for another baby atween you an' me. Still what's done is done and God willing all will go well this time.'

'And . . . how is Ben?' Niamh asked, trying to keep her voice casual.

'Same as always, working hard.' Maeve sighed. 'I wish he'd find himself a nice lass though. I know he's accepted your marriage now and there's no lack of wee girls queuing up for him but he don't seem interested. Still, no doubt he'll meet the right one someday. But now tell me all about what's been going on back at home.'

So Niamh did exactly that as they sat at either side of the cheery fire.

The next morning, Niamh woke to a leaden grey sky full of rainclouds and the sound of rain drumming on the window; it was dancing off the cobbles in the yard and streaming down the gullies, and the wind was fierce, making the windowframe rattle.

Shivering, she pulled her dressing gown on and hurried

down to the kitchen where she found Roddy sitting at the table tucking into soft-boiled eggs and fresh baked bread smeared with Maeve's home-made butter.

'I'm going to see Roisin after breakfast,' he informed her with his mouth full. 'An' then this afternoon me an' Maeve are going to put the baubles on the Christmas tree, aren't we, Maeve?'

'We are that,' Maeve agreed, smiling at him affectionately. The boy was shooting up now and it was hard to believe that he would soon be starting school, but then as she knew all too well, they didn't stay children for long. It seemed no time at all since her own sons had been his age.

Niamh helped herself to a glass of milk, saying carelessly, 'I thought I might go for a nice long walk after breakfast, unless there's anything you want me to help you with?'

'A nice long walk!' Maeve glanced towards the window. 'Why, you must have taken leave of your senses, lass, so you must! Have you seen what it's like out there? You'll be soaked to the skin in seconds so you will and you might catch your death.'

Niamh grinned. 'Rubbish, Gran'ma. As long as I wrap up I'll be fine and the fresh air will do me good.'

'It's fresh all right. In fact it's enough to blow your head off out there but you're old enough to please yourself, I dare say,' Maeve huffed. Niamh chuckled as she placed a slice of bread on the toasting fork and held it out to the fire. Perhaps her walk could wait until later. She and her gran'ma had a lot of catching up to do.

# *Chapter Thirty-One*

'Hello, Father.'

'Hello, darling.' Max settled further back into the chair to enjoy his conversation with Olivia. She had rung right on time as she'd promised and now he was eager to know when she would be coming home for Christmas. It seemed such a long time since he'd seen her and he was looking forward to the family being all together again.

'So have you sorted out train times, et cetera? I can meet you at the station if you like,' he said. 'Mrs Pegs has your room all aired and ready for you.'

In the large hallway in Queenie's house in London, Olivia bit down on her lip before answering. 'I'm sorry, Daddy, but I won't be making it home for Christmas this year. It's work, you understand? We only get Christmas Day off so there's no point in going all that way for just one night.'

'But you *must* come home!' Disappointment was sharp in her father's voice and tears sprang to Olivia's eyes. 'We've always spent Christmas together. It wouldn't be the same without you.'

'I know and I'm sorry, but it can't be helped.' Olivia was missing her family so much it was like a physical pain but she kept her voice light. 'I should be able to get back towards the end of January or early in February, and we can have a belated Christmas meal together then.'

One of the girls who lodged there passed Olivia at that moment on her way to the front door and glanced at her curiously as she saw the tears in the girl's eyes, but Olivia forced a smile.

'But what about your presents? Isn't it about time you gave me the address of where you're staying? I could at least post them on to you then.' There was an edge of irritation in Max's words now but Olivia remained firm. She had no choice.

'There'd be no point. They probably wouldn't get here in time anyway now. Let's wait and open them together, eh? It'll be so much nicer.' There was only silence at the other end of the line as Max grappled with his confusion so Olivia said hastily, 'Look, Daddy, there's someone here waiting to use the telephone so I'm going to have to go, but do give my love to everyone there and tell them I'm thinking of them.'

'But, Olivia . . .'

'Bye, Daddy. I'll phone again very soon.' With that she slammed the receiver down as if it had bitten her and as Queenie appeared and saw her distress she placed a comforting arm about her shoulders.

'Come on, luvvie. Let's go an' scrounge a nice cup o' tea off Cook, eh? You'll be goin' home again soon enough.'

Olivia nodded numbly. She hated lying to her father – but what else could she do?

*

Back at the shop in Nuneaton, Dilly kept glancing anxiously towards the window for a sight of Max. Olivia had promised to phone him that morning to tell him when she intended to come home for Christmas and Dilly was all fingers and thumbs. Thankfully the shop was so busy that she barely had time to think, but even so when the bell above the door tinkled and Max stepped in late morning, she hurriedly finished serving her customer.

The second the door had closed, Dilly demanded eagerly, 'Well? Did she ring? When is she coming?'

Max shook his head sadly. He'd been looking forward to seeing Olivia as much as Dilly had.

'Yes, she did ring but I'm afraid she's not coming back for Christmas. She says she's far too busy with her theatre work but promised that she'll be able to take a few days off towards the end of January or early in February.'

'That's something, I suppose.' Dilly was trying desperately hard not to show how disappointed she was. 'But has she still not given you her address? No? Don't you find that strange?'

'She does ring regularly every week,' Max said heavily. 'And she says we can share presents when she comes home. I think we both know how low she was when she left and I think she just needs this time to come to terms with things, which is why I haven't pressured her into giving me an address. I think I'd know if anything was wrong but she sounds fine, I promise you.'

'I suppose we'll just have to wait until she feels ready to come home then,' Dilly answered regretfully and he could only nod in agreement.

In Enniskerry, Niamh was battling against the wind and rain as she picked her way through the muddy puddles in the rough track that led to the town. The weather was quite as bad as her gran'ma had warned, but she would have walked through fire to catch a glimpse of Ben. The wind was whistling through the trees and they bent towards her as she passed beneath them, but never once did her footsteps waver until the town came into sight. Then at last she was outside the smithy. After the bitter cold the heat inside made sweat pop out on her forehead but she didn't even notice as her eyes settled on Ben, who was leaning over an anvil hammering away at a tin bucket he was making.

'Niamh!' He instantly stopped what he was doing to rush over to her and take her hands in his. 'You look wonderful.'

She chuckled. 'I hardly think so in Granda's waterproof and with my hair all over the place.' She could only begin to imagine what a sight she must be.

'You'd look beautiful in a paper bag, so you would,' he joked, but then became serious as he said, 'Your poor hands are frozen. Come over to the cottage and I'll make us a hot drink. You don't have to rush back for a while, do you?'

'No, but what about this place?' she asked doubtfully. 'I wouldn't want you losing trade on account of me.'

He waved his hand airily as he led her towards the door at the back. 'Don't be worrying about that now. Trade is always quiet this time of year.' With that they walked the short distance to the cottage and Niamh grinned as she looked around at the chaos. There were dirty clothes and pots everywhere and the furniture was covered with dust so thick that she could have written her name in it.

'Sorry about the mess,' he said sheepishly as he followed her eyes. 'I didn't think you'd be able to get away until tonight so I was going to close early this afternoon and come over and have a good clean-up, so I was.'

Niamh lifted the kettle and filled it at the sink then pushed it onto the fire and took her coat off. 'Once I've had a hot drink and thawed out a little I'll have it straight in no time,' she told him.

'No, you will not,' he said, wagging his finger at her. 'I don't expect you to come here and clean up after me. Maeve is always telling me I'm big enough to look after meself but I don't seem to have got the hang of this housework lark.'

Niamh smiled as she began to collect the dirty clothes into a pile then warmed the teapot and prepared two mugs as Ben cleared the pots from the table into the deep stone sink.

'I've had a letter from me mammy today – look.' He took it from his pocket, and Niamh noticed that he'd referred to the woman as Mammy for the first time in her presence. It was a good sign. She knew how much Ben had always longed to know where he had come from, and she was glad that they were getting on so well.

'Has she gone to New York yet?'

He shook his head. 'No, she postponed her journey till the New Year. Maeve has invited her to spend Christmas Day with us at the farm, so you'll get to meet her. Won't that be grand?'

'It certainly will – I can hardly wait.' Niamh was delighted to see how his face lit up when he spoke of her. Elizabeth McFarren must really be a lovely woman indeed to have won him over so quickly. Niamh was just relieved that he hadn't agreed to go to New York with her. She didn't know how she could bear that. At least now they got to see each other occasionally, which was better than nothing. Niamh was writing to him regularly now and so she wasn't surprised when he asked, 'And is Samuel still at home?'

'Yes, he is.' She couldn't help but smile as she went on, 'And not at all happy about having to sweep floors for a living in his father's mill. I think he knows though that he's on his last warning so he's doing as he's told – for now anyway. Goodness knows how long he'll be able to keep it up.'

'Serves him right.' Ben had no sympathy for him whatsoever. From where he was standing, Samuel had asked for all he'd got – and more besides.

'Anyway, let's not waste what time we have together talking about him any more,' Niamh said then. 'Tell me what you've been up to.'

Ben was more than happy to oblige and they were so at ease with one another that anyone glimpsing them working together to tidy the room could have taken them for a married couple. Niamh felt at home there as she never had in the lovely house that Max had provided for her and once again she sighed wistfully as she thought of how things might have been.

'But *why* won't you come and have dinner with us?' Max asked on Christmas Eve as Dilly was closing the shop up.

'Because it wouldn't be right,' she answered primly, turning the Closed sign on the door. 'I am still your former servant, you know. What would people say? Mrs Pegs for a start-off.'

'Nonsense. You are now a businesswoman in your own right and you know how much Mrs Pegs thinks of you,' he coaxed.

Still Dilly stood firm. She'd decided she wanted to spend the day alone, and upstairs was a small chicken waiting to be cooked. She'd catch up on her bookwork and have a rest before she re-opened the shop the day after Boxing Day, and nothing was going to sway her. Mary and Seamus would be dining together and Max was having the whole family, apart from Olivia, to his house; even Samuel was included. Dilly didn't want to encroach and was actually quite looking forward to having a little time to herself.

'Then if you're sure I can't persuade you I'd better give you this now – but don't open it until tomorrow,' he told her sulkily as he handed her a small, beautifully wrapped box.

'You really shouldn't have,' she told him, then scuttled away to fetch his gift. It was a fine cashmere scarf with matching leather gloves and she hoped that he'd like them. When she'd bought them from the finest menswear shop in town, she'd smiled ruefully at the price. They'd cost more than she had used to be able to spend on the whole of the family put together, but she didn't begrudge a penny of it. Sometimes she wondered how she would have got through the past few years without Max.

'Will Camilla be coming down to join you for dinner?' she asked him then.

'No. It's highly unlikely. She'll probably have her meal in her room with Bessie. I really don't know what I'd do without that young woman. I dread to think how I'd manage Camilla now if Bessie were to leave, but I'm realistic enough to know that she's going to want to get on with her own life at some stage. I believe that she's been looking around for a small property to buy and I wonder if that will be the start of her wanting to take control of her own life again. I do worry about Roddy though. I've grown very fond of the child, as you're aware. He is my grandson, after all, the same as George is.' He smiled then. 'Oscar informed me that Penelope didn't want to accept my invitation to dine but when he put his foot down and told her that he was coming anyway, she relented. She's not the best of company as you know, but at least I'll get to spend a few hours with George. I doubt Patty and Lawrence will be much company either. They're still too busy mooning over each other. It's ironic when you think of it, isn't it? I have one son who can't stand his wife, another who can't keep his eyes or hands off his and another whose wife won't even be there – no insult intended for Niamh, of course. Between you and me I don't blame her for going away. Then there will be the absence of Olivia and Harvey . . . I sometimes wish we could just cancel Christmas, don't you?'

'Oh, stop being such a misery guts,' she laughed, patting his hand. 'If you come upstairs I'll treat you to one of Mrs Pegs' delicious mince pies and a glass of sherry – but only if you promise to smile.'

'I think I could manage that.'

They had just reached the sitting room when someone hammered on the shop door and Dilly sighed. 'Help yourself to a drink while I go and see who it is,' she told Max as she ran downstairs again.

He had poured two glasses of sherry and was just sitting down when Dilly reappeared carrying the most enormous bouquet of flowers he had ever seen.

'What's this then? Have you got a secret admirer?' The words were said jokingly but Dilly detected that he was none too pleased as she read the little card that was tucked inside them.

'They're from Henry Price wishing me a Happy Christmas.'

Suddenly the atmosphere was tense.

'I'll just go and pop them in some water and fetch those mince pies,' Dilly said, but draining his glass in one gulp, Max shook his head.

'Not for me, Dilly, thank you,' he said stiffly. 'I really ought to be going.'

'So soon?' she said disappointedly.

'Yes. I've just remembered something I have to do, but thank you for the present.' He shrugged his coat on and paused before crossing to her. Then very gently he placed his lips on hers and she felt a tingle throughout her body.

'Merry Christmas, Dilly.' And then he was gone, leaving her to touch her lips with tears in her eyes.

Suddenly the thought of a lonely Christmas was daunting although she knew she should be used to it by now. It seemed a long, long time since she'd had someone special to share it with and her mind slipped back to when she and Fergal had first been wed. They would go to Midnight Mass together on Christmas Eve then return to their little cottage full of hope for the future. Soon the children had started to come along, each one wanted and beloved, and their routine had changed slightly. Instead of spending the evening in church they would spend it sitting around the Christmas tree telling the children stories and putting out milk and mince pies before they went to bed for Santa Claus and his reindeers. Such happy times!

Dilly sighed wistfully as she gazed around her small rooms. It hadn't seemed worth going to the trouble of buying a tree when there was only her to see it, and the room suddenly looked bare. Still, she consoled herself, she had a lot to be thankful for. Her shops were doing a brisk trade and the following year they would no doubt do even better. Crossing to a drawing pad that lay open on the table, she looked at some of the designs she'd been working on. She would get the seamstresses to put them together in the New Year and see how they sold. Feeling slightly better, she went to make herself a light meal.

# Chapter Thirty-Two

'That's it,' Queenie encouraged the girl on the bed. 'Shouldn't be long now an' the midwife will be here any minute. Fiona, run downstairs and check would you?'

Fiona fled gratefully. If this was what giving birth entailed then she decided there and then that she was never going to have a baby, ever!

Ten minutes later she showed a plump middle-aged woman carrying a large black bag into the room.

'She's nearly a month early accordin' to her dates,' Queenie informed the midwife the instant she appeared.

Nurse Bourne, not the prettiest of creatures but very kindly, slipped off her coat and rolled up the sleeves of her dress before washing her hands with the soap and water Queenie had ready.

'Right then, young lady, let's have a look at you,' she said as she approached the bed.

Olivia stared up at her from frightened eyes. The midwife's hair was steel grey and pulled into a bun on the back of her head, but it was the hairs sprouting out of her chin that the girl focused on.

'Hmm.' She ran her hands across the swollen stomach and asked, 'How long has she been like this?'

'The pains started mid-mornin' an' they've got worse as the day's worn on. Is everyfink all right?'

'It seems to be.' The woman glanced at the third finger of the girl's left hand. There was no wedding ring there but then Nurse Bourne didn't hold it against her. She'd delivered her fair share of babies born out of wedlock during and since the war, which just went to show how the world was changing.

'You should feel the urge to push soon,' she told the girl calmly. 'When you do, tell me and don't panic. Just try to do as I tell you and it should be over in no time.'

The girl groaned and held fast to Queenie's hand as another contraction gripped her. Sweat was beaded on her brow and she was exhausted but still she didn't cry out. The way she saw it she'd got herself into this mess so she just had to make the best of it somehow.

Minutes later she leaned slightly up and gasped, 'I want to push!'

'Excellent! Let's have a peep at you then.' Nurse Bourne swiftly parted Olivia's legs and smiled with satisfaction. 'Good girl, now do exactly what I tell you. Pant . . . that's it, then push when I tell you – with all your might!'

She was impressed with the girl. Most young first-time mothers were usually screaming the place down by now but this one was doing exactly as she told her. 'Good . . . good . . . that's it, now *push*!'

The girl obliged, going red in the face with the effort before flopping back onto the pillows when the contraction passed.

'Now when the next pain comes I want you to do exactly the same again,' the nurse ordered.

The minutes, although they seemed like hours to the mother-to-be, ticked away until she was sure that the labour was going to go on for ever. But then at last, the midwife told her, 'The next one should do it if you really try hard.' As she spoke, the church bells began to peal and she said, 'Why, it's Christmas Day!'

The girl heard the bells from a world of pain and didn't think she had another push in her. Even so, as the contraction seized her yet again and she was sure that she was about to be torn in two, she gritted her teeth and with Queenie shouting words of encouragement in her ear she pushed with every ounce of strength she had left. She felt the baby slide out of her and as the midwife bent to it and slapped its bottom soundly, a mew like that of a kitten filled the room, mingling with the sound of the church bells.

'Aw luvvie!' Queenie had tears in her eyes. 'You've got yourself a fine baby girl an' she's a little beauty, the double o' you!'

The midwife expertly cut the cord attaching the child to its mother and then after wrapping the baby in a towel that Queenie held out to her, she placed her on the girl's chest.

Olivia stared at her in awe, wondering how anything so perfect could ever have come from her body. Suddenly all her doubts and fears dissolved and she knew that from this moment on, her child would be the most important person in her life. She didn't care now about the stigma of being an unmarried mother, nor of what people would say; nor did she worry about how she would manage.

'Is she all right?' Queenie asked the nurse anxiously.

'A bit on the small side, but then she would be if she's early. But she appears to be healthy enough. She's certainly got a good pair of lungs on her.'

Queenie sighed with relief. The last few months had not been easy but all the worry seemed worth it now. 'Have you got a name for her, duckie?' she asked Olivia as she tenderly stroked the thatch of reddish downy hair on the baby's head.

'Her name will be Jessica Camilla Farthing,' Olivia announced quietly.

# Chapter Thirty-Three

'Well done, Olivia. Now let me take her and get her bathed and dressed for you while the nurse tidies you up.'

Olivia reluctantly handed her baby to Queenie and lay back against the pillows feeling exhausted but strangely at peace.

'Well, you certainly won't forget her birthday,' Nurse Bourne chuckled as she deftly delivered Olivia's afterbirth. 'It's the first baby I've ever brought into the world on Christmas Day, bless her.'

But Olivia had retreated into a world of her own as her mind raced back across the last few anxious months. To begin with, she had enjoyed her stay in London. It would have been hard not to. The flower-sellers on the street corners, the sights and smells of Covent Garden and the boats chugging along the River Thames were so different from the market town in which she'd been brought up. But always underneath she'd worried about what would happen to her when she could no longer hide the fact that she was with child. She'd known when she left home that soon her condition would become obvious, but then Queenie had allowed her to stay in the lodging house and she'd got a job in the theatre and tried to block her situation from her mind as if by not thinking about it, the problem might go away. It didn't go away, of course, and one day Queenie had asked her quietly, 'Is there anythin' yer want to tell me, luvvie?'

Olivia had been mortified as she spilled out the story of her short affair with Roger, but she hadn't told Queenie what had driven her into his arms in the first place. She was too ashamed to tell anyone of her feelings for her brother, or of how she couldn't bear to see him married to someone else. She'd expected the landlady to give her her marching orders – and she wouldn't have blamed her – but instead Queenie had drawn her into her plump, soft arms and told her, 'When you get too big to work, you can help out here until after the birth and then we'll take it from there.'

Olivia had stared at her, astounded. 'Do you mean it?' she'd gasped.

Queenie had nodded. 'Yes I do, although personally I think you should go home. Your father sounds a reasonable man and though I've no doubt he'll be shocked at first, I reckon he'll forgive you.'

Colour had flooded into Olivia's cheeks as she'd shaken her head vehemently. 'No . . . he'd be so ashamed of me.'

'So what will you do then? Stay away from home for ever?' Then, seeing that the girl was becoming agitated, Queenie had patted her hand. 'Why don't we just get the birth over with and see how you feel then, eh? You might decide you don't want to keep the baby, in which case there are places you can go to where they'll arrange an adoption for you. There again, you might decide that you can't bear to part with the little 'un – so let's just cross each bridge as we come to it.'

That was exactly what they'd done. Olivia had worked for as long as she could, but when she began to waddle like a duck and her ankles began to swell alarmingly, Queenie had put her foot down.

'That's enough,' she said firmly one morning when Olivia came into the kitchen for breakfast looking, as Queenie tactlessly put it, 'like death warmed up'. 'I reckon you should finish work now. You've been having pains an' it's far too early for the baby to come yet. If you won't do it for yourself, do it for the little mite you're carryin'.'

Olivia had agreed. She had been feeling unwell and she was quietly relieved not to have to be on her feet all day. Instead she helped out around the house, although Queenie watched over her like a mother hen and made her put her feet up and rest at regular intervals.

And then this morning she'd started to have twinges and Queenie had gone into a flap. 'But you've got another four weeks still to go. It's too soon. I've heard of babies comin' two weeks either way, but surely four is too much?' She didn't know that much about childbirth never having had any children of her own.

'Perhaps – you-should-tell-this-one-that,' Olivia had gasped as a pain took her breath away.

And now at last the birth was over. Suddenly she desperately wanted to see her mother and father – not that her mother would probably have even known her. The birth of a child should be a special event for anyone, but Olivia had given birth miles away from her family. Worse still, they didn't even know that she was going to have a child. The dear familiar faces that she so missed flashed in front of her eyes. Her mother, father, brothers and of course Oscar – he was never more than a thought away despite all her

291

best efforts to estrange herself from him. And then there was Mrs Pegs, and Mrs Carey. Dear Mrs Carey, she'd always been a part of Olivia's life from as far back as she could remember, and she felt a special bond with her, probably because Dilly had always been so kind to her . . .

The birth now presented another set of problems that she had so far refused to think about. Queenie had been kindness itself over the last two months, refusing to take any money for her board and keep, in exchange for help about the house. But now Olivia would have to consider how she was going to manage financially. The allowance she received each month from her grandmother would not stretch to keeping two people without her working, and who, she fretted, would care for the baby if she got herself a job? No doubt Queenie would volunteer like a shot but the huge woman had not been in the best of health and Olivia didn't feel that she could hoist that responsibility onto her.

Her thoughts suddenly jerked back to the present when Nurse Bourne said, 'Right, that's all done. Let's get you washed and changed now and then you can have a cuddle of the new arrival.' She removed Olivia's stained nightgown and washed her from head to toe, and in no time at all Olivia was propped up in a nice clean bed with her hair brushed looking neat as a new pin. Apart from the fact that she was still pale and feeling a little weak, no one would have believed that she'd recently given birth.

As the midwife started to pack her bag, Queenie reappeared carrying the baby wrapped in a white shawl. The infant's cries were louder now and Queenie chuckled.

'I reckon this one wants a feed. Do yer feel up to it, luvvie?'

Olivia nodded as she unfastened the buttons on her clean nightgown and in no time at all the baby was nestled against her, greedily sucking at her mother's breast.

'She looks just like you,' Queenie commented as she looked happily on. 'Apart from the fact that she has blue eyes.'

'Almost all new babies have blue eyes,' the midwife informed her as she shrugged into her coat. 'There's plenty of time for them to change and they probably will if her mother's are anything to go by. But now I'll be on my way if you don't mind. It is Christmas Day and my family will be waiting for me.'

Olivia thanked her profusely for all she'd done, then as Queenie saw her out she turned her attention back to her daughter, feeling like the luckiest woman in the world. She had another little person to care for now and she knew that from this moment on, her life would never be the same again.

Samuel left the house at eleven o'clock on Christmas morning to dine at his parents', and from that moment on Mary and Seamus began to enjoy themselves.

'I'd better go and prepare the vegetables. The goose is already in the oven,' Mary said but Seamus argued with her.

'Come and have a glass of sherry first then I'll help you with the vegetables.'

Mary looked positively horrified at both suggestions. 'I can't do that! I don't drink and I certainly can't let you help. I'm the servant here.'

Because it was a special day, Mary was wearing the dress Dilly had had made for her as a Christmas present. It was in a lovely shade of blue, and with her hair shining and loose about her shoulders Seamus thought he had never seen her look so pretty. Yet strangely he wouldn't have cared if Mary had still been clad in her work clothes. Mary would never be a conventional beauty, she was a little too plump and didn't make the best of herself for most of the time, but her main beauty came from within. She was gentle and kind, and in that instant the young man realised that he was developing feelings for her. It hit him like a ton of bricks as he hastily turned to pour a small amount of sherry into two glasses.

'Not at all,' he replied, trying hard not to let her see that his hand was shaking. 'There are just the two of us here, so for today we can do as we like – and we're going to start with a drink. Just try it for me, you might like it.'

Mary hesitantly took the glass from him and sipped it. 'It's quite nice actually,' she admitted, 'but I won't have any more if you don't mind. I'll not be in a fit state to cook the dinner if I do.'

Once she'd drained her glass and hurried off to the kitchen, Seamus sat down heavily, feeling deflated. Now that he'd acknowledged that he was drawn to Mary, he realised that the attraction between them had been growing for some time. But what good would it do him? Why should a girl like Mary consider tying herself up to a wreck like him? Admittedly he was far better than he had been, but he still had dark times when he would shake uncontrollably and suffer from horrendous nightmares. It would start with no warning whatsoever, then the following day he would be fit for nothing, unable to cope with even the most mundane tasks. He was now able to work for his mother part-time, fetching and delivering stock to the shops, but a part-time post would not secure somewhere for himself and a wife to live and he was too proud to expect a woman to keep him.

Seamus stared moodily into the fire, deciding it would be better to leave things as they were. Mary was a lovely lass and no doubt soon she'd meet some healthy young chap who would be able to offer her far more than he could. With his mind made up he settled in the chair and kept well away from the kitchen.

In the Farthing household the family were now assembled in the drawing room and little George was the centre of attention.

'He's a lovely baby,' Patty cooed as she tickled his chubby legs. She would have liked to have held him but Penelope was hanging possessively on to him.

Max was pleased to note that Samuel was looking more like his old self again. Max had paid the tailor in town a considerable amount of money to restock his son's wardrobe. Samuel would have preferred to have the money in his hand, but not wishing to rock the boat he had held his tongue. The way he saw it, if everything went to plan it wouldn't be for much longer and then his father – and the whole damn lot of them, if it came to that – could stew in their own juice!

He glanced around at the gathering. Lawrence , his twin, and Patty were still behaving like lovesick schoolchildren and Oscar looked thoroughly wretched as Penelope hovered over their son. There was clearly no love lost there. Camilla had been brought downstairs and Bessie had done her best to make their mother look nice but had failed miserably. Camilla sat staring vacantly into the fire, her clothes hanging loosely off her, her face lined with pain and her mouth hanging slackly open. Then there was Bessie who stood protectively behind her, openly glaring at Samuel every time he so much as caught her eye.

Bessie was bubbling with rage. Every time she saw the way Penelope was billing and cooing over her son, guilt sharp as a knife lanced through her. Why couldn't she feel that way about Roddy? She'd actually looked forward to his birth, and yet once he'd arrived she'd never been able to bond with him. She knew it was because he was like a smaller version of his father to look at, but it didn't stop her hating herself. He was her flesh and blood, after all, no matter how he had been conceived – and she knew that she must be unnatural to feel as she did. Now here was his father strutting about in his fancy new clothes as if he owned the place, yet he'd been set on sweeping floors, which in her eyes made him no better than she was. When she thought back to the magical Christmases she had spent with Malcolm, this one didn't measure up at all.

Even Mr Farthing seemed on edge. He was obviously trying far too hard to make the atmosphere cheery and was not succeeding. Samuel was making it more than apparent that he could hardly wait for the meal to be over so that he could escape, in no mood to play happy families.

'Would you like a little glass of wine?' Max asked his wife then, breaking Bessie's chain of thought, but Bessie shook her head firmly.

'Best not, sir,' she advised firmly. 'Not with the tablets she's on.'

'Oh, of course. I'm sorry – I didn't think. But will you have one, Bessie?' Max backed away to get her a drink, feeling uncomfortable. Christmas wasn't the same without Harvey and Olivia, and he doubted it ever would be again. He felt so sad as he thought back to Christmases past when the house had been full of laughter.

At that moment Dilly was popping a small chicken into the oven in her rooms above the shop. She'd spent the morning drawing sketches of designs that she wanted the seam-stresses to make up in the New Year and hardly felt it was worth cooking a meal just for herself, but then she supposed she should make some sort of effort.

She was just about to start peeling some vegetables when there was a loud rap on the shop door. She frowned, wondering who it could be come calling today of all days. And because she'd thought she wouldn't be seeing anyone she was wearing comfortable rather than smart clothes. It was too late to worry about that now though, so with a sigh she went down to see who was there.

When she opened the door she was astonished to find Henry Price standing on the step with a broad grin on his face.

'Merry Christmas, Dilly!' He dragged off his hat and gave a gallant little bow. 'You haven't eaten yet, have you?'

'Well, no, but . . .'

'Ah, good. In that case may I ask you to join me for dinner? My cook has done us proud and everything is in the car all ready to eat in a hamper. I swear she's piled the dishes with enough to keep us going for at least a week.'

'But . . . I thought you were having dinner with Eleanor and her fiancé?' she said, astounded.

'Last-minute change of plan. Her future in-laws begged her to spend the day with them and as I didn't like to think of you all alone, I was only too happy for her to go. You're not going to send me away, are you?'

Before Dilly could reply he sprinted across to the car and removed the most enormous hamper she had ever seen.

'Do you see what I mean?' he chuckled. 'Please take pity on me, Dilly.'

'You'd er . . . better come in,' she whispered. 'But I'm afraid I'm looking rather a mess. I wasn't expecting company today.' How could she send him away?

'I was just thinking how lovely you looked.'

She blushed at the compliment as she flicked a stray lock of hair behind her ear.

By the time he'd carted the hamper upstairs he was breathless and panting. He plonked it down on the table and laughed.

'I think the cook must have stuffed this goose with a house brick,' he joked as he opened the hamper. First to be taken out was a large silver salver, and when he removed the lid Dilly gazed at the most enormous goose she'd ever seen still steaming fresh from the oven. Another dish contained roast potatoes, another a selection of vegetables, various sauces and so it went on until the small table was covered with food. There was even a huge Christmas pudding and a jug of creamy custard.

'So . . . will you help me do it justice then?' Henry rubbed his hands together as Dilly hurried away to fetch plates, cutlery and a sharp knife. She didn't really feel as if she had much choice, although she had to admit that the food did look delicious.

'The staff will be glad to get me out of the way,' he confided as he began to carve the bird. 'They can have a bit of a knees-up now.'

In no time at all Dilly was seated with a loaded plate of food in front of her.

'I shall never manage to eat all this, Henry,' she objected but he merely laughed.

'Just tuck in and eat what you can. I know I shall,' he said, raising the glass of wine she had poured for them both. They clinked glasses and Dilly found that she was beginning to enjoy herself.

'I'd just put a chicken in the oven,' she told him with a grin. 'But I must admit this rather beats it.'

Henry was an amusing companion and by the time they'd eaten Dilly was totally at ease with him.

'I must wash all the dishes before you put them back in the hamper,' she said.

Henry glowered at her. 'You most certainly will not. We'll put them back in just as they are and they can be done when I get them back home. You're having the rest of the day off – I insist. I bet you've been working this morning, haven't you?'

'Well, I did do a little bookwork and a few sketches,' she admitted. It was quite nice to be spoiled for a change, she was discovering.

'I thought as much,' he said mock sternly, then reaching into his pocket he withdrew a small box. Dilly suddenly realised that she hadn't unwrapped Max's gift yet and suffered all manner of guilt because she hadn't bought anything for Henry, but then she hadn't expected to see him and they didn't really know each other that well so she hadn't given it a thought.

'I hope that isn't for me,' she said, deeply embarrassed. 'Because I didn't think I'd be seeing you and I haven't got you anything. The flowers were enough anyway. Thank you, they're gorgeous. '

He glanced across at them in the vase where they were displayed and made a mental note to thank the florist. He'd asked for something special and the woman had certainly done him proud.

'Nonsense,' he said, waving aside her objections. 'It's nothing much, so please accept it.'

Reluctantly she sprang the lid then gasped. A gold brooch in the shape of a filigree leaf nestled in tissue paper, and if she wasn't very much mistaken the stones set into the leaves were diamonds.

'But I *can't* accept this,' she croaked. She knew it must have been very expensive and she had never owned anything like it in her whole life.

'Of course you can. May I?' He calmly plucked the brooch from the box and leaning over he fastened it to her dress before saying admiringly, 'It suits you.'

Dilly was speechless as she stared down at it. The stones were reflecting the light from the fire and sending rainbows all around the walls.

'It's beyond beautiful, but really I . . .'

'Please, don't say anything more. Just accept it with the grace with which it was given. Now shall we have another drink? Oh dear, we've finished this bottle. It's a good thing Cook thought to put two in.' Then without another word he uncorked the wine and carried on talking as Dilly sat there speechless.

Henry left at seven o'clock that evening and only then did Dilly think to open Max's present. It was yet another item of jewellery – a lovely bracelet set with emeralds – and her eyes welled with tears as she stared at it. She realised with a little shock that she'd thoroughly enjoyed her day but it had brought home to her what a lonely existence she led. Henry had made it more than obvious that he was fond of her and she'd grown fond of him. They were at ease in each other's company and could talk about anything together. Even so, Dilly had been on her own for a long while and she wondered if she could ever share her life with a man again. There were times when she thought it would be nice to have someone waiting upstairs for her and to snuggle up to at night. Even as the thought occurred to her it was Max's face that flashed in front of her eyes and angrily she set about clearing the table. There was no point in thinking along those lines. She had her business and her family to think of, and they would have to be enough. She was far too old to be having romantic notions, she told herself sternly.

# Chapter Thirty-Four

As Henry was leaving the shop, the party was just starting in the farmhouse in Ireland. The family had spent a wonderful day together and now their guests, families from the surrounding farms, were arriving bearing gifts of homemade wine, fresh baked bread and all manner of treats. In no time at all the place was heaving at the seams and Roddy was dashing about with the neighbours' children having the time of his life.

'He'll go out like a light when he goes to bed this evening,' Ben commented with amusement to Niamh. 'He hasn't stopped all day.'

'Well, it's not as if he's got to get up early tomorrow, is it? So I'll let him stay up for as long as he likes,' Niamh said indulgently.

Ben had arrived shortly before with his mother, who had spent the day at the blacksmith's cottage with him, and Niamh had taken to Elizabeth instantly. She and Ben appeared to be getting along like a house on fire and Niamh was so pleased for him. He'd waited a long time to feel he truly belonged to someone, although his devotion to Maeve and Daniel was clear to see.

'So did you have a good day?' he asked, noticing that she was wearing the little sapphire and diamond ring he had once given her next to her wedding ring.

'Yes, I did, thanks – and I've no need to ask if you did. You haven't stopped smiling since you got here.'

'Well, everyone's allowed to be happy at Christmas,' he answered as Patrick flew past him in hot pursuit of Bridie.

One of the neighbouring farmers started to thump out a tune on Maeve's rather old, out-of-tune piano then, and before they knew it everyone was dancing and laughter echoed from the rafters.

Maeve observed the couple from the corner of her eye. She loved both Niamh and Ben dearly and it hurt her to know that they'd missed their chance at happiness. Still, at least for now they could enjoy each other's company.

At half past nine the children were drooping and Shelagh and Liam left the party to put them to bed, although how they'd sleep in the adjoining cottage with all the racket going on they had no idea.

'I think I might go and tuck Roddy in too,' Niamh told Maeve. He was red in the face from dashing about and could scarcely keep his eyes open.

'Good idea.' Maeve was secretly relieved. Niamh had been stuck like glue to Ben's side all evening and she was worried about what the neighbours might say.

Maeve was not the only one who had been observing Ben and Niamh throughout the evening and when Niamh took Roddy off to bed, Elizabeth McFadden stared thoughtfully through the dark window into the black night. The spark of love that had once existed between them was still there for all to see, burning as brightly as ever, and she thought Niamh was a charming girl, just the sort she would have chosen for her son. How sad it was that through no fault on either side they could not be together. She could only blame herself for the mistake she had once made and the path she had chosen to go down, which had cost her her son, but she had suffered for it every single day of her life. They didn't deserve to suffer as she had.

As she stood there lost in thought, the first flakes of snow began to fall and she just wished that she could stay in this peaceful place for ever. The whole of the short precious time she had spent with Ben had been magical and now she dreaded having to tell him that the day after tomorrow she must leave to begin the journey to New York. Her sister's health had deteriorated and Elizabeth was aware that she could delay her departure no longer, but it would be harder than she'd ever thought possible to have to leave her son again so soon after finding him.

'Penny for your thoughts, lass. You were miles away then.' Maeve's voice made Elizabeth start.

'It's just beginning to snow,' she said for want of something to say, and feeling her pain, Maeve nodded.

'Aye lass, it is,' then in a gentle tone, 'I'm glad you got to join us today. It'll mean a lot to Ben to have you here, so it will.'

'It's meant a lot to me too, more than you can ever know – but I'm afraid I shall be leaving the day after tomorrow. I haven't told Ben yet.'

'He'll accept it,' Maeve assured her. 'And there'll be other times.'

'I hope so – I sincerely do. But you'll continue to keep your eye on him for me, Maeve, won't you, please?'

'Always. Ben's a part of our family now and so are you. If ever you want to come back there'll always be a place here for you, but I know you have to go. Your sister worse, is she?'

When the woman nodded, Maeve rubbed her arm sympathetically. 'Then go – but write to him often. It would break his heart to lose you again now.'

'That will never happen.'

The words were said with such sincerity that Maeve didn't doubt her.

'So what are you two planning on doing for the rest of the week?' Samuel asked casually the next morning at breakfast.

Mary was just placing a dish of devilled kidneys in the centre of the table.

'Well, nothing much apart from going to the market to do the shopping on Wednesday,' she shrugged. Christmas Day had started so well but then all of a sudden Seamus had become very quiet and withdrawn and had barely said a word to her since. No doubt it was to be expected. She was only a servant, after all, and Seamus could surely have any girl he wanted. She'd been foolish to believe that he could ever return the feelings she had for him – and she did have feelings, deep feelings. In fact, she loved him and had done almost since the first moment she had clapped eyes on him. Not that it would do her any good now, she thought forlornly.

'And what about you?' Samuel said then, addressing Seamus.

'Oh, I dare say I'll just get back to delivering the stock to the shops once we've got today over with,' Seamus answered as he pushed his food about the plate, avoiding Mary's eyes. 'And I was also thinking that it's about time I moved back in with Mammy. I don't really like the idea of her being above the shop all alone at night since the fire.'

Mary was so shocked that she almost dropped the dish of

bacon and sausages she was carrying to the table, but she didn't say anything. She could only think that she must have upset Seamus somehow, but for the life of her she couldn't think how. Everything had been so wonderful between them yesterday and then suddenly he had closed up like a clam and it had been all she could do to get a word out of him. She quickly finished putting the food on the table then fled back to the kitchen with tears in her eyes. It just reinforced what a fool she had been, daring to think that Seamus would ever look at the likes of her. But now that she knew where she stood, she would be more careful in future. She still had her pride!

Meanwhile Samuel was feeling quietly delighted. Seamus would be gone soon and with Mary out of the way on Wednesday he could start to put his plan into action. He stabbed at a sausage with a grin on his face. He'd show his father what he thought of being made to sweep floors! And he still had his ace card up his sleeve, of course, because up to now he had kept quiet about what he had discovered regarding his sister Olivia's real parentage. It was a shame in a way that Olivia hadn't been there for the holiday. Their father would have been fretting that he'd open his mouth to her if she had been, but Samuel hoped it wouldn't come to that. All in all, the New Year 1921 looked set to be a good one.

That night, the sound of Seamus screaming brought Mary from a deep sleep. Disorientated, she sat up and blinked as she scrubbed the sleep from her eyes. Suddenly realising what it was, she snatched up her dressing gown and raced along the landing towards Seamus' room, her gown flying out behind her like a cape.

'What the bloody hell is going on?' a bleary-eyed Samuel demanded as he appeared in his bedroom doorway.

'Don't worry – it's just Seamus having a nightmare. You go back to bed, I'll see to him.'

'I bet you will!' Samuel leered and, outraged, Mary turned on him.

'You have a mind like a sewer rat,' she stated coldly, her dislike of him spilling out of every pore, and with that she continued on her way.

She found Seamus thrashing about like someone demented on the bed and instantly the promise to distance herself from him flew out of the window. Sitting beside him, she drew him into her arms, revelling in his closeness as she gently tried to wake him. 'Come on now,' she soothed, wiping the damp hair from his brow. 'Wake up, Seamus, you're havin' a nightmare.'

His eyes sprang open, enormous in his pale face. He was wet through with sweat and shaking like a leaf in the wind.

'You're safe now here at home.' She was rocking him to and fro as she would have rocked a child and suddenly he sagged against her.

'I – I thought I was back on the battlefield,' he said hoarsely. 'A German was coming towards me and there was murder in his eyes . . .'

'Hush now, it was just a bad dream. It's all over.'

They sat there in the deep silence for some time until with an enormous effort Seamus straightened and sat up.

'Sorry I . . .'

'You don't ever need to apologise to me.' Her voice was like warm ointment on his soul. Mary could always calm him, but he knew that she was only being kind. She would do the same for anyone.

'You can go now – I shall be fine.'

'No. Come downstairs and let me make you a nice cup of cocoa. It will help you to sleep and then I'll change the bed for you. The sheets are damp.'

He opened his mouth to refuse and thought better of it. He didn't feel like being alone just yet and it would be warm down in the kitchen. She slipped away then and when he joined her she was standing at the stove warming milk in a copper pan.

'Sit yourself down, it'll be ready in a minute.'

Drawing his dressing robe tightly about him he did as he was told, and when the cocoa was made she joined him and said gently, 'It must have been awful out there.'

He sat silently and she began to think that he wasn't going to answer, but then he began to speak and suddenly he was spewing out the horrors he had seen as she sat and listened sympathetically.

'It's no wonder you have nightmares. No one could have seen what you did an' come through it unscathed.'

He hadn't been after sympathy, merely understanding. 'At least I came home,' he said. 'So I suppose I was one of the lucky ones. Kian didn't and neither did Mr Farthing's son, Harvey.'

It was then that a thought came to her, and speaking impetuously, she said, 'I hope you're not feeling guilty because you survived an' they didn't!' Instantly she saw that he did feel that way, and she went on, 'That should make you all the more determined to honour the memory o' those that didn't come home an' have a good life. If you don't do that, then they all died for nothing and you might as well have died with 'em!'

He blinked as if what she had said had never occurred to him before. 'I never thought of it like that,' he admitted. 'But I suppose you're right.'

'I am right, so let's 'ave no more o' this feelin' sorry for yourself,' she said sternly. 'Your Kian would want to know that you were well and happy.'

He gave her a wobbly smile as he sipped at his cocoa,

307

feeling like a fool, and she surprised him then when she said, 'Would you do me a favour?'

'Of course, anything.'

'The thing is – you mentioned today that you were thinkin' of movin' back to live with your mam. Would you mind very much hangin' on till Niamh an' Roddy get home? See, I don't fancy bein' here by meself with Samuel. I doubt he'd ever look at the likes o' me, o' course but—'

'Of course I will,' Seamus responded. 'And I think any man would look at you!' He blushed then as she glanced at him curiously before sliding out of his seat and rising hastily. He'd almost let his mouth run away with him and he couldn't bear it if she realised how he felt about her and then pitied him.

'Good night, Mary – and thanks again.'

'Good night, Seamus.' She stared thoughtfully down into her cocoa as he left the room, wishing with all her heart that she had been brave enough to confess how she felt about him. But then perhaps it was just as well she hadn't. She would have died rather than embarrass him.

'So this is it then,' Ben said shakily as he stood outside the smithy with his mother. The carriage he had hired that would take her to the ferry was already loaded with her luggage and it was time for her to leave.

'I've really enjoyed having you here,' he mumbled self-consciously.

'And I've enjoyed it too.' Elizabeth was crying unashamedly and didn't know how she was going to bear to leave him. 'You will write regularly, won't you?'

'I'll do me best but I ain't much of a letter-writer,' he confessed as the driver climbed up onto the seat and took up the reins.

'We'd best be goin' now, missus, else you'll miss the ferry, so you will.'

This was it – the moment of parting could be postponed no longer. Elizabeth leaned forward and kissed him soundly on the cheek then blinded by tears she clutched at his hand as he helped her into the carriage.

'Take care,' she told him through the window.

'I will, Mammy.'

Her heart soared. He had called her Mammy at last and it meant the world to her but then the carriage was pulling away and she was waving to him as the snow fell softly about her.

Later that day, Ben visited the farm and Niamh saw how low he was feeling. She could understand it. He'd waited so long to discover his real mother but circumstances had all too soon torn them apart again. She and Maeve were having a huge tidy-up but she told him cheerfully, 'There's tea in the pot. Granda's out seeing to the animals but he'll be in soon for his so sit yourself down and I'll pour you one.'

For the first time that morning she'd noticed how her gran'ma was slowing down and it worried her. But then her grandparents were both in their seventies now so she supposed it was to be expected. Thankfully, Roisin and Shelagh were always on hand to help, and Liam and Declan had taken on most of the outside work, but Niamh knew that being as independent as they were it must have gone sorely against the grain for the elderly couple.

Ben plonked himself down at the table and Maeve asked tenderly, 'Did your mammy get off all right then, lad?'

'Aye, she did,' he answered as he sipped at the tea Niamh had placed before him.

'And how long does she expect to be away?'

Ben shrugged. 'Who knows? Her sister is suffering from some sort of muscle-wasting disease so she could hang on

309

for years, then again she could go tomorrow. Mammy clearly expects to be gone for a good while – that's why she sold her house. But then she said if she comes back she'd want to buy one closer to us anyway.'

'Everything happens for a reason,' Maeve said stoically, but then Roddy and Liam's children skipped into the kitchen.

'Any mince pies left, Gran'ma?' Patrick chirped and Maeve chuckled.

'I dare say I could find you all one or two, though how you can be hungry so soon after breakfast beats me. I reckon you've all got hollow legs. And don't tell your mammy I've given you any afore dinner else she'll be telling me off, so she will.' Maeve obligingly fetched a tin from the pantry and handed out some of the mince pies she and Niamh had baked on Christmas Eve, and then Ben crossed to the tiny picture that Niamh had painted for her grandparents for Christmas. It was quite a small canvas as she'd never have managed to carry a larger one on the journey. She had painted the farm nestling in the dip from a vantage point on the hill and it was so good that Ben's eyes stretched wide.

'You really should think o' getting some of your work displayed,' he commented.

Niamh said shyly, 'Oh, I just do it to pass the time since I lost Con— well, it's just a hobby really.'

'And when were you and Roddy thinking of going home?'

'After we've seen the New Year in,' she told him. 'I'm planning on going to work back at the school. Why, are you trying to get rid of us?' Her eyes sparkled as she teased him.

'Of course I'm not. Maeve and Daniel love having you here, so they do, but I dare say you miss your mammy.'

'I do,' she admitted. 'Although she has a "friend" now so I hope he'll have kept her company over the holidays.'

'"A friend"? Who's this then?' Maeve asked with raised eyebrows.

'His name is Henry Price. He's a solicitor and quite wealthy. Mammy is making all the outfits for his daughter's wedding in June and he's taken her out a few times.'

'Has he indeed.' Maeve felt hurt as she thought of her son but then she acknowledged that she was being unreasonable. Fergal had been dead for a long time now and Dilly was still a comparatively young and very attractive woman. Maeve knew she should have been aware that Dilly would meet someone else eventually, and yet until that moment the thought had never occurred to her. Begrudgingly she had to admit that Dilly deserved some happiness. She was one of the most hard-working women Maeve had ever known, and sometimes when Maeve thought back to how Dilly had toiled when Fergal was ill and the children were small she wondered how she'd coped. It hadn't ended there either, for look at her now! Two dress shops on the go and still working hard. Yes, it was time for her daughter-in-law to move on, and Maeve wished her well – although it would be strange seeing another man in her beloved Fergal's place.

# Chapter Thirty-Five

*January 1922*

On a day early in January, the shop door suddenly flew open and Mary spilled into the shop, startling Dilly and the customer she was serving.

'I'm so sorry, would you excuse me?' Dilly said to the woman, then leaving her to browse through the rails she hurried towards Mary. The girl was shivering with cold and her hair was plastered to her head. It was no wonder, Dilly thought. She had no coat on and it was wet and windy outside.

'Whatever's the matter, lass?' She drew her towards the other end of the shop and waited patiently as Mary tried to get her breath back. She'd clearly been running.

'Th-there's a man – at the house,' Mary gasped. 'He has a cart there wi' all his furniture on an' he reckons he's come to move in!'

'What do you mean, come to move in?'

'Just what I say. He says he's bought the house an' I didn't

312

know what to do. I've no idea where Mr Farthin' is so I ran here to fetch you.'

Dilly frowned. 'Right then – here, borrow my coat and run back and tell this gentleman that I shall be there as soon as I can. On the way, call in at the Farthings' and get Mrs Pegs to ask Mr Jackson to track Mr Farthing down.'

Mary nodded and after struggling into Dilly's coat she shot off to do as she was told.

Meantime, Dilly hastily finished serving her customer, turned the Closed sign on the window and after grabbing her old coat she set off for Niamh's house. She was sure that it must be a misunderstanding but it needed to be dealt with until Max could be found.

Sure enough as she approached the house she saw a large flat-backed cart loaded with furniture parked outside and a rather irate gentleman pacing up and down the pavement outside.

'May I help you?' Dilly asked as she came abreast of him, smiling politely at the woman who was still sitting at the front of the cart beneath a large black umbrella.

'I've bought this house fair an' square an' I've the paperwork to prove it, but the maid who answered the door to me won't let us in. I shall call the police if this isn't sorted soon,' the man ranted.

'I don't understand,' Dilly told him. 'This is my daughter's house, sir. She's in Ireland at the moment but I assure you it is.'

'Would her name be Farthing?'

'Well, yes . . . it is,' Dilly said uncertainly as he snatched a legal-looking document from inside his overcoat pocket.

'Then argue with this.' He thrust the paper at her. 'I bought the house from Mr Samuel Farthing and the deeds are now in my name. Look, if you don't believe me. Me and the wife have also bought the grocery shop on the

Green and we liked this house because it's only a stride away.'

'I . . . I don't understand,' Dilly stuttered as she stared at the paper. It certainly looked legal enough.

Thankfully, Max's car pulled up at that moment. He got out and, striding towards them he demanded, 'What's going on here?' Mary was with him and she came to stand beside Dilly, her eyes fearful.

The man repeated what he had told Dilly, growing more irate by the minute until Max said, 'Look, why don't we go inside to discuss this? Mary can make us all a nice hot drink.'

'Humph!' the man snorted but he helped his wife down from the cart, tethered the horse to the railings and followed Max inside just the same.

'So.' Grim-faced, Max went to stand with his back to the fire as the man and his wife took a seat in the sitting room. 'Could you tell me what's going on, please, Mr Er . . .'

'Harding,' the man responded. 'Howard Harding. I met your son just before Christmas. Me and the wife had been staying at the inn in the town centre and I'd put the word about that I was looking for a suitable property to buy. It was then that your son came to see me and said he had a house for sale that might suit me on Abbey Green. I agreed to come and view it and he showed us around last Wednesday. It was just what we were looking for so he got the necessary deeds drawn up at his solicitors and I paid him for it yesterday, five hundred pounds in cash. Here's the receipt – look.' He took yet another piece of paper from his overcoat pocket and after he had passed it over, Max frowned.

'We agreed then that me and the wife could move in today, so here we are,' Mr Harding ended irritably.

'I see.' Max studied the receipt. 'Luckily I have been at the office in my mill this morning, where the foreman informed me that Samuel hasn't been in today. Ah, Mary,' he said then as she entered carrying a tray of tea. 'Where did Samuel say he was going when he went out this morning?'

Placing the tray carefully on the table she told him, 'I ain't seen him since last night, sir. An' he never come down for his breakfast today. I checked his room afore I ran to fetch Dilly, but his bed ain't been slept in an' all his clothes are gone out o' the wardrobe.'

Dilly saw Max visibly pale but he remained calm as he told Mr Harding, 'I cannot explain what's going on without speaking to my son, sir, who clearly is not here. What I can say is that I shall see you are fully recompensed for this misunderstanding.'

'*Misunderstanding!*' the man spluttered. 'But there *is* no misunderstanding. I have the deeds to the house and the receipt for the sum I paid for it here in my hand!'

'Should you take the deeds to a solicitor I think you will find they are a forgery,' Max said unhappily. 'I can only apologise for my son's devious behaviour – but as I said, I will more than happily repay whatever this has cost you.'

'Max, a word please.' Dilly smiled apologetically towards the couple before taking his elbow and leading him out into the hallway. There she closed the door firmly behind them and hissed, 'You can't really be going to lay out all that money, Max? Samuel was clearly trying to cheat those people and he shouldn't be allowed to get away with it. You must involve the police and let them deal with it. Samuel has gone too far this time. What he's done is illegal!'

He stared at her strained face and sighed. How could he tell her that Samuel knew that Olivia was her daughter? If she knew that, she would worry herself sick and he would pay any price to prevent that so he merely said, 'You're quite right, Dilly, but he is still my son. What would you do in my position?' When her lips pursed he went on, 'I think you would do exactly what I am about to do. Am I right?'

'I suppose so,' she muttered reluctantly although she thought it was high time Samuel was taught a lesson.

'Then let me handle this in my own way,' he ended, and without another word he turned and went back to his visitors.

When they left an hour later, Max gave a sigh of relief. As well as the money Samuel had cheated them out of, Max had also promised to pay their hotel bills whilst the couple searched for another property, so although they were not exactly happy, at least they had to admit that Max had done right by them.

'The young bugger ought to be horse-whipped – an' I'll do it meself if I ever get me hands on him!' Mr Harding was heard to say as Mary let them out. She would secretly have liked to help him do it although she couldn't say that, of course.

In the sitting room Dilly was pouring Max a large tot of whisky. It wasn't even lunchtime but he looked as if he could do with it.

'He's really excelled himself this time, hasn't he?' Max said wearily. 'I really thought he was trying. How wrong could I be? Now God knows where he is.'

'Well, he's certainly got enough money that you won't need to worry about him,' Dilly pointed out.

'I dare say you're right. But I never thought even Samuel would stoop so low, Dilly. I despair of him, I really do. I'm at the end of my tether.'

'I doubt you'll see him for some time now, not until the money has run out at least and surely that should take some time.'

'Huh! Not necessarily so. Money runs through his hands like grains of sand and he could lose that much in a single card game. The problem is, he doesn't know when to stop.'

She could think of nothing to say to console him, so instead she simply squeezed his arm before preparing to return to the shop. It wouldn't do to leave it shut for too long.

# Chapter Thirty-Six

On a blustery night in early February when Dilly had just settled down to enjoy a cup of cocoa before retiring to bed, a loud rattling sounded below on the shop door. Dilly had already washed from head to toe and changed into her nightclothes after spending the evening working on Eleanor Price's bridesmaids' dresses, and she frowned with misgiving as she tightened the belt on her dressing gown and headed down the stairs. Who could be calling so late? Perhaps Camilla had taken a turn for the worse or something had happened to one of the children? All she could see through the gloomy shop interior was the outline of someone standing outside on the pavement, and it looked like that of a woman. Perhaps it was Niamh? She fiddled with the bolts on the door then after cautiously inching it open a little she gasped with delight.

'Olivia!' Reaching out, she yanked the girl inside out of the stormy night and it was all she could do to stop herself from throwing her arms about her.

'Why didn't you tell us you were coming?' she gushed. 'But no, don't answer me yet. You look frozen. Come upstairs to the fire and get warm and I'll make you a nice hot drink.'

Olivia gently laid down the large bag she was carrying and obediently followed the other woman upstairs as her heart beat a wild tattoo in her chest, suddenly wondering if this had been such a good idea, after all.

'Now take that wet coat and hat off,' Dilly ordered bossily when they were in the sitting room.

She was pleased to see that Olivia looked quite well. She appeared to have lost a little weight and was pale and tired, but that was probably due to the long journey if she'd only just arrived from London. It did seem strange that she'd come to see her first though, instead of going home. Not that Dilly was complaining.

'Now you must tell me all you've been up to,' she encouraged when she'd placed a steaming mug of cocoa in the girl's hands. 'Then we'll telephone your father to come and fetch you if you haven't already been home. I've had a phone installed now, you know. It was your father's idea. I don't want you walking the streets late at night all on your own. You never know who you might bump into, a pretty girl like you. Failing that I'll get Seamus up. He won't mind walking you back but he's gone for an early night. Are you home for good or is this just a visit?'

She chuckled suddenly and flushed. 'I'm rambling on, aren't I? Do forgive me, it's just that I'm so pleased to see you. We've all missed you so much, lass.'

To her horror, Olivia's face suddenly crumpled and she burst into tears as she fumbled in the sleeve of her dress for her handkerchief.

'Oh, my dear Mrs Carey . . . I've missed you too but I'm afraid I'm in a terrible mess which is why I've come to you

319

for advice. Please send me away now if I'm being a trouble.'

'I would *never* send you away, lass,' Dilly told her with feeling, anxiety gripping her. 'But now try and calm yourself down and tell me what the problem is. I'm sure it can't be as bad as you think.'

'Oh yes, it is,' Olivia choked, crying harder than ever. 'You see I . . . I . . .'

Dilly forced herself to keep her hands clasped tightly in her lap as she looked on. She so wanted to hold the shaking girl in her arms but was afraid of overstepping the mark.

'In your own time, there's no rush. We can sit here all night if it helps,' she told her softly.

Eventually, Olivia managed to compose herself enough to say, 'I'm afraid that what I'm about to tell you may make you turn your back on me, Mrs Carey.'

'*Never!*' Dilly repeated emphatically. The girl was clearly in so much pain that she could almost feel it coming off her in waves. 'There is nothing you could tell me that would ever make me turn my back on you. I've . . . known you since you were a baby and you must know how fond I am of you.'

'The thing is . . . well, there's no easy way to say this so I'll just come out with it. I left home because I was having a child. I gave birth on Christmas Day and I have a little daughter.'

Dilly's hand flew to her mouth as shock coursed through her but then unable to contain herself any longer, she placed a comforting arm about the girl's thin shoulders.

'Oh, my poor girl. What you must have gone through, facing such a trial all on your own.'

'You – you don't think I'm wicked?' Olivia asked incredulously.

'Anyone can make a mistake,' Dilly answered. 'But where is the child?' Her heart was thumping with delight. She had a brand new baby granddaughter, although of course she couldn't admit this to Olivia.

'She's being cared for at the moment by the lady who owns the lodging house where I've been staying in London. She's been wonderful to me but I can't stay there for much longer.' Olivia sniffed. 'When I first went there I thought I'd perhaps go into one of these mother and baby places and then have the child adopted when it was born. But then as the pregnancy went on I knew that I wouldn't be able to go through with it. I thought that after the child was born I would go on working, but it isn't as easy as it sounds. Queenie, the lady I'm staying with, is very kind but she's too old to look after my daughter while I'm at work, and the allowance I get from my late grandmother won't keep us both without me working. Everything is so expensive in London. There's no one else I would trust her with, so you see I'm in a terrible pickle.'

'What is the baby's name?' Dilly managed to ask calmly.

'I called her Jessica, then Camilla after my mother and she's quite beautiful.' Olivia grew tearful again then. She had never been parted from her baby since the day she had given birth, and she was missing her dreadfully.

Dilly rolled the name round in her head. Jessica. She had a little granddaughter called Jessica.

'But what can I do to help you, pet?' she asked then.

'I don't quite know but I thought perhaps you might know of someone trustworthy who might be able to foster her for me. Someone close by so that I could come home but see her regularly without anyone realising that she was mine, especially Daddy or Oscar. I would die of shame if they ever found out. I could go back to work then, and with my wages and my allowance I could manage comfortably.'

'But your father would help you financially if he knew what position you're in,' Dilly said.

'*NO!*' Olivia shook her head dramatically. 'You must promise me that you'll *never* tell my father about her. He'd disown me and the shame would kill him. And Oscar . . . what would he think of me if he knew I had an illegitimate child? I couldn't bear it.' She began to rock backwards and forwards with distress then.

'All right, I promise,' Dilly told her hastily. 'But I have to say I disagree with you. I'm sure your father would stand by you, once he got over the shock. He loves you, Olivia.'

'I know he does, that's why I can't do this to him,' Olivia answered chokily and then, 'Do you think you may be able to help me, Mrs Carey? I have no one else to turn to that I can trust with my secret.'

'I shall have to give the matter some thought,' Dilly answered truthfully. 'This has rather taken me by surprise. But in the meantime you must stay here tonight. You can't go home at this time with your eyes all red and swollen. Your father would guess straight away that something was wrong. You can sleep in my bed and I'll sleep out here on the sofa.'

'But I can't put you to all that trouble,' Olivia objected although she saw the truth in what Dilly said.

'Oh yes you can, and it's no trouble at all,' Dilly answered in a no-nonsense kind of voice. 'Now come along with you. Let's get you settled. Everything will look better in the morning, you'll see.'

Yet deep inside she doubted her own words. She had just discovered she had a granddaughter. It should have been a joyous time but she would never be able to lay claim to her, and she felt almost as bad as she had on that long-ago night when she had given her own newborn daughter away.

## Chapter Thirty-Seven

Dilly slept little that night as she tossed and turned thinking of Olivia's dilemma. Long before Seamus rose she had tidied the room and cleared the sofa of blankets so that he wouldn't know that they'd had an overnight visitor. Thankfully, he was aiming to get an early train to Birmingham to visit Dilly's suppliers and when he left immediately after breakfast, Dilly heaved a sigh of relief before taking Olivia a cup of tea in.

'I heard you talking to Seamus and I didn't like to come through while he was there,' Olivia confessed, taking the cup gratefully from Dilly.

'It's perhaps as well,' Dilly agreed, perching on the end of the bed. 'The fewer people who know about this the better, if you're quite sure that's the road you want to take. I have given the matter a lot of thought and without wishing to raise your hopes I think I may have come up with a solution.'

'Really?' Olivia's smile was ecstatic.

'Really, but I don't want to say any more until I've spoken

to the person I have in mind. All I can tell you is, I would trust this woman with my very life, so if you're quite sure about this, with your permission I'll go and see her this very morning.'

'Oh yes – yes, please,' Olivia said emotionally.

Dilly nodded. 'Then in that case I suggest you go home now. They'll be so pleased to see you and I'll get back to you later if it's possible. But first I've made you some breakfast, so please come and eat something or you'll make yourself ill.'

Olivia gave a wan smile. 'You sound just like my mother,' she said innocently, and she would never know how much those few words cut Dilly to the quick.

''Ello, 'ello! To what do I owe this 'onour then?' Nell teased when Dilly visited her later that morning.

'Are we alone?' Dilly asked as she placed her bag on the table and glanced around Nell's neat and tidy kitchen-cum-sitting room.

'Course we are. The old man left fer work hours ago.' Nell was serious now. After knowing Dilly for as long as she had, she could sense that something was wrong as her old friend began to pace up and down, clearly agitated.

After a time Dilly said tentatively, 'Nell, I've come here to ask you for a favour. You're the only one I can trust with this, but it's a *very* big favour, so I'll quite understand if you don't want any part of it.'

'Lordie, yer gettin' me nervous now. An' will yer please stop pacin' – yer makin' me bloody dizzy!'

'Sorry.' Dilly stared at her for a moment then after taking a deep breath she told her about Olivia's unexpected arrival the night before and the girl's confession.

'Strewth! So what you're tellin' me is you're a grandma again?'

Dilly nodded. 'That's about the long and short of it, but Olivia obviously doesn't know that. Now she needs someone nearby that we can trust to foster the child so that she can come home to live. Someone who will let her see the baby regularly. Olivia is prepared to pay well, so I wondered . . .'

'You wondered if I'd take the little mite on.' Nell scratched her head and sighed. 'Well I, ain't no spring chicken, as yer know, Dilly. I'm goin' on fifty. That's not to say I'm past it, o' course. But my brood flew the nest a long time ago an' I never considered another one.'

As she glanced at Dilly's anxious face her heart went out to her. She'd been through so much over the years. Denied the right to bring up her own daughter and now she was in danger of being denied access to her granddaughter, unless . . .

'I suppose I could consider it,' she said cautiously.

Relief lit Dilly's face and Nell hurried on, 'But who would we say the child was? We'd have to come up with something believable.'

'You're right, I hadn't thought of that.' Dilly chewed on her lip for a moment. Then: 'Couldn't you spread the word that the baby had been orphaned and that she was your niece's child or something? Most people who know you are aware that you have family living at the coast. We could perhaps say that the mother was widowed and then died herself whilst giving birth. That sounds fairly plausible.'

Nell nodded thoughtfully. 'I dare say it does, but it would mean me lettin' the old man into the secret.'

'Would he mind you taking on the care of another baby?' Dilly hadn't considered Nell's husband until now.

Nell chuckled. 'Would 'e 'ell. Yer know what he's like! Long as his dinner's on the table 'e'll put up with anythin', God love 'im.'

'So does this mean that you'll seriously consider it? I'd do all I could to help, I promise, Nell, and no one would think anything of it with us being friends for so long.'

Nell let out a deep breath before saying, 'All right then. Bring Olivia to see me and we'll discuss it.'

'Oh Nell, thank you *so* much.' Dilly flew across to her and hugged her so hard that Nell almost overbalanced.

'Steady on,' the woman chuckled. 'You'll 'ave me on me arse at this rate.'

Dilly mopped at her eyes before snatching up her bag. 'Right, I'd better go and see if I can catch Olivia alone then. She'll be overjoyed and so grateful. We both are.'

'Get off wi' you,' Nell muttered, greatly embarrassed. 'I'd best go an' look at the back bedroom. I dare say it'll need a whitewash an' some new curtains. A new bit o' lino wouldn't go amiss either if there's to be someone sleepin' in there again.'

'I can make you some new curtains and of course I'll reimburse you for anything you have to spend,' Dilly said immediately. If Nell did this for her, it would be like the answer to a prayer.

'Well, I'm sure I've still got the cot I used fer my kids. It's up in the attic if I remember correctly 'cos I couldn't bring meself to part with it. Happen it'll only need a lick o' paint an' it'll be as good as new. An' then I'll need a pram . . .'

'Please don't get worrying about things like that just yet. Olivia may already have one, and if she hasn't I'll see to it that you have everything you need,' Dilly promised. 'But now I must get round to the Farthings' so I can tell Olivia the good news. But are you *quite* sure about it, Nell? I do realise it's a huge commitment and I wouldn't think ill of you if you felt it was too much.'

'I wouldn't agree to it if I didn't want to,' Nell said firmly. 'The more I think about it, the more I realise it'll actually be quite nice to 'ave a little 'un in the house again. Now be off with you and bring Olivia to see me when you can. There's arrangements to make.'

Later that afternoon, Henry brought Eleanor to the shop for a fitting. 'You seem chirpy today, Dilly,' he commented. 'What's put the smile on your face?'

'Nothing really, I'm just feeling happy,' Dilly answered through a mouthful of pins but his remark made her think – really think for the first time about what it would be like to have her new granddaughter so close. She supposed she should be disgusted at Olivia for having an illegitimate child, but Dilly had always been broad-minded and believed that anyone could make a mistake. The war had changed people's attitudes anyway and there were hundreds of children that had been born out of wedlock during that time. Even so, she felt guilty about Max being kept in the dark about the little girl. She felt she knew him well enough to be sure that he would have accepted Jessica, but Olivia was still adamant that he should never find out.

'So how is the dress coming along?' Henry enquired when Dilly emerged from the fitting room a short time later, leaving Eleanor to get dressed.

'Beautifully, even if I do say so myself – but don't ask for a peep. You're not allowed to see it until the day of the wedding.'

'I thought that only applied to the groom,' he said with a grin.

'Then you thought wrong,' she answered mock sternly. 'You'll just have to wait but I promise it will be worth it. She's going to look stunning on the day.'

'Actually, at the weekend I found the tiara my wife wore for our wedding in one of her cupboards,' he told Dilly on a more solemn note then. 'It was Emma's mother's and her

327

grandmother's before her, so Eleanor is going to wear it too.'

'How lovely. I'm sure it will bring Eleanor's mother closer to her.' Dilly smiled at him sympathetically, thinking again what a thoroughly nice man he was. Most brides would be shopping for wedding clothes and going for fittings with their mother, but Henry had willingly stepped into his late wife's place to ensure that the time would be as special as it could be for his daughter. Remembering how Fergal had hated to go shopping, she was full of admiration for him.

'I was wondering if you'd like to come to lunch with me on Sunday,' Henry said then. 'I thought we could go for a ride out to that new eating house that everyone is on about on the way to Tamworth . . . if you've nothing else planned of course.'

'I'd love to,' Dilly agreed readily. She would only spend the day working if she didn't accept his invitation, and she thought perhaps it would be nice to have a break.

The rest of the week flew by. Olivia was thrilled that Dilly had managed to find someone to care for Jessica; the girl felt as if a huge weight had been shifted from her shoulders. Dilly had taken her to meet Nell and despite the woman's brash ways, Olivia trusted Dilly's judgement implicitly and felt sure that Jessica would be happy with Nell. It was almost perfect. She would be able to call in and see her daughter on her way to and from the hospital where she intended to work again, and she didn't know how she would ever be able to thank Dilly enough. Little could she have known that just having the baby close by would be all the thanks that Dilly would need. She could hardly wait.

'I shall be in touch, but I intend to return at the end of January with the baby,' Olivia told Dilly. 'We can make the arrangements over the phone. Oh, it's so handy now that you've had one installed. I shall be able to ring you.' She had then kissed Dilly impulsively, and Dilly's heart had swelled with love for the girl. Now she knew that Olivia was coming home for good she was even able to accept her going back to London, although she still felt bad about having to keep such a momentous secret from Max. He adored little George and Roddy, just as he had adored Constance, and Dilly felt sure that he would feel the same about Jessica. However, she loved Olivia too much to break her trust even for Max.

The week progressed happily until on Friday Dilly received some devastating news in a letter from Ireland. It was from Niamh.

*Dear Mammy,*

*I hope you are well and not working too hard? I just wanted to let you know that I am planning on bringing Roddy home towards the end of next week. As I told you in my last letter, Gran'ma has been very poorly. The heavy cold she came down with settled on her chest and I was worried that it would turn to bronchitis or pneumonia, but thankfully she is on the mend now so I feel able to leave her in the capable hands of Shelagh.*

*Sadly, I also have to tell you that Roisin has lost the child she was carrying once more. Everything was going along well but then suddenly she got stomach cramps and by the time Declan had fetched the doctor it was all over. Obviously they are both upset but not quite as much so as last time. They both say that they will try again as soon as possible and we can only pray that it will be a case of third time lucky. I know that they will make wonderful parents and it seems so unfair – but then as Gran'ma is so fond of saying, 'That's life!'*

*Ben is well and sends his love, as do Granda and the*

*children. I am so looking forward to seeing you now. Until*
*then take care.*
  *With love,*
  *Niamh xxx*

A tear raced down Dilly's cheek as she read about Declan and Roisin's loss and she angrily swiped it away. How strange life was indeed. Here was Olivia who had openly admitted that she hadn't been at all sure that she wanted her baby until she had held her in her arms – and there was Declan and Roisin desperate for a child. Tutting, she folded the letter and put it in her pocket then went about her business.

Dilly woke on Sunday morning to thick freezing fog. Surely Henry would want to call off their lunch date, she thought. She wondered if she should ring him but then thought better of it. He might deem it intrusive if she started ringing him at home; worse still, what would his servants think? So she started to get ready just in case, deciding that if he wished to postpone the trip, he would let her know. Luckily, Seamus was round at Niamh's house fixing a dripping tap for Mary who had invited him to stay for lunch, so she didn't have to worry about his meal.

Dilly brushed her hair until it shone before fixing it into an elegant chignon, then she selected a blue dress that the seamstresses had made up from one of her own designs. Eyeing herself critically in the mirror, she was quite pleased with what she saw. The dress was plain admittedly, but the beautiful cut and the simplicity of it were what made it so stylish. Yes, I'll get the women to make up a few in different colours and sizes for the shop, she decided as she slid her arms into her coat and fastened her hat on. She then added a lovely warm woollen scarf and gloves, feeling that she was probably going to need them should Henry turn up. He did, exactly on time, and when Dilly tripped out of the shop to him he looked her up and down appreciatively.

'You look lovely,' he said as he helped her into the car and tucked a cosy rug across her knees. Unfortunately the fog hadn't lifted and the pavements were covered with frost.

'Perhaps we should go somewhere a little closer to home with the weather conditions?' Dilly suggested but he waved aside her concerns.

'You'll be perfectly safe with me,' he promised her. 'I'm a very cautious driver and I won't take any chances, especially with you in the car.'

She felt warm colour slide into her cheeks. Henry had inferred that she was special and again she was forced to look at him through different eyes. He was certainly a handsome man, and kind too. Any woman would be lucky to have a man like Henry and she had a sneaky feeling that she would only have to give him a little encouragement for their relationship to continue to the next stage – and yet still she held back. Was it because she'd been on her own for so long? she asked herself. But then they were motoring along and Henry was telling her all about the recession he feared the country was heading for, and any romantic thoughts she'd had flew straight out of her head. If he was right it could severely affect her shops and that was the last thing she needed after she'd worked so hard to get them off the ground.

Henry drove through the town and on through Weddington, then they were passing the village of Fenny Drayton and Dilly stared appreciatively from the car window at the open countryside. She had rarely been out of the town, apart from her frequent trips to Birmingham and her occasional visits to Ireland, so this was a real treat. Even with the fields shrouded in mist and frost glistening on the trees it was beautiful and she felt herself relaxing.

They stopped for a drink on the way at The Cock Inn at Sibson, reputed to be one of the oldest inns in England and said to be a favourite haunt of the notorious highwayman of bygone years, Dick Turpin. It almost took her breath away. The ceilings were low and heavily beamed, and Dilly felt as if she was stepping back in time. The wooden bar was polished to a mirror-like shine and an enormous log fire was roaring up the chimney, making the whole place feel welcoming.

They then drove on to an eating house where they ordered piping hot home-made parsnip soup with fresh-baked bread followed by a roast leg of lamb that was so tender it fell from the bone, served with a selection of vegetables. When that had been cleared away Henry insisted that they should try the pudding, although Dilly felt as if she might burst at that point. She was feeling pleasantly tiddly after the wine that she'd drunk with the meal but when the pudding was served – a delicious trifle affair – she managed to eat some of that too. When Henry then ordered coffee and cheese and biscuits she held her hands up in defeat.

'No more, *please*,' she implored with a giggle. 'I shall be the size of a house at this rate.'

'Nonsense, you're as slim as a reed.' He leaned across the table and took her hand then before adding sincerely, 'And very beautiful too.'

Dilly gently withdrew her hand, but then thankfully the waiter was there with a tray bearing their coffee and the moment was gone.

On the way back to the shop later that afternoon, Dilly was in good spirits. She'd enjoyed herself more than she'd imagined she would and was just beginning to realise what a rut she had fallen into. Her life centred on her family and her shops, no bad thing, but now she was beginning to acknowledge how lonely this situation could be at times. It was nice to have a man dance attendance on her, nice to have someone to pay her compliments and make her feel good. Wickedly she suddenly thought how nice it would be to have someone to curl up to at night, and the thought made her blush as she hastily looked away from Henry.

When they pulled up outside the shop it was gone four o'clock in the afternoon and already getting dark as she told him, 'Thank you so much for today. I've really enjoyed myself.'

'It should be me thanking you, Dilly,' he said soberly. 'After I lost my wife I was beginning to think that life wasn't worth living any more but you've shown me that it is. I suppose I should feel guilty but I'm sure that Emma would have wanted me to be happy – and you do make me happy. Do you think you might ever be able to look on me as anything more than a friend?'

Dilly gulped, then choosing her words carefully she answered, 'I'm very fond of you, Henry, but as you pointed out, it is still very early days. It could be that you're on the rebound because you're lonely, so let's just take things slowly and get to know each other properly, eh?'

He nodded then got out of the car and came round to open her door for her. He was smiling again now and gave a gallant little bow as he said, 'Would you like me to escort you inside, madam?'

'No, thank you, sir. The lights are on upstairs so Seamus must be home – but thank you again for a lovely meal.'

He kissed her hand then clambered back into the car, and as he drove away she watched him go with a thoughtful expression on her face. Could it be that it was time to move on? Only time would tell.

# Chapter Thirty-Eight

Over the next few weeks, Olivia made two more trips to Nuneaton, loaded down with baby things each time. Dilly always met her at the railway station and between them they then transported the things to Nell's house before Olivia caught the next train back to London. Now at last the day had arrived when she would bring Jessica home with her and both Nell and Dilly were almost beside themselves with excitement.

It had been agreed that Olivia would arrive on the night train. There was less chance of her being spotted carrying a baby at night, and as Dilly waited for the train to arrive on the platform, she shuffled impatiently from foot to foot.

At last a dull roar in the distance heralded the train's approach, and soon after it puffed into the station in a huff of steam. Dilly hurried along the platform gazing into each carriage window as she passed, then ahead of her she saw Olivia trying to manoeuvre the bundle she had clutched in her arms and a large bag through the door.

'Here, let me help you,' Dilly said breathlessly as she rushed up to her. 'Give the baby to me.'

Olivia handed her precious bundle into Dilly's waiting arms as she climbed down the steps, hefting the large bag behind her. They then went and stood in the shadows as Olivia said solemnly, 'Dilly, this is Jessica Camilla Farthing.'

Olivia's eyes were red and swollen. The girl had found it harder than she had anticipated to say goodbye to Queenie and Fiona and the good friends she had made in London, and she knew that if she had gone there under other circumstances she could have been very happy there. But Jessica must be her first priority now.

Dilly twitched aside the white shawl enveloping the baby and as she looked down on her tiny face her heart was lost instantly and a rush of love swept through her.

A pair of blue eyes gazed steadily back up at her from beneath a thatch of soft downy copper hair. Her eyes had never changed colour as the midwife had said they might, but apart from that Dilly felt as if she was holding Olivia again on that faraway night.

'Oh, she's just beautiful,' Dilly breathed trying very hard to keep a rein on her emotions.

Olivia nodded in agreement. 'I think so too, and now that you've met her you'll see why I couldn't bear to let her go.'

'Yes, I can, but we'd better be getting along now. Nell has everything ready for her and it's far too cold for her to be out any longer than necessary.'

Dilly had noticed that Olivia's eyes were bloodshot, and the reason for it was explained when Olivia told her, 'It was very hard to say goodbye to Queenie and Fiona and the rest of the girls. They've been so good to me, but I still think I'm doing the right thing in coming home. At least this way I shall be able to work and still see Jessica.'

The women moved out of the station, relieved to see that

there were few people about. It was hardly surprising. It was a bitterly cold night and Dilly pressed the child tightly against her to keep her warm as they hurried along.

When they reached Nell's cottage they found her anxiously peering from the front window, and by the time they'd reached the door she was holding it open for them.

'Come on in quick out o' the cold,' she ordered. 'I've had the kettle on the boil this past hour and a bottle all ready fer the baby. But give 'er 'ere an' let's 'ave a look at 'er.'

Dilly reluctantly parted with the child, and when Nell unfolded the shawl her reaction at first sight of the infant was much as Dilly's had been.

'Why, what a little sweet'eart,' she sighed. 'She'll break a few hearts she will, for sure.' Then to Dilly, 'Pass me that there bottle, would yer, pet. I bet she's hungry.'

Dilly obediently lifted a glass banana-shaped bottle with a rubber teat at either end of it full of warm milk, and as Nell offered it to the baby she latched on to it greedily with her rosebud mouth.

As Nell settled down in the chair and smiled contentedly, Olivia heaved a sigh of relief. The woman had clearly taken to the child, and whilst circumstances were not ideal and she wouldn't be able to spend all her time with her baby, at least this way she would get to see her often. Nell had already put the word around about her niece's orphaned child and the neighbours had accepted it unquestioningly. Olivia gave Dilly a teary smile and Dilly smiled back encouragingly.

'She tends to be a bit windy. You need to pat her back halfway through a bottle.' Suddenly Olivia was panicking. Leaving her baby in Nell's care wasn't going to be as easy as she had thought, as lovely as Nell was.

'I know 'ow to wind a baby, never you fear. I've fed more babies than you've had hot dinners,' Nell assured her.

'Of course – I wasn't meaning to interfere,' Olivia answered in a choked voice.

'We really ought to think of getting back to the shop now,' Dilly told her. She of all people knew just how painful it was going to be for the girl to leave her child in the care of another.

'Yes, of course.' Olivia crossed over to the baby and kissed her tenderly.

'Just come whenever yer want, pet,' Nell said, her voice kind. 'An' don't you be worritin' about her none. Me an' this little 'un are goin' to get along just fine.'

'I believe you will,' Olivia answered in a wobbly voice, but she allowed Dilly to lead her blindly out into the yard.

'At least she's close by and you can still see her often,' Dilly pointed out sympathetically, but too upset to answer, Olivia merely nodded, wondering how on earth she was going to be able to bear the separation from her baby.

Dilly was busily working in the shop one afternoon when the phone rang. She picked up the receiver and heard her father-in-law's voice. 'It's Maeve, lass. Can you hear me?'

'Yes, yes, I can hear you, you don't have to shout,' Dilly informed him gently. 'What's wrong with Maeve, Daniel?'

'She's had a stroke – a bad one. An' Declan reckoned I should let you know,' the old man shouted with a catch in his voice.

Dilly's heart did a somersault. Maeve was no youngster now and she realised instantly how serious this could be.

'It's my fault,' Daniel said wretchedly. 'I should've made her slow down, so I should, but you know what Maeve's like, she's so bloody independent.'

Dilly held the phone slightly away from her ear to prevent herself from being deafened.

'I'm sure it's no one's fault,' she assured him. 'And the

337

only way you'd get Maeve to slow down would be to tie her to a chair.' Her mind was racing and she felt guilty. The Price wedding was rushing towards them, and although she was on target for getting all the outfits ready, should she take any time off she would soon fall behind with her deadline. There were other bridal outfits ordered as well now. Yet Maeve clearly needed her – what was she to do?

'Do you want me to come?' she asked then.

'No, lass, no – I know how busy you are, but Ben thought perhaps Niamh might be able to come over? I know she's not been home long, God love her, and I wouldn't ask, but . . .'

'I shall speak to her tonight and then phone you back,' Dilly promised. 'In the meantime, give Maeve my love and tell her I'm thinking of her, of all of you.'

'I will, lass, I will,' Daniel said then the phone went dead in her hand.

Dilly sighed. Everything had been going so well. Olivia had gone back to nursing at Weddington Hall Hospital, and the arrangement with Nell taking care of Jessica was working far better than any of them had dared hope. The baby was thriving. The shop was doing well too, so well that Dilly had now been able to employ Seamus on a full-time basis as well as another seamstress to help keep up with demand. And now this blow!

As soon as she shut the shop that evening she went round to Niamh's and was relieved to see that she'd returned from the school. Niamh had recently started working part-time again and was clearly enjoying it. Dilly wondered how she would feel about having to let them down again so soon after starting back, but she needn't have worried. Niamh was keen to go.

'If it's a choice between helping Gran'ma and Granda out or working at the school I'd choose to go to them every time,' she said earnestly. 'But I'm sure when I explain the circumstances the headmistress will understand why I have to have more time off. Leave it with me, Mammy, and I'll speak to her first thing tomorrow. All being well I'll be able to get a ferry across to Dublin the next day.'

Dilly wrung her hands, feeling useless. Maeve had come to mean a lot to her over the years and she felt all manner of guilt because it wasn't she herself that was going. But how could she let everyone down?

She voiced how she felt to Niamh, before ending, 'This has decided me. I've been thinking of taking on another assistant full-time to help me in the shop. It would free me to do more sewing or to take a little time off when emergencies like this crop up. I shall put a sign in the window advertising for one first thing tomorrow. But in the meantime, are you sure that you don't mind going? And what about Roddy? He won't be able to come with you this time now that he's started school.'

'Mary is more than capable of looking after Roddy. She already takes him to and from school anyway, now that I'm back at work. And no, I truly don't mind going, so stop fretting. I shall phone you just as soon as I get there to let you know how Gran'ma is and I'll keep you updated.'

Dilly agreed reluctantly. Sometimes she felt angry at the way Bessie had just abandoned her child. The young woman didn't even bother going to stay at Niamh's on her evening off any more, preferring to stay at the Farthings' with Camilla, to whom she was clearly devoted. It was perhaps as well, for Camilla had deteriorated so badly now that she didn't even know Max when he went to her room to visit her. Poor Max. Dilly knew that many men in his position would have put Camilla into an asylum long ago, but he was too loyal to contemplate that and she admired him for it. He still visited Dilly regularly, and although he knew that she now saw Henry Price at least once a week neither of them mentioned it.

'Poor Gran'ma,' Seamus said when he arrived back from Birmingham that evening and Dilly told him what had happened. 'Did Granda say how bad it was?'

'Very bad apparently,' Dilly told him truthfully. 'And the problem is her age is against her now. I think we should prepare ourselves for the worst.'

'Rubbish!' Seamus answered heatedly. 'Gran'ma is a fighter, bless her! She'll be back on her feet in no time, you'll see.'

'I hope you're right,' Dilly told him with a weak smile but deep down she had grave misgivings. 'It will mean though with Niamh gone again that Mary will be left alone to keep the house running and care for Roddy, but you'll keep your eye on them for me, won't you?'

She saw the dull flush creep up his neck before he muttered, 'I suppose so – if I have to.'

'Whatever is wrong with you two?' Dilly asked then. 'You always seemed to get along so well then suddenly you've moved back here and barely seem to be on speaking terms! Have you had a row?'

He shook his head, looking decidedly uncomfortable, as Dilly sighed. 'Do you know, there are times when I feel like banging your two heads together,' she declared. 'Ever since you came home you've been moping about with a face on you like a wet weekend, and Mary looks as if she's ready to burst into tears at the drop of a hat. A blind man on a galloping horse could see that she thinks the world of you. Is that why you're keeping away – because you don't have feelings for her?'

Seamus looked shocked. 'It's because I *do* have feelings for her that I'm keeping away, if you must know,' he spat sullenly. 'You must be wrong about her caring for me. Mary is such a bonny lass. She could have anybody she wanted, so why would she want to saddle herself with the likes o' me who sometimes jumps at me own shadow an' has nightmares like a bairn! Why, I even still wet the bed from time to time, as you're well aware.' He hung his head with shame.

'Oh, sweetheart,' Dilly said despairingly as she grasped his two large hands in her small ones and gently shook them up and down. 'You've got it so wrong, truly you have. That girl understands why these things happen and I'd stake my soul that she'd walk through fire for you. Just open your eyes and you'll see, and I'll tell you now you could do a lot worse than young Mary. She's got a heart of pure gold.'

Denial and hope vied for first place in his eyes as he stared wonderingly back at her. 'Do you really believe that, Mammy?'

'With all my heart,' she nodded. 'So why don't you wait until Niamh has left for Ireland and then go round there one evening when Roddy is in bed and tell her how you feel? I'm sure you wouldn't be disappointed at her reaction, trust me. Faint heart never won fair lady, you know.'

'I'll think about it,' he answered and Dilly went away with a little smile on her face. She'd promised herself that she wouldn't interfere in any of her children's lives but this, as far as she was concerned, was an exceptional circumstance.

Niamh left for Ireland two days later and that evening Seamus plucked up his courage and went to see Mary whilst Dilly nervously waited for his return. Max came as she was working on the Price wedding outfits and she was thrilled to see him. Anything was better than sitting there wondering how the two young people were getting on.

She told Max all about it and he grinned ruefully.

'Sometimes people can't see what's right in front of their noses, can they? But you know I have a feeling things will turn out well for those two. They seem to be very well suited.'

'I think so too,' Dilly agreed as she poured them both a drink, a whisky for him and a small glass of sherry for her. It was funny now that she came to think about it. She never touched drink unless Max or Henry called, but then she was usually too busy to stop work.

'How is the baby your friend adopted?' he asked after a time and Dilly squirmed uncomfortably as she avoided his eyes. She was still certain that Max would fall in love with Jessica if he met her, as everyone else did, but Olivia was still adamant that he must never know about her. Everyone had accepted Nell's story unquestioningly, and if anyone thought it strange that Olivia was rarely off her doorstep no one had commented on it up to now.

'She's an absolute little darling.' At least Dilly didn't have to lie about that. 'And as good as the day is long. I think Nell is quite enjoying having a baby in the house again. I thought I might take her to see Mrs Pegs on Thursday on my afternoon off to give Nell a little break.'

'Oh, I'm sure Mrs Pegs would enjoy that,' Max answered amiably. 'And Jessica will get to meet George. Penelope is bringing him to see me on Thursday.'

'Are she and Oscar getting along any better?' Dilly ventured to ask.

Max shook his head. 'I don't believe so. She's a bit of a shrew, from what I can gather – but then I shouldn't lay all the blame at Penelope's door. I just don't think Oscar measured up to her expectations. She was clearly in love with him when they got married but her feelings weren't returned so I can sympathise with her up to a point.'

Dilly sighed. It was so sad, but what could anyone do about it?

'Did Niamh get off all right?' he went on, and just as the words had left his lips the phone rang. Dilly raced down the stairs to answer it.

'It's me, Mammy.' Niamh's voice crackled along the line. 'I just wanted to let you know that I've arrived safely.'

'Good, and how is Gran'ma?' Dilly asked worriedly.

There was a short silence then Niamh replied, 'Not good at all, to be honest. The stroke has taken all the feeling from her left side and her mouth has dropped too. It's awful to see her like this. Bless her soul, she can't even feed herself. Granda is almost beside himself with worry.'

'Then it's a good thing you're there to help. Does the doctor have any idea how long her recovery might be?'

'None at all,' Niamh admitted. 'So I shall stay for as long as I'm needed. But are you all right, Mammy? And has anyone applied for the job in the shop yet?'

'I have two ladies coming to see me tomorrow evening,' Dilly told her, 'and one of them sounds just right. She's already worked in a shop before so she wouldn't need training up, and with someone here to help full-time I'd have a lot more time to concentrate on the sewing and the sketching.'

The line began to crackle dangerously then so they bade each other a hasty good night and Dilly went back upstairs to Max to pass on what Niamh had said.

It was as he was preparing to leave sometime later that he suddenly asked, 'How are the outfits for the Price wedding coming along now?'

'Very well, thank you.'

'And Henry? I hear that you go out regularly together now.'

'If you can call about once a week regularly.' Dilly wondered why she should feel so guilty.

'Good – I'm pleased for you. You should have someone special in your life, Dilly. You deserve it.'

'But we're nothing more than very good friends,' she hastened to tell him.

He smiled sadly and she stifled the urge to take his hand. 'Henry's no fool. He knows a good woman when he sees one. But now I must be off. I've no doubt you're itching to get back to work.'

She walked down the stairs with him to the shop door and once he had gone the loneliness closed around her like fog. She was very fond of Henry and he made no secret of the fact that he admired her, and yet something always stopped her from letting their relationship progress beyond friendship. Despite enjoying his company, she couldn't help comparing their time together with the ease she felt with Max. But Max was married.

With a shrug she trooped back upstairs and concentrated on her sewing again. She was in the process of stitching hundreds of tiny crystals onto the long trailing veil that Eleanor would wear on her wedding day, and it seemed to be taking for ever. But then as Dilly thought of how the girl's outfit would shimmer as she walked down the aisle on her father's arm, it all seemed worth it.

# Chapter Thirty-Nine

'So where did you get to last night then?' Dilly asked Seamus with a smile the next morning at breakfast. 'I didn't go to bed until way after eleven o'clock and there was no sign of you.'

'Me an' Mary got talkin',' he answered sheepishly then his face stretched in a grin that seemed to reach from ear to ear. 'She's agreed to be me girl, so we're officially walkin' out now.'

Dilly let out a hiss of relief. 'And about time too,' she said delightedly, then on a more solemn note, 'But don't go planning the wedding for too soon, for goodness sake. I'm stacked out with work as it is.'

Hearing the teasing note in her voice he laughed, looking happier than he had for months – years in fact. 'We're just goin' to take things slowly an' see how it goes,' he confided. 'But not too slowly . . . do you know somethin', Mammy? I'd marry her tomorrow if she'd have me. I reckon I'm the luckiest chap alive.'

There's one I shan't have to worry about in future, Dilly thought as she stirred the pan of porridge. It looked as if both Seamus and Declan would be happy in their marriages. She just had to worry about Niamh and Olivia now.

That evening, Dilly went to bed a happy woman, or at least as happy as she could be whilst worrying about Maeve. The second woman she had interviewed for the job at the shop had turned out to be perfect and would be starting the following Monday. Nora Jenkins was middle-aged, attractive and exactly what Dilly had been hoping for. She had an easy way with people and a good sense of what would suit them, and Dilly was sure that her customers would love her. Nora lived within walking distance of the shop with her husband, which was another plus, so all in all Dilly was feeling quite pleased with herself, despite the fact that she would be paying out another full-time wage. The two shops were now earning more than enough to support it, and Dilly was beginning to realise that her time might be better spent on her designs. They were certainly proving to be very popular and the seamstresses were struggling to keep up with the demand for them.

On a beautiful warm day in May, Eleanor Price visited the shop for the final fitting of her wedding gown. Just as Dilly had hoped, Nora had proved to be a godsend and Dilly wondered how she had ever managed without her. Dilly carefully pinned the chiffon about Eleanor's slender waist into place while Nora adjusted the lacing on the bodice and Eleanor cried with delight as she twirled in front of the cheval mirror.

'It's absolutely lovely – easily the most beautiful dress I've ever seen! Thank you *so* much, Mrs Carey. I know how hard you've worked on it.'

'It was worth every second to see you so happy,' Dilly told her, smiling broadly. 'Now all we have to hope for is sunny weather. Early June is usually pleasant. It won't be much fun being stuck in a marquee in the grounds of your home if it's raining.'

'It won't rain,' Eleanor answered serenely. 'Everything is going to be just perfect – I know it.'

Dilly beamed at her. She'd grown fond of the girl, and once she'd helped her out of her dress and carefully hung it up she left her to get dressed and went to join Henry in the shop. Nora was busy serving a customer so she asked Henry, 'Would you like to come upstairs for a cup of tea?'

'I'd love to,' he responded, adding in a lower voice. 'Between you and me, I shall be glad when it's all over now. I'm nervous as a kitten. But I know I shall miss her when she's gone. It's hard to believe that she'll be in Venice on her honeymoon soon. I always just see my little girl when I look at her, not a grown-up, almost married woman. Actually, I'll be glad of a few moments alone before Eleanor joins us because I was wondering . . . well, I was wondering if you'd consider being one of the guests at the wedding?'

'*Me?*' Dilly was astounded.

'Why not you?' Henry answered. 'After all your hard work surely you'd like to be there to see everything finished? Besides, there will be someone there whom I'd like you to meet. My friend Philip is a fashion designer in London. He has his own string of shops and I have an idea he'd enjoy meeting you. I'm sure he will be impressed with your creations so it could work very much in your favour.'

'I'm not sure that I have anything grand enough to wear,' Dilly fretted, quite in awe at the thought of meeting a successful fashion designer. Surely he would sneer at her efforts?

Henry threw back his head and bellowed with laughter.

347

'Why, you have three seamstresses working for you around the corner! Surely if you give them one of your splendid designs they could have something ready on time, between them? Oh, please don't refuse the invitation, Dilly! It would mean so much to Eleanor if you were there.'

'Then in that case, I'd love to accept your invitation,' she told him primly.

'Wonderful! I shall send a car to take you to the church. But now where's that tea? A man could die of thirst around here!'

Dilly bustled away in a state of shock wondering if she'd done the right thing in agreeing to attend. There would be some very wealthy influential people at the wedding. Would she feel like a fish out of water? Even if she did, it was too late to renege now. She was going to the wedding and she would have to make the best of it.

Just as Eleanor had prophesised, the day of the wedding dawned bright and clear with powder-puff clouds floating across the calm blue sky.

Dilly had bathed and washed her hair the night before. She'd visited the hairdressers two days previously and had her long hair cut into a fashionable shoulder-length bob and now she brushed it until it gleamed before slipping into the dress that the seamstresses had worked flat out to finish for her. It was made of satin, in a very becoming shade of blue, with a low waist and floaty elbow-length sleeves that fluttered as she moved. She had found a very pretty straw hat in Max's hat factory that she'd trimmed with silk flowers and a ribbon the same colour as the dress, and she'd even treated herself to some dainty high-heeled shoes. She felt a little guilty at her extravagance and wondered when she would ever get the chance to wear such a dressy outfit again but even so, now that the day had come she was determined to enjoy herself. The fact that she would at least be as well dressed as some of the wealthy guests gave her confidence, and as she placed her hat at a jaunty angle on the side of her head she was satisfied with her efforts, even if she was only a former maid. The florist had delivered a corsage of cream and pink rosebuds from Henry earlier in the morning and once she'd pinned them to her dress she was ready to go. As she came downstairs and into the shop Nora smiled at her admiringly.

'Why, you look absolutely lovely,' she declared and Dilly blushed self-consciously. But then a smart car pulled up outside and Nora ushered her out, saying, 'Now you go off and enjoy yourself and don't get worrying about anything here. I've got everything under control and I shall be sure to lock up safely when I leave.'

When the car drew up close to Holy Trinity Church in Hartshill, Dilly saw that people were pouring into it and she was suddenly very aware of the fact that she was alone and knew no one apart from the wedding party. Once inside, she was amazed at the beautiful floral arrangements. Freesias were everywhere she looked and she couldn't help but be impressed. Henry had skimped on nothing. Eleanor was a very lucky girl. At the end of the aisle she spotted a very nervous bridegroom with his best man, but then she edged into a pew towards the back of the church and after bowing her head she said a prayer. Soon the church was full to capacity. People were exchanging pleasantries and chatting but then the vicar took his place in front of the holy altar and a hush fell as the organist began to play The Wedding March.

Dilly peeped across her shoulder and caught her breath as she saw Eleanor seemingly float down the aisle on her father's arm. She was touched to see that there were tears in Henry's eyes and he looked so proud. The bride looked positively stunning. Her dress and veil shimmered in the lights pouring through the stained-glass windows and Dilly felt a lump form in her throat as she saw the expressions on everyone's faces and heard the murmured words of admiration from the assembled congregation.

'Why, she looks just like a film star,' Dilly heard a woman behind her whisper. 'And what about the flower girls? I've never seen anything like their dresses. They're fit for royalty.'

Dilly felt a glow of pride and held her head a little higher, but then Eleanor reached her groom and silence descended as she smiled adoringly at her handsome groom and the service began.

Dilly shed a tear as she saw Henry give his daughter away. She knew how much he loved her and guessed that he would be thinking how proud his late wife Emma would have been if she had been there. Once the service was over and the register had been duly signed, everyone left the church to the joyous sound of the bells for the official photographs to be taken. Rice and rose petals were thrown amidst laughter and Henry snaked through the crowds to stand at Dilly's side.

'I have a feeling you're going to be inundated with work after this,' he told her. 'Everyone is so impressed with the outfits. Philip, my friend from London – the one that I told you about – has already said that he simply must meet you. But hold on, I think the photographer is calling for me again. Do excuse me, Dilly. I'll see you back at the house. The car should be waiting for you.'

When all the photographs had been taken, and everyone finally dispersed to head off to the reception, Dilly found her car waiting for her, and was driven to the Prices' beautiful home.

The house took Dilly's breath away. It was an old black and white timbered building behind heavy iron gates, and the gardens seemed to go on for ever. A huge marquee had been erected on the lawn to one side of it and the second Dilly stepped out of the car a waiter politely greeted her, balancing a silver tray full of brimming champagne glasses. Dilly had never tasted champagne in her life but she found that she liked it.

'Ah here you are, I've been looking for you.'

She turned to find Henry striding towards her.

'Come along and I'll show you where you're going to be sitting.' He took her arm possessively and led her into the marquee, which was unlike anything she had ever seen before. A number of round tables were laid with snow-white cloths, silver cutlery and sparkling cut-glass goblets, and in the centre of each one was a magnificent flower arrangement.

The head table where the bridal party would sit was even more magnificent with trails of ivy and fresh flowers all along the length of it.

'I've put you on this table with Philip. I'm sure you'll get along and then I'll come and join you just as soon as the meal and the speeches are over. Will you be all right, Dilly?'

'Perfectly,' she assured him as the waiter drew out the chair for her to take a seat. Seconds later, a tall dark-haired man sat down next to her. He was impeccably dressed and very handsome, and he immediately introduced himself.

'Philip Maddison.' He held out his hand with a broad smile and as Dilly shook it he said, 'Henry informs me that we are to sit together and you, I believe, are the renowned Mrs Carey.'

'I am Mrs Carey but I'm not so sure about the renowned bit,' she told him, returning his smile. It was very infectious and she liked him instantly.

'So it is you who was responsible for the bridal party's impressive outfits today?'

When Dilly inclined her head and blushed prettily he rushed on, 'May I say they are superb? Never have I seen a more ethereal bridal gown and the little ones look adorable, like something out of a fairy tale. But did you really design them all?'

'Ye – yes, I did.' Dilly was feeling thoroughly embarrassed as other people were joining them at the table now and listening with interest.

'Then perhaps you would be willing to talk to me later on about showing me some of your designs?'

Why a successful man like him should want to look at her designs Dilly had no idea, but she nodded politely all the same. He was probably just being friendly, she told herself, and as the afternoon wore on he'd forget all about her.

The meal that followed was exquisite, course after course of it, and by the time it was over Dilly was sure she wouldn't be able to eat so much as another mouthful for at least a month. She was also feeling quite tiddly as her glass appeared to be magic, insomuch as it never seemed to empty. An army of waiters prowling around the tables made sure of that. The cake, a towering three-tier affair, was cut, the speeches were made and then everyone walked out into the sunshine whilst the waiters prepared the marquee for the band that was due to arrive.

Dilly was standing alone admiring the house when Henry found her, a grin like the Cheshire cat's on his face.

'Phew, thank goodness everything went well,' he said, glancing across at the happy couple who only had eyes for each other. 'All your painstaking work paid dividends in the end, Dilly. Thank you so much. When I got my first glimpse of Eleanor in her wedding gown today she looked so beautiful that she took my breath away and I was moved to tears.'

'Eleanor would look beautiful in anything,' Dilly

answered as her eyes followed his. 'You must be feeling so very proud today. She's a credit to you – and to your late wife, of course.'

'Dilly, there's something I've been meaning to say to you.' He took her hand, looking vaguely uncomfortable. 'You see—'

His words were interrupted when Philip Maddison strode purposefully towards them and Henry hastily dropped her hand looking like a guilty schoolboy who had been caught kissing a girl in the playground.

'Ah, here you are,' Philip said pointedly to Dilly. 'Henry, may I intrude, old friend? I was afraid Dilly here had gone without my having the chance to talk to her properly. Dilly, my dear, I shall be staying in Nuneaton this evening and I was wondering if you would allow me to come and look at some of your designs tomorrow before I return to London?'

'Well, yes of course you may,' Dilly told him, 'but I must warn you they are very amateurish.'

'Not if what I've seen today is anything to go by.' Philip smiled at them both. 'So may we say at ten o'clock then?'

'Er . . . yes.' As Philip strode away, Dilly turned her attention back to Henry. 'What were you saying before we were disturbed?' she asked.

'Bride's father to the marquee, please!'

The photographer was about to take yet more photos and Henry grinned wryly. 'Excuse me, Dilly. It seems I'm needed yet again.'

Once Henry had sprinted off, Dilly strolled around the garden. It was quite beautiful, with sweeping lawns that rolled down to a small lake where two snow-white swans were gracefully swimming. Weeping willows trailed their branches into the water, and it was so peaceful that she felt she could have lingered there for ever. Glancing back towards the house, she was sure that she had never seen

353

anything more beautiful. Virginia creeper and ivy clambered up the walls, and sunshine was glinting off the leaded windows. Her thoughts then turned to Philip Maddison. Her designs would surely look very crude when set against the ones he was used to. Still, she consoled herself, she wouldn't have long to wait to find out what he made of them – and on that thought she returned to the wedding party.

Once the photographer had finished, the band that Henry had hired struck up a tune and soon people were dancing both inside the marquee and outside on the grass. The whole day had been a roaring success and Dilly was satisfied that all her months of hard work had been worth it. Henry soon sought her out again and she found herself in his arms being swept along to a waltz. It felt nice to be held in a man's arms again. She'd almost forgotten how nice, and she relaxed and gave herself up to the pleasure of the moment.

Late that afternoon the waiters and waitresses began to load the tables with yet more food and the wine flowed like water.

'No, no more for me, thank you,' Dilly told a waiter hastily as he tried to refill her glass yet again. 'I shall never be able to get up to open the shop in the morning at this rate.'

'So have a day off then,' Henry told her. 'That's the beauty of being your own boss.'

'But closed shops don't earn money,' she pointed out. Then, 'I really should be going soon. I promised Nell I would call in and see Jessica this evening.'

Henry raised an eyebrow, clearly disappointed. 'Must you? I was hoping you would stay until the end. And aren't you spending rather a lot of time with the little girl that your friend has taken in?'

Dilly visibly bristled. 'I suppose I am, but why shouldn't

I? Jessica is a beautiful child and I enjoy seeing her. Now that my own children are grown up and we've lost Connie . . . Well, I just like helping Nell out.'

'Of course, forgive me, I shouldn't have interfered,' he said contritely. 'It's just that I worry about you, Dilly. You work so hard and when you're not working you seem to be rushing round to Nell's to help her out. You've even stood me up lately a couple of times to go and see that young lady.'

As she looked into his twinkling eyes her annoyance vanished. He was only concerned about her, after all, and she supposed he did have a point. She saw Jessica on an almost daily basis now and couldn't get enough of her. It was as if she was making up for all the years that she had been deprived of Olivia. Jessica was healing the empty place inside her that had existed for so many years – and that couldn't be a bad thing, surely?

# *Chapter Forty*

Dilly was tidying the glove drawer in Dilly's Designs when Philip Maddison's car drew up outside the shop promptly at ten o'clock the following morning.

Hastily smoothing her skirt, Dilly asked Nora, 'Are you all right to watch the shop for a while, Nora, while I take Mr Maddison upstairs to look at my drawings?'

'Of course I am,' Nora told her with a grin. 'And good luck. Who knows where this might lead, eh? Your designs could be in the London stores if he likes them.'

'Hmm, we'll see.' Dilly didn't dare let herself think about that but then she was holding her hand out to Philip as he entered the shop. 'Good morning,' she greeted him. 'Would you like to follow me? I have everything ready for you to look at.'

'That's what I like, efficiency.' He shook her hand warmly and trailed up the stairs behind her. Once in the small living room he glanced around in astonishment. The place was spotlessly clean but tiny, and he wondered how she managed – but then his attention was drawn to the sketches she had laid out ready for him on the table. He began to study them one at a time as Dilly stood nervously by.

'I think I'll go and make us a cup of tea and leave you to it,' she bumbled. She really couldn't stand there much longer waiting for his verdict and needed something to do.

'That would be most welcome,' he answered absently without even looking up.

She scuttled away and when she returned a short time later with the tea tray he turned and addressed her.

'Dilly, these are just . . .' He paused trying to find the right words. 'Excellent!' he said eventually. 'There are some that I am particularly enamoured of. This one for instance.' He lifted a sketch. 'And this one and this one. I think these would sell really well in my shops and so I think we should talk business.'

Hardly able to believe her ears, Dilly stared at him blankly. 'What do you mean, talk business?' she asked when she found her voice again.

'I am quite prepared to buy these designs off you and have them made up to sell in my shops.' When she failed to respond, he took it that she wasn't particularly interested and hurried on, 'I will of course pay a generous price for them.' Still no response from Dilly so he added, 'And I would also have your name sewn into the label so that everyone who buys them will know who the designer is. It could prove to be very beneficial to you.' He then named a price for each design that made Dilly's mouth gape.

'It's a good job there are no flies about,' he teased.

Dilly instantly clamped her mouth shut. 'I must admit I'm shocked that you're interested,' she said modestly.

'I don't know why – they're quite brilliant. So now put me out of my misery and tell me if you are prepared to do business with me.'

Dilly gazed at him thoughtfully. The amount he had mentioned was far more than she had ever dared dream of, but Max had taught her to be an astute businesswoman and she wanted to achieve the maximum return possible.

'I er . . . I'm not so sure that I want to sell them,' she heard herself say as her heart thudded painfully. She was aware that she could be shooting herself in the foot. 'Once I've sold them to you I shan't be able to use them myself as you'll have sole rights to them.'

He tapped his lip with his forefinger as he stared back at her.

'You drive a hard bargain,' he said as he returned his attention to the sketches. They really were original and highly commercial – and he knew that he must have them. 'All right,' he said eventually. 'How about if, in addition, I give you ten per cent for every dress that is sold?' When she still hesitated he went on, 'I really can't go beyond that. You must realise I have to take into account the cost of manufacturing the garments. The money for the sales would be paid to you on a monthly basis.' His voice was firm now and Dilly realised that she had pushed him as far as he would go. With what he was offering and what she was already making from the two shops she would be able to buy a third shop in Coventry. She'd had her eye on an empty premises in Primrose Hill for some time now and this would bring it within reach.

When she nodded he sighed with relief, held his hand out and they shook. 'It's a deal then. And I also want to see any more designs you may do. Would you allow me to do that? I haven't been so excited for many a long day.'

When he left the shop a short time later to return to London with the sketches he'd selected placed safely in his briefcase, Dilly was reeling with shock. She was also considerably richer.

The following week, whilst Dilly was in the shop, a neighbour came in from the courts where she had used to live to tell her that Nell's husband Fred had died suddenly of a massive heart attack while he was at work. Leaving the shop in Nora's hands, Dilly rushed straight around there to see how Nell was. She found her friend sitting huddled in a chair in a state of shock and Jessica fast asleep in the crib that Dilly had provided for her, with her tiny thumb jammed in her mouth.

'I can't take it in,' Nell muttered, shaking her head. 'We had our ups an' downs but my Fred weren't a bad old cuss.'

'Of course he wasn't,' Dilly agreed sympathetically as she began to make tea. 'But you must leave everything to me now and don't worry about a thing. I shall organise the funeral.'

'I can't let you do that, lass,' Nell protested but Dilly wasn't prepared to take no for an answer.

'Will you still be able to manage financially?' she asked eventually when she had pressed a steaming mug into Nell's shaking hands.

The woman nodded. 'I think so. I'll get a small pension from the pit, an' wi' that an' the money Olivia pays me for lookin' after the baby I should be all right.'

'Well, Jessica can come and stay with me for a while till the funeral is over,' Dilly told her.

Nell frowned. 'But what will Olivia think to that?'

'If she's with me she'll be perfectly fine about it,' Dilly assured her. 'She can come and see her just as easily there as she can here. And it's only temporary, after all. Nora is more than capable of keeping the shop going on her own for a time, and even if she isn't I'm only upstairs, aren't I?'

Too numb with grief to argue, Nell made no protest as Dilly piled everything the baby would need into the end of her pram. She was secretly delighted to be having little Jessica all to herself for a while, although she wished for Nell's sake that it could have been under happier circumstances. Neighbours were already popping in and out to pay their condolences and once Dilly was sure that Nell would not be alone, she lifted Jessica, tucked her into the pram and set off for the shop again.

She was changing the wrapping on Jessica's plump bottom that evening when Max knocked and came inside the flat. 'I see you haven't forgotten how to do it,' he teased, then on a more serious note, 'I was so sorry to hear about Nell's husband. What a blow it must be for her.'

'It is,' Dilly agreed as she fastened the nappy pin and lifted the baby onto her shoulder, then feeling that she should offer some explanation for Jessica's presence she added, 'I offered to take the baby to give her some peace and quiet to get over the shock.' Could Max have known it, Olivia had already called in to see Dilly on her way home from the hospital after Nell had told her of the arrangements. But Dilly didn't tell Max that of course.

'Here, would you just hold her for a moment for me while I warm her milk up?'

Max willingly held out his arms for the mite and Dilly's throat was full as she watched him smiling down at the baby. If only she could tell him that Jessica was his granddaughter, but that would be betraying Olivia's trust and she would never do that.

'How are things at home?' she asked when she was giving the child her bottle.

'Much the same,' Max said. 'But at least I get to see George every Thursday afternoon now when Oscar brings him round. Why don't you bring this little one as well? She and George will be good company for each other – if Nell is planning on keeping her, that is.'

'Of course Nell will keep her, where else would she go?' Dilly asked. 'And how are Patty and Lawrence getting on?'

His shoulders relaxed. 'Oh, still love-struck and long may it last. Olivia still isn't herself though. She seems to have lost all her sparkle and she never ventures out any more apart from to go to work. It doesn't seem natural to me.'

They then went on to speak of other things and were completely at ease together until Dilly casually mentioned that Henry was calling around later that evening.

'I think he's desperately missing Eleanor,' she confided. Eleanor and her new husband were on their honeymoon in Venice by now and she hoped that they were having a good time.

'And is there still no word from Samuel?' she asked hastily, seeing the way his face set at the mention of Henry.

Max shook his head. 'Nothing – and between you and me I don't *want* to hear from him. The last trick he played on me with the house cost me dearly and I shan't forget it in a hurry this time.'

Despite his words, Dilly knew that even now he would forgive the young man eventually. Samuel was his flesh and blood, after all, and hard to turn his back on.

Once Jessica was tucked back into her cot, Dilly made Max a drink and he was halfway through it when there was a rap on the shop door.

'That'll be Henry,' Dilly mumbled as colour crept up her neck and into her cheeks.

'Then I'd best be off,' Max said shortly, tossing his drink back in one swallow. 'Stay where you are, Dilly. I'll let Henry in on my way out. Good night, have a good evening.'

As he disappeared off down the stairs, Dilly had to bite back unexpected tears. Max still had his family about him and yet he always looked so lonely. She felt sad for him. He deserved so much better.

Henry bounced up the stairs seconds later, his usual cheerful self, only to stop abruptly as his eyes settled on the sleeping baby.

Dilly hastily explained who she was and why she was there, and watched as disappointment settled across his face.

'Does this mean we shall have to postpone our trip to the theatre this week then?'

'I'm afraid so,' she told him gently. 'Nell is my dearest friend and I couldn't let her down in her hour of need, could I?'

'I suppose not,' he answered reluctantly. 'But I do wish you'd think of yourself more, Dilly.'

How could she tell him that it was an absolute pleasure to care for her grandchild? Instead she answered, 'Nell once helped me when I lost my husband. It's my turn to help her now.'

Aware that he might have appeared rather churlish, Henry was instantly contrite. 'Of course you should,' he agreed. 'Take no notice of me, I'm just being selfish because I'm being deprived of your company for a time.'

She instantly forgave him. Henry was such a genuinely nice man that it would have been hard to stay annoyed with him for long.

'I'll tell you what – seeing as we can't go out, how about if I was to cook you a meal tomorrow evening?' she found herself saying. 'I'm afraid it won't be anything fancy as I'm just a very plain cook, but you'd be more than welcome. If you don't mind having the baby here, of course.'

His face broke into a smile. 'That would be lovely. And I shall bring the wine. Shall we say about six-ish?'

'Seven would be better,' Dilly answered. 'Jessica should be settled for the night by then.'

'Seven it is then,' he said delightedly and so it was agreed.

Olivia called in the following evening as usual on her way home to find Dilly all of a dither as she tried to prepare a meal for herself and Henry and keep an eye on Jessica. The child was sitting on a blanket on the floor chewing on some wooden bricks that Dilly had bought for her and at sight of Olivia her lovely face broke into a smile displaying a lone tooth and painfully red gums.

Scooping her into her arms, Olivia exclaimed happily, 'Oh, her first tooth!'

Dilly smiled indulgently. 'She's chewing on everything in sight like a dog with a bone,' she chuckled, thinking what a pretty sight the pair made.

'I just popped in to see Nell,' Olivia told her soberly. 'Poor thing – you don't think this will make her want to give up on Jessica, do you?'

'Absolutely not.' Dilly threw her a clean towelling wrap as she juggled with a pan of potatoes and Olivia expertly began to change the child's bottom.

'But what if she can't cope?' Olivia's voice was heavy with worry.

'Actually I've been giving that some thought,' Dilly said. 'And I think I may just have come up with a solution.' When Olivia waited expectantly she went on, 'This place is barely big enough to swing a cat around in, and now the shop is doing so well I desperately need more storage space for materials. Then today when I took Jessica for a stroll I saw a lovely house for rent up in St Edward's Road. It's a grand house three storeys high and right close to Riversley Park. An ideal place for Jessica to grow up in. So I got to thinking, Why don't I suggest to Nell that we all move there together?'

'But how much is the rent?' Olivia asked worriedly. 'I'm not sure that I could afford to pay rent *and* the money I give Nell to care for Jessica.'

Dilly chuckled. 'You've misunderstood me. I would rent the house and let Nell move in with me. There's more than enough room for all of us, Seamus included. I've been looking around for somewhere suitable for a while as it happens and this would be the ideal solution. Truthfully, I don't envisage Seamus being with us for too much longer. I rather think there might be a wedding in the offing.'

B-but I couldn't let you do that for us,' Olivia stammered.

Crossing to her daughter, Dilly bent and tickled Jessica beneath the chin.

'To be honest, I wouldn't just be doing it for you two. Nell's remaining children and their families have recently informed her that they are all planning a new life in America in the not too distant future. This means that Nell will be quite alone then, now that her husband Fred has passed away. Nell and I have been friends for a great number of years, more than I care to remember, and she helped me through some of my darkest hours after my late husband had his accident. She has become the big sister I never had and now I want to do something for her. Can't you see, this would be perfect? I would be at hand to help Nell with Jessica should she need it, and it would be company for me too.'

Olivia was still uncertain so Dilly hurried on, 'I've become very attached to your lovely daughter and that would be a much nicer environment for her to grow up in. Plus it's only a few minutes' walk away from the shop for me. Also, Olivia, since the fire I tend to get quite nervous in the rooms above the shop when Seamus is out at night – and something Henry said made me realise that I've become rather reclusive since I've lived here. It will be good for me to have people around me again. And so with your permission I intend to go and enquire about the lease first thing tomorrow morning. But now if you'll excuse me I'll give you a few moments alone with madam here while I go and put the finishing touches to this meal. It's only lamb cutlets, potatoes and vegetables, I'm afraid. A far cry from what Henry is used to his cook producing.'

The smile returned to Olivia's face as she said teasingly, 'I'm sure it will be delicious, and perhaps Seamus won't be the only one with a wedding on the horizon? I rather think Mr Price is quite taken with you, Mrs Carey.'

'Oh, get away with you. We're simply friends.' Dilly blushed becomingly as Olivia giggled. It was nice to see her girl smile again.

# Chapter Forty-One

That Thursday afternoon, Dilly wheeled Jessica round to Max's house in her pram to find Oscar already there with George. He was sitting in the middle of the floor in the drawing room surrounded by toys that Max had bought for him, and the second she saw him, Jessica started to gurgle and laugh.

'Put her down here with George, they can keep each other company,' Oscar invited as she made to wheel the pram through to the kitchen to Mrs Pegs.

Dilly glanced at Olivia who was sitting primly in a chair and Dilly realised how difficult it must be for her to see Oscar with his son. Olivia had taken the afternoon off from the hospital where she was happily working again, and when the girl nodded her agreement Dilly lifted Jessica from the pram and placed her gently down on the carpet next to George.

'Right – I'll leave you two to keep your eyes on these little rascals,' she said as brightly as she could. Olivia was looking vaguely uncomfortable, she noted. 'I'm going to go and scrounge a cup of tea off Mrs Pegs then I'll pop upstairs to see Bessie and your mother.'

By now, Olivia was down on her hands and knees playing with the babies, and as Dilly glanced across her shoulder at them all a cold chill ran up her spine. They looked for all the world like a happy family – and perhaps they could have been, had it not been for the terrible secret she and Max had been forced to keep all these years. The injustice of it made her feel nauseous.

'So what's this I'm hearin' about you movin' into a posh new house then?' Mrs Pegs questioned with a grin the second Dilly walked into the kitchen. 'Goin' up in the world, ain't yer, gel? An' long may it last, that's what I say. You've worked hard enough fer it an' that's a fact. But now come on, Gwen, get that kettle on an' dig out them biscuits I made. Me mouth feels like the bottom of a birdcage. Yer could perhaps take a tray through to Miss Olivia an' Oscar an' all. Don't let them babbies get anywhere near it, mind.'

Gwen obligingly did as she was told as Dilly took a seat. It was a glorious day and stifling hot in the kitchen despite the fact that the back door was wide open.

'So when will yer be movin' in then?' Mrs Pegs asked.

'I shall be picking the keys up tomorrow and then it's up to me and Nell,' Dilly told her as she spooned sugar into three cups. 'But I'm also going to look at a shop in Primrose Hill in Coventry on Saturday, so it won't be over the weekend, that's for sure. Perhaps early next week. Max – Mr Farthing – has told me that he'll get Mr Jackson to help me and Nell move our stuff on the cart, which was very kind of him, wasn't it?'

'Not really,' Mrs Pegs answered unexpectedly. 'I don't reckon there's owt he wouldn't do fer you. In fact, I often think if it weren't for the fact that the missus were still alive,

367

he'd . . .' Suddenly realising that she was letting her mouth run away with her, she hastily changed the subject to ask, 'An' how is little Jessica?'

'Very well.' Dilly kept her smile firmly in place and soon the awkward moment passed and they were chatting easily again. Eventually she made her way back to the drawing room to find Oscar and Olivia still playing with the babies.

'These two have really taken to each other,' Olivia informed her. 'Jessica just had quite a tantrum when I tried to lift her up away from George.'

'I seem to recall you being just the same when your mother tried to take you away from Oscar.' The second the words had left her lips Dilly wished she could have bitten her tongue out. Olivia had flushed a dull brick-red but worse than that, as Dilly watched the way the babies were interacting, a cold hand closed around her heart. Surely history couldn't be about to repeat itself with these two little innocents?

'I think I'll just pop up and see how your mother is today while the babies are happy,' Dilly said, pulling herself together with an enormous effort. She then shot from the room leaving the two young people to themselves.

'So how are things with you?' Olivia asked eventually as she offered a brightly coloured rattle to George, who instantly proceeded to batter Jessica with it.

Oscar remained silent for a while as if he was deciding how to answer. Then: 'Not brilliant, if you want the truth. Within days of marrying Penelope I realised that it would never work. She is not the one for me. I actually feel quite sorry for her. She isn't a bad person, not really, but I haven't measured up to what she expected of a husband. It's no wonder she's become so stiff and starchy. But what about you? I was quite surprised when you came back from London. I thought you were enjoying living there.'

'I was,' Olivia said, avoiding his eyes. Oscar had always been able to read her like a book and she was afraid that he would guess the truth. 'I made some wonderful friends and there was always so much to do there, but there's no place like home at the end of the day.'

They then went on to discuss everyday matters and gradually the ease that had once existed between them began to return again.

Upstairs, Dilly found Bessie giving Camilla a drink through a long funnel device attached to a beaker. The sight brought tears to her eyes when she thought of the woman Camilla had once been. This sad drooling creature in no way resembled her. She was clean and tidy, thanks to Bessie, but apart from that she was almost unrecognisable.

'How is she today?' Dilly asked as she took a seat beside Camilla. What a stupid thing to ask, she silently scolded herself then. Anyone with eyes in their head could see how Camilla was.

'Oh, she's havin' a good day today. What I mean is – good for her. At least she's calm this afternoon and hasn't tried to attack me. She went for Mr Farthing like a wild-cat last night when he popped his head round the door. Trouble is, when she's like that she's got the strength of ten and it took both of us to get her into bed.'

'I'm sorry to hear that,' Dilly said sincerely, then went on to tell Bessie of her proposed move. 'Then once we're settled in and I've got this new shop up and running I really must get over to Ireland to see how my mother-in-law is,' she ended.

'Yes, you should,' Bessie agreed. 'And weren't you also planning to visit your son's grave in France this year?'

'Yes I was.' Guilt pierced through her. 'It's just that with the fire, the Price wedding and one thing and another I haven't been able to spare the time yet. But I will,' she said stoically. 'Now what about your long-term plans? Have you given any thought to yours and Roddy's futures yet? You won't be nursing Camilla for ever.'

Bessie's hands began to flutter like birds' wings as she quickly began to fold some bedlinen. 'Well no, I haven't as yet,' she said. 'Things are all right as they are for now, ain't they? What I mean is, Roddy seems as 'appy as Larry wi' Niamh an' Mary lookin' after him, so there's no rush to make a decision just yet, is there? An' I am grateful to 'em for takin' such good care of him.'

'Roddy's fine,' Dilly said kindly. It always hurt her to see the way Bessie struggled with her feelings for her son. She clearly wanted to love him, but couldn't.

Shortly afterwards, Dilly went back downstairs to find Oscar and Olivia chatting animatedly. Jessica was getting tired by then so she reluctantly laid her in her pram and set off back to the shop. Somehow she was going to have to find time to start her packing, and she thanked God for Nora and Jayne who had the two shops running like clockwork.

Early in July the day of the house move dawned bright and clear. All was frantic activity at the shop. Nell was still grieving for her husband following the funeral, which had been a modest affair at her request, but the thought of moving to a new house had cheered her up considerably.

With Mr Jackson and Seamus along to help there was no shortage of strong men to move the heavy items from the rooms above the shop.

By the time they arrived at the shop to help Dilly shortly after eleven o'clock in the morning, Nell was already at the house with Jessica, arranging her own furniture with a huge happy smile on her face.

'I think you're going to have to buy some new things,' Mr Jackson joked as he helped Seamus manoeuvre Dilly's table down the narrow staircase. 'That house is positively huge compared to this place and you'll 'ave nowhere near enough furniture for all those rooms.'

'It will come in time,' Dilly panted as she followed on with a large box of pots and pans in her arms. 'And at least we'll have enough between us to get by for now. I might go to the auctions when I get time. There are some bargains to be had there.' Although when she would find the time she had no idea, she thought ruefully. Since taking the lease on the house she had also secured one on the shop in Coventry and then promptly employed shopfitters to prepare it for opening. She'd also taken on a Coventry woman to manage it and hoped to open this new branch of Dilly's Designs within the month, so everything had been fairly hectic.

'You'll be richer than me at this rate,' Max had teased her, but Dilly could never see that being the case. Even so, she was happy with the way things were going and was more determined than ever now to get over to Ireland for a visit just as soon as she and Nell were settled in. Thankfully, Niamh had reported that Maeve had recovered slightly from her stroke. She had partly regained her speech but was still bedridden, and it looked doubtful now if she would ever again be the woman she had once been. Even so, the family were just grateful that she had survived, for she was much-loved, and none of them could bear to think of life without her. Niamh had shown no signs of wanting to return home but Dilly knew that she was happy in Enniskerry and so put no pressure on her, although she missed her dreadfully.

An hour later, Mr Jackson stood back to survey the loaded cart with a sigh. 'Phew, I reckon that's the lot,' he gasped. 'However did you manage to cram all this lot into those three tiny rooms? There ain't space for another pea on that cart!'

Dilly chuckled. 'Right, I think we're ready then. I'll just pop in and check on Nora, and then we'll be on our way.'

Mr Jackson set off. Dilly was to travel to the new house with Max, who had called to pick her up in his car. Unbeknownst to him, Henry had also offered to help with the move but Dilly had gently declined. She had guessed that Max wouldn't be too thrilled to have Henry about, so instead he was going to call around to see her in her new home later that evening.

Nell met them at the door when they arrived with Jessica sitting on her hip, a beaming smile on both their faces.

'Eeh, lass. Whoever would 'ave thought that the likes o' meself would ever end up livin' in a place like this?' Nell said wonderingly.

In truth it was a beautiful house and Dilly was pleased that Nell was so excited about it. It was a large Victorian terrace with a good-sized back garden where Jessica would be able to play to her heart's content when she was old enough.

Dilly took Max for a tour while Nell rummaged amongst a pile of boxes to try and find the kettle. He too was delighted with it. 'It's a much more suitable residence for an up-and-coming businesswoman,' he commented as they went from one room to another. 'And the rent is quite reasonable too.'

'Oh, I don't intend to rent it for long,' Dilly informed him airily. 'I've already worked out that if the Coventry shop does as well as the other two are doing, and if my designs sell well in London, I shall be able to afford to buy it by this time next year.'

Max stared at her admiringly. He had no doubt at all that she would do it if she set her mind to it.

The ground floor consisted of a large drawing room, a dining room, another sitting room and a large kitchen. On the first floor were four enormous bedrooms and an indoor bathroom, and on the second floor were two further bedrooms.

'I really am going to have to buy some more furniture,' Dilly sighed. 'The things Nell and I have brought will look lost in this place.'

'As it happens there are quite a few bits and pieces up in our attic,' Max said thoughtfully. 'Items that Camilla has had taken up there over the years when she's changed things. They might not be the height of fashion any more but they're good sturdy pieces and you're welcome to them if you can use them – they're only sitting up there gathering dust. Shall I get Mr Jackson to get them down and bring them round for you?'

'I'd be most grateful,' Dilly said as they went back to join Nell in the kitchen. Jessica was fast asleep in her pram by the open back door that led directly into the garden and Nell had found the kettle and placed it to boil on the range.

'I reckon this room alone is almost as big as the whole o' me old cottage put together,' Nell told them. 'That fireplace is goin' to look grand wi' a few nice copper pans hangin' above it. And where's them curtains yer had made, Dilly? I'll set to an' get them hung after we've had us tea.'

Dilly and Max exchanged an amused glance. It was nice to see Nell look more her old self and Dilly was sure that she'd done right in renting the house.

Henry was very taken with it too when he arrived that evening bearing a great armful of flowers.

'It's a lovely place,' he acknowledged when they were back down in the kitchen after Dilly had given him a tour. 'But don't go getting too comfortable. You might decide to live elsewhere in the not too distant future.'

Dilly raised an enquiring eyebrow but Henry wasn't able to expand on his comment because Nell bustled through then with her arms full of clean bed linen and Jessica began to stir.

'Just got to get the beds made up now an' then I'm callin' it a day. I'm fair worn out, and that's the truth,' she huffed.

'She certainly seems happy with the move anyway,' Henry chuckled when she'd gone. 'But I wish you'd let me help you.'

'Oh, we had more than enough willing hands without troubling you,' Dilly said cagily, unwilling to tell him that Max had already been there. She had no wish to hurt Henry's feelings. 'But now if you'll excuse me I should really get on. The little miss there will be wanting her last feed and poor Nell hasn't stopped all day.'

'All right, I can take a hint – I know when I'm not wanted,' Henry responded but his eyes were twinkling as he headed for the door. 'I'll pop into the shop and see you tomorrow shall I?'

'That would be nice. Good night, Henry.'

Once he was gone, Dilly lifted Jessica and cuddled her warm little body to her. From now on she would get to see her every single day. She'd be there to see her get up in the morning and go to bed each night, and she'd also see much more of Olivia. Just the thought of being able to spend so much time with both of them made her tingle with pleasure.

# Chapter Forty-Two

It was mid-August before Dilly found time to visit Ireland. The Coventry shop was now open, the new house was in some sort of order and she felt that she could put it off no longer.

Daniel met her off the ferry and as the trap rolled through the lush green countryside of County Wicklow Dilly asked, 'So how is Maeve now?'

'Hmm – well, let's say better than she was, but you ought to prepare yourself. She won't be the same as you remember her. She's partially regained her speech but not the feeling in her left hand and she can get very frustrated.'

'I can imagine,' Dilly said. 'She's always been so hard-working and independent. It must be so difficult for her to have to lie there and be waited on.'

'That's an understatement, to be sure,' Daniel answered. 'But Niamh has been wonderful, God bless her. Nothin's too much trouble for her gran'ma.'

'She's always been a good girl,' Dilly agreed. 'I can't

begin to tell you how much I've missed her – not that I begrudge her coming to you, of course. But how does Niamh seem to be in herself?'

'Chirpy as a leprechaun,' Daniel chuckled. 'An' Ben's been a right good help an' all. He's over at the farm every spare second he gets.'

A little alarm bell suddenly sounded in Dilly's head. Surely Niamh wouldn't be silly enough to renew their relationship? She'd be aware that it was doomed to failure surely, for she was a married woman now, even if it was in name only. No, she told herself then. Niamh was an intelligent lass and she'd know what the consequences of that would be. Much as Maeve loved her, she would see it as a mortal sin and turn her back on her granddaughter. She was of the old school and firmly believed that once you had made your bed, you must lie on it.

Dilly shrugged off her gloomy thoughts to admire the passing countryside. She was missing Jessica already. She was now seven and a half months old and was into everything. As yet she hadn't mastered the art of crawling but had found out that she could get exactly where she wanted to be by shuffling about on her bottom, which frequently had them all in fits of laughter. For the first time in her life Dilly had the pleasure of spending time with her daughter and her granddaughter every single day, and she was loving every second of it.

'Mammy!'

When Dilly entered the farmhouse a short time later Niamh hurtled towards her and caught her in a bear hug.

'Oh, I've missed you so much. It's so lovely to see you!'

'I've missed you too,' Dilly responded, holding her at arm's length. Niamh was positively blooming. Her hair was shining, her eyes were bright and Dilly was pleased to see that there was a glow in her cheeks that had been absent since little Constance's death. The country air was clearly suiting her, or something was.

'You're looking grand!' Dilly exclaimed, but then her attention was caught by a noise from the other side of the room and she saw Maeve lying in bed holding her right arm out to her. The other lay uselessly on the sheets to the side.

Forcing a smile to her face to hide the shock that shivered through her at first sight of her mother-in-law, Dilly hurried across to her and gently took the outstretched hand. 'Maeve, how are you?'

'I . . . s . . . all . . . right,' Maeve answered with a lopsided smile.

Dilly could have cried at the change in her but kept the smile firmly in place. The poor woman was almost unrecognisable. Gone was the busy little person Dilly remembered. She seemed to have shrunk to half her size and her hair, which had always been her crowning glory, was thin and grey now. But it was her face which had altered the most. Dark circles ringed her eyes and lines of pain were etched into her cheeks.

'Ha . . . ppy to see . . . you.'

'And I'm happy to see you too.' Dilly leaned forward to hug her, to hide the tears that were threatening. 'I'm glad to see you're on the road to recovery,' she said throatily as she straightened.

'Sl . . . ow job . . . to be sure.'

Dilly could see the frustration in her mother-in-law's face. 'Ah, but you have to be patient. These things take time.'

Thankfully Declan bounded into the room then. He lifted Dilly off her feet and swung her about as if she weighed no more than a wean. Like Niamh, he too looked a picture of health and Dilly could hardly believe that this big strapping man was really her son.

'I was so sorry to hear about the baby,' she told him when he'd placed her back on her feet and a shadow fell across his face.

'Aye, we were too, sure we were, but we won't stop trying,' he said with a determined lift of his chin. 'Roisin wants a child more than anythin' else in the world an' we won't give up till she gets one. But now tell us all about the new house an' the new shop. Sure we can scarcely keep up wi' you, Mammy.'

So as Niamh made a large pot of tea and buttered some soda bread to keep them all going till dinner time Dilly did just that. She told them all about Jessica and Nell moving into the house with her, although she was careful not to mention Olivia's relationship to the child, and all about the new shop in Coventry, and they all listened enthralled.

That evening, Ben arrived bright and chirpy. Dilly found herself watching him and Niamh closely and soon decided that her suspicions must be unfounded. True, they were once again at ease in each other's company but there didn't appear to be anything more than friendship between them, for which she was extremely thankful. Roisin came in too, keen for news of Roddy, and before Dilly knew it the evening had passed in a pleasant blur.

'How long can you stay for, Mammy?' Niamh asked as Dilly helped her to wash up the supper pots.

Ben and the others had left for their own homes some time earlier, Maeve was already asleep – she tended to tire easily – and Daniel was napping in the chair at the side of the fire, so they were careful to keep their voices low.

'Only for three or four days at the most, I'm afraid,' Dilly told her apologetically. 'I only came to see how your gran'ma was for myself, but as you can appreciate I need to be back home to keep my eye on what's happening.'

'I can see that.' Then with a wicked grin Niamh asked,

'And how are things going between you and Mr Price now?'

'Going?' Dilly blushed to the roots of her hair and almost dropped the plate she was in the process of drying. 'Why, I'm sure I don't know what you mean, lass. Henry Price and I are just companions, nothing more, although I confess I enjoy his company. Until he came on to the scene I'd almost forgotten what it was like to have a night out.'

Niamh looked at her knowingly. 'I reckon it might be a bit more than companionship Mr Price is looking for, Mammy. Surely you've realised that he has strong feelings for you. And don't frown at me like that. From where I'm standing that's no bad thing. Daddy's been dead for a long time now and you're still young enough to get married again and enjoy life.'

'Why, I . . . I *do* enjoy myself,' Dilly blustered indignantly. 'I think you've been reading too many romance novels, my girl!'

'We'll see,' Niamh said with a smug little grin and for then the subject was closed. Even so as Dilly snuggled down in her crisp white sheets later that night she thought on what Niamh had said. On a few occasions she had felt that Henry was on the verge of saying something to her but they had always been interrupted. Could it be that he had been going to profess his feelings for her? And if he did, how would she respond? Furthermore, how would Max respond? She gave herself a mental shake. What did it matter what Max thought! He was a married man and her personal life was her own affair, after all. Burrowing further beneath the blankets she gave a sigh and tried to sleep. She was just too tired to think about it all for now.

In Plymouth, Samuel was sitting in the corner of a noisy bar near the docks with a jug of ale in his hand. In his pocket was a roll of money and he was feeling pleased with himself. He'd fulfilled his dream of owning a tattoo shop and was making cash hand over fist thanks to the tattooist he'd employed. Tod Fellows was a little on the thick side, very easily taken advantage of, but he was a brilliant tattooist and the local dockers and seamen were happy to pay good money for his work. Tod had had little or no education so it was easy for Samuel to sit in the shop each day and take the customers' money whilst Tod did all the hard work. His tattoos were becoming very popular despite the fact that the shop wasn't particularly clean or hygienic. Samuel didn't give a great deal of thought to things like that, and if the odd chap got an infection from dirty needles, so what? He could get away with paying Tod a pittance although Samuel charged high rates for his work, and now he was raking the money in. He'd found himself a nice lodging house to stay in as well, just beyond the docks, where the blowsy widow who owned it was more than happy to cater to all his needs, so all in all things were going well. If occasionally he thought briefly of Niamh and his father it was with no affection. For now he had no thoughts of returning to his home town; he had it far too cushy where he was. Perhaps one day he might go back, if the money ran out or he needed to boost his coffers – after all, he still had his so-called sister's secret to reveal – but for now he was quite content where he was.

Oscar arrived at his home that evening to find Penelope waiting up for him. He'd informed her that morning that he'd be late and wouldn't require an evening meal as he was dining with a prospective client for his father.

He was mildly surprised to find his wife in the drawing room still, since she usually retired early, but he nodded at her politely as he went to help himself to a glass of sherry, asking, 'Is everything all right? George isn't unwell, is he?'

She shook her head. 'George is fine – although in a way it's him that I wish to talk to you about.'

Samuel was vaguely surprised. They barely passed the time of day with each other now and Oscar had been sleeping in a single bed in his dressing room for some time.

'Oh?'

She licked her lips before saying, 'The thing is . . . I have decided that I'd like George to have a brother or sister. I have no wish for him to be an only child so I'd like you to return to our bedroom.'

Oscar's stomach sank as a picture of Olivia floated in front of his eyes. He'd long since come to terms with the fact that he had feelings for her, sister or not, and there wasn't a damned thing he could do about it. Even so, he was an honourable man and felt he had a duty to his wife.

'Very well.' Ignoring the sherry, he poured himself a generous tot of whisky from the decanter and tossed it back in one gulp, already dreading what lay ahead. 'Perhaps you would care to go up to our room then and I'll join you presently.'

She inclined her head as two spots of colour flamed into her cheeks, and as she departed, closing the door quietly behind her, he couldn't help but compare her to Olivia. For all her expensive clothes – and he'd soon discovered that Penelope was used to the best of everything – she couldn't hold a light to his sister. She had about as much grace as a carthorse, but then no one had forced him to marry her so he had no choice but to meet her demands. The thought of it made him break out in a cold sweat and he hastily poured himself another drink. It was the only thing that might help in this situation.

Things were very different in the small cottage in Caldecote where Patty and Lawrence were curled up together on the sofa. Although they'd been married for some time they still couldn't get enough of each other and whenever Dilly saw them together it made her feel sad to think of what her own daughters had been denied.

'Lawrence, I have something to tell you,' Patty murmured as she snuggled into his chest and he raised an eyebrow. Patty usually just came straight out with whatever she had to say.

'Well, spit it out then, I shan't bite you,' he laughed as he twisted a lock of her flame-red hair about his finger.

'The thing is . . .' She gulped. 'I know we both agreed when we got married that we'd wait for a few years until we started a family, but I'm afraid something's gone wrong.' She held her breath as she stared into his face waiting for his reaction.

'Gone wrong?' he repeated uncomprehendingly and then as realisation dawned, he held her at arm's length. 'What? you mean you're . . .'

'Yes, I think so although I haven't seen a doctor yet. I wanted to find out how you felt about it first. I'm so sorry – we've been very careful but we've slipped up somewhere. I was so determined to become a Sister before I became a mother, and now . . . Are you very angry, Lawrence?'

'Angry?' He was laughing and crying all at once. 'No, I'm not angry. I'm bloody delighted, if you must know. Oh, you clever girl!' Jumping up he snatched her into his arms and began to waltz her about the room. 'But how do *you* feel about it?' he asked anxiously as he pulled her to a halt. 'I know how much your promotion means to you, and you're so close to getting it.'

'Actually, I'm thrilled about it too,' she admitted shyly. 'And seeing as you're a modern-minded man I can always go back to work when the baby is a little older to continue with my nursing. We could perhaps get a nanny in to look after him or her?'

'That's a marvellous idea,' Lawrence agreed. He couldn't seem to stop smiling. 'I'm going to be a father,' he said wonderingly and Patty laughed as she nodded her head in agreement.

The following evening in Enniskerry Father Doherty arrived as he did each week. Since Maeve could no longer attend church he made the journey each week to see her. Over the years he had become almost a member of the family and he was thrilled to see Dilly there.

'I hear you're a woman of substance now, Dilly,' he said as he shook her hand warmly.

'Well, I wouldn't go quite that far but I do have three shops now,' she admitted modestly.

'I'm pleased to hear it.' And he was. He could still remember when she had been so poor that she had been forced to leave her children in Dublin with her in-laws for a time. She'd had a hard life though no one would have guessed it. She was still a fine-looking woman, with skin the colour of milk and scarcely a grey hair on her head. He was just surprised that some chap hadn't snapped her up before now, but from what he could make of it, Dilly had shown no interest in remarrying after Fergal had died. She'd been too intent on seeing to the needs of her family, which was all credit to her.

'They must keep you very busy.'

'They do,' she agreed.

'Hmm, building an empire is all well and good but you know you should look to yourself more, so you should, especially now the children are all grown and don't need you so much.'

'I lead a very full life,' she answered in amazement.

'But full of what?' His words were said so kindly that she found it hard to take offence. 'There's more to life than work, so there is,' he went on gently. 'And you are still young enough to find happiness again. There must be many an admirer out there. Surely you don't want to face a lonely old age?'

'I shan't be lonely. I still have my family,' she said defensively but he shook his head.

'Your family are grown with families of their own now, Dilly. Look to yourself, lass.' And with that he went off to chat to Maeve while Dilly made her way out into the farmyard. She picked her way through the chickens who clucked indignantly at being disturbed and headed for the orchard. Once there she sat beneath an old apple tree and chewed thoughtfully on a piece of grass. Perhaps Father Doherty was right? The prospect of growing old and lonely was not very appealing. Her thoughts ran on to Henry. He had made it clear in a thousand ways that he was fond of her, but being the gentleman he was he had never tried to push their relationship beyond friendship. Perhaps it was time she showed him that she was fond of him too. He was, after all, an extremely kind man. Any woman would be proud to be seen on his arm. She knew that she'd sadly neglected him recently – ever since the wedding, in fact. She'd cancelled many of their outings through one thing and another and he'd patiently put up with it. But there always seemed to be so much to do. Getting the new Coventry shop up and running; preparing to move to the new house; settling into the new house – but, she decided, when she got home things would be different. Eleanor and her husband were settling blissfully into their newly-wed status and she sensed how lonely Henry was. So, she decided, when I get home I'll be kinder to him and make more time for us. And with that thought still in mind she rose, dusted off her skirt and headed back to the farm.

'Where's Niamh?' she asked when she entered the kitchen. Daniel had come in from the fields for a cup of tea and a brief rest, leaving Liam and Declan to the more back-breaking work.

'Gone for a walk into town,' Daniel answered as he stirred the tea in the pot and put the cosy on it. He did like his tea to mash. 'She often goes walkabout this time o' day, so she does. And why not indeed? The lass works hard enough while she's here and that's the truth.'

Dilly merely nodded as the niggling suspicions returned. Was Niamh going to visit Ben? But no, she reassured herself, her girl would never be so silly. Even though Niamh had no idea where her husband was, and the fact that theirs was a marriage in name only, still in the Church's eyes she was a married woman and to commit adultery was a sin.

Dilly's visit passed all too quickly and as she was packing on the evening before she was due to leave, Niamh got tearful.

'I shall miss you, Mammy,' she croaked.

'But it won't be for much longer now,' Dilly soothed as she hugged her. 'Shelagh was only saying today that Maeve should be well enough to get up and sit in the chair soon, then she and Roisin can manage things here between them. She also confided some wonderful news,' she went on, dropping her voice to a whisper. 'She's just discovered that she and Declan are to have another baby, but she doesn't want to tell the rest of the family just yet because of Roisin recently losing hers again.' She sighed then. 'It's so sad, isn't it, that Shelagh can have babies like shelling peas yet poor Roisin can't carry one to full term? Still, we have to stay positive that it will happen for them one day and be glad for Declan and Shelagh.'

'Of course,' Niamh agreed and she then helped her mother with the rest of the packing.

It was late the following evening when the train Dilly was on pulled into the station at Nuneaton. She found Henry waiting on the platform for her. He had phoned her on a number of occasions while she was in Ireland and she'd told him what train she was hoping to catch.

'But you didn't have to put yourself out to come and meet me,' she protested as he gave her a chaste kiss on the cheek and took her bag from her.

'Nonsense, I won't have you walking home after such a long journey. The car is outside – come along.'

Dilly happily slipped her arm through his as he led her from the station and in no time at all she was back at the house in St Edward's Road.

'It still feels strange to come here,' she confided, 'and not to the rooms above the shop. It doesn't feel quite like home yet.'

'Perhaps it was never meant to be your home,' he commented, and although Dilly found that rather a strange thing for him to say, she didn't reply but mutely followed him into the house.

# Chapter Forty-Three

'Oh I've missed you so much, little one,' Dilly cooed to Jessica the next morning at breakfast. The tiny child had been fast asleep in her cot when Dilly had arrived home the evening before, and Dilly had been reluctant to disturb her.

'I reckon she's missed you an' all,' Nell chuckled as she carried Jessica's porridge to the table. 'Oh, and by the way, there's a letter came for you. It's on the mantelpiece and it's got a London postmark on it.'

'I bet it's from Philip Maddison,' Dilly answered. 'He's had my designs made up and in his shops for the last month so it's probably to tell me how they're selling – or not, as may be the case.' She had been horrified when Philip had told her what the cost of the dresses would be, but then as he had explained, his seamstresses were highly qualified and would work with only the finest material. On top of that, the cost of clothes was much more expensive in the capital so she had kept her opinions to herself, trusting him to know what he was doing.

She tore open the envelope and nodded at Nell. 'Yes, it is from Philip.' She then began to read aloud.

*Dear Dilly,*

*I am delighted to inform you that your designs are selling out almost as quickly as I can get them made up. The money order I have enclosed is for 10 per cent of each garment sold to date. I would be delighted to look at any more designs you may have ready and hope you will be pleased with the first month's profits.*

*Yours sincerely,*
*Philip Maddison.*

Dilly tentatively took the enclosed money order from the envelope then gasped and held it out to Nell with a shaking hand. 'My God, it's over fifty pounds,' she breathed. Never in her wildest dreams had she expected that much.

'Lordie . . . it's a bloody fortune,' Nell said disbelievingly. 'You're gonna be rich at this rate, gel.'

Dilly plonked down heavily on the nearest chair and Jessica began to coo and giggle as Nell did a little dance before slapping a wet kiss on Dilly's cheek, saying, 'Well done, you!'

'I can't quite believe it,' Dilly answered in a daze. 'I shall be able to pay for the house and the shops sooner than I thought, if the dresses continue to sell at this rate.'

'You will that,' Nell chortled. 'An' buy even more if you've a mind to. Things are finally goin' your way, an' it's not afore time.'

'I think I might just ring Max and tell him the good news, if he hasn't already left for work,' Dilly said as she headed for the telephone on the small table in the hallway. She was delighted when it was Max himself who answered the phone and she quickly passed on her good news.

'Why, that's marvellous! And so well deserved. I shall pop round to see you this evening and we'll have a drink to celebrate. Congratulations.'

'Thank you, but actually I've already made arrangements for this evening,' she said guiltily.

'Oh . . . I see. Then in that case I'll call in at the shop tomorrow if that's convenient?'

'Of course it is. You are always welcome, you should know that, Max.'

There was silence for a moment before he said quietly, 'Bye for now, Dilly – and well done again.'

As the phone went dead in her hand she felt strangely bereft.

The whole day was spent travelling between the three shops to check that all was well, but she needn't have worried. Seamus was doing a grand job of keeping them all supplied with stock and the three manageresses she'd appointed had each one running smoothly.

'I was thinking today how much time it would save if I were to invest in a motor car for you,' Dilly told Seamus that evening before she went to get ready for her evening out with Henry. 'You're having to hump everything about on the trains and it must be very tiring. I shall ask Henry's advice this evening.'

Seamus beamed, 'Me, driving a motor car? Crikey, Mammy, we are goin' up in the world! But as you quite rightly say, it would save a tremendous amount o' time.' His face became straight then as he said nervously, 'Actually there's somethin' I'd like to talk to you about.'

'Then fire away,' she answered. 'Since when have you been afraid to tell me anything?'

'The thing is, me an' Mary have decided to get wed at Christmas. There doesn't seem any need to wait, as we both feel sure of our feelin's. How do yer feel about it, Mammy?'

'I think it's wonderful,' Dilly beamed. 'But where will you live? Will you go to join her at Niamh's house? I'm sure Max wouldn't have any objections.'

'We haven't got that far yet,' he admitted. 'But it's somethin' to think on.'

'And what about Roddy? Mary is his main carer.'

Seamus shrugged. 'Well, I don't see a need for that to change. I've no objections to the little chap, but again we haven't discussed that so far. We only decided on the date a couple o' days ago an' Mary hasn't even had chance to tell her mammy yet.'

'Finally, where will you be getting married?' Dilly was aware that Mary was Church of England. 'Will Mary be converting to your faith?'

Seamus hung his head. 'To be honest we're not overly worried about that. We thought we might just have a quiet do at the register office like Niamh an' Samuel did. Times are changing, Mammy, and people don't worry so much about things like that any more. Mixed marriages are becoming more commonplace an' we have to move with the times.'

Dilly nodded. She supposed he was right, although she dreaded to think what Father Brannigan would have to say about yet another of her children marrying outside their faith. Fergal would have turned in his grave, God bless his soul, but then she had to accept that Seamus was right – times *were* changing – and if marrying Mary made her son happy then she herself would have accepted him marrying a heathen.

That evening, Henry took her to a new eating house that had opened in the town and between courses Dilly told him about Seamus' forthcoming marriage.

'It won't be anything like the lavish do Eleanor had. They want it quiet,' she told him as she sipped at the champagne he had insisted they should have to celebrate the success of her designs in London.

'So what?' He shrugged. 'Seamus has been through the mill since he was injured in the war but I've seen a marked difference in him since he started walking out with young Mary. She makes him happy and that's the main thing. Sod the difference in their religions! Lots of things that were unacceptable before the war are accepted now. You're a prime example. Who would have thought that women would become successful in business? Look at you now, Dilly. You've come a long way and I'm very proud of you. In fact . . .' He hesitated before going on cautiously '. . . I would be more than happy to accept my wife working for a few hours a day to occupy herself and earn some pin money.'

Dilly looked at him thoughtfully. Was he trying to tell her something? Then a waiter stepped forward to replenish their glasses and once again the moment was lost.

'Bessie is worried about what will happen to young Roddy when Seamus and Mary get married,' Mrs Pegs confided to Dilly later that week when Dilly took Jessica round there for her usual rendezvous with George on Thursday. It was a regular thing now and the babies would coo and gurgle with delight when they caught sight of each other. Often, Dilly would leave Jessica in the care of Olivia and Oscar once she got there so she could go into the kitchen and catch up on the gossip with Mrs Pegs.

'I can't see that things need change,' Dilly answered. 'I've had a word with Max and he's more than happy for Seamus to stay at the house and live there with Mary. Whether Roddy is recognised as such or not, he is Max's grandchild after all and I know that Max thinks the world of him.'

'It's all right sayin' that now, but a young couple settin'' out on married life may not want someone else's little 'un to care for, at least they might not when bairns o' their own start comin' along. I love Bessie like me own but I wish she'd take more responsibility fer the poor little lad,' Mrs Pegs said in a low voice. 'I know Bessie *wants* to love 'im, an' I know she feels guilty because she can't, but I reckon it's because he looks so like his dad. Every time she looks at him she sees Samuel an' remembers the way Roddy come about.' She shuddered as she thought of the rape.

'Well, things have a way of coming right in the end usually,' Dilly said philosophically.

'I just hope yer right,' Mrs Pegs answered but she sounded doubtful.

At that moment there was a terrible commotion from upstairs and both women and little Gwen rushed out into the hallway to see what was going on. Olivia was there too with Jessica in her arms and Oscar was holding George.

'I thought it came from my mother's room,' Oscar said, holding George out to Dilly as he glanced towards the ceiling. 'Will you hold him while I go up and see what's happened?'

The second the child was in Dilly's arms, Oscar raced up the stairs, to find Bessie almost hysterical as she pointed towards the bed.

'I only left her for a few minutes to go to the w.c.,' she sobbed. 'An' look what she's done. Run an' get a doctor quick while I try an' stop the bleedin'!'

Oscar gulped and fought down vomit as he stared at his mother. She was sitting on the edge of the bed completely unconcerned as blood gushed from her wrists with a broken glass flower vase at her feet. Pulling himself together, he flew from the room leaving Bessie to deal with her and sped downstairs to the phone.

'It's Mother, she's cut her wrists,' he told them all when

he had got through to the doctor. 'She must have broken a vase and used some of the glass to do it.'

Both of the infants were beginning to whimper as they picked up on the tension in the air and Dilly and Olivia hurriedly took them back into the drawing room to play with their toys.

'Wait by the door to let the doctor in, would you, Gwen?' Oscar said grimly. 'And Mrs Pegs, would you phone my father? He should be at the Atherstone factory – please ask him to come straight home.'

'Ooh!' Mrs Pegs flew into a panic. She'd never got the hang of the phone and almost jumped out of her skin every time it rang, but all the same she quickly looked in the phone book for the number she needed and dialled the operator with a trembling finger.

'He's on his way,' she told Oscar minutes later when she joined him and Bessie in Camilla's bedroom. By then Bessie had bound both of the poor woman's wrists tightly to try and stop the bleeding but Camilla was rocking back and forth and wailing, an unearthly sound that made the hairs on the back of their necks stand on end.

Thankfully the doctor arrived within minutes and ushered everyone apart from Oscar from the room while he examined her.

'Fortunately it's only surface cuts,' he informed them some time later. Max was there by then, white-faced and trembling. 'I believe it's time we had a talk, don't you, old chap,' the doctor said and Max nodded miserably, for he had an idea what was coming.

They left Camilla to Bessie's tender mercies and went down to the day room where the doctor stood in front of the empty fireplace with his hands clasped behind his back.

'I think you already know what I'm about to say to you, don't you, Max?' he said.

Max dropped onto the sofa and nodded mutely.

'I feel that I can speak to you openly because I've tended your family for many years – in fact, I was just a young man when I first met you,' Dr Beasley went on. 'But surely you must see now that Camilla is becoming a danger not only to other people but also to herself? Bessie does an admirable job of caring for her, but with the best will in the world she can't be with her every second. It would have been a very different outcome indeed today, had Camilla sliced through her veins rather than just the surface skin. You must realise that?'

Deep down, Max knew that the doctor was right. He had only been postponing the inevitable but he could be signing Camilla's death warrant if he didn't heed what the kindly man was trying to tell him now.

'It – it's just the thought of her being shut away in one of those dreadful asylums,' he mumbled brokenly as he leaned forward and clasped his hands between his knees.

'I can assure you that not all asylums are bad places. In fact, Hatter's Hall on the outskirts of the town has a reputation for excellence. I visit there regularly and I can vouch that the patients have the best of care. Particularly the ones like Camilla whose family can afford to pay well. You must be able to see it makes sense, Max! How much longer can you keep her here? Bessie is only a young woman and sooner or later she's going to want to get on with her own life – then where will you be? There are not many that would be as committed to Camilla as she has been, and you know how upset your wife gets at strange faces.'

Max knew that it was time. He nodded slowly. 'Very well, but I'd like to go and see the place before I make a final decision. Would that be possible?'

'Of course. If I make a phone call now I can take you there myself this very afternoon if you like.'

When Max opened his mouth to protest the doctor rushed on, 'It can't be delayed any longer, man. How will you feel if she does herself or someone else serious damage?'

Max's shoulders sagged in defeat. 'Very well, make the call.'

As the doctor passed him on the way to the phone he patted his shoulder and Max blinked to hold back the tears that were threatening as he thought of Camilla as she had once been. Unbidden, a picture of her lying in bed with their firstborn in her arms flashed in front of his eyes. She had been glowing with pride and he had never loved her more than he had at that moment. She had taken to being a mother like a duck to water, and as their family had increased he had thought he was the luckiest man in the world. She had been beautiful, loving and intelligent, but now he asked himself when had it all gone so wrong and he wept for what he had lost.

# Chapter Forty-Four

'I feel as if it's all my fault,' Bessie said thickly as she sat in the kitchen with Gwen and Mrs Pegs enjoying a cup of cocoa before bedtime. 'If only I hadn't left her perhaps—'

'You can stop that sort o' talk right now,' Mrs Pegs scolded her. 'Everyone has to listen to the call o' nature. What else could you 'ave done? You've been marvellous to 'er an' that's a fact, even Dr Beasley said so, but . . . Well, the thing is she's gone beyond the help any normal person could give 'er now. And didn't you 'ear what Mr Farthing said when he got 'ome? He felt a lot better after seein' the place she's goin' to himself. She'll 'ave somebody wi' her every second o' the day there an' they're used to nursin' people wi' mental illnesses so she'll get the best o' medication an' all. She ain't goin' to be locked away in a straitjacket, yer know – this ain't the Middle Ages.'

'I suppose you're right.' Bessie wiped her eyes. 'And I suppose I should start to think what I want to do now. I shan't be able to stay here, shall I?'

Mrs Pegs looked shocked. She hadn't thought of that and the prospect of losing Bessie again was painful.

'After all you've done fer the missus I can't see the master chuckin' you out on yer ear,' she stated.

'I'm sure he wouldn't,' Bessie agreed. 'But I don't need to become a charity case just yet, Mrs Pegs. Now that there's only Mr Farthing at home, you and Gwen are all the staff he needs. The money that Malcolm left me is tucked safely away in the bank and I've even added to it since I've been here. It's not as if I go out to spend me wages, is it?'

'Do you 'ave any idea what you might want to do, pet?'

'As it happens I do,' Bessie said. 'But first I need to speak to Mr Farthing and Dilly.'

Mrs Pegs was consumed with curiosity but she knew better than to question Bessie. She could be a stubborn little bugger when she wanted to be.

'I reckon I might go round and have a word with Dilly tomorrow if you or Gwen wouldn't mind sittin' with the missus for me for a while? Dilly was sayin' that she spends most of her time workin' on her designs at home now that she's got reliable staff to keep the shops goin'.'

'Yes, I believe she does, an' o' course me an' Gwen wouldn't mind sittin' upstairs. God bless 'er. There were times when I could quite willingly 'ave wrung Camilla's neck when she were younger 'cos she could be terrible stuck-up! Even so, she weren't all bad an' she certainly didn't deserve to end up like this. It's a good job that we don't know what's round the corner for us, ain't it?'

Gwen and Bessie nodded sombrely in agreement.

Bessie set off for Dilly's new house mid-morning the next day and was met at the door by Nell, who ushered her inside.

'I shall 'ave to show yer around,' she tittered. 'You ain't

been 'ere before, 'ave you, Bessie? Eeh, it's a grand house, I can tell yer.'

'I'd love to 'ave a look round,' Bessie answered pleasantly. 'But I was hopin' fer a word with Dilly if she's in?'

'Oh, she's in all right,' Nell assured her. 'She's in her office. Well, it were one o' the downstairs reception rooms really, but she's turned it into an office. It's dead smart. She 'as a long table she can draw on an' everythin' she needs in there. Shall I go along an' tell her you're 'ere?'

'If you wouldn't mind, Nell.' Bessie glanced around. It was a lovely kitchen as Nell had said and she could understand why she was so happy to live there. After the tiny cottage in St Mary's Road it must seem enormous. Jessica was asleep in her pram by the open window and Bessie strolled over to take a peek at her. She really was a bonny little lass and she could see why Dilly was so taken with her.

Then suddenly Dilly walked in with Nell and pecked her on the cheek, saying, 'Why, what a nice surprise. We'll have some fresh lemonade if you've time. Is there something I can help you with, Bessie?'

Colour burned into Bessie's cheeks as she lowered her eyes and glanced towards Nell but Dilly assured her, 'Don't worry. I would trust Nell with my very soul. You can say anything you came to say in front of her, and I can assure you it will go no farther. Now what's wrong? You look all upset.'

'You er . . . probably know that Mrs Farthing is going to be committed into Hatter's Hall next week?'

Dilly nodded. 'Yes, I do know. Mr Farthing called by and told me last night. It's very sad but I think we all knew that this was inevitable. You mustn't blame yourself, Bessie. No one could have cared for her better than you have. In fact, I'm sure if it wasn't for you she'd have had to go there long ago.'

'Thank you.' Bessie gulped and licked her dry lips before going on, 'The thing is, I won't be needed once Camilla is in Hatter's Hall. Oh, Mr Farthing has told me that I'm welcome to stay on but I reckon it's time I sorted myself out. I've been thinking that I might enjoy nursing – proper nursing, I mean. I've already spoke to Miss Olivia and she's been very helpful. But the long an' the short of it is, I won't be able to take Roddy with me. I'm plannin' on goin' to train in London, see? An' who would care for him while I was at work? So I got to thinkin'. All I ever hear off him is Roisin this an' Declan that. He seems to be at his happiest when he's over in Ireland wi' them so I wondered if perhaps they'd consider takin' him on for me? It's not fair to expect Seamus and Mary to start married life with someone else's little 'un hangin' round their necks. I could afford to pay them, and I would do so regularly. What do you think?'

'I think you've taken me completely by surprise,' Dilly said as she hung on to the back of a chair. Her legs had gone all of a wobble. Then as something occurred to her she said, 'But what about Mr Farthing? How would he feel about this? Roddy is his grandson, after all, and I happen to know that he's very fond of him.'

'But he could come back to stay with his grandpa in the school holidays,' Bessie answered calmly. It seemed she had thought of everything.

'Hmm, do you realise exactly what you would be doing?' Dilly asked then. 'Roddy is your son. Are you quite sure that you want to relinquish all care of him? It's an enormous step to take, Bessie, and one that you might well live to regret for the rest of your life.'

Bessie lowered her eyes. 'I've thought of nothing else for months,' she said unhappily. 'I know you think I'm unnatural, but I can't help how I feel about him. I've tried to love the poor little chap, really I have – after all, he didn't ask to be born, but all I'll ever see when I look at him is Samuel. I can't help it, Dilly, really I can't.' She began to sob bitterly then and Dilly hurriedly took her in her arms.

'All right then, if you're quite sure this is what you want to do I'll speak to Max this evening, then I'll phone Roisin and Declan and see how they feel about it, but I can't make you any promises mind.'

'I . . . know,' Bessie hiccupped. 'And I'm grateful to yer Dilly, really I am.'

Nell, who had overheard everything, was scooting about preparing a pot of tea. She'd always condemned mothers who didn't love their children, yet strangely she found herself feeling sorry for Bessie. The way she saw it, it should be the swine who'd raped her that should be feeling guilty – but he was long gone and as far as she was concerned it was a case of good riddance to bad rubbish.

'Come an' sit yerself down an' have some o' this lemonade an' a piece o' parkin,' she told Bessie kindly. 'Things'll all come out in the wash, lass, they allus do.'

Dilly had crossed to lift out Jessica, who was stirring in her pram, and as Bessie watched her with the baby she remarked, 'She's a lovely little lass, ain't she?'

'She is that,' Dilly murmured, planting an affectionate kiss on the child's springy copper curls. 'I'm afraid we all rather spoil her, especially me.'

'I just wish I could be the same wi' my Roddy,' Bessie grieved and not knowing how best to answer, Dilly and Nell remained silent.

'Why, Dilly, what a lovely surprise,' Max said that evening when she paid him an unexpected visit. 'Is everything all right?'

'Sort of,' she answered cautiously as she took a seat beside him. 'But I need to speak to you about something,

Max. You see, Bessie came to see me today and it's like this . . .' She then went on to tell him of the conversation she'd had with Bessie and his face grew grave.

'So what you're telling me is, Bessie wants your son and his wife to foster my grandson and for him to live in Ireland with them?'

'That's about it.' Dilly reached out to pat his hand as he stared sightlessly at the window. 'I think given the circumstances it might be for the best, if Roisin and Declan are agreeable to the idea. There are only a handful of people who know that Roddy is your grandson so you can't have him here to live openly with you.' Or Jessica, she thought sadly. How awful that he had two adorable grandchildren that he couldn't openly acknowledge because they were both illegitimate.

'Then I suppose you must go ahead and put the idea to them,' he said eventually but his eyes were dull at the thought of the little chap being so far away from home. As Dilly had pointed out, Roddy could come back to Nuneaton during school holidays but it wouldn't be quite the same as being able to see him whenever he wanted.

It was a beautiful evening and through the open window bird song was the only sound to be heard as they both sat lost in thought.

'I'll get back and give them a ring then,' she said quietly and he nodded, too full of emotion to speak as she left the room. It seemed that he was going to lose his elder grandson as well as his wife, and Dilly felt heart sorry for him.

When Dilly got through to Roisin later that evening and put Bessie's idea to her, the girl shocked her with her immediate response. 'Sure we'd love to have the little chap, so we would.' She could scarcely keep the delight from her voice.

'But don't you need a little more time to think about it?

And shouldn't you be talking to Declan first to see how he feels about it? It's a big step to take, although Bessie would make sure that you were well paid for looking after him,' Dilly said worriedly.

'I've no need to ask Declan,' Roisin crowed. 'I know he'll be thrilled, an' there's no need for Bessie to pay us either. We're doin' well an' one more little mouth to feed will be neither here nor there, so it won't. Oh Dilly, this is wonderful!'

'In that case I'll tell Bessie that you accept and we'll talk to Roddy. Of course we shall all have to leave the final decision up to him. He doesn't even know about it yet.'

'Of course,' Roisin agreed on a more sober note. 'But will you tell me what he decides as soon as possible? If he wants to come I shall have to speak to the teacher at the village school and start getting a room ready for him, to be sure. We can't have the darlin' wee chap without his home comforts, can we? Goodbye, Dilly.'

The very next day Dilly went with Bessie to see Roddy at Niamh's house. Mary had just fetched him from the park and he was sitting at the kitchen table with a large glass of milk and some jam tarts fresh from the oven in front of him. He smiled at Dilly but looked at his mother nervously and in that moment Dilly knew that Bessie had made the right decision. He would be far happier in Ireland.

'I was wondering,' Bessie began cautiously as she joined him at the table, 'how you might feel about going to stay with Roisin and Declan in Enniskerry?'

His eyes lit up as he asked excitedly, 'When? And how long could I stay?'

'You would be staying . . . for a long time,' Bessie said lamely. The child had made it clear that he had no more feelings for her than she had for him, but then she didn't blame him. She could never remember kissing him or stroking his hair as she frequently saw Dilly do to Jessica. They were almost like strangers.

'You would be going fairly soon. You see, I've decided to go away and train to become a nurse and I couldn't take you with me.' There was a catch in her voice and Dilly felt sorry for the girl. Samuel had a lot to answer for.

'But what about school?'

'You would be going to the village school over there and I'm sure you'd soon make lots of new friends.'

'I already have friends there,' he told her proudly. 'Patrick is my best mate an' Bridie ain't so bad for a girl.'

'Is that a yes then? I mean, do you want to go?'

'Not 'alf!' His face momentarily fell then as he thought of something and added, 'But I'll miss Mary.'

'She's already said that you'd be able to come back here and stay with her and see everyone else during the school holidays,' Bessie assured him.

He nodded so vigorously that Dilly was afraid he'd make himself dizzy, and so it was settled. The child had thrived in Ireland and he needed some stability in his life. Roisin and Declan would be able to provide that.

Once Roddy had skipped outside to play in the garden, Bessie and Dilly decided that it might be better if he went during the next couple of weeks so that he was in Enniskerry for the new school term which started in September.

'I'll take him over,' Dilly volunteered, much to Bessie's relief. 'Everything is running smoothly in the shops at the moment and I've an idea Niamh may be ready to come back with me. Then I'll have to get busy on Mary's wedding dress. The wedding will be on us before we know it.'

'But I thought they were only having a quiet wedding?' Bessie queried.

'They are, but that doesn't mean to say that she can't wear a lovely dress, does it?' Dilly said determinedly. She was still dreading bumping into Father Brannigan who would no doubt have got wind of the forthcoming marriage by now. She knew that he would be incensed when he discovered that yet another of her brood was marrying outside the Catholic Church – but what could she do about it?

'Have you got everything prepared for Camilla's move?' she asked then and Bessie nodded.

'Yes. Mr Farthing and I are taking her to Hatter's Hall on Monday. She's to have her own suite of rooms there and he's employed two nurses who will give her round-the-clock care.' She sighed sadly then. 'I've become fond of her. You wouldn't believe the strange things she comes out with though from time to time, and I hate to tell you this, Dilly, but she really doesn't seem to like you for some reason. She keeps telling me that you wanted her baby and she had to keep her safe from you. Poor soul. I know it's only the ravings of a lunatic.'

Nell and Dilly exchanged an anxious glance but neither of them commented. Instead they went on to speak of the things Roddy would need to take to Enniskerry with him.

As Dilly lay in bed that night watching the full moon suspended in the sky through the open curtains her heart was aching. Within just a few days Camilla would be locked away from the world in an asylum, albeit a very grand one, and little Roddy would be embarking on a new life in Ireland. It seemed that nothing ever stayed the same – but at least she would still have her little lass here. And that was how Dilly looked upon Jessica now although she knew that she shouldn't. All the love that she had longed to heap on Olivia was now heaped on her granddaughter and she couldn't imagine her life without her.

# Chapter Forty-Five

'You're going to Ireland *again*?' Henry's face fell as Dilly nodded. It was Sunday afternoon and he was taking her to lunch at a little country inn he had come across in Fenny Drayton, the village on the outskirts of Nuneaton.

'Unfortunately I have no choice,' Dilly answered calmly. She had already explained about Roddy and had hoped that Henry would be a little more sympathetic and understanding.

'But why can't Mary take him – or Bessie herself?' he asked.

'Because,' she said patiently, 'Mary has never set foot out of Nuneaton in her life and would get lost in no time, and Bessie is in no fit state to do so. For all her hard front she hasn't made this decision lightly, poor girl. She just wants to do what's best for Roddy and she wants him to be happy.'

As he drove along, Henry tapped the steering wheel irritably. Dilly always seemed to be at everyone's beck and call.

'You know, you have shops to run, designs to do, yet still you're running around after one or another of them. Isn't it time you made a little more time for yourself? Your family are all grown up now, you know.'

'Are you implying that once our children are grown we shouldn't help them? That we should turn our backs on them and leave them to it?' Dilly asked coolly as she stared straight ahead through the windscreen. She was so annoyed that she wasn't even looking at the passing scenery.

'Of course I'm not. But Bessie and Roderick aren't family, are they? Neither is Jessica for that matter. It's supposed to be Nell looking after her, yet you spend a tremendous amount of time with her.'

'If you must know, Jessica is . . .' Dilly stopped herself just in time from telling him that she was her granddaughter. 'She's just a poor innocent little soul who through no fault of her own cannot be with her own mother,' she said in a trembling voice. 'Surely you wouldn't begrudge a child like her a little attention? And as for Bessie and Roddy – no, you are quite right, we are not related but Bessie and I go back a long way and I want to help her.'

'I'm sorry, Dilly,' he said contritely. 'I've made myself sound like a spoiled child, haven't I? But it's only because I get frustrated that you can't spare me a little more of your time.'

Despite his apology, Dilly suddenly wished that she had never agreed to come. Camilla would be moving to Hatter's Hall the following day and she knew that Max was struggling with his conscience even though he had accepted that it would be the best and safest place for her.

'Actually, Henry, I have an awful headache coming on. Would you mind very much if I were to miss out on the meal today? And would you very kindly take me home?'

'Of course.' He silently cursed himself as he turned the

car around. He'd really gone and put his big foot in it now by being too possessive, but it was getting harder and harder to be with Dilly without telling her how he felt. Dilly had filled the huge hole in his heart that his wife had left when she died, and more than anything he wanted her to become the next Mrs Price. Yet somehow whenever he tried to tell her, they always seemed to get interrupted. Today he had intended to propose over lunch. A precious diamond ring was nestling in a tiny box in his pocket but it would be no use doing it now. She clearly wasn't in the right frame of mind after his thoughtlessness, so with a sigh he drove her home.

Dilly made sure that she was at the Farthing house bright and early on Monday morning. She knew that it was going to be a difficult day for Max and that he was going to need all the support he could get.

'I know me an' the missus ain't always seen eye to eye but I hate to think o' the poor lamb bein' locked away fer the rest of her days,' Mrs Pegs sobbed into her pinny as Dilly entered through the back door.

'I'm sure the place really isn't as bad as you think,' Dilly said as she gave her a hug. Seamus had had to spend time in hospital after the war, and while Dilly couldn't wait to get him home the nurses were kind and he'd been well cared for. She was sure the nursing staff would be just as caring at Hatter's Hall. 'She'll have a whole suite of rooms all to herself and round-the-clock nursing. Max has made sure of that.'

'It still don't seem right though,' Mrs Pegs sniffed.

'Look, I'm off upstairs to help Bessie with the last-minute packing, then when Camilla is all ready to go, you and Gwen can come and say goodbye to her. You can even go and see her in Hatter's Hall, if you like. She'll have open visiting and I'm sure Mr Farthing would drive you there.' Dilly patted the cook's arm and hurried away.

Camilla was dressed when she got upstairs. Bessie had somehow managed to do her hair for her and she looked neat and tidy although her eyes were blank. Max was there looking pale and unhappy as he carried his wife's cases from the room and down to the car. He'd chosen to drive her there himself with Bessie rather than have the asylum ambulance call for her. He wanted Camilla to retain as much dignity as she could. He owed her that much at least.

'Right, I think that's everything,' Bessie said as she glanced around the room. She too looked tired and strained. The doctor had prescribed a mild sedative which Bessie had administered that morning so that Camilla would not become distressed on the journey, and now all she could do was hope that it would last until they arrived at Hatter's Hall. With Dilly's help she got Camilla's arms into her coat. It was far too big for her now but the woman didn't object or even seem to notice.

'Come on, we're going for a little ride in the car,' Bessie told her gently as she assisted her to her feet. Suddenly Camilla's eyes rested on Dilly and recognition dawned in them.

'*You! Keep away from my baby!*' she cried as she pointed a trembling finger at her.

'Best leave quickly,' Bessie instructed as she sprang towards Camilla and placed a comforting arm about her.

Dilly instantly retreated onto the landing, her heart thudding wildly as tears pricked at the back of her eyes.

Seconds later, Bessie led a docile Camilla from the room. She walked woodenly with no comprehension of where she was going and Dilly stayed on the landing, unwilling to cause her any more distress. It was amazing that even after all these years, Camilla still resented her and feared that Dilly wanted to reclaim Olivia as her own.

Downstairs in the hallway, Mrs Pegs, Gwen and Mr Jackson were waiting to say their goodbyes to their mistress, and then she heard Max enter and lead her outside to the waiting car. Camilla climbed meekly in and sat unblinking as Bessie wrapped a rug around her knees and clambered in beside her. Dilly was watching from the landing window and felt a great wave of sadness as Camilla was driven away from her home for the very last time. Sadder still was the fact that she wasn't even aware of it and didn't even once look back. Her children had all said their goodbyes the evening before on the doctor's advice and now Dilly felt that a chapter of her life had closed. It was doubtful that she would ever see Camilla again.

That evening, Dilly went round to Niamh's to help Mary with Roddy's packing. It seemed that this was the week for goodbyes and she was feeling very low, but her spirits sank even lower as she approached Abbey Green to see Father Brannigan striding towards her.

'Ah, Dilly, I was wondering when I was going to catch you,' he said with a frown. 'I've not seen you in church for a while.'

'No, Father, I've been rather busy,' Dilly blustered guiltily.

'You should always make time to visit the House of God,' he scolded then went on, 'And what's this I'm hearing about young Seamus and Mary? Is it true that yet another of your brood is to wed outside the faith?'

'Yes, Father, it is,' she said humbly.

'Poor Fergal must be turnin' in his grave, so he must,' the priest muttered sadly.

'Ah, but what I was going to ask you was if you would bless the marriage in church,' Dilly said quickly, hoping to placate him. 'I can't force my children to wed in a place of my choice as you can perhaps understand. They are all grown up now and make their own decisions, but I know it would make their daddy happy if you would bless them.'

'Hmm, well, I suppose I could do that,' he agreed reluctantly. A blessing was better than nothing at all. Then: 'And how are you settling into the new house? I hear you have Nell and her little orphaned niece living with you.'

Colour raged into Dilly's cheeks. 'Yes, they are with me and we're settling in very well, thank you. I was hoping you would call round when you have some spare time and bless the house for us.' She hated lying to the Father but what else could she do? One lie had turned into another and then another – and yet she would have told them all over again to protect Olivia's reputation.

'I dare say I could do,' he agreed again, looking a great deal happier this time. 'But remember, you must not neglect your faith for gain, Dilly. Building up your businesses is one thing but not at the cost of your immortal soul. I shall expect to see you in church again very soon. Is that understood?'

'Yes, Father,' she answered meekly, and as he strode away with his cassocks flapping about his skinny legs she heaved a great sigh of relief and offered up a silent prayer asking God to forgive her for the lies she had told.

Mary was tearful when she reached the house. She had grown very fond of Roddy and hated the thought of him being so far away, although he himself could hardly wait to go.

'It will be very quiet here without him,' she sniffed as she packed some of his freshly washed and ironed clothes into a large jute bag.

'Try to think of the wedding,' Dilly encouraged. 'Roddy will be absolutely fine in Enniskerry. He'll have Patrick and Bridie to play with and he loves Roisin and Declan.'

'I know, he hasn't stopped talking about them but I'll miss him all the same.'

Dilly gave her a warm cuddle before asking, 'Is Seamus not back yet?'

'No, he's delivering stock to the Birmingham shop and said he might be late back. It's doing very well by all accounts.'

'All of the shops are,' Dilly said. 'And Philip Maddison phoned yesterday to say that my bridal designs are selling well in London and do I have any more ready for him to look at yet. Who would ever have thought it, eh?'

'I would,' Mary said stoutly. 'You have a flair and an eye for fashion, which is why I'm so pleased you've agreed to design my wedding dress. If it were left to me I'd end up looking like a sack of potatoes.'

'Nonsense,' Dilly replied. She already had an idea in mind. Mary was on the plump side so Dilly was thinking of something straight and simple that would flatter her figure. But first she had to get Roddy over to Ireland and settled, then hopefully Niamh would come home with her and life would return to some sort of normality.

Once the packing was done, Dilly again made her way to the Farthing house. She felt that Max might be in need of a friend that evening and she was right. She found him sitting in the drawing room looking pale and gaunt, but his face lit up on seeing her.

'I've just asked Gwen to make us a pot of tea,' she told him, tutting at the glass of whisky he was holding. 'And although it's not my place to say it, I think you should make that your last one. It won't solve anything.'

'I know you're right but I'm just feeling so . . .' He sought for the right words to explain and finding none, he shrugged.

'Sad? Lonely?' she ventured quietly.

He nodded. 'Yes, I suppose I am. It's silly really because

Camilla and I haven't lived as husband and wife or shared a room for years. Yet the house feels strange without her.'

'Of course it will. You were married for a long time – and you still are,' Dilly pointed out. 'What you have to do now is hang on to the happy memories. Remember her as she was then, not as she is now. And also accept that you've done the best thing for her. Bessie did a marvellous job but she doesn't have eyes in the back of her head. At Hatter's Hall Camilla will have the best of care.'

'I know you're right but I just feel so wretched,' he said brokenly, and Dilly did something then that she had longed to do for a long time. She hurried across to him and held him close to her trying to relieve his pain.

By the time Gwen appeared with the tea shortly afterwards they were both sitting a discreet distance apart but Dilly's heart was thumping so loudly that she felt sure they would hear it. It was all so unfair! Max was a good man and deserved so much better than life had meted out to him. She just hoped he would find the courage to carry on. He might well have to live the rest of his life alone, for as the doctor had told him, Camilla could live for years and whilst she did they were still tied to each other.

'Will you be coming to Niamh's to say goodbye to Roddy before we leave tomorrow?' she asked as she laid out the tea cups and saucers. She hated to heap yet more heartache on him but it had to be done.

'Yes, of course. In fact, I was hoping you'd let me drive you both to the station. I would gladly have come to Ireland with you if you'd allow it, but I knew what you'd say if I suggested it.'

'It wouldn't appear right, us travelling together,' she said primly and he grinned.

'That's exactly what I thought you'd say.'

She returned his smile as she passed him his tea.

*

Max appeared at Niamh's first thing the next morning to find Roddy in a state of high excitement and Mary wailing like a banshee.

'Don't cry, Mary,' the boy said. 'I'll come an' see yer often, won't I, Mrs Carey?'

'Very often,' Dilly said solemnly, keeping a close eye on Bessie who had also come to say her goodbyes. Dilly could only imagine how bad she must be feeling and it was mirrored in her eyes.

Eventually all the goodbyes had been said apart from Bessie's and she stooped to her son's level, but even then she couldn't bring herself to take his hands.

'I'll write to you often,' she promised in a choky voice, whipping herself as she stared into his handsome little face. He was such a bonny boy. *Why* couldn't she love him?

'Will I see you again?' he asked, his own voice quivering now. She might not have been much of a mother but she was the only one he had known.

Bessie blinked rapidly. 'Of course you will. Just as soon as I've finished my nurse's training I'll either come to Ireland or come to see you here,' she told him. 'But in the meantime promise me that you'll be a good boy for Roisin and Declan and try hard at school.'

'I will, Mammy.'

'Good boy, then off you go . . .'

He took Dilly's hand and left the room as Bessie turned away to hide the tears that were racing down her pale cheeks.

Seamus and Mary went outside to wave them off and soon after that they were at the railway station.

'Safe journey,' Max said, once he'd carried the bags onto the platform for them. The train was already drawing into the station. 'And here, Roddy, this is for you.'

413

Roddy crowed with delight as he stared at the silver coins in his hand while Max ruffled his hair, his eyes overly bright.

'Goodbye, Max.' Dilly herded Roddy onto the train and Max waved until it was out of sight, then he turned slowly and made his way back to the house. He didn't feel like working that day.

Both Roisin and Declan were waiting to meet them when they alighted from the ferry that evening. Roddy flung himself into Roisin's arms with a rapturous smile on his face.

'Oh, it's wonderful to have you here, so it is,' Roisin told him as she kissed him soundly and Dilly's heart warmed. At last it seemed that Roddy would know love.

Declan was beaming from ear to ear too, and as they led the lad to the trap where the horse was contentedly munching the grass at the side of the lane she thought they already looked like a little family and it did her heart good to see it.

# Chapter Forty-Six

Roddy kept up a non-stop stream of chatter all the way to the farm as Roisin listened indulgently with her arm about his thin shoulders. Dilly had a feeling that the two fulfilled a need in each other and she sat back to enjoy the journey feeling strangely drained. It had been an emotional couple of days, one way and another.

Bridie and Patrick were waiting in the farmyard for them and Roddy instantly scampered away to play in the orchard as Declan carried Dilly's luggage into the farmhouse. She had only brought an overnight bag for herself as she couldn't stay long, so the rest of the bags were Roddy's.

'I'll take them straight round to our place and start to put his things away for him,' Roisin said happily. 'His room is all ready for him and I've cooked him his favourite dinner today.'

She went off with a spring in her step and a smile on her face as Dilly sped over to give her mother-in-law a fond kiss.

'That was a turn-up for the books, so it was,' Maeve

commented once they'd greeted each other. 'Our Roisin has been like a different girl since she knew Roddy was coming. But how are you, lass? You look fair worn out.'

Before Dilly could answer, Niamh appeared from the stairs door with her arms full of dirty laundry, and after dropping it all in a pile she and her mother embraced.

'My, you look well,' Dilly told her, holding her daughter at arm's length. Niamh was glowing. She'd gained weight, her hair was shining and her eyes had a sparkle to them that had not been there for a long time.

'I'm grand,' Niamh answered, 'but now tell me all about what's going on at home.'

So for the next half an hour Dilly filled them in on all the gossip. The men were working out in the fields and so they were uninterrupted.

'Anyway,' Dilly said eventually when they were all up to date, 'I'm afraid this will only be an overnight stay for me and I was rather hoping that you'd be coming back with me, Niamh. That's if you feel well enough to manage, of course, Maeve.' She'd noticed that Maeve's speech had improved tremendously and she'd progressed from her bed to sit at the side of the fire now, but she still looked frighteningly pale and fragile.

Dilly saw Maeve and Niamh exchange a look before Niamh said hesitantly, 'Actually, Mammy, there's something I need to talk to you about.'

'Oh, and what's that then?' Dilly raised an eyebrow, suddenly feeling that she wasn't going to like what she was about to hear.

Niamh glanced towards the pile of dirty sheets she had just stripped from the beds then shrugged. There was no point in putting this off; the washing could wait until later.

'The thing is,' Niamh lowered her eyes and began to twist her fingers together, a habit she'd adopted as a child when she was nervous about something, 'I won't be coming home.'

'Oh? Do you mean your gran'ma still needs you for a little longer? Well, that's fine, of course. I just thought—'

'No, Mammy,' Niamh interrupted firmly. 'I mean I won't be coming home – ever. You see, I'm having a baby – Ben's baby.'

'*What!*' Dilly stared at her daughter in disbelief but rather than look ashamed Niamh answered her proudly.

'I'm sorry, truly I am. I tried so hard to accept my lot, but in the end I couldn't stand it any more. Ben and I love each other.'

'But Niamh, you *know* you can never divorce Samuel!' Dilly gasped. 'The Catholic Church would never allow it. You'll be shamed and the child will be branded. You'll never be able to hold your head up again.' She looked at Maeve for support but strangely the woman said nothing.

'I'm quite aware of that,' Niamh said calmly. 'And that is why we've decided to go away.'

'Go away where?' Dilly was reeling with shock.

'We are going to live in New York close to Ben's mother. It will be for the best. We can go to America as a married couple and no one need ever know any different. Ben's mother is aware of the baby. She's given us her blessing and has already found us a house to live in. The blacksmith's is sold and we're sailing out there next month.' She held out her hand to show Dilly the shiny new wedding band that Ben had bought her and went on, 'As far as we're concerned, we *are* married! We belong together, and while I've no wish to hurt anyone I'm not prepared to spend the rest of my life at home with a man I detest. Once Constance died I felt I had nothing left to live for but now I have a rosy future ahead of me again and I intend to seize it with both hands. *Please* try to understand, Mammy,' she begged with tears in her eyes. 'It would mean the world to us both if you could give us your blessing too.'

'I . . . I just can't take it in,' Dilly croaked. And then she appealed to Maeve. 'You must be shocked too, surely.'

'I'll admit I was when I first found out,' Maeve said. 'But then I got to thinking, what happened to Niamh wasn't her fault. She only married Samuel Farthing to give the child he'd forced on her a name. Sadly, wee Constance didn't have a long life, God bless her tiny soul. But now why should this precious girl be forced to live the rest of her life in a loveless marriage? Oh, I'll confess I wish things could have been different, but love doesn't choose where it strikes an' we've all said Ben an' Niamh were made for each other. I knew that the very first time I ever saw them together. I've no doubt Father Doherty would be horrified were he ever to find out – but he isn't the one whose life has almost been ruined, is he? So what I'm saying is, I hope you'll find it in your heart to forgive them as well, Dilly. I've a feeling my Fergal would have done so under the circumstances, had he still been alive. They've a bright new future ahead o' them an' Ben is even going to try an' find Niamh a little studio where she can start her painting again.'

Dilly stared numbly down at her hands which were folded neatly in her lap, and when she finally looked up her eyes were wet. She was about to lose her daughter. Who knew if they would ever see each other again? Niamh was about to go to the other side of the world, or at least that's how it felt, and Dilly wouldn't be there for the birth of her new grandchild. And yet she had always known how unhappy she was, so was it fair to condemn the girl to a life of loneliness and misery in the name of religion? *No, it isn't,* her heart told her, much as Maeve's heart had told her, and when she opened her arms, Niamh tumbled into them and their tears mingled.

'I shall miss you so much,' Dilly told her daughter in a wobbly voice.

'But we can write to each other – and who knows, you might be able to come and visit,' Niamh choked.

'Who else knows?' Dilly asked then.

'Everyone here, but no one outside the farm,' Niamh said. 'People will assume that I've returned home and that Ben has gone to America. We wanted to do it that way so that no shame would fall on the family here.'

Even now Niamh was still thinking of others and it made her mother love her all the more, if that was possible. But then something else occurred to her.

'What shall I tell Max?' she asked. 'There's been no sign of Samuel for months and he can't be expected to keep paying the bills on the house if you and Roddy aren't there either.'

'I've already thought of that. I wondered, seeing as their wedding isn't so far away, if Mary and Seamus might want to rent it from him. It's already very comfortably furnished so it would give them a good start, and I'm sure they'd be happier there than I ever was. That house holds nothing but unhappy memories for me now since I lost Constance.'

'That would be an ideal solution,' Dilly said thoughtfully. 'I'll put the idea to them just as soon as I get home. Oh, but lass, I'm going to miss you so much. And the child who is on its way.' The tears came faster than ever then as they clung to each other.

'I'll miss you too, but you'll still have little Jessica. You seem to have taken a rare shine to her,' Niamh smiled.

Never had Dilly been closer to confiding her true relationship to the child than she was at that moment, but again she remained silent, unable to break the promise she had made to Max all those long years ago. How very different all their lives would have been if Fergal hadn't had his accident. But that was all in the past and she had to look to the future now. One without her daughter in it. The thought was painful.

'How do you feel about this, Maeve?' she asked again and the sick woman shocked her when she answered.

'The Church teaches us that the Good Lord is all-forgiving of our sins. But this girl is in the position she's in through no fault or sin of her own – and true love is a powerful thing. So I reckon He'll forgive her and the innocent life that she's carrying. I've forgiven her an' it's right glad I am that you have too.'

'How could I do any other,' Dilly whispered as she stroked Niamh's soft hair. 'For I've loved her since the second she drew breath and I think I would forgive her anything.'

'And that's just how it should be, to be sure,' Maeve answered emphatically. 'So now all your brood will be settled, Dilly, an' mebbe it's time you concentrated on your own life. I miss Fergal every single day, so I do. But he's been gone an awful long time now, so perhaps when you get home you should concentrate on your own future. It's what my son would have wanted. He'd not have wished you to grow old alone.'

A picture of Henry came into Dilly's mind. Perhaps Maeve was right? She was so tired of being lonely and when she got home she'd take steps to change it.

The goodbyes next day were bittersweet, for neither Dilly nor Niamh knew when or if they would ever see each other again. Even so, now that Dilly was over the shock she was pleased for her daughter. She deserved to have a good life, with children to love and bring up. Ben clearly adored her and all Dilly could do now was wish the couple well, even though her heart was breaking.

'I'll phone you every day until you leave,' Dilly promised as Niamh sobbed on her shoulder. But then Ben came and put his arms around her and as Dilly saw the deep bond between them she was more than ever sure that they were doing the right thing.

She turned to Maeve then to hug her tenderly, and the older woman whispered, 'Remember what I said, lass. It's time for you now. And Dilly, I need to tell you I couldn't have wished for a better daughter-in-law. I've come to love you like me own, so I have.'

'Oh stop it or you'll start me off again,' Dilly sniffed, mopping at her streaming eyes. 'You talk as if I'm never going to see you again.'

She had already said her goodbyes to Roddy and the rest of the family and now Maeve pushed her gently towards the door with her one good arm. 'Go on – be off with you,' she told her sternly with a strange little smile. 'Sure my poor Daniel sittin' out there waitin' for you in the trap will think you've got lost.'

Dilly made her way blindly to the door and as the trap pulled away she turned to wave, to see Niamh and Ben still standing close with their arms tight about each other.

Henry had phoned the farm the night before and when the train pulled into the Trent Valley railway station he was waiting for her on the platform, impatiently walking up and down.

Ignoring her puffy eyes, he took her elbow with one hand and her bag in the other and marched her purposefully out to the car.

'Now then,' he began. 'I'm going to make you sit here while you hear me out. There's something I've been wanting to say to you for months, but every time I try we seem to get interrupted.' All the time he was talking he was fumbling in his waistcoat pocket and eventually he withdrew a tiny leather box.

'Dilly Carey, you must know by now that the feelings I have had for you, ever since the first day I met you, have been steadily growing.' He snapped the lid to reveal a beautiful diamond ring that flashed fire. 'And so, before you can escape, or before we get interrupted again, I want to ask you – will you do me the very great honour of becoming my wife? I know I'm not as young as I was and—'

'Yes, Henry, I will be your wife!' she interrupted.

'*What* did you say?' His face was incredulous.

'I said yes.' Dilly slowly withdrew the thin gold band that Fergal had placed on the third finger of her left hand on the day they had wed and placed it in her purse. It had never been off her finger since and she felt strangely naked without it as she held her hand out to Henry.

'I would be proud to be your wife.'

'Oh Dilly, you've just made me the happiest man on earth,' he exulted as he slipped the ring onto her finger and kissed her soundly on the lips. 'I was all ready to persuade you. I never dreamed you'd agree.'

Dilly smiled as she admired the ring. She'd never owned anything like it in her entire life and she watched in fascination as it caught and reflected the street lamp, all the colours of the rainbow.

'That will be just the start,' Henry promised. 'From now on you'll be dripping in jewels and fine clothes and I'll give you anything you ask for, I promise.'

'I already *have* everything I need,' Dilly told him practically. 'I'm not marrying you for your money, Henry. I make enough of my own now. And speaking of that, I hope you won't try to stop me working?'

'Of course I won't,' he told her as he draped an arm about her shoulders. Dilly felt her cheeks grow hot. It was a long time since a man had openly shown her affection in public.

'Just so long as you know that you don't *have* to work. My housekeeper is excellent, she keeps the house running like clockwork. And so is my cook and the general maid. Oh, I must think about getting you a lady's maid of your own.'

'A what?' Dilly snorted. 'I've always dressed myself and seen to my own toilette, Henry, so I see no reason to change that now. A lady's maid indeed! Don't you think they're rather outdated now?'

'But my wife had one.'

'Yes, that was then – but times are changing. And as for not having to work, I think I'd die of boredom if I didn't. What would I do with myself all day if you have a full staff to do everything about the house?'

'It's entirely your choice,' he said quickly then, not wishing to upset her. The way he saw it, Dilly had worked hard enough all her life and he wanted to make her life easier but he wouldn't force the issue, not yet anyway. 'Now we must go out for a meal tomorrow evening to celebrate, as it's a little too late this evening – and then I'll organise a party,' he said happily.

Dilly bit her lip. 'I'm so sorry but I'm afraid I won't be able to dine with you tomorrow,' she apologised. 'There's something I have to do. And to be honest, I don't fancy a party. I'd rather keep the news just to ourselves and close friends and family for now, if you don't mind. You see, I don't want to take the shine off Mary and Seamus' wedding.'

'Very well – but what's so important that you can't have a meal with me tomorrow?'

Realising that he would have to know, Dilly told him all about Niamh and Ben. He whistled through his teeth.

'So you see, I really must go and tell Max tomorrow

evening,' she explained. 'As you rightly said, it's a little too late to pay him a visit tonight, but Niamh is still legally married to his son, after all, and he has a right to know. I need to speak to Seamus and Mary too, to see if they wish to rent the house – unless Max decides he wants to sell it, that is,' she finished.

Henry wasn't happy at all about it but he could see that Dilly did have a point and there would be many more nights for them to celebrate. 'We'll go out for our special meal the next night then?' he said hopefully and when she nodded, he sighed with relief, started the car and drove his brand new fiancée home.

# Chapter Forty-Seven

'You've just done *what*?' Nell gasped when Dilly walked into their new house a short while afterwards.

'I've just agreed to become Henry Price's wife.' As Dilly flashed her ring at the astounded woman Nell oohed and aahed over it.

'It must be worth a pretty penny an' if that's what yer want then I couldn't be more pleased fer you,' Nell declared. 'But are yer really sure about this, luv? What I mean is, I've never said this to yer before 'cos it weren't my place to but I always felt that you an' Max had feelin's fer each other.'

'Camilla may be locked away in an asylum now but she and Max are still married,' Dilly pointed out sadly.

'I know all about that, but I still thought . . . Well, what does it matter what I think? I'm right pleased fer you, but . . .' Nell chewed on her lip for a moment before asking uncomfortably, 'Where will this leave me an' little Jessica? What I mean is, where will we live?'

'Why, you'll continue to live here, of course. This house

will be an investment for me and you'll live here as the caretaker.' It was the first time she'd thought of going to live in Henry's house. As his wife she would be expected to, but the thought of leaving Jessica pierced her like a knife. But I can still come and see her regularly, she told herself as Nell bustled off to put the kettle on while Dilly kicked her shoes off. The past few days were catching up with her now and she felt utterly drained.

'So Niamh didn't come back with you then?' Nell said a few minutes later when she had pressed a steaming mug into Dilly's hand.

'No, she didn't.' Dilly then went on to tell her about Niamh and Ben's plans to move to America and Nell was shocked yet again.

'Well, good fer her, that's what I say,' she said stoutly when the whole tale was told. 'She's far too young an' good to tie 'erself down to that good-for-nowt she's married to. I hope they'll be very 'appy!'

'Thanks, Nell, I knew you'd understand. But do you mind keeping it to yourself? The whole point of them going is to save her good name. People here will just assume she's decided to stay in Ireland. That's what I'm to tell the teacher at the school where she worked. I don't know what Max will make of it though.'

'I reckon he'll be fine about it,' Nell told her. 'Between you an' me I think he were ashamed o' what his son did to the poor gel an' he'll want her to be happy.'

'You're such a good friend,' Dilly said with a catch in her voice as she squeezed Nell's hand affectionately. 'I really don't know what me and my family would have done without you over the years.'

Nell's cheeks flamed to the colour of beetroot. 'Get away wi' yer. You've just got to concentrate on gettin' a bit o' happiness back into your own life now, an' hopefully

Henry'll be the man to do it. Now get that tea down yer an' this sandwich I have ready an' then get yerself off to bed. You look all in.'

Dilly was only too grateful for once to do as she was told.

The next day, Seamus drove Dilly to visit all three of her shops and after checking the books she came away feeling very satisfied. She also posted off some more of her designs to Philip Maddison, who couldn't seem to get enough of them. All in all, things were going wonderfully well yet she couldn't help dreading her meeting with Max that evening. Seamus and Mary were thrilled at the possibility of renting the house, should Max agree to it, but Dilly had told them not to raise their hopes until she had spoken to him.

As it was, she didn't have to wait until the evening because late that afternoon as she sat busily sketching in her little room at the house, he knocked and then walked in.

'Oh, Max!' Dilly felt apprehensive and happy to see him, all at the same time. 'I was going to pop round and visit you this evening.'

'Then I've saved you the trouble, haven't I?' He plonked himself down onto the chair in front of the table with a cheeky grin on his face, looking far better than he had the last time she'd seen him. On the day Camilla had been committed to the asylum he had looked like death warmed up. He's coming to terms with it, she thought thankfully and just prayed that the news she was about to impart wouldn't set him back.

'So how are they all over in Ireland then? Was Roddy all right when you got there?'

'They were all very well, thank you, and I've never seen Roddy so happy. He didn't even shed a tear when I left. He was too busy chasing chickens and playing with Bridie and Patrick. They're trying to teach him how to ride a bike, but . . .

427

look, Max, there's something else I have to talk to you about.'

Haltingly, she told him of the latest developments with Niamh and Ben and he listened carefully without interrupting her once. When she'd done she waited for the storm to erupt but surprisingly it didn't.

'Well, I can't say I'm sorry,' he said eventually. 'Niamh didn't deserve what my son did to her and I hated to think of the life she was being forced to lead while he went on his merry way with not a care for her. I'm just sorry that your religion doesn't allow divorce. It would have been nice for her and Ben to start their new life together properly married. Do tell her I wish them both all the best when she next phones you, Dilly.'

'Thank you,' she said humbly. Max was so kind that he never failed to surprise her. 'But now we need to speak about what you intend to do about the house. Obviously you won't want to keep paying the bills since neither Niamh nor Samuel are there. Mary and Seamus have already said that they are more than prepared to pay you a fair rent for it – unless you want to sell it, that is?'

'Not at all,' he assured her. 'And I'd be very happy for them to rent it. Tell Seamus to come and see me – and don't worry, I shall be very fair with him.' It was then that his eyes fell on the diamond ring on her finger and he stopped talking abruptly.

'I er . . .' Dilly squirmed uncomfortably. 'Henry bought it for me. He's asked me to marry him and I've said yes.'

The silence seemed to stretch between them for ever but then after a time Max rose and held out his hand. 'Then I must offer my congratulations, Dilly.'

She thought she detected a catch in his voice but couldn't be sure.

'Henry is a good man, none better, and I hope you'll be very happy together. But now if you'll excuse me, I really must be on my way. Things to do, you know?' And with that he stumbled from the room leaving her to stare after him, feeling strangely empty.

Before they knew it they were racing towards Christmas and the plans for Mary and Seamus' wedding were almost complete. Mary had flatly refused to wear a conventional wedding gown, saying that a register-office wedding didn't warrant it and that she'd look like a beached whale in one anyway. But the outfit Dilly had finally designed for her was now ready on a mannequin in Dilly's design room and she was sure Mary was going to look beautiful in it. The dress was long-sleeved, a thick ivory satin that would keep out the cold. Ankle length, it skimmed her figure with a high neckline and a dropped waist adorned by a band onto which Dilly had painstakingly sewn crystal beads and tiny pearls. Over it, Mary would wear a short white cape and a matching muff in cream fur. Instead of a veil she would be wearing cream and pink hothouse rosebuds in her hair to match those in her bouquet.

Henry and Dilly had had their first little row over where the reception should take place. Henry had kindly offered for it to be held at his house and was most upset when the young couple had thanked him sincerely but declined it.

'We'd feel like fishes out o' water wi' waiters an' whatnot hoverin' round us in a strange place. Not that we ain't very grateful for the offer, o'course,' Mary had explained. Dilly could understand that and so had finally got them to agree to a small reception at the Bull Hotel in the marketplace. A nice back room there was often hired out for weddings and parties, and she knew that the couple would feel more comfortable somewhere familiar.

'I'm not so sure that that place is grand enough for your son,' Henry had said doubtfully. 'After all, you are going to be my wife, Dilly. We have to think what people will say.'

'I don't much care what people say,' Dilly had responded, her eyes fiery. 'I care about making my son and his future wife happy.'

Henry had gone off in a huff but soon came back with his tail between his legs. He was fast discovering that Dilly had a mind of her own when it came to her family, and he supposed that he had better get used to it. He'd been badgering her constantly to set a date for their wedding but as yet she'd refused to even discuss it, saying that one wedding at a time was more than enough to worry about, thank you very much.

Max still called in occasionally to see Dilly in the shop or at the house but nowhere near as frequently as he had done and Dilly knew that this was only right now that she was engaged to be married; however, it didn't stop her missing him. She had never felt that she had to stand on ceremony with Max. After all, he had seen her down on her knees scrubbing floors many years ago, whereas with Henry she always felt that she had to look her best. Even so, Henry went out of his way to make her feel special and spoiled her shamelessly, despite her telling him he had no need to. The house was always full of flowers and she had more jewellery now than she had ever owned in her whole life before, although she rarely wore it.

Niamh was now settling into her new home in New York and from the letters Dilly regularly received she sounded happy and content. The pregnancy was proceeding without problems and she was blooming. Ben's mother had found her a small studio where she could display her artwork, and from what she wrote, the paintings were selling well. Dilly wasn't surprised. Niamh had always been a talented artist and was so glad that her girl had finally found the peace she deserved.

Thankfully, Dilly still had Olivia, who she saw on an almost daily basis, and Jessica continued to be the apple of her eye, so much so that Dilly sometimes wondered how she was going to feel when she had to leave her with Nell to go and live in Henry's house. She had never quite felt at ease there, possibly because she wasn't used to being waited on.

It was one evening early in December and just a week away from the wedding as they sat in front of a roaring fire surrounded by a heavy brass fireguard in Nell's cosy little kitchen, that Dilly said to Olivia, 'You know, pet, your father took the news about Niamh moving away to live with Ben remarkably well. I wonder if you're doing him any favours by keeping the fact that Jessica is his granddaughter from him? I know he's desperately lonely since your mother went into the Hall and Roddy left to live in Ireland. He does love children so. I think he'd adore her as we all do, once he was over the initial shock.'

But Olivia set her lips in a straight line and shook her head.

'I couldn't bear to think he was ashamed of me,' she said. 'And what about Jessica, even if he did accept her? People would call her a bastard and I don't want that for her. At least this way, thanks to you I get to see her almost every day, although I have to admit it tears my heart out not to be able to be with her all the time.'

Dilly's eyes strayed to the little girl who was moving around, holding on to the furniture, as fast as her chubby little legs would take her, trying to catch the cat Nell had recently adopted.

'Well, the decision must be yours,' she told Olivia gently. 'But I think you are making a huge mistake.' And with that the subject was closed again – for now, at least.

# Chapter Forty-Eight

On the day of the wedding, Dilly woke to find her bedroom shrouded in an eerie grey light. Crossing to the window, she swished the curtains aside to be confronted by a completely white world. It had snowed during the night and everywhere looked clean and brand new.

'Bloody stuff, it'll play 'avoc wi' me posh new shoes,' Nell grumbled when Dilly joined her in the kitchen. 'An' where's Seamus? His breakfast is ready. Let's hope the car can get through this lot to get him to the register office on time.'

'Stop worriting. I think everywhere looks perfect for a white winter wedding,' Dilly said cheerfully as she went upstairs to stir Seamus. Mary had returned to her parents' house the night before to get ready and Seamus had stayed over with Dilly.

'Come on, sleepy-head,' she called when she reached his room. 'Rise and shine.'

A strangled groan came from beneath the blankets. Her

son had been out the evening before with some of his pals to celebrate his last night of freedom and it seemed he'd had a few too many glasses of ale.

'You'll get no sympathy from me,' she chided, but there was laughter in her voice as she hauled the blankets off him. 'Come on now, a few cups of Nell's strong coffee will have you right in no time. We can't have the groom turning up late for his wedding with a hangover, now can we?'

Half an hour later, after two cups of coffee and a quick sluice under the cold tap, Seamus was looking much better and was beaming from ear to ear. 'Who'd ever have thought that a lovely lass like Mary would marry the likes o' me, eh?' he said perkily. 'I must be the luckiest chap on two legs.'

'You won't be if yer don't get a shufty on an' yer miss the bride,' Nell told him, waggling the porridge spoon in his face. 'Now get some o' that down yer to line yer stomach, an' go an' start to get ready. I'd better an' all, else we'll be late an' I don't want to miss the chance o' wearin' the lovely new frock Dilly's had made fer me!'

Dilly grinned from her seat in the fireside chair where she was getting Jessica dressed. Dilly had sewn her a tiny dress from the leftover material of Mary's and trimmed it with red ribbons and she knew the child was going to look just adorable, but then she always did to Dilly.

She too had had a new outfit, a smart costume in pale lilac trimmed with cream lace. Max had presented her with a hat that complemented it perfectly from his hat factory in Atherstone, so all in all Dilly hoped that they would all look the part.

At last everyone was ready and Max arrived to transport Seamus, Nell and Jessica to the register office, leaving Dilly to wait for Henry to arrive.

As always he was spot on time and when Dilly opened

the door to him he gazed at her admiringly. 'You look wonderful,' he told her. 'And perhaps when we've got today over we can think about making plans for our own wedding?'

'One thing at a time,' she said, and the hopeful expression on his face died instantly. Dilly always seemed to avoid setting a date but then that might change now. He knew how busy she had been trying to make sure that everything was just as perfect as it could be for the couple today. Dilly always tried to put everyone else before herself.

The snow had stopped falling and when they arrived at the register office everyone was in fine spirits. Olivia was there holding Jessica for Nell, and once or twice Dilly saw Max glance towards them with a thoughtful expression on his face. Then there was no more time to ponder on it, for the bride was due to arrive and they were all ushered inside to take their seats for the ceremony to begin. She was sad that the family in Ireland hadn't been able to attend but Maeve had recently suffered another stroke and they couldn't leave her. Dilly had assured them that it was only going to be a quiet wedding, but now as she walked inside on Henry's arm she hoped that Maeve was all right.

As the bride joined her groom a short time later, a gasp rippled through the assembled guests. Mary looked as if she was lit up from within and everyone agreed they had never seen a lovelier bride. Max caught Dilly's eye and somehow she sensed that he had known what she was thinking – *I won't have to worry about these two in the future!* They exchanged a smile and Dilly turned her attention back to the happy couple.

As Seamus and Mary were saying their vows the family in Enniskerry were gathered about Maeve's bed in the cosy farmhouse kitchen.

'They'll . . . be getting wed now,' Maeve whispered as she looked towards the clock on the mantelpiece.

'Aye, they will that, lass,' Daniel agreed as he gently squeezed her hand.

As she looked back at him she saw the tears glistening on his lashes and she weakly squeezed his hand back. 'Now let's be having none o' that,' she warned him, each breath an effort. 'We've had a long an' happy life together, so we have, Daniel Carey, but now it's me time to go an' I want to remember you smiling. To be sure, no one has a smile quite like you.'

Unable to stop it, a tear rolled down Daniel's cheek as Maeve turned her attention to the rest of the family. Roisin and Shelagh were crying too and Declan and Liam looked as pale as ghosts.

'You're to promise me you'll keep an eye on this old devil for me till it's his time to join me,' she said breathlessly, and they all nodded solemnly. 'And also promise me that you'll not be in touch with Dilly until tomorrow. I want nothing to spoil the day for Mary and Seamus.'

Again they all nodded and watched as Maeve's eyes grew glazed. 'I've had the best life an' the best family a woman could ever wish for, so I have,' she sighed contentedly, and then as she looked beyond them she became aware of a white light and her heart lifted – for there in the light was Fergal. But not Fergal as he had been when he passed. This was Fergal in his prime, tall, strong and handsome. Her son held his hand out to her and with a little cry of joy she went to join him.

'I don't think I've ever been to a lovelier weddin',' Nell sniffed as they all arrived back at the hotel. 'An' the blessin' in the church by Father Brannigan were just beautiful.'

'You old romantic, you,' Dilly teased but she too was

thrilled at how smoothly everything had gone. Seamus and Mary were radiating happiness and as Dilly remembered back to the state her son had been in when he had first come back from the war, she offered up a silent prayer of thanks that Mary had come into his life to heal him. And she *had* healed him, far more than any of the medicines or pills he had been prescribed had ever managed to do.

'This all looks very nice,' Nell commented then, glancing around at the tables laid with snow-white cloths and silver cutlery. In the centre of each one was a bowl of holly with bright red berries and everywhere looked very festive.

The meal that followed was a delight, one delicious course following another, but eventually the cake was cut, the speeches were made and the tables were cleared to the edges of the room ready for the evening reception. Dilly had booked a small local band to come and play, and the guests were looking forward to the dancing.

'When do you think we may be able to slip away?' Henry asked, cornering Dilly and grasping her elbow in a gesture of ownership.

Dilly raised an eyebrow. Henry had become increasingly possessive over the last few months and it had begun to get her down. 'Slip away? Why would I want to do that? This is my son's wedding day and I want to share it with him.'

'Oh, I should have guessed you'd want to see it through to the bitter end,' Henry said peevishly. 'You always seem to have time for other people rather than me!'

One glance at her face told him he might have overstepped the mark again.

'Sorry,' he said shamefacedly. 'I just get so frustrated, Dilly. We don't spend nearly enough time together. I'll go and get us another drink, shall I?'

As he hared away, Dilly watched him go with a thoughtful

expression on her face. How could he have thought that she would want to leave her own son's wedding reception? She couldn't imagine him wanting to have left Eleanor's, but then she'd noticed lately that he seemed unhappy if they weren't together every day – and there was nothing she could do about that. She had a full life and that was how she liked it.

As the evening wore on, Dilly watched indulgently as people began to let their hair down. The wine and ale were flowing like water and everyone was enjoying themselves.

'It's been a grand do, you've done them proud,' Max told her when she managed to escape Henry for a moment at one point. 'Olivia seems to be enjoying herself too, although I haven't seen her without Jessica in her arms once today. I'd never really noticed before, but their hair is exactly the same colour, isn't it?'

When Dilly flushed and looked quickly away Max's heart did a somersault. Could the suspicions he'd been harbouring for some time be true? But there was no time for further questions then, for Henry appeared from nowhere at Dilly's elbow and led her away without a word.

'That was very rude,' Dilly said crossly. 'Max and I were having a conversation, Henry.'

'So I noticed, but in case you'd forgotten it's *me* you are engaged to.'

Dilly stared at him, incensed, as she shook her elbow free from his grasp. 'And does the fact that I am engaged to you mean that I can no longer speak to old friends?'

'Well, I'd rather you weren't so pally with menfriends.'

It was then that the truth hit her between the eyes and suddenly she knew what she must do. She'd known deep down for some time if she were to be honest with herself, but things had gone far enough.

'May we have a word, Henry? Outside please?'

'Of course.' He instantly reached out to take her arm again but she hurried ahead of him.

Once outside in the marketplace Dilly shuddered from the intense cold and wrapped her arms about herself. The marketplace was almost deserted and she dreaded what she was about to do, yet in the long run she knew that she would be doing Henry a kindness.

'So what did you wish to speak to me about, darling?' he asked expectantly. 'Is it about setting the date for our wedding at last?'

'No, it isn't. In fact it's quite the opposite,' she answered softly. 'You see, Henry, I've realised more and more of late that I would be doing you no favours whatsoever if I were to become your wife.'

He opened his mouth to protest but she gently placed a finger on his lips.

'You are a lovely man,' she said sincerely. 'But the thing is, I've been alone for a long time now. I've become independent and I'm totally the opposite of your late wife. Emma was happy to stay at home and care for you and Eleanor, but I have my businesses to run.'

'And I've already told you that I would be happy for you to continue to run them,' he objected.

'I know you have, but think about it – would you *really*? Furthermore, I don't think I'd be happy to be waited on by maids. I was a maid myself not so very long ago in case you'd forgotten. Even of an evening when the shops are shut I tend to work on my designs, but you need someone who can accompany you to all the functions you attend and host dinner parties for you. That's not for me, Henry, and deep down I think you know I'm right.'

Very slowly she withdrew the sparkling engagement ring from her finger and placing it in his hand she closed his fingers around it.

'I'm very, very fond of you,' she told him truthfully. 'But you deserve someone who will love you with all their heart.'

'So you're telling me this is the end then?' he said brokenly.

She nodded. 'I'm afraid so. But I hope that we can remain friends.'

He gazed at her for a moment before saying quietly, 'I think there's someone else, isn't there, Dilly? Someone you *do* love with all of your heart? I've felt it right from the start and I have a good idea who it is.'

She looked away from the hurt in his eyes as he dropped the ring into his pocket.

'Then if that is your decision, it only remains for me to say goodbye, Dilly.' He raised her hand to his lips and kissed it tenderly before striding away into the cold white world without another word.

Dilly stood there chilled to the bone till long after he had disappeared from sight. She had thought she would feel sad, yet strangely all she felt was relief. She had just avoided making one of the biggest mistakes of her life: to fall into the trap of marrying for the wrong reasons. Loneliness could be a terrible thing, but better that than tying herself to someone whom she didn't love. No, she promised herself, if ever I do marry again it will have to be whole-heartedly because I love the person as I once loved Fergal. Nothing less would do. Sadly, that person was already spoken for. That was why Henry had never quite measured up. It was always someone else's face she thought of first thing in the morning and the last thing at night. It was someone else's smile that could brighten her day – so she knew she had been right to release Henry. One day he would find someone who would return his feelings tenfold – he deserved that at least.

With a sigh, Dilly turned and straightened her back, and

fixing a smile on her face, she returned to the heat and noise of the wedding party.

Max was watching for her and as she helped herself to a glass of champagne from the tray that one of the waiters offered, he noticed that she was now alone and the engagement ring was missing from her finger. She was calm and there was no trace of tears, but he couldn't help but see that she looked sad too.

As the evening drew to a close the guests began to leave, many exclaiming loudly that it was the best knees-up they'd attended for a very long time.

Max had taken Nell and Jessica back to the house earlier on when the baby began to get tired. Olivia had gone with them, which hadn't surprised him. He'd also taken the newly-weds back to their house to spend their first night together, and now as Dilly saw off the remaining guests he returned to take her home too. He was looking forward to having her to himself for a short while. They'd spent little time together lately. He frequently worried about what would happen if Samuel should turn around and tell Olivia about her true parentage. How would the news affect her and Dilly: all of them, if it came to that? But this evening he pushed his worries aside as he strode back into the hotel.

Dilly was alone by then, gathering the wedding presents into a pile that the hotel staff had assured her could be picked up the following morning.

'Ah, that reminds me, I have my gift to them here.' Reaching into his overcoat pocket Max withdrew a large brown envelope. 'Would you mind giving this to them for me?'

'Of course not, but I'm curious. Aren't you going to tell me what it is?'

'Well, I daresay they'll tell you soon enough. It's the deeds to their house, in their name.'

As Dilly gasped he shrugged self-consciously. 'I couldn't think of what to get them and this will give them a good start to married life I hope.'

'But it's too much,' she croaked.

He laughed as he lifted her coat and helped her into it. 'Nonsense. Now are you ready? I'll give you a lift home. You must be quite exhausted by now. I know I am, I'm just beginning to realise that I'm not as young as I used to be.'

She followed him out of the hotel with the precious gift clutched to her chest thinking how very generous he was, but then she'd always known that. As they reached the steps of the hotel they noticed that it had started to snow again and the whole town looked like something off a Christmas card.

'Oh, it's magical,' Dilly breathed, then she was laughing as they ran towards his car hand in hand and clambered inside. It was warm and cosy in there and she felt that she could have sat there all night.

Max didn't immediately start the engine but said quietly, 'Can I ask you something, Dilly?'

'Of course.'

'It's about Olivia and Jessica. Is the child my grandchild?'

Dilly looked straight ahead, watching the snow falling. She hesitated. 'How would you feel about it if she was?' she answered cagily.

Leaning his arms on the steering wheel, he gazed at the snowy windscreen. 'I suppose if you'd asked me that a few years ago I would have said I'd be horrified, but now . . . Well, times are changing and it's lonely at the house.'

'Then why don't you ask Olivia right out?' she suggested.

His heart caught at the idea that Jessica might belong to his beautiful daughter. His eyes shone as he laughed. 'Do you know, I rather think I will? But the other thing I wanted to ask you was – is everything all right between you and Henry?'

'Actually I ended our engagement this evening,' she said, and when he looked at her questioningly she shrugged. 'I wasn't right for him. I'm too ambitious. You see, I don't want to stop with just three shops, Max, and I don't think Henry wholly approves of working women. I've been speaking to Philip Maddison about the possibility of opening a store in London and I've also thought of having one in New York. It would mean I would get to see Niamh and Ben from time to time.'

Max chuckled. 'Have I told you lately, Dilly Carey, that I think you are a truly remarkable woman?'

'Yes, but I don't mind if you want to tell me again. Now take me home, will you? Before we get stuck in the snow.'

'Certainly, m'lady.' He winked at her and started the car, and as they drove along she snuggled down into the seat and dreamed of the little empire she was going to build.

Dilly's story continues in

*Dilly's Hope*

# *Chapter One*

*Changing Times*
*Nuneaton, May 1926*

'Whatever are you doing, Dilly?'

Glancing up from the basket she was in the process of filling, Dilly saw Max Farthing standing in the open kitchen doorway.

'I'm just putting a basket of food together for the people of the courtyard where Nell and I used to live,' she explained as she placed a cabbage in the basket. 'Nell visited them the other day and with the miners' strike some of them can't afford to eat, let alone pay the rent.'

'Hmm, it must be very grim for them,' Max agreed. 'And it will only get worse if the strike goes on for any length of time. What you're doing is a very kind gesture but I fear it won't sustain them for long.'

'Well, as they say, "every little helps",' Dilly replied.

Some years before, Dilly had lived side by side with the people she was trying to help but now she was a successful

businesswoman who owned a string of dress shops –
*Dilly's Designs* – that were doing very well indeed. Max
found it endearing that she could still concern herself with
those who were not so well-off as herself. Not that it
surprised him. Dilly had a heart of pure gold and always
went out of her way to help people, which was just one of
the things he loved about her.

Nell, her one-time neighbour who now shared the fine
house Dilly had purchased in St Edward's Road, entered
the kitchen then and she smiled a greeting at Max. He was
a regular visitor and they were all at ease with each other.

'Bad do, ain't it, this strike?' Nell remarked with a sigh.
'An' there but fer the grace o' God would go I, if it weren't
for our Dilly 'ere.'

'Rubbish,' Dilly chided. 'I don't know what I'd do
without you, pet.' Nell flushed at the praise as Dilly then
commented, 'And you're looking very smart today.'

Nell self-consciously ran her hands down the sides of
the black skirt Dilly's seamstresses had made for her. With
it she was wearing a crisp white cotton blouse; she liked to
look neat when she was going to work in Dilly's Nuneaton
dress shop, but it hadn't always been that way. Once upon
a time Nell could only have been described as slatternly –
but Dilly had changed all that. She'd changed Nell's whole
life, in fact, and the woman would have walked through
fire for her if need be. Their friendship stretched back
many years, and at one time it had been Nell who had
helped Dilly through the most difficult period of her whole
life.

When Dilly's family were young, her husband Fergal
had been crippled in a terrible accident at work on the
railways, and for a while, Dilly had feared that she would
have to place her children in the workhouse. But Nell had
helped in any way she could until a terrible solution was

2

found. In 1900, Dilly had given her newborn daughter to Max's wife, Camilla, following the death of Camilla's own little daughter, Violet, in exchange for a sum of money, which she had used to get her remaining children safely over to their grandparents in Ireland. In addition Dilly had been given a permanent full-time position as a maid in Max's home, Mill House, which had enabled her to earn enough money to get the family back on their feet and eventually fetch the children home again. Dilly had worked tirelessly to keep her family together, and she had made a grand job of it.

Max had marvelled at the way Dilly had coped with seeing another woman bring up little Olivia, with never a word of complaint, and over the years his esteem of her had grown. Sadly, Dilly's decision to give up her baby daughter had had disastrous consequences. Both Dilly and Max had suffered because of their deception to Olivia, but neither felt that they could admit to her true parentage because of the oath Dilly had made to Camilla. Even now, when Camilla was incarcerated in Hatter's Hall, the local mental asylum on the outskirts of the town, Dilly couldn't bring herself to break her promise – and Max doubted that she ever would. Dilly Carey was a woman of her word.

'Right then, if you're goin' to take those round to the courtyard I'll go an' open the shop, shall I?' Nell said, after checking her hair in the mirror. She'd been helping Dilly in the shop for some time now and it seemed to have given her a new lease of life and made her take pride in her appearance again.

'I'd be very grateful if you would,' Dilly answered, lifting and testing the weight of the basket.

Nell took the shop keys from the hook above the sink and with a smile at them both she left, as Max told Dilly, 'Here, I'll carry that for you. I walked this morning so I'm

3

'going back that way anyway. It'll give us a chance to talk.'

'What about?' Dilly enquired curiously as she shrugged her slim arms into the sleeves of her coat.

'Well, I was wondering if you'd reached a decision about taking on the lease of that shop in London.' Max hoisted the heavy basket and followed Dilly outside, waiting patiently while she locked the door before falling into step with him.

She shrugged. 'I'm not sure what to do, to be honest, what with the current situation. The sales in my other shops are down already and if the Strike goes on I can only imagine things will get worse – although Philip assures me that my designs are continuing to sell well in his shops.'

'Ah, but Philip Maddison caters to a different clientele in London,' Max pointed out. 'Most of his customers are wealthy and the strike won't really affect them.'

'You could be right, which is why I've been toying with an idea,' Dilly told him. 'As you know, I already sell a broad range of clothes varying in price, and the bridal shops are still doing good business, but I wondered if I shouldn't introduce a new budget range of clothing. What do you think?'

Max pursed his lips as they strode along, deep in thought, but finally answered, 'It does sound plausible, but how would you afford to do it? You still have to pay the seamstresses and the shops' overheads.'

'I know that, but if I bought slightly cheaper material, that would reduce the cost of the clothes at a stroke. I'd be aiming the range at the working classes.'

'Then I suppose it's worth a try.'

Dilly changed the subject then. 'And how is my favourite little girl this morning?' she asked with a grin. 'Was she up when you left the house?'

'She certainly was.' Max knew exactly who Dilly was

4

referring to: Olivia's four-year-old daughter, Jessica, who was their mutual granddaughter. 'And as usual she had everyone running around after her. I'm telling you, that little minx has the entire household wrapped around her little finger.'

Dilly chuckled, thankful that Max had accepted the child despite the fact that she was illegitimate.

Soon they were at the entrance to the courtyard and Max handed Dilly the basket asking, 'What on earth have you got in there – house bricks?'

'Just some slices of pork and some vegetables, but it's hardly going to be enough to fill all their bellies, is it?'

'Here.' Max opened her hand and dropped some silver coins into it. 'Share them out as well for me, would you?'

She smiled at him, remembering a time when she had been hungry and thinking how grateful she would have been.

'Thanks, Max, that should get them all another meal each at least. I've had a word with the Salvation Army. They're thinking of setting up a soup kitchen if the Strike goes on, so at least then everyone will get at least one hot meal a day. But let's hope it won't come to that, eh?'

'I'm rather afraid it will,' Max replied solemnly. 'The General Council of the Trades Union Congress has voted to back the miners after the breakdown of their negotiations so this could be a long and bitter battle. But you go ahead and deliver those things now and I must get off to work. Lawrence will think I've disappeared. Will you be coming around to the house later?'

'Of course I will – it's Thursday, isn't it? Oscar will be bringing George to play with Jessica and you know I love to see them together. I think Patty might be bringing William too. Goodbye for now, Max.' With that she swung about and headed for the entrance to the courtyard.

Max watched her go. With the sun shining on her copper hair, which was showing only the slightest hints of grey, Dilly looked nothing like a woman who was fast approaching her fiftieth birthday. But then she had always been attractive as far as he was concerned. When she finally disappeared from view, Max turned and headed towards his mill in Attleborough. His son, Lawrence, and the father to his three-year-old grandson, William, was also his right-hand man and had teased him the day before saying that he was developing a middle-age spread . . . so Max had decided that a walk would do him good.

# *Chapter Two*

'They're as close as two peas in a pod those two, ain't they?' Mrs Pegs, Max's cook, commented to Dilly. The kindly woman had just taken Jessica and George some home-made jam tarts and a glass of milk each for their mid-afternoon snack and now she and Dilly had settled down in the kitchen to enjoy a cup of tea while Gwen, the young maid, prepared the vegetables for the evening meal.

'I'm rather afraid they are.' Dilly and Mrs Pegs exchanged a look and without a word being said they each knew what the other was thinking. It was like watching Olivia and Max's son Oscar at that age all over again, and both women hoped that there wasn't more heartache ahead. Olivia and Max had fallen in love – a love that was taboo, since they believed they were blood-related, brother and sister. But because of Dilly's oath to Camilla, no one would tell them the truth.

'Have you heard from the family in Ireland lately?' Mrs

Pegs asked then, keen to change the subject as she took a noisy slurp of her tea.

'Yes, I have. As a matter of fact, a letter came this morning. I'm afraid Daniel still isn't too well. He can't seem to shake off the cold he caught in the winter, by all accounts. Still, on the bright side, Roisin tells me that they're all taking very good care of him. I intend to go over for a short visit as soon as I can spare the time. Between you and me he's never been the same since Maeve died. Those two were inseparable and I think he still misses her terribly, bless him. Roisin also told me that Roddy is growing like a weed. I wonder what Bessie will think when she next sees him?'

'I had a letter from Bessie only last week,' Mrs Pegs told her. 'She's almost completed her nurse's trainin' now, an' then she's comin' back to Nuneaton and hopes to get a job at the Weddington Hall Hospital. I reckon she'll use some o' the money her husband left her to buy herself a little place then.'

'Hmm, I wonder if she'll want Roddy back when she does return?' Dilly mused worriedly. 'I think it would break Declan and Roisin's hearts to part with the little chap now. Roisin had another miscarriage recently – that's six in all, poor soul – and she and Declan look on Roddy as their own now.'

'Huh! I reckon there's little chance o' Bessie wantin' him back,' Mrs Pegs snorted. 'You an' I both know she never took to the poor little chap. He's a million times better off where he is than wi' his real mother, but then I don't want to be too harsh on the girl. She didn't ask to be raped an' end up pregnant, did she? Talkin' o' which . . .' She lowered her voice at that point and glanced towards the door. 'Do yer happen to know if the master's heard from that no-good son o' his?'

'Not a dickey bird as far as I'm aware – and we can only hope that it stays that way. Life around these parts has been so much more peaceful without Master Samuel Farthing about. He has a lot to answer for.'

Dilly remembered the terrible shame he had brought down on her own daughter, Niamh, after he had raped her as well as Bessie, also leaving her with child. Admittedly, Max had forced him to do the right thing by marrying her, and the result of the rape had been Constance – a beautiful little girl who had sadly died when she was two years old. From then on, the farce of a marriage had gone from bad to worse and when Bessie, Max's former maid, had reappeared and disclosed that Roddy, her young son, was also the result of her being raped by Samuel, Niamh had refused to have anything more to do with him. Now she was happily living in New York with Ben, the love of her life, but it hurt Dilly to think that she was still legally tied to Samuel. Niamh and Ben had been meant for each other and it seemed a shame that they were forced to live in sin.

'As well as going to Ireland, I'd also like to go and see Niamh and Ben in New York,' she confided to Mrs Pegs. 'I've never even set eyes on James, my grandson, and he's almost two years old now. And I've also got to find time to visit Kian's grave in France.'

'So why don't yer just do it instead o' keep harpin' on about it?' Mrs Pegs said bluntly.

'Because now I have the other three shops I never seem to find the time.' Dilly sipped at her tea as she gazed from the window. Primroses were peeping from beneath the hedge and tender green leaves were just beginning to sprout on the trees.

'Six shops, eh?' Mrs Pegs whistled out a breath. 'Who'd ever have thought it, eh, lass? It don't seem so long ago since you were workin' here as a maid wi' not two pennies to rub together. You've worked damned hard to get where you are. The only thing I'd say is, don't go puttin' the businesses afore things you'd like to do. Life is passin' by an' one day you might regret it if you do. Your Seamus is more than capable o' keepin' things goin' while you're away – so think on it.'

Dilly knew that Mrs Pegs was right and a stab of guilt pierced through her. But if and when she decided to go, where would she go first? She knew that she would never forgive herself if anything happened to her father-in-law before she'd seen him for one last time. Daniel and Maeve his late wife had been very good to her over the years. Then there was Niamh and little James. It hurt to have a grandson she had never even met, although Niamh always sounded happy in the letters she wrote. She now had her own small art gallery in Manhattan and appeared to be doing very well. It came as no surprise to Dilly. Niamh had always had a talent for painting and now it appeared she was actually making a living from the pictures she sold.

Finally, Dilly's thoughts turned to the lonely grave in France where her beloved son Kian was buried after being killed in the war. Every year she promised herself she would visit it to say her last goodbyes, but somehow she had never seemed to spare the time. Perhaps Mrs Pegs was right? On top of everything else, Philip Maddison was badgering her to visit him in London. She'd long thought of opening a shop there too, since the designs she did for Philip were selling like hot cakes in the capital, but again she never seemed to get around to it . . .

Just then, the door leading into the hallway burst open and Jessica and George raced in, closely followed by Olivia and Oscar.

'I'm afraid they've come to try and con you out of some

more of your delicious jam tarts,' Oscar warned the cook with a grin. 'There'll be hell to pay from his mother though, if he doesn't eat all his dinner tonight.'

'Huh, a bit o' spoilin' never hurt anyone,' Mrs Pegs responded indulgently as she loaded some more jam tarts into the two tiny pairs of waiting hands. 'An' what his ma don't see won't hurt her, will it, George?' She winked at him conspiratorially and he giggled with delight as she affectionately ruffled his fair curls. 'He looks so like you did at his age,' Mrs Pegs said to Oscar, sighing nostalgically. 'It make me wonder where all the years have gone.'

Jessica meanwhile had clambered up on to Dilly's lap and Dilly promptly planted a kiss on her springy copper curls. Jessica had jam smeared all around her mouth and on the end of her nose, and Dilly thought she looked delightful.

'Mrs Pegs here was just saying that she thinks it's time I got round to paying a visit to Ireland,' Dilly told Olivia and Oscar. 'And I also think I should make plans to get to New York and France.'

'I thoroughly agree,' Olivia said instantly. 'Seamus and Mary are more than capable of holding the fort while you're away and a break would do you good. You're always working.'

'They're more than capable of keeping the shops supplied,' Dilly readily admitted, 'but what about my designs for Philip in London?'

'Now don't get looking for problems,' Olivia scolded gently. 'I'm sure Philip has enough to keep him going for a while. You're always sketching, and anyway, he'd be the first to say you work too hard.'

'Hmm . . .' The thought of a break was very tempting, Dilly had to admit.

'Why don't you telephone Declan in Ireland right now and tell him that you're coming while you're in the mood?' Olivia encouraged. 'I know what you're like. You'll go home, get sketching again and postpone it once more. Go on – ring him. Daddy won't mind you using his telephone.'

Dilly lifted Jessica on to the floor and headed for the telephone on the hall table before she could change her mind. Luckily she knew the number off by heart and Roisin answered it almost immediately.

'I've decided it's time I paid you all a visit,' Dilly told her and Roisin was delighted.

'Wonderful! When will you be coming? It'll do Daniel a power of good to see you, so it will.'

'I'm going to try and book the ferry for tomorrow,' Dilly promised and after chatting for a few more minutes she went back to the kitchen with a spring in her step.

When she got home later and told Nell of her plans, her friend was pleased too. 'You've been lookin' tired lately an' a break away will breathe new life into yer. Just stay as long as yer like, luvvie. Me, Seamus an' Mary are more than able to keep things runnin' smoothly 'ere.'

And so after ringing Philip Maddison, the designer who sold her designs in London and telling him of her plans she hastily packed a small case and prepared for leaving the very next day. There was no time like the present, and Dilly knew that if she didn't go now she'd only find an excuse to postpone the visit – yet again.

Max ran her to the station the next morning and insisted on carrying her case on to the platform for her although it wasn't heavy and contained only the basic essentials.

'I feel almost envious,' he told her as they stood together

12

waiting for the train to arrive. 'I could do with a little break myself.'

As Dilly glanced at him she saw that he looked tired, and a little shiver of fear ran through her. Max was an important part of her life and she didn't like to think what she would do without him. For years he had been her friend, her confidant and her rock.

'So why don't you arrange to take a little time off and have a short holiday, then?' she said. 'If I can do it, so can you.'

He laughed. 'Oh? And where would I go? It's different for you. You're going to visit family but I don't think it would be much fun on my own.'

'So take Olivia and Jessica away with you. I'm sure Jessica would love a few days at the seaside.'

He chewed thoughtfully on his lip for a moment before saying, 'You could be right there. I might ask Olivia how she feels about the idea this evening. It's been a few years now since I've wielded a bucket and spade but I suppose it's a bit like riding a bicycle. Once you've learned you never forget.'

'Oh, get away with you,' Dilly grinned but then their attention was distracted by the sound of the train approaching. 'Here we are then,' she said, trying to ignore the look of sadness that had settled on his face.

'Any idea how long you might be staying?'

'Not long,' she assured him. 'I've only packed enough clothes for a few days.' She was missing him already although her journey hadn't even begun and she could see that he felt the same.

He lifted the case into the carriage for her and she pulled on the brown leather strap to let down the window.

'Ring me and tell me when you're coming back,' he said, 'and I'll be here to meet you.'

13

She nodded, but then there was a hiss of steam and the train began to move, so after a hasty wave she closed the window. By the time she had placed her case on the overhead luggage-rack and settled herself, Nuneaton station was already far behind her.

## About Rosie . . .

Becoming an author has opened up yet another new world to me, and I am now the patron of three establishments for which I fundraise. One of them is Bulkington Community Library, where a willing team of volunteers work tirelessly to keep the village library running smoothly and open to the public (bulkingtoncommunitylibrary@btconnect.com) and the local Mary Ann Evans Hospice, who do a wonderful job working with people who have life threatening illnesses (www.maryannevans.org.uk).

I was also thrilled when local people voted for the children's Assessment unit at the George Eliot hospital to be named after me.

Two years ago, my husband and I moved into a wonderful, character-filled house with a large garden, and ever since we have been in our elements making it into our own.

Another huge part of my life is our dogs, Alicia, Mowgli, Bonnie and Beau. Alicia is a shih tzu, Bonnie is a Chinaranian and Beau and Mowgli are chihuahuas. We did have six (two more shih tzus) but sadly we lost Honey and Sassy.

I am delighted to say I am now amongst the Top 50 most borrowed library authors.

With love
Rosie x